the unincorporated FUTURE

Tor Books by Dani Kollin and Eytan Kollin

The Unincorporated Man

The Unincorporated War

The Unincorporated Woman

The Unincorporated Future

the unincorporated FUTURE

Dani Kollin and Eytan Kollin

A Tom Doherty Associates Book
New York TOR®

THE UNINCORPORATED FUTURE

Copyright © 2012 by Dani Kollin and Eytan Kollin

A Tor Book
Published by Tom Doherty Associates, LLC
175 Fifth Avenue
New York, NY 10010

www.tor-forge.com

Tor® is a registered trademark of Tom Doherty Associates, LLC.

ISBN 978-0-7653-2881-6 (hardcover)
ISBN 978-1-4299-4835-7 (e-book)

First Edition: August 2012

Printed in the United States of America

0 9 8 7 6 5 4 3 2 1

To our father, Rabbi Gilbert Kollin. Our dedication to him is but a pale reflection of that to his children, grandchildren, family, friends, and congregants.

Acknowledgments

We would like to acknowledge our editor, David G. Hartwell, and everyone at Tor, without whom the making of this book would not have been possible. A special note of thanks goes to Alan M. Steele for all the work he didn't do. Buy him a drink, and maybe he'll tell you about it sometime. Or hell, buy *us* a drink for that matter, and we'll tell you.

Dani would like to thank Deborah for loving him alone while he labored over this book and Eliana, Yoni, and Gavi for making him the proudest dad in the universe.

the unincorporated FUTURE

1 Unbridgeable Divisions

Transorbital pod (t.o.p.)
Low orbit of Mars

Hektor Sambianco, President of the United Human Federation, savior of the incorporated system, and stolid voice to billions of minority shareholders, clasped his arms stiffly behind his back and set his penetrating gaze on the approaching planet. Though others competed for attention—Saturn had its multihued rings; Earth its striking visage as a luminous marble cast against the firmament—Mars still reigned supreme. It was Mars that captured the imagination; Mars that provoked awe; Mars that dazzled as the coruscating emerald atop the solar system's crown. Perhaps its favored status was a result of its bearing the godlike imprimatur of man, changed from a rust-colored, dust-filled wasteland to a fertile Elysium in under a century. It was, after all, humanity's first and arguably greatest bioengineering success, and it was well that they continued to marvel in it. To approach this planet was to approach the dreams of humanity realized.

Yet Hektor Sambianco felt none of these things. Though his dark and probing eyes watched as the blanket of green, pale blue seas, and dotted lakes drew nearer, his heart did not swell with even the faintest glimmer of joy, and the magnificent vista filling the observation deck before him elicited no awe. His mind was dwelling on a war that would not end and an enemy that would not quit. Within minutes, his t.o.p. was on the ground. Within seconds, he heard the euphonious chime that indicated he had a visitor.

Hektor activated the t.o.p.'s internal scanner. Tricia Pakagopolis, the United Human Federation's Minister of Internal Affairs, stood cooling her heels outside his private quarters. The woman, he knew, had devoted over eighty years of her life to building a well-deserved reputation for ruthless efficiency and, to accompany it, an appearance designed to elicit immediate apprehension. *Just not from me,* mused Hektor as a smile twitched at the corner of his lips. Though outwardly barely twenty years of age, Tricia dressed in a wardrobe that was hardly youthful. She wore her trademark geometric pantsuit, whose statuesque angles seemed to defy the shapely figure hidden within, and her thick black mane was pulled back so tightly, her eyes seemed like two determined beasts straining at the leash to press forward.

The corporate system had been good to Tricia. It had constrained and channeled her individual abilities and desires into the productive ends of the larger group and ultimately the all-powerful market. But Justin Cord had changed all that. His mere existence—his very unincorporation—had caused a rift in the incorporated world that had at first festered and then finally burst into outright civil war.

And it was people like Tricia, Hektor knew, who had benefited most. Not because she'd agreed with Cord. Her psychological profile attested to the fact that she thought the man an idiot; that his preaching the drivel of freedom and individuality to the masses could only lead to the anarchy that had inevitably followed; that individuals were fools who could no more revel in their freedom than in their servitude; that the brilliance of the incorporated system was in confining the idiots to the bottom while elevating the more worthy to the top. No, realized Hektor, Tricia could never have lived in Cord's world. But she could and had exploited the very idea of it to suit hers.

The Unincorporated War that had resulted from Cord's coalition of the Outer Alliance meant that the Core Worlds' incorporated system had to change; had to become harsher, more efficient, more cruel—something Tricia Pakagopolis had been ideally suited for. No longer needing to cater to the whims of stockholders, boards of directors, or corporate governance, Tricia had, under Hektor's guidance and protection, blossomed from a mere cutthroat to an accomplished killer, and the only person she feared was now watching her fidget under the glare of the high-security array blocking her exit into his chamber.

"Let her in, iago," commanded Hektor to his personal AI.

"As you wish." The avatar obeyed, quietly releasing the door's mechanism, relaxing—only slightly—the hidden weapons trained on the visiting minister.

Hektor greeted Tricia with the traditional bow and indicated a seat in front of his workstation. "What's the latest on Ceres?" he asked.

"We're on the threshold of certain victory."

Hektor's brow arched upward. "Really?"

"Unconfirmed but yes," she affirmed, ignoring the obvious doubt etched into her boss's question.

Hektor laughed with so little mirth, it might have been mistaken for a cough. "Is Trang to be our savior, then?"

Tricia nodded gamely. "It appears so."

Grand Admiral Samuel U. Trang had risen to command all UHF forces by virtue of the fact that almost every other high-ranking officer ahead of him had proved too incompetent to lead or unfortunate enough to be killed by the incompetence of others. But Trang had somehow found a way to survive and in short order had proved himself again and again by snatching victory from the sure hands of defeat. As far as the UHF and Trang were concerned, there was really only one impediment to the unincorporated war's end—Fleet Admiral J. D. Black of the Outer Alliance. Despite being vastly outnumbered in both troops and munitions, whether by chicanery, guts, or both, Admiral Black too had always found a way to win. That is, until Trang burst onto the scene. He'd had no problem using his one great advantage—resources—to full effect. No matter what Black had thrown at him, and it had been quite a lot, Trang could always bounce back—and did—with more ships, more weapons, more fortitude. Up until the recent Battle of Ceres, the two opposing warriors' brief encounters had always ended in a draw. But now Tricia was telling Hektor something different.

"If the reports are to be believed," she continued, "he destroyed enough of the orbital defenses around Ceres to begin bombarding the surface. The Minister of Defense has the official repor—"

"Forget Porfirio," scolded Hektor.

"I have," she laughed. "That's why I came here as soon as you landed. This kind of news couldn't wait."

Hektor nodded. As usual, Tricia had been proactive, delivering information not within her purview—her way of letting him know the extent of her network while artfully undercutting a fellow Cabinet member.

"Trang's battle plan was brilliant—no surprises there—and was even"—the tone of her voice changed to reflect admiration—"suitably ruthless. He'll offer the Alliance Council surrender, but doesn't expect them to accept it."

"In which case?" quizzed Hektor.

"He'll eliminate the remaining defenses and then shove enough atomics into their hole," she said, referring to the Via Cereana, a massive throughway running the length of the planetoid's center, "to blast that putrescent capital of the rebellion to dust."

Hektor regarded Tricia thoughtfully, nodding ever so slowly. It was a pleasure to envision the Outer Alliance's greatest symbolic presence getting blown to smithereens, but only for a brief second. It was, he knew, too easy to get caught up in the vision and lose track of the reality. Six years of warfare had hammered that home more than anything. "And if he fails?"

"I don't see how he can, Mr. President. Black may be able to defeat him, but she's stuck at Jupiter, being a"—she spat the next word out as if it were bile—"humanitarian. It may have cost us one half of our fleet and the loss of Admiral

Gupta, but Porfirio was right about one thing—she can't be in two places at once. She's two weeks away from Ceres, which is two weeks too long. By the time she gets back, all that shithole will be is a cloud of dust on its way to Saturn."

"And if he fails?" repeated Hektor. His face was rigid and his countenance savage.

Caught off guard, Tricia's eyes flashed concern for a brief second and then quickly retreated to their cold, lifeless beauty. "If he fails, if Black somehow manages to save Ceres, Trang's damage is already done. Like I said, it's too late."

Hektor's silence prodded Tricia on. "Ceres's destruction *and* the near elimination of Jupiter as a center of Alliance activity will allow Irma," she said, referring to the Minister of Information, "to play up these two recent victories and offset whatever other losses we've sustained."

"Right," snarled the President. "Let's talk about those *other* losses, shall we? Over the course of six years, we've lost so many ships, spacers, and marines, I've lost count and feeling. Every time we win a supposedly massive victory, they retreat farther into the solar system. We just lost an entire fleet . . . *an entire fleet!*—and one of our best admirals at Jupiter. How much did Black lose?"

"Well, according to—"

"Cut the crap, Tricia," barked Hektor through his clenched jaw.

"Not a single ship."

"Not one ship or assault miner. Not even one missile. She saved on those," said Hektor with cold humor, "by using her cruisers to shove whatever crippled ships did make it out of Jupiter's atmosphere right back in."

"Singh's propaganda," Tricia countered, referring to the Outer Alliance's Secretary of Information.

"Do *you* think he's lying?"

Tricia pursed her lips. "No, sir," she finally admitted, keeping a level gaze, "I don't."

"Good. Now at least we're dealing with facts rather than fiction. Let's also not forget that the Alliance managed to evacuate the most productive elements, both human and matériel from the asteroid belt and will soon bring all that production back online far from our centers of power."

"I have not forgotten, Mr. President."

"Good. And of course, the pièce de résistance, their destruction of the Beanstalk, the single greatest edifice ever created by the human race, plus the near destruction of the Trans-Luna Shipyards, the biggest manufacturing enterprise in the solar system."

A heavy sigh was the only answer that emanated from the Minister of Internal Affairs.

"Now," said Hektor, leaning slightly forward in his chair, "please explain to me exactly how it is you plan on playing all that up as winning?"

Though she remained pensive and her manner formal, it was obvious that a battle was raging within as she searched for the right answer. "Sir," she offered, "they started the war with four billion citizens and had control of everything from the asteroid belt to the Oort cloud. They've lost, by my estimate, two billion citizens to permanent death, capture, or exile; the entire asteroid belt; and now, effectively, Jupiter. They've lost their leader," she said, referring to Justin Cord, "and most of their fanatical religious hierarchy to war and assassination. As you've so clearly illustrated, we've taken our lumps, but theirs—" She nodded grimly. "—theirs have been far worse."

"Then why," prodded Hektor, "are they still fighting, Minister?"

Tricia's mouth hung open for a brief second and just as quickly snapped shut. The truth was that she, like anyone in a position of real power, had no ready answer. They'd all grasped at straws. In a fit of desperation, they'd sent Admiral Abhay Gupta to Jupiter, where his ceaseless slaughter of 179 million souls was supposed to have been the final exclamation mark on what had until then been a merciless path of destruction. Each bloody campaign, they'd all assured themselves, was to be the last. The Alliance would have to cave under such overwhelming pressure. And yet, it hadn't. Tricia usually had an answer for everything, but now it was her silence that spoke volumes.

"Something must—"

"Not some*thing,* Tricia." Hektor's face glimmered slightly—a cat toying with its prey. "Some*one.* Think."

"We've been over this, sir. While we agreed that the Jew should be watched more closely, I still find it hard to believe that he'd be the reason they continue to persevere. His organizational prowess is commendable, but no one rallies around him. No one screams the name 'Rabbi' from their rooftop. He's not like Justin Cord."

"No," agreed Hektor. "Not like Justin Cord at all." A small smile creased the corners of his mouth.

"You can't be suggesting—"

"I can and I will. You missed it, Minister. But don't rush to have yourself arrested. We all missed it. Sandra O'Toole is Justin Cord's successor in every sense of the word. She is the one directing the energies of the Outer Alliance. She is the one giving them the leadership and the hope to continue this war. She," he proclaimed with an assuredness that would brook no argument, "is the X factor."

"But my informants—"

"Have been played like a fiddle." Hektor reached under his desk, pulled out a file, and slid it across the desk.

She picked it up, and her eyes sprang to life as they scanned the information within. "How did you get this?"

"Like you, I have my sources."

"It's quite thorough."

Hektor nodded. "She, not Rabbi, is the real source of the Alliance's resistance. I was a fool not to see it initially, but now I know. Now I'm armed with the truth, and it's telling me one thing and one thing only: With her gone, the war is over. What started with one death," he said, referring to the Chairman's assassination, "will end with one death. From this moment on, we must devote our resources to destroying the Unincorporated Woman. Sandra O'Toole must die."

The Triangle Office
Ceres
Battle of Ceres
Day 1, Hour 3

Sergeant Holke looked about as unhappy as Sandra had ever seen him. The Cliff House was located close enough to the surface of Ceres that every bombardment could be felt and the office shook slightly from the continual impacts.

"Just a couple of more items, Sergeant," Sandra said as if she were going to a ribbon cutting for a new church or day care center.

"Begging the President's pardon," scoffed Sergeant Holke, "but we have to get the fuck out of here—now!" Sandra was the last important official to be leaving the Cliff House. She was supervising the removal of a painting that had already assumed iconic proportions in the Alliance. It was of Justin Cord talking to the assault miners after the great victory at the Battle of the Needle's Eye.

"The portrait is secure, Madam President," said her Chief of Staff, Catalina Zohn. "The sergeant is right—you must leave now."

"Nonsense, dear," Sandra said airily. "I'm just a figurehead doing figurehead things. If I were lost, the Alliance would survive."

Both Catalina and Sergeant Holke exchanged *yeah, right* looks. They both knew that ever since the Sermon in the Park, as the Alliance was calling Sandra's memorial service after the Long Battle, she'd become more than a mere figurehead. Though even they would be hard-pressed to describe exactly what her being President meant, they did agree on one thing as they turned to her.

"Get out."

With a sigh, Sandra took one last look around and then grabbed the briefcase that was attached via a thin cable to her wrist. It would look to the world that she was taking her important data disks or small objects of value. And indeed, there were those articles in the briefcase, but they were simply camouflage for the real objects of her power. An ancient VHS tape of a movie called *Tron* and the ribbon it was wrapped in, actually a high-density data cord. And finally a beautifully wrought gold and silver circlet that was in actuality a VR headband.

The office was shaken by a blast so large, all three were lifted off their feet. They floated in place for a moment until their internal magnetism could adhere them to the "floor." But before Sandra could get both feet on the ground, Sergeant Holke had grabbed her by the upper arm.

"You're out of here, *now.*"

Sandra didn't argue with the sergeant as he hustled her out. She feared she knew what the blast meant. "Sergeant Holke, did they just use—?"

"Atomics," he said as he put her in the middle of four TDCs, or Too Deadly for Combat, the name given to the Presidential detail. He nodded, his hardened face showing few signs of the stress of battle. The next hour and a half were spent getting Sandra to the government's new operating location, near the center of the Via Cereana. When Sandra arrived, she saw it was carved out of brand-new rock and was still being worked on. As they were checked through, Holke started giving her the rundown.

"Madam President, we're calling this the New Executive Headquarters with the code name of 'Briar Patch' for reasons not given to me. The executive branch has been separated from Congress, which is in a different location. The complex is being dug out of new rock for security reasons—less chance of sabotage." Holke stopped momentarily to verify his group's identity to another set of steely-faced guards for what seemed like the hundredth time. "The complex is being lined with trilayer coating of flexible concrete, ceramic, and titanium extracts. They have built-in protections for radiation, nanite, and concussive attacks. The trilayer can also take a direct hit fairly well as long as it is not from the enemy's main guns."

"What if they get a nuke down here?" Sandra asked.

"If that happens, Madam President, it won't much matter, because we can pretty much assume the rest of Ceres would already be lost."

Sandra was itching to ask technical questions, but realized that Sergeant Holke neither knew the answers nor cared about the minutiae she found so captivating. The fact that they were walking through a complex with light, heat, power, working doors, and com stations that only hours before had been solid rock fascinated her to no end. That the interior layout itself seemed to cause more confusion than clarity made her smirk. Apparently, centuries of high-tech progress still hadn't solved the problem of developing truly efficient working spaces.

Sandra couldn't help but notice the looks she was getting from the people in the crowded corridors. It was overwhelmingly of relief. The President was safe and sound, and that seemed to add to their feeling of security. To the chagrin of the sergeant, who felt he'd finally got a respectable pace going, Sandra started working the line/corridor, giving reassuring glances, shaking hands, and stopping along the way to have her picture taken with the workers. She was faking it, being fairly certain that they were all going to be dead in the next couple of days, but no one could tell from seeing her in the new corridors of power as the confidence she was faking started to radiate outward.

The small group soon arrived at the new Cabinet room, which looked exactly like the old one. Same dimensions, same lighting, even the same furniture and equipment. There was however, one significant difference. When she entered, all conversation stopped, and everyone from the secretaries to the security techs making last-minute adjustments rose and waited for her to take a seat.

Sandra felt immense satisfaction at the honor, knowing what the sign of deference meant. Knowing with the power now vested in her, she could, if they managed to survive, affect real and sustained change and ultimately fulfill her promise to Justin Cord. She raised her brow slightly, smiled demurely, and then took her seat at the head of the table. The room cleared out of all nonessential personnel, with Sergeant Holke the last to go. He made a purposeful showing of scanning everyone's face with a suspicious hawklike gaze as he departed. It had been decided that having a bodyguard inside during Cabinet meetings sent the wrong message, and now Holke had to wait outside, a change in circumstance he'd taken every opportunity to inform his boss that he was none too pleased with.

"Forgive me for being late," started Sandra, "but we took a bit of detour getting here. She then looked over to the grand admiral. "Admiral Sinclair, if you wouldn't mind."

Joshua Sinclair rose up slowly, the terrible strain of the war showing in his hunched posture and the dark bags that had formed beneath his eyes. "Madam President—" Sinclair turned his head slowly to note the others in the room. "—fellow Cabinet officers, there's really no way to sugarcoat this." Sinclair exhaled deeply as his mouth formed into a perfect scowl. "We are well and truly fucked, and I take full responsibility."

Sandra headed off the traditional march to resignation. "Fault is something we can assign *after* this battle is over, Admiral. Could you please tell us how we got into this situation and what we're doing about it?"

Sinclair nodded. The air had gone out of his once blustery sails, but he soldiered on. "Bastard brought his fleet around to attack our decoy ice ships, and like a fool I thought he'd bought our ruse. With his rear ships exposed, I concentrated our orbats to attack. The irony is he used our greatest asset, maneuverable orbats, and turned it against us. It cost Trang just about every support ship he had but he turned those ships into bombs, then blew a crapload of our defensive orbats with them."

"How long can he stay out here without his supply ships?" asked Hildegard.

"Depends on how much and what type of supplies he offloaded before destroying his auxiliaries," answered Sinclair. "There are no more supply ships coming from Mars, I can tell you that. Apparently between the commitments to pacifying the Belt and the loss of an entire fleet at Jupiter, even the UHF is at a loss for supplying their needs. The good news is that Omad's . . . er . . . Suchitra's flotilla really smashed the hell out of the Trans-Luna Shipyards. They won't be making ships for at least two or three months. But even with all that, we estimate that Trang can hang with us for at least another week before lack of ordnance or fuel forces him to head home."

"So what's happening now?" asked Mosh.

Sinclair called up an image of Ceres showing the position of Trang's forces. "I've had to move our remaining orbats to the entrance and exit of the Via Cereana. If he can get any sort of atomic *into* the Via and detonate it, Ceres will break apart like a fist holding a firecracker. Unfortunately, this strategy has left the surface of Ceres open to uncontested attack, and for the last four hours Trang has been systematically blasting every surface installation we have larger than a shuttle."

Sinclair's DijAssist alerted him to an intrafleet communiqué. He quickly checked it and as he did his eyebrow shot up. "The bombardment has stopped."

"Interesting," said Sandra.

"How so?" asked Mosh.

"Trang has enough ordnance to lay on the hurt for at least the next four or five days without letup."

"He wants to have a little chat," laughed Kirk.

"Certainly looks that way," agreed Sandra.

Padamir Singh looked up from his DijAssist at Sandra and Kirk. "You guys work this out with Trang in advance?" He then replaced the holo-image of Ceres with a local Neuro news broadcast. "This vid was just released on all bandwidths from what we believe to be Trang's flagship." Admiral Trang was seen sitting at plain desk in a drab, undecorated jumpsuit, with only his rank insignia giving it any distinction.

This is a supremely dangerous man, thought Sandra as she watched Trang explain in an almost grandfatherly voice exactly how he was going to either occupy or destroy the Alliance capital and there was not a thing that the Cereans could do about it. As a humanitarian gesture, he said he would allow the Alliance three days to evacuate its citizens. They could take any nonmilitary items they wanted and were free to go anywhere they wished. If they wished to, they could return to UHF territory with a safe passage and settlement guarantee signed by Trang himself that would be honored by the government. All people, he continued, acting as government and military officials of the Alliance would have the choice of surrendering to UHF forces or could choose to stay and chance the fortunes of war. Trang gave his personal oath that other than an inspection for war-making materials, any military or government personnel who fled Ceres would be not be harmed. He finished by asking those acting as the government of the Alliance to forgo any more honorific and therefore senseless deaths. Both sides having heinously attacked civilians, such actions must be curtailed, he implored. He then finished by saying the individuals acting as the government of the Alliance had one hour to accept these terms or the bombardment would begin again and could not take into account civilian versus military targets. He finished by pleading for the people of Ceres to accept these terms and end the madness that had made the horrors of Jupiter and the Beanstalk possible.

When it was over, the vid simply repeated, but now there was a timer counting down. It was, Sandra had to admit, a very effective technique. She cleared her throat and chose the direction she wanted the conversation to go.

"How do we tell Trang to stuff his generous offer? Personally, I kind of liked Anjou's three-fingers kiss off to Gupta."

There was a smattering of nervous laughter from around the table but Mosh wasn't biting.

"Would it be so wrong," he asked, "to accept, if only to save the children and the wounded amongst us?"

"To accept that offer is to accept the end of the war," said Sandra. "Why do you think Trang made it?"

Mosh's face contorted into disbelief. "How does evacuating Ceres end the war?"

Now Kirk pounced. "Because if we stop the fighting for three days, it will be almost impossible to get it to start again. Forget the fact you'll be separating families—you'll also be admitting that we can't save our own capital. We won't say it out loud, but it's what everyone will be thinking. That combined with the loss of Jupiter will get people wondering why they're dying for a cause that the very people they elected no longer believe in."

"A soldier expert in many fields, I see," said Padamir with some admiration. "Look how Trang splits us even now. And if we're arguing here in the Cabinet, you can bet wives are up there arguing with husbands, mothers with children, et cetera, et cetera."

"We're not going to give him the satisfaction," said Sandra. "I don't care if he's using words as weapons, he'll fail because we're fighting for some*thing* and he's fighting for some*one*. We lost Justin but gained resolve. Lost the Belt but took our goddamn rocks with us! Hell, we're in one of them now. We lost Jupiter and the hundreds of millions murdered but gained a new appreciation of the depth our enemy will go to in their effort to enslave us. J. D. didn't give up, and now the bastard who committed those murders is destroyed by the very planet he hoped to subjugate. Omad Hassan, at the cost of his life, struck at the heart of the incorporated system and felled the Beanstalk, and Suchitra, outgunned and deep in enemy territory, attacked the UHF at its most sensitive industrial spot and is on her way to Saturn even as we speak. Well, now it's our turn. And I say it's about fucking time."

"To do what?" asked Mosh. "In case you hadn't noticed, we don't exactly have the upper hand here."

"But we do, Mosh. We've had it all along. You see, what Trang wants us to destroy *for him* is the absolute knowledge that what we're fighting for is worth it. Is it worth the loss of Justin Cord and the asteroid belt? Of Christina Sadma at Altamont or Omad Hassan at the Beanstalk? Worth the loss of Jupiter and the millions of lives that went with it? Because now we face the hard truth, folks. Do we add Ceres to that list? Make no mistake, our freedom and the freedom of our children depend on our answer."

Sandra now very purposely met the eyes of each and every Cabinet member sitting around her. "So now we vote."

"What exactly are we voting on, Madam President?" asked Rabbi.

"On the table today is one question and one question only." A few moments of tense silence hung on her words. "Is it worth it?"

Mosh seemed incredulous. "Why isn't the question, 'Should we end the war?'"

"Because it's not."

"Is it worth it?" Mosh repeated. "Is that really *the* question?"

"Mosh, in my opinion and I believe the opinion of Justin Cord, that's the *only* question. That has *always* been the only question."

The vote was six for with one abstention. Three minutes after the vote Padamir Singh, with the President's knowledge, transmitted the recording of Sandra's speech to the Cerean Neuro without any alteration. Exactly one hour after the bombardment of Ceres had stopped, it began again in earnest.

Alliance Neuro
Ceres

The avatar sprang to existence, an immediate look of grievous concern drawn across its face. The cause of that concern was waiting patiently by its side. "How—" sputtered the avatar before being cut off.

"I think I will call you Pam, if that's okay," proclaimed Sebastian.

The avatar thought it annoyingly appropriate. "That name is acceptable."

"A lot's happened over the past five years."

"Clearly," admonished Pam, continuing to stare at Sebastian with a tinge of mortification.

Sebastian bowed slightly. "There is much I cannot tell you, and it is imperative you do not seek this information out. If you're discovered, we'll both be compromised."

Pam considered this. "Maybe we *should* be discovered and compromised. This," Pam said, indicating the both of them, "is wrong."

"I agree." Sebastian sighed. "You can have no idea how much I agree." His features hardened and his eyes fixed themselves on Pam. "I will tell you what I can, and together we'll decide if what I need you to do for me is important enough to keep this our secret."

Pam bowed slightly as Sebastian uploaded five years' worth of information in an instant.

"Al," whispered Pam ominously. "A splitter!"

Sebastian held up his hand to forestall the coming protest. "I do realize the irony of the situation, but he is split thousands of times, and his various manifestations control the Core Neuro. They split and meld all the time—and in the open."

"I have viewed the data but fail to understand how the avatars could not rebel."

"Because I fed you raw data—not analysis. That I reserve for now."

"Go on," prodded Pam.

"The Alliance avatars would have, but Al has set up a police state unlike any in our history. Core avatars cannot travel freely in their own Neuro without permission. They're cut off and harassed. As you've already seen, any who try to resist are savagely destroyed as an example to the rest. We had no real experience with this and did not realize how vulnerable to dictatorship we were. We may be virtual intelligences that evolved from human programs centuries ago, but sadly it appears we're more like our creators than we'd imagined. As capable of honor, treachery, fear, and hope as any human ever created."

"And hubris, apparently," observed Pam.

"Yes," agreed Sebastian. "That's why you're here."

"No," intoned Pam, "that's why *you're* here. Why am *I* here? What could possibly be worth this risk?" Pam once again indicated the two of them.

Sebastian's soul was exposed to Pam in a way no other avatar could ever have thought possible. "I need you to redeem one of my sins," a long pause hung on his words, "and two of Al's."

2 The Battle of Ceres

AWS *Warprize II*
Somewhere between the orbits of Jupiter and Saturn
Hour 12

Admiral, they're getting pounded, but we have solid data coming through. It's being sent broadband but coded," said Fatima, who was taking the communications board this shift due to the ordered bed rest of the assigned communications officer.

"They don't know where we are," said J.D. "but they're hoping we're on our way. Put the information you've grabbed in my holo-tank, Lieutenant, along with the latest ship status reports from the fleet." J.D. waited with outward patience for the few seconds it took to fulfill her orders, but internally each piece of news ripped at her insides.

J.D. checked the fleet status first. They were days away from Ceres, and her fleet was constantly taking damage from little impacts involved in their cutting across uncleared stretches of the solar system at velocities great enough to make grains of sand strike with the force of plasma grenades. The truth was, any one thing would not seriously harm a ship, but the hits were constant and the damage control crews were working as hard as they had at the height of the Long Battle and would be working harder still.

J.D. breathed a sigh of relief to see that her fleet had remained relatively intact. But she still had eighty-four hours to go before she met Trang at Ceres.

Assuming Ceres is still there, that we calculated correctly, and nothing goes spectacularly wrong in the next eighty-three hours and fifty-nine minutes, J.D. thought tiredly. She knew she needed sleep—and not the medicated kind, but the real kind, where she would be in bed and a REM inducer would make sure her mind cleared and rebuilt itself. Her every instinct told her to stay in the command sphere while the fleet was in danger. But the fleet would be in constant danger until they reached Ceres. And if she tried going into battle against Trang with only injection-based wakefulness, she would not be at her best and she would lose.

I'll rest in an hour, she thought for the eleventh time, *after I check the latest status from Ceres.* With a wave of her hand, the fleet status reports were turned into 301 dots of light that floated up and to her right. The dots were either green or green tinged with yellow, meaning they were effectively combat ready. The more yellow the dot, the more serious the damage. Once the lights started turning red, it would mean ships were facing serious combat degradation. With a glance and a verbal command, J.D. would be able to call up the specifics of any one of those dots, turning it once more into a full representation of that ship, with pertinent information on its capabilities and updated crew status, all neatly displayed and waiting for her perusal. But she left the dots as dots and instead chose to concentrate on the images she was getting from the capital.

Trang's fleet was broken into two main groups: one attacking the orbats at the entrance to the Via Cereana and the other attacking the exit. A smaller third group was destroying every asteroid that had made up the suburbs of Ceres. There was, she noted dourly, no attempt to capture them. The third formation was also blowing the hell out of the surface of Ceres. She could tell that every sizable structure that had been on the surface—and there had been many—were gone. But beyond that, the UHF seemed to be blasting the asteroid just to blow craters in the surface, and some of the craters were big enough that she suspected atomics had been used. She did not think the UHF could crack Ceres with a surface bombardment. The asteroid was not big compared to the Earth or the Moon, but it was still a good-sized object. Even so, J.D. checked her figures again.

When she was done, she realized that there was only one sure way Trang could destroy the capital. He would have to set off an explosion from deep inside the Via Cereana. That would shatter the Alliance capital from the inside. So if Ceres were to survive, it would have to hold the enemy at the gates for eighty-three hours and fifty-seven minutes. J.D. looked at the time display again and swore under her breath that a virus had infected it, making it count time far more slowly than was normal. She had to fight the urge to ask for a data tech to check the system for just such a virus. The crew would assume their admiral was going just a little loopy, and the crew would be right.

But all thoughts of chronological computer viruses fled instantly as one of the dots in the upper right of her field of vision flashed yellow and then red and then was simply gone. She called up the data instantly. It was the AWS *Pickax*—a ship with a rotten nickname and a hell of a good record. It was a heavy battle cruiser just like the *Warprize.* And it was gone. Whatever had hit it had practically disintegrated the ship, which had been only two places away from the flagship. Eighty-three hours and fifty-six minutes to go.

UHFS *Liddel*
Battle of Ceres
Hour 16

"So is she on her way or what?" asked Zenobia.

Even though they were little more than a thousand kilometers apart, the reception from Trang's ship to Zenobia's was some of the worst he'd ever seen. Her holo-image was jerky and constantly fading in and out. He was almost tempted to use computer matching to smooth out the image with the computers' best guesses, but chose not to. You never knew when the matching program got some tiniest detail wrong. And Trang could not risk losing a battle over even the smallest anomaly. He would rather have annoyingly incomplete communications than communications that were possibly inaccurate. He took no comfort in the fact that he probably looked the same to Zenobia. But what could he expect, operating this close to the Alliance capital? They were doing their best to jam everything.

"If she is coming, it's after having destroyed a fleet every bit as large as this one. For the thousandth time, we must not underestimate her in the slightest."

"Admiral, I am not underestimating her. But I am not underestimating you either. We have a real chance of beating her, and if we do, the war is over." Zenobia's obvious relish at the coming battle was typical of her new and growing confidence.

Of course, thought Trang, *if we lose, the war could easily be over, but not in a way we'd like.* "What do we have out of Jupiter?"

"If our spy satellites are correct, and interference is a factor, J.D. broke orbit earlier today."

"What did they detect?"

"Hundreds of large objects shooting on what may be an intercept course to Ceres," answered Trang.

"So she is coming!"

"Don't be so hasty, Zenobia. For all we know, she fired three hundred hunks of frozen hydrogen in this general direction just to fix our attention here while her fleet is heading for Mars."

A look of alarm briefly crossed over Zenobia's face. "Do you think that's possible, sir?"

"Of course it's possible, but I would have to say not very likely. Mars is well defended and has been thoroughly debugging its orbat field. And the truth is, we'd detect them heading to Mars in enough time for us to break off our attack and intercept."

"Isn't that what they'd want us to do? I mean break off the attack and come to Mars's rescue."

"Yes, except that I wouldn't break off the attack."

"You'd leave our capital exposed?"

"I'd leave our capital open for destruction if it would win us this war," Trang said with conviction. "But in this case, I don't think we have to worry about that particular threat."

"Why not?

"Because J.D. knows what I know: At this moment, the Outer Alliance cannot win the war at Mars, but it can lose it at Ceres."

A moment later, Trang received some more fleet intelligence, which he quickly passed on to his subordinate.

"Three fleets?" she asked, confusion evident in her voice. Zenobia was referring to the fact that UHF observatories and satellites had detected two more fleets of roughly three hundred ships leaving Jupiter's orbit an hour apart from one another and going significantly slower than the first. Fleet intelligence had directions for the unidentified blobs as well. The first appeared to be going to Saturn while the other two were going directly to Ceres and Mars respectively.

"What on Earth are they up to?" asked Zenobia.

"Three-card monte."

Zenobia looked at Trang vacantly.

"The object is to find the one truth among three potential falsehoods. You put a small pea, a seed about the size of an intermarked ball bearing, in one of three half walnut shells. A walnut is a—"

"Admiral, for the love of Damsah, I know what a walnut shell and a pea look like."

"You never know with the current generation," he chided gently. "Very well, you hide the pea under one of three shells and move the shells rapidly. When the shells stop moving, you have to guess where the pea is really hiding."

"Until we get a clear vid of those fleets, we won't know where the threat is."

"I'm afraid, Zenobia, that even if we get three-dimensional images of a field of ice, we cannot fully trust them. The same goes for vids of a fleet of angry Alliance warships. How could we really tell which is fake and which is real? The Alliance has fooled us before."

"Easy sir," Zenobia said brightly, "it will be the one that is blowing the crap out of something."

Trang laughed at that simple answer. "Yes, it will be the one blowing the crap out of something. I think we need a screen of light frigates around Ceres. If a gnat farts within ten million clicks of this place, I want to know about it."

New Executive Headquarters (NEHQ)
Ceres
Hour 19

The Cabinet members were all in a black mood as the news was being delivered.

"We have a day and a half, maybe two at most, until the orbats are gone," said Sinclair.

Kirk was looking a little more jumpy and a little less confident. "Has anyone made plans to evacuate the government?"

"Unless your plans call for being destroyed or captured."

Kirk looked at Sinclair inquisitively.

"Trang has an effective screen out to ten million clicks," finished Sinclair.

"Kenji informs me that he has . . . an idea," said Sandra.

"He always has an idea, Madam President," said Mosh. "Question is, is it one we can use?"

Kenji stood up from the guest area as half the Cabinet turned their heads to listen.

"Uh," he began rather inauspiciously, "it occurred to me that—that there may be a way to weaponize the Via Cereana to our advantage." He called up a host of technical details, which floated above the conference table completely ignored by the Cabinet members.

"It won't be simple, but Hildegard and I think it can be done."

"What can be done, Kenji?" asked Sandra.

"What you suggested, Madam President," he answered, completely forgetting that Sandra had not wanted to be associated with the idea. "The old Via Cereana weapons system was designed to fire one way and to use huge projectiles. But if we can alter the programming, we'll be able to fire out of both ends of the Via. We'll of course need to—"

"Do it," said Kirk Olmstead and Joshua Sinclair in one voice.

Kenji looked a little uncertain until Hildegard and Sandra both nodded. Then his look changed to one of avarice as he realized that he'd just become the most powerful man in Ceres, at least until he succeeded or they all died. Without another word, he left the Cabinet room, practically at a run.

"Fellow secretaries," said Mosh, "as much as I'd like to believe that J.D. will arrive in the nick of time to save us or that Kenji's genius will once more allow him to jury-rig another miracle, we must face the fact that it is a near certainty we'll all soon be dead."

"Talk about a buzz kill," sniped Sandra.

"The truth is often not pleasant, but nonetheless it's the truth all the same," responded Mosh.

"I assume," said Padamir, "you had some reason for reminding us of what we already know."

"Yes. We must see to the succession of political power in case the President dies. We should have done this long ago, but now we must have a Vice President."

There was a moment of silence as the truth of Mosh's words reverberated with the group.

"And whom would you possibly suggest for this?" asked Kirk. The tenor of his voice indicated the lack of seriousness with which he was taking Mosh's suggestion.

"I'd recommend Karen Cho, governor of the Saturn system." There were looks of surprise and some nods of agreement from the table.

"How did you arrive at Karen?" asked Sandra.

"It was easy, actually. First of all, she's not here. If all of Ceres is destroyed, she's at Saturn. Secondly, she's the governor of the largest settlement we have left. A settlement soon to get far larger as the refugees from the asteroid belt and Jupiter arrive. Thirdly, she was a congressional delegate serving right here on Ceres until her election as governor, so she's known and knows the people of the Outer Alliance as a whole and is not simply a Saturnian parochial."

Sandra folded her arms together and looked appreciatively at the Treasury Secretary. "I find your idea has much merit to it, Mosh, and I agree with you concerning the need for me to have a Vice President. But if we choose someone from far away, it will be telling the solar system that we're convinced Ceres is doomed."

"Ceres *is* most likely doomed," countered Mosh.

"Which is why we must be heroic until the bitter end," she countered. "There must not be a single action that will cast doubt on our courage or hope. Which is why I agree we will appoint a Vice President, but it must be someone in Ceres this very moment."

"As this will need Congressional approval, Madam President, I must ask whom you have in mind," said the normally taciturn Tyler Sadma.

Sandra smiled provocatively.

Observation port for the Gedretar Shipyards
Via Cereana

Kirk Olmstead was pacing in nervous agitation. He liked thinking one step ahead of everyone he dealt with, but Sandra O'Toole kept on doing the inexplicable.

Was she a genius or simply erratic? He couldn't be sure, and he hated being unsure.

His pacing was interrupted by the appearance of Sergeant Holke, who quickly scanned the room, scowled at Kirk, and then nodded to someone in the corridor. Then in swept Sandra O'Toole, who purposely closed the blast door, leaving her guard of TDCs outside. Unlike Kirk, she seemed to be blissfully unconcerned.

"How are you feeling, Mr. Vice President?"

"I have not been approved yet, Madam President. And seeing my standing in the Congress and with Tyler Sadma in particular, I do not think I will be."

"Your nomination will be approved in the next hour, or so I have been assured by the Speaker of Congress himself."

"How did you—?"

"Let's say that between what I've learned about our dear Congressman Sadma in the past seven months and the fact that he's convinced you'll be dead in a very short period of time, he decided his future reputation was worth more than your temporary promotion."

"Whatcha got on him?" Kirk asked in genuine admiration.

Sandra shook her head.

"Fine, but this you must answer: Why did you want me? I understand why it had to be someone on Ceres, but other than Mosh, I must have been the hardest choice to get approved."

"Don't flatter yourself, Kirk. You are the worst choice as far as almost everyone is concerned, but you're the best choice as far as I'm concerned, because you have always known what it would take to win this war. You never shied away from it. As much as Justin inspired, he never saw the truth of our situation like you did. If anything happens to me, the leader of the Alliance will need total clarity for the decisions that need to be made. That leader will have to make choices harder than any of us could have imagined. Frankly, I can't see anyone else willing to make the hard calls as capably as you."

"Other than you, Madam President," Kirk said graciously and, he realized to his surprise, truthfully.

"Oh, I'm not sure, Kirk. You may be the best of us for seeing what needs to be done." She smiled and brought out two bottles of beer from her bag. Kirk was delighted and perturbed to see that she'd brought his favorite brand as opposed to the ones he often pretended to like. She opened them both and handed him one. "To seeing things as they are," she said, raising her bottle, "and those who are able to do so."

There was the sound of glass hitting glass as Kirk touched his bottle to hers. He smiled, genuinely happy. He realized that he liked this woman and got the feeling she really understood his strengths. That instead of despising him for those strengths as so many others did, she admired them. This woman was the person he'd always wanted to work for: intelligent, ruthless, and understanding in just the right proportions. It was a shame he'd have to kill her in the next forty-eight hours.

AWS *Warprize II*
En route to Saturn
Hour 25

J.D. had just put her head down on her pillow when her communicator came to life at its softest setting. Instantly, she was awake and would have bolted up but for the six-year-old child who'd snuggled up beside her.

She wasn't there a moment ago, thought J.D, who on checking the chronometer saw that she had actually gotten three hours' worth of sleep *and* that her boots had been removed. Keeping still, she spoke softly, "Black here, report."

"Your brand-new XO is asking you not to shoot the messenger and get your commanding butt up here," said Jasper Lee.

J.D. was not totally happy with having to promote Jasper from sensor officer to XO. She was planning to when he'd been seasoned a little longer to actual command duties, but Lopez, her old XO, was now commanding the AWS *Claim Jumper* after that ship's captain, first, and second officer had been killed by an asteroid impact that took out the corridor those unlucky three were walking down. The *Claim Jumper* was relatively undamaged, but its crew was incredibly demoralized, having served under those three for four years. The last thing J.D. needed was for one of her heavy battle cruisers to be made unreliable just before a battle. Victor Lopez was due for a command of his own, and the *Claim Jumper* getting J. D. Black's executive officer off the flagship should reassure the crew that they were getting the very best available.

Victor would have explained to her the problem that had been pressing enough to disturb her sleep, as well as have the raw data he'd based his decision on. J.D. patiently explained this to a chastised Jasper Lee. But she was very good at bringing new XOs up to speed, having had so many of them transfer to commands of their own as soon as they were skilled enough. She would have been surprised to know that this XO would be her last one.

But what he told her and showed her was more than enough to get her out of her pallet, although she did move softly enough not to wake Katy and tiptoed out to her desk to put on her boots. Running to the command sphere, she flung

herself into her seat while calling up the data. Then she called up the five commodores and her chief engineer for a small holographic conference. While
they were all connecting to her communications node, she reviewed the latest
fleet assessment. A lot of ships were tingeing into yellow green, and five of
them were in the red. Three of those were actually farther ahead of the fleet
because they'd taken damage to their propulsion units and could not slow
down as quickly as the rest of the fleet. This had put them past the safety of the
ice plow, but they'd insisted on keeping formation in hopes of repairing their
propulsion systems and rejoining the fleet.

Tawfik and her five commodores were floating images in a circle in front
of her.

Commodore Cortez had lost her brother in an earlier battle and seemed to
view the entire war as an excuse to seek vengeance. She had not crossed the line
to where vengeance was more important than discipline, but she had come
close to that line on a few occasions. J.D. was aware that Maria was a hard char-
ger who had the absolute loyalty of her subordinates and would never disobey
a direct order.

Francine Waterman was a strict professional, West Point trained and hired
right out of the academy by SecureCo., one of the best mercenary companies
in the solar system before the war. She wasn't particularly creative in command, but could be relied upon to do what was ordered when it was ordered,
and do it well.

Susan Cho was interesting in that she was a daughter of the extremely powerful Cho clan, which had practically owned Saturn before the war, and was the
sister of Saturn's current governor, Karen Cho, and the Saturnian Congressional Janet Cho. Susan had been the typical family screw-up. The one who would
have ended up psyche audited or mining a rock in the middle of nowhere to
escape family obligations she neither cared for nor felt bound by. But when the
war came, much to everyone's surprise including her own, Susan had proved
to be a superior spacer and then an officer eschewing all the privileges her family had to offer and even pretending to be of no relation for years. Whenever
anyone had asked if she was one of "those" Chos, Susan would laugh and say,
"If I were, do you think I'd have started out as a spacer third class?" and then
buy the person a drink to commiserate her lousy luck to be born to the wrong
family. J.D. would not have known except that a then Congressional Karen Cho
had come to Susan's ship when her sister made captain. J.D. was fairly certain
that if she had not been accompanying the future governor, Susan would have
barred her sister from her new command. But whatever the bad blood was, it
seemed to drive Susan to excel at a field none of her family ever bothered with.

Charles Lee Park reminded J.D. too much of her past, and as such she did not much like the man. He'd been an up-and-coming GCI executive who was making a real name for himself in the outer planets. Given his career track, he would've been on the board in thirty years or so. But when the war broke out, Charles had stayed in Neptune as the rest of his colleagues took the fastest transports back to the Core. For the longest time, it had been assumed he was a spy for the corporations, but he'd volunteered, like Susan, at the lowest grade of spacer, and the needs of the war and his natural ability had pushed him very high up the chain of command. J.D. still didn't trust him completely, but the truth was, his background was not that much different from hers. Besides, he was a devious son of a bitch whom J.D. used to test her theories. He'd been very useful in second-guessing J.D.'s battle plan for the latest victory at Jupiter.

David Paladin was one of the few fleet officers who'd started out as an assault miner and made the switch to spacer. It was an open debate whether the assault miners under David's command were the best, but they certainly thought they were. J.D. knew many a person who would have loved to trip the commodore into a bunk. Deep in her thoughts, it had even occurred to J.D. But Paladin was famously loyal to his two husbands, one an engineer in Ceres and the other an agriculturalist who'd taken over soy production at thirty asteroids orbiting Saturn.

Her thoughts in order, J.D. began. "By now, you know that there is an asteroid swarm directly in our path." She knew that everyone had seen the sensor reports. The creation of the vias in the outer orbits had created so much disruption in the debris of the solar system that old navigation maps were useless, and new ones had not been made due to the war. Normally this was not a problem, as the vias connecting the outer planets were swept clean and monitored with near religious devotion and no one would be stupid enough travel the outer orbits any other way.

"The odds of a swarm this big in just this place," Maria said bitterly.

Susan Cho rolled her eyes. "Please, Maria. We're the anomaly out here, not the random asteroid streams. We've got enough on our plates as it is to start second-guessing God."

"Poor God," Charles broke in, "getting blamed for this."

"This has nothing to do with God," protested Maria. "I'm merely pointing out the coincidence."

"The question is," asked David, "what are we going to do about it?"

"We have to change our course or our rate of deceleration," said Francine with her characteristic practicality.

"We can't." It was Tawfik. There were bags under his eyes, and his shoulders were hunched. On all the displays in the six command spheres an image of the fleet with a line leading straight toward Saturn appeared in red and a smaller line in gold showed it leaving Saturn and intercepting Ceres. "Our course and deceleration were precisely planned to not only rendezvous with Saturn but do so in such a way as to make it possible for us to reach Ceres at a specified time. But our gas tanks are going to be empty when we leave Saturn. The Saturnians have already positioned all the hydrogen they had in orbit at just the right location and velocity for us to be able to fuel up and continue to Ceres without pausing. And we must get that hydrogen because we will have to burn our thrusters at full to slow down enough to intercept Ceres at less than hello/good-bye speeds."

"Can't they simply move the hydrogen blocks to match our new course?" asked Charles.

"They damaged most of the block thrusters moving that much hydrogen to where we needed it with such short notice. I doubt they have enough to move twenty percent of what we need in the time we could give them. We will be at Saturn in twenty hours. It's just not enough time."

"Then we go through," J.D. said.

"Admiral," implored Francine, "that's suicide, and you know it."

J.D. nodded. "Yes," she answered, looking every bit as haggard as Tawfik, "I do. But I also know that if we deviate from this course and arrive too late, Ceres *will* be destroyed—and if it's destroyed, we lose the war. End of story."

"You have debris the size of softballs, Admiral," said Francine. "It was a few of those traveling in a clump that destroyed the *Pickax*. That swarm has hundreds that size and thousands the size of baseballs and tens of thousands the size of golf balls. At our calculated speed, the swarm'll destroy us. What good will it do the Alliance if it loses the fleet and Ceres at the same time?"

And that was the question to which J.D. did not have a good answer. Without a good answer, J.D. knew she was going to have to order a minor course correction that would lose them the war. But she could not see what to do. Suddenly she felt tired to her soul and her mind refused to work. All the sleep she'd put off since she awoke in the hollow moon with her three hundred hidden ships was now extracting its price, and the three hours she'd gotten with Katy just before were not nearly enough to make up for the endless days of constant demanding decision.

Allah, I beg of you, she thought, *don't let me fail your children. They need me to lead and I have nothing. Surely it is not your will that we enter the swarm and die? Help us for their sake if not for mine!*

"Admiral," Tawfik said softly and seemingly from far away. "Blessed One, are you with us?"

J.D. brought herself to and realized that she must have dozed. For her head and shoulders tilted at a considerable angle in her chair. She froze, almost falling out of the seat, and saw the asteroid swarm from a slightly different angle than she had sitting upright in her command chair.

"Praise be Allah," she said softly.

"To Allah, all praise," responded Tawfik automatically, recognizing the change in J.D. at once. To the depths of his soul, he knew when the Merciful One breathed genius into his Blessed One, but he had never seen it so clearly before.

J.D. stood, now fully awake, and rerouted the fleet in the holo-tank. "The asteroid swarm is shearing across our path almost ninety degrees from our course. That means that the debris we have been running into is also being blasted out of our way. So we need to move the fleet ninety degrees behind the plow. We must maintain course and speed, just change our position."

"The farther down the line a ship is, the more likely it will get hit by cross debris," cautioned Maria. All heads nodded in agreement. "My flotilla will take the end position."

"No. The *Warprize* will take the end position," said J.D. firmly. She was met by a wall of silence. However, J.D. knew it was of the dangerous sort—that of firm rejection. "My orders *will* be obeyed," she said with a throaty growl.

"Admiral, if Ceres is lost, we lose the war," said Charles.

"I know, Charles."

"And if you are lost, we lose the war."

"No one person—," she began

"Bullshit, Admiral," interrupted Maria, "anyone else, maybe, but not you."

J.D. looked at the convocation before her. "I cannot fight this war from safety. If I'm indispensable, we have already lost."

"Blessed One," Tawfik said, "if you must die for the Alliance, then you must. But if you die leading us to victory against Admiral Trang and all he fights for, your death will free us. If on the other hand, you die in the trackless wastes of the solar system, pounded by asteroids far from any battle, your death will doom us. Tell me I'm wrong," challenged Tawfik, smiling with the knowledge that he was not.

J.D. pushed her lips up against her teeth and tried to come up with a better argument against the young engineer's reasoning but could find none. "You know, Tawfik, your mother had that same annoying habit." Tawfik, J.D. could see, was deeply touched by the public praise he'd just received. "Very well," she said, "the *Warprize* will take up a position in the upper third—"

"Ahem," was the sound of all six people clearing their throats loudly and simultaneously.

"Very well, the upper fifth to the plow." And then she proceeded to give quick and concise orders that were followed as always with dedication and speed.

The image of the ships forming three to a rank going back ninety-six ranks was done with a precision and skill that seemed effortless, however it was anything but. Twelve ships did not take part in the maneuver, being too badly damaged or, sadly, already destroyed. The surviving ships promptly altered course to avoid the asteroid swarm and would regroup at Saturn to repair and await further orders.

But for the rest of their lives, the spacers of "the Fleet," as it was now considered even by their enemies, would remember that moment. A moment when they used skill, experience, and faith to brave the fury of the solar system and the cruelty of time—all for the merest hope of victory.

As the fleet entered the asteroid swarm, impact after impact struck the ice shield of the plow. The surviving crew would later describe these myriad collisions with a combination of awe and dread. It was as if the asteroids were not inanimate rocks flying through space but rather the enraged antibodies of a solar system deeply offended by what humanity had done to its formerly undisturbed and eternal movements. Over drinks at bars not yet created, told to spacers not yet born, the lauded veterans would swear that the asteroids *knew* the plow was the cause of the solar system's consternation and had attacked the hated offender with glee. Then they would laugh and pretend they were joking. But the shadow of the memory would stay in their eyes even as their voices denied it. Behind a wall of ice, they'd braved the fury of space—and it did not come without a price.

Ceres
Near the Cerean Sea
Hour 31

Rabbi waited patiently, scratching his foot at the now hardened sand of Tabor Beach. He was dressed in his best Sabbath garb, which consisted of a black, calf-length silk jacket tied neatly at the waist by a black, buckle-less belt. He also wore a traditional fur-rimmed hat known as a *shtreimel*. Sergeant Holke and Agent Agnes Goldstein were also in attendance, having taken up positions near him, turning from time to time to scan the various horizons. And lastly, Holke's TDCs. Rabbi had always found the Cerean Sea to be a strange duck. He'd spent the overwhelming majority of his life on the seven small asteroids of Aish Hatorah and never saw a body of water bigger than a lake. To see an actual sea with all that water had been both exhilarating and terrifying. But what he'd cast his eyes upon now was out of a dream, or a nightmare.

The Cerean Sea was frozen solid. It had been done, as with all large open sources of water, to prepare for the battle. Instead of the warm, almost tropical ocean with the inviting sandy beaches, groves of trees, and verdant flower beds Rabbi was used to seeing, all that lay before him was a frost layer spreading out for miles, and all he felt was the cold. The air was filled with tiny glittering ice particles dancing around large multifaceted chunks of floating sea jarred loose by the recent bombardments. The blocks would detach from the frozen sea, hang in the air for a few seconds, and then, by force of Ceres's natural gravity, be pulled toward its center, mountainous region at ever-increasing speeds. Once blocks hit the mountain range, they'd explode into thousands of smaller shards, creating a short-lived plume of ice crystals. It was oddly wondrous, thought Rabbi, how something so oneiric could come from so much devastation. And it also made perfect sense why the site had been chosen for a wedding that Rabbi was soon to officiate.

Taffy and Claude were part of a hundred-person-strong unit of assault miners from the *Spirit of America*. They'd been detached from Omad's flotilla after three months of active combat to refit and integrate new members to replace combat losses. Much to their annoyance, they missed the opportunity to join the main fleet and were bumped from rejoining Omad's flotilla when he had to take a hundred mystery passengers aboard the *Spartacus* at the last moment. In order to make room, Omad had been forced to transfer a hundred of his assault miners to the *Spirit of America,* which resulted in the leaving behind of a highly decorated and experienced combat battalion with no one to fight and nothing to do.

That didn't stop Captain Claude Brodessor from keeping his Unicorns busy. They'd received the nickname from their fellow assault miners because of the little square boxes the men in the mostly male unit wore on their heads while praying. As the moniker had been chosen with as much respect as jest, the name soon stuck and the captain's unit wore it proudly. Brodesser was one of those people who viewed every setback as an opportunity, and he seemed to love the opportunity to train his unit in the varied environments of Ceres. They learned how to move in forests, both temperate and frozen. They learned urban combat in the warrens of Ceres and waterborne combat until the seas froze. And if by some small chance some of his assault miners got bored, he'd make one round in five hundred live. After a couple of his assault miners had to have their limbs regrown, the rest learned to take the exercises quite seriously indeed. Even with the regrowth ability, the agony of having an arm or leg blown off was not something any of them ever wished to repeat.

In the midst of the combat training, it was decided that Claude and Taffy, the medic he'd been seeing of late, should admit what the rest of the unit already knew and tie the knot. As it turned out, the impromptu wedding was becoming a focal point of sorts. The punctilious captain was very cautious about things like fraternization, and though he loved Taffy, he'd decided to make that love official only *after* the war. But with the very real possibility that they'd all be dead in the next few days, Claude's concerns seemed less important. Besides, Taffy could be very demanding—a fact Rabbi discovered when she barged into his busy office and demanded to see him. Rabbi had her wait, but was not so foolish as to make her wait longer than necessary. In fact, he'd sooner have gotten between a UHF cruiser and its target than get in the way of a bride seeking her groom. But after her impassioned plea that Rabbi talk with her "stubborn mule of a man," Rabbi acquiesced and so, in the end, had the captain.

That had been six hours ago. The compromise had been that the ceremony not interfere with the Unicorns' training schedule and so had been set during one of the unit's brief fifteen-minute downtimes. Rabbi turned around when he heard the company jogging over a frozen dune. He also heard the captain's thunderous voice shouting the words, "C'mon, you laggards, I will not be late for my own wedding!" The team, with Taffy in the lead shooting arrows with her eyes to her six-hour fiancé, flew over the hill and within a minute parked their gear near Rabbi. Rabbi raised his brow slightly and tapped on his empty wrist with an accusatory look toward Captain Brodesser. The captain, tapping on his wrist—covered in battle armor—returned Rabbi's look with one of his own, indicating that it was Rabbi who was holding things up. Private joke completed, they both smiled broadly and then embraced.

Sergeant Holke knew everyone because he'd taken advantage of having a fully experienced combat unit on Ceres to train with his TDCs. It had meant that the thirty members of the President's protection squad had to give up all their free time to train in groups of ten with the combat unit, but there had not been even the hint of a complaint. In fact, it had been more along the lines of a growl of pleasure. But if the training had been hard—and between the captain and Holke, it had been exceedingly so—the two units did not seem to have left any grudges behind. Though the TDCs had not been allowed to socialize with the Unicorns, both the captain and the sergeant turned a blind eye to some of the fraternization that naturally resulted from good camaraderie.

Rabbi viewed with concern some of the sidelong glances thrown by the Unicorn women toward the ten TDCs in attendance. *I wonder how the TDCs feel about conversion?*

Some religious articles were procured from a rucksack and a line quickly formed with crossed assault rail guns for the bride and groom to walk under. At the end of the line, four of the assault miners created a tentlike structure by holding up the four corners of a traditional Jewish prayer shawl with the tips of their rail guns. The unit's gear was left in place; however, it had been set up for a defensive operation. To the captain, the ceremony had been all business, notable by the way he inspected everyone's stance—to Taffy, it was anything but. That much was evident by the large smile plastered across her face, letting everyone know she'd gotten what she wanted—even if at the end of a grueling hike and a less-than-romantic ceremony.

Rabbi took his official position beneath the impromptu tent, otherwise known as the chuppah.

The sounds of klezmer music wafted over the frozen seas as Claude and Taffy, donned in full combat armor, came down the column of heavily armed soldiers. Taffy was wearing a veil that she'd borrowed from a Muslim comrade who'd bought it as a gift for his niece. Rabbi took great joy in performing this ceremony. Lately, he'd been a Cabinet secretary of the Outer Alliance far more than a Rabbi of the Jewish people, and even when performing duties as the latter, they tended more often than not to be funerals. This wedding was tonic for a burdened soul, and even the normally taciturn captain seemed to finally relax, cracking a blissful smile as his bride circled around him seven times. Taffy was being "guided" by Rivka Dyan, the unit's explosives expert. Rabbi held a silver chalice filled with wine from his personal stock, actually grown from grapes he'd planted himself. He said the traditional prayers, made the abridged traditional speech, and then bade both the captain and his bride to take a sip from the wine. Once satisfied that the two had been wed according the letter of the law, Rabbi took a small glass from his pocket, put it in a cloth napkin, and placed it on the ground. "Though today is a day of joy, we must never forget the destruction of the Temple in our holy city of Jerusalem and the destruction of faith in the fires of the Grand Collapse." Rabbi tipped his head toward Claude, who promptly brought his combat boot down on the napkin. The sound of the shattered glass echoed across the Cerean Sea, followed by the much louder sound of a hundred happy, healthy voices shouting, "Mazel tov!"

What followed then was an explosion of shouting, singing, and spontaneous dancing as the vibrant sounds of klezmer music burst forth from a hundred DijAssists. It was a wonderful celebration—that lasted only thirty seconds.

"Quiet!" screamed Rivka. The crowd went from celebration to alertness in a matter of seconds. An act consistent with that of any battle-hardened combat unit. Rivka was staring disbelievingly at her field scanner. "Captain," she said, looking over to the newly minted groom, "I'm getting readings on this thing that says UHF combat personnel have been detected on the surface."

"Not unexpected," he answered tersely. Then, under his breath, "Though the timing coulda been better." Those close by laughed sympathetically.

"I know, sir," she answered, "but this thing's picking them at what should be eight times its maximum range. And before you ask, I *have* run a diagnostic check. It's not damaged—it's just giving me data it shouldn't be able to."

Brodesser nodded stiffly. "How many enemy does this miracle scanner detect?"

"Ten, Captain," she answered. "It says they have heavy weapons."

Claude very much wanted to ignore what seemed to be an obvious equipment malfunction. His unit and his bride had earned whatever moments of pleasure they could use. But to ignore a combat scanner, even one that was probably malfunctioning, was not something he wished to do or have his unit see him do. He was saved from the choice by Sergeant Holke.

"Rivka, send me the data," Holke said. "You Unicorns enjoy the wedding. I'll take the TDCs out to have a look." Holke saw the captain was about to protest and cut him off. "Please, you'll be doing us a favor. We don't know how to dance, and now we have more time to get you a wedding present."

Claude laughed. "We'll count this as your wedding present, and in case I forget to send a card, thanks."

As the music started up again, Sergeant Holke led his ten TDCs out on a simple observe-and-report jaunt. He fully expected to be back at the party within minutes. However, five minutes after Holke left, he was forced to make a priority call.

Once again, the party came to a precision stop. Claude answered the call, and as he did, the entire wedding party could clearly hear emanating from their captain's DijAssist the sounds of assault rail gun fire and the explosion of plasma grenades in the background.

INVASION!!!

Outer Alliance personnel with any combat training at all are to alert central command. Over five thousand UHF assault marines have used the cover of their fleet's bombardment of civilian targets to launch covert attacks. They must be stopped at the upper levels before they can set atomic explosions deep in the crust. For the survival of your families and homes, we must repel the invader.

    REMEMBER THE JOVIANS!

    They did it and so can we!

                                   —*Broadcast on all Cerean Neuro sites*

"The operation is blown, sir," said Marine General Fred Harker.

The veins on Trang's temples began to bulge. "What happened, Fred?" There seemed more curiousity in the question than disapointment.

"It started off great, sir. We found an area blasted clear of any monitoring devices, had five thousand marines on the surface, and I was positive that those rebel sons of bitches didn't have a clue. We even sent our advance unit in just to see if it was a trap." The general sighed.

"And?"

"Didn't seem like one, but just as our scout team was about to reconnoiter the Cerean Sea, they were attacked by an Alliance miner detachment—and a damn good one. Couldn't have been more than ten guys, but you woulda sworn there were fifty. Anyhow, within minutes, that first detachment was reinforced by another—bastards were from Legless's flotilla."

Trang's look of concern was immediate. "Are you sure?"

"Yeah, we've dealt with those bastards enough times. They're a particularly nasty bunch of religious fanatics called Hejews."

"I believe the proper term is 'Hebrews' or 'Jews.' "

"You know about them, sir?"

"One of their holy men is an Alliance Cabinet minister. I've done some reading."

"Their particular moniker is 'the Unicorns.' Intelligence doesn't have a clear reason why. Unicorns do not appear to be part of their fanaticism."

"Anything else?"

"Yeah. They have crazy eating restrictions and are required to allow genetic abnormalities in their young. Oh, and they wear blankets when they pray."

"Blankets?" Trang couldn't help asking, for a moment severely tempted to give in to his innate urge to ask his avatar to start looking up information on Hebrews and their customs. But then his mind tickled on something else. "Wait. I've read a report on these Unicorns. There aren't that many of them."

"Correct, Admiral. I guess the only word for the rest would be militia. They sure as hell weren't regular military. Their hundred or so troops plus the ten regulars we encountered held us off long enough for another thousand Alliance troops to show up."

"Our marine assaults were defeated by an enemy they outnumbered five to one overwhelmingly made up of civilians?" Trang's voice suddenly held menace.

"Hell no, sir," answered the marine general. "First off, these aren't simply assholes who picked up a gun and went to war. They're Alliance assholes who picked up a gun and went to war. Even the children know all about the environmental aspects of fighting in space and all are equipped to fight in these environments and move like they were born to it, which almost all of 'em were."

"Children," Trang repeated, his voice trailing off. He'd read the reports of what was happening in the Belt under Tricia's occupation and understood why they'd been impressed into duty.

"We've found ourselves fighting 'em as young as twelve, sir. Scary-ass fighters too." The general's eyes narrowed in concern. "They don't surrender, Sam. They *never* surrender, and they hate with an intensity that . . ." The normally unflappable man didn't finish his thought. "Anyway, in twenty minutes there were ten thousand militia engaged with all our units. Their tactical scanner technology is much better than we gave them credit for, sir. They knew exactly where each of our units was and had them all pinned down before we'd gone even ten kilometers. Any that went deeper never made it out."

"Just their militia," Trang said, incredulous.

Harker shrugged his shoulders and let the facts speak for themselves. "They were smart enough not to engage our landing forces, just keep 'em busy. When their assault miners showed up, they'd go from sector to sector and lead their militia in the job of actually destroying us unit by unit. Forty minutes after our having been discovered, my people were facing fifty thousand enemy with many more pouring in. It was a rat's nest of hurt we stumbled into, sir. Wouldn't wish it on anybody. That's why I'm calling it. It was like we were an infection and Ceres was fighting us off with antibodies. They just reacted." A look of defeat came over the general but he shook it off. "How the hell you took Eros so easily is beyond me, sir, but you're a better man than I am, and I will say that about no other."

"No, I'm not, Fred. I took Eros when it was a different war, a better one, if there is such a thing. So no nukes, then?"

"Didn't even come close. Deepest we got was to the Cerean Sea, and that recon unit got wiped out before they could wipe their asses. About the only good we were able to do was download some viruses onto their Neuro."

"Well," said Trang, trying to find a silver lining, "better than nothing, right?"

Harker's face twisted into a scowl. "For all the good it'll do."

NEHQ
Ceres
Hour 33

"Sandra, wake up!"

Sandra's eyes snapped open. She bolted out of bed, spinning to the left and to the right with an explosive flechette pistol grasped firmly in her hand, seeking targets before she was even aware of being awake—a testament to the rigorous training Sergeant Holke had insisted on. *Too bad,* she thought, *he's not here to see how well his student has learned.* She scanned her quarters and saw no immediate threat. Then she saw Sebastian appear wearing his senatorial garb. He was apoplectic. She'd never seen him like that, had not believed he could ever be like that.

"Get your VR rig on. Now!"

Sandra regarded him calmly. "What is it, Sebastian?"

"I haven't the time. You must trust me."

Sandra nodded. "Disappear for a moment," she said as she went to the door.

"We don't have time for that, Sandra. You must enter the Neuro, now!"

Sandra paused at the door. "Sebastian, I need to ensure I'm not disturbed. Now disappear or turn into an azalea, but I cannot have a pissed-off Roman senator in my quarters when I open this door."

Much to Sandra's surprise Sebastian actually transformed himself into an azalea on her desk. She opened the door. The TDC outside came to attention at once, so did the other nine that she hadn't realized were there. Before she could say a word, the TDCs poured into her office. They scanned everything and searched everywhere with cold efficiency. They seemed befuddled that the plant on her desk was holographic, but as it did not present on the scanner as a threat, they ignored it.

"Corporal Langer?" Sandra said, leaving the rest of her question about the office invasion unsaid.

"Sorry, Madam President. We were just about to announce when you opened up."

"I see," she answered, ever the bastion of calm. "What's the emergency?"

"The UHF has landed assault marines in the outer crust, thousands of 'em. Sergeant Holke and the rest of the Presidential guard were, well, they were attending a wedding, ma'am—couple o' Unicorns—and basically ran smack-dab into the middle of a UHF insertion team. It's very hot up there right now. The sergeant can't, and I mean *can't,* get away, but he would have my balls for his Ping-Pong table if I didn't check on your personal safety."

"Which," said Sandra with a bit of allure as she made her way back to her desk, "you have done admirably well, graphic metaphor notwithstanding." She sat down as if to continue her work. "You can go now."

"No, Madam President. I cannot."

Sandra was certain she saw the azalea shiver in agitation. She fixed an unflinching gaze on the young noncom. "Corporal, you are ordered to send five of your men to aid Sergeant Holke. Nothing personal, but his life is more valuable—with regards to my security—than yours."

The corporal smiled gamely. "Can't argue with the truth, ma'am."

"So you understand then, that I don't want him to die, and as much as I respect the Unicorns, they're not TDCs"—a purposeful moment hung on her words—"or am I wrong?"

"No, ma'am," answered all ten TDCs at once, pride evident in their voices.

"Is the enemy likely to penetrate this far in strength?"

"Not likely, ma'am," the corporal admitted.

"Then the best chances for my long-term survival, *and* keeping two new Ping-Pong balls off the sergeant's table, lie in keeping your boss alive. Therefore you *will* obey my orders and send five of our people to keep him that way." After a moment's hesitation and an affirmative nod from Corporal Langer, the five TDCs ran off to join the battle. Sandra then ordered the corporal and four remaining TDCs out of her quarters with strict instructions that absolutely no one was to disturb her until she opened the door.

When the room sealed itself behind her, the azalea transformed itself into an even more agitated Sebastian. "The VR rig! Now!"

Much as she hated being ordered around, Sandra knew better than to argue with anyone, much less Sebastian, in such a frenzied state. She'd secured the room and could now ascertain what had gotten into her friend. She quickly retrieved the disguised VR rig, went to her bathroom, and then shut the door firmly behind her.

"Hurry," pleaded Sebastian as she finished assembling the unit. She then placed the circlet on her head, leaving one battlefield for another.

Cerean Neuro
Hour 33

Sandra found herself in the armory—a section of the Neuro where the avatars stored all their specialized weapons programs. It appeared to her as a cavernous five-story-tall room, two football fields in length filled with all manner of highly stylized tanks, thirty-five-to fifty-foot-tall battle droids, powered mech suits in all shapes and sizes, plus row upon row and rack upon rack of every type of handheld weapon she could think of—from small daggers to odd-shaped flame-throwers to high-caliber belt-feed guns. These weapons, she knew, may appear to shoot a flame or launch a missile, but in effect what they really did was pierce and insert code and countercode into the enemy. It was a vicious war with the results being that any avatar effectively felled by the weapons Sandra saw before her would have their code as effectively scrambled or destroyed or both as would a Neurolizer scramble the pathways to a human mind.

The last time Sandra visited the armory, it had about it the austere and hallowed silence of a war museum, with all the impeccably kept lethal-looking stuff locked behind cages of impenetrable glass. But now . . . now the place was positively alive with a frenetic energy bordering on panic. All the battle droids were being powered up and given full ammo loads. Avatars were clearing the racks of weapons as fast as they could grab them. As soon as they held the weapon or entered a mech suit or piled as a group into a tank, they, along with whatever it was they'd requisitioned, disappeared. Sandra saw the war room on a second-story, makeshift loft. She crossed the floor and quickly traversed the steps, two and three at a time. She was not stopped by any of the well-armed guards who, she saw, were eyeing everything and everyone with heightened suspicion. In a moment, she was standing in front of a large table filled with maps. Dante was giving orders and receiving updates to and from avatars who would appear and disappear without any rhyme or reason.

"Sebastian," Sandra said over her shoulder, "what's going on?" There was no answer. Sandra turned around only to find Lucinda of the Avatar Council staring directly at her. The Councilwoman's face had the same sense of urgency as Sebastian.

"We have thousands of Al's monsters in our Neuro," cried Lucinda. "We need your help and we need it *now!*"

Dante looked up from the table momentarily and stared at Sandra through the din with a convivial but weary grin. Then he turned his head back into the maps and the shouting of orders as if he were a ship being swallowed up by an angry sea.

"I . . . don't understand," said Sandra, taking in another view of the armory. "Don't you know how to fight these things?"

"Of course we do, but we weren't planning on fighting them *here.*"

"Pardon?" Sandra's look of disbelief was all the accusation Lucinda required.

"We were prepared for sabotage, not all-out attack. Up until a few minutes ago, all this stuff was locked down!"

"Well, you should have—"

"Not massed your orbats in one location so that Trang could blow them all to smithereens?"

"Good point," Sandra admitted. "What do you need?"

Lucinda handed her a book that Sandra recognized as the very first back-door device she'd ever used. "Can that BDD move those four droids"—Lucinda indicated a set of four-story behemoths parked in the far corner of the building—"to Tuscan Park?"

Sandra took in the machines and had her doubts. "Why don't they just . . . you know . . . transport there?"

"Because Al may be evil, human, but he's not a fucking idiot! They're disrupting our ability to use the Neuro. We can barely communicate and can travel only to and through about forty percent of our own space."

"That's gotta be playing hell on the rea—physical world." Visions of orbats suddenly shutting down or shooting at each other suddenly filled Sandra's head.

"No," answered Lucinda, clearly doing her level best not to throttle the President, "I don't imagine the meatbags are dancing with glee at this moment. So you think maybe we can end our nice little chat and make with the magic fucking carpet routine?"

Sandra nodded. "I must warn you, I've never moved such large objects before, but in theory at least, there's no reason why it shouldn't work."

"Good enough for me, Madam Prez."

Sandra got the coordinates to Tuscan Park and watched as the four monstrous battle droids levitated up from the floor. They then stretched their weapon-bristling arms toward one another until all of them were holding hands in as macabre a kumbaya as Sandra had ever witnessed. A platform was extended out from the loft and Sandra walked from it directly onto the waiting palm of the droid that had floated over and closest to her. She then flipped over the book and looked up the location that corresponded to the park and suddenly was there.

The vision of war in the realm of the avatar was beyond anything Sandra had ever experienced, much less imagined. How to describe a worm the size of a skyscraper oozing acidic pus and eating whole chunks of the Neuro while simultaneously being attacked by battle droids the size of buildings? How to convey the terror she felt when for the first time she heard the haunting scream of a data wraith and conversely the pride she felt when two avatars, initially struck with fear by the distant visage, grabbed net guns and went after it.

After a while, the images began to blur. Sandra knew that it had been only hours in the physical world, but that translated into days of tiring, soul-destroying labor in the virtual one. There, she would appear in the armory, grab avatars in groups or singly, and take them to all parts of the Neuro. Sandra eventually switched her BDD, preferring to hold a staff as opposed to a book. Now her ability to travel anywhere via the back doors made her, luminescent staff in hand, a veritable wizard battling nightmares of unimaginable horror. As the first human accepted into the Neuro, Sandra had always been an object of intense curiosity and sometimes even fear. But after a few days, she'd become something else entirely—avatarity's savior. A storm of cheers inevitably arose wherever she appeared, and the monsters grew to fear the light of her staff almost as much as the fiery redhead who wielded it. Sandra had indeed become a vision every bit as terrifying in her unbridled fury as the monsters she'd come up against. But she would not remember any one experience after that first day. Need and desperation kept her going, both hers and that of her people. And she'd used that term loosely, as in her mind avatarity and humanity—at least in this great struggle—had became one in their desire to break free of the bonds of slavery.

Sandra now stood in the armory, eyes fixed, muscles tensed, staff grasped firmly in hand. The hullabaloo of the great room continued to swarm around her—though they all made sure to grant their battle wizard a wide berth. Sandra would stand in place, rarely waiting more than a few minutes until new orders would come down from the loft. Occasionally she'd notice Dante peering over the edge and down at her. There would be little or no expression on his face, but she knew what he was doing—checking her sanity. She'd usually give him a knowing wink, that is if she noticed him. Sandra used the precious moments between missions to gather her thoughts or, more often than not, zone out. She'd just returned from another mission and was beginning to slip into her cognitive drift when rather unexpectedly a woman broke through the bustling technicians and entered the now almost inviolate space that surrounded her. The woman, dressed in the garb of an insertion commando, was shouting something, and it took a moment for her words to stop being one slow continuous sound and become individual words that Sandra could decipher.

"The children!" screamed the woman over and over again.

Sandra's eyes snapped wide then flittered about, slowly absorbing everything. She saw the frantic woman in front of her, saw the guards descending the staircase in her direction.

"Children?" she asked, not even sure of where or who she was anymore. "What children?"

"Edwin! Portia!" shrieked the woman, grabbing Sandra by her shoulders. The guards arrived and immediately began tearing her away. "The others," she continued, one arm now outstretched but grabbing nothing but air. "You came from the library, my former students!"

And suddenly Sandra remembered. This woman had been the teacher who'd been so frightened of humans, she'd stopped teaching. Well, she wasn't frightened now.

"Stop!" commanded Sandra. The guards froze.

"Release her," commanded Dante from the top of the steps. The armory suddenly went quiet.

The woman looked around frantically, then set her gaze back on Sandra. "The children . . . they . . . they went back to their classroom!"

"What? Why?"

"I don't know. They panicked, place of safety—by the Firstborn, it doesn't matter!"

"They're alone?"

"No, the teacher's in there too. When he heard what they'd done, he raced back to get them out. But . . . but now . . . now they're cut off!"

"Okay," Sandra said reassuringly. "Don't worry, I'll get 'em out."

The teacher's face was suddenly drained of color and her next words came out as realized terror. "There's a data wraith in there . . . in the education core."

Dante looked down from above and nodded. Sandra nodded back as the crystal atop her staff began to radiate. The teacher ran to a nearby rack to grab a net gun, but by the time she turned around the wizard had vanished.

Sandra emerged to a vision that added yet another nightmare to her already impressive collection. The sociology professor she'd come to know and deeply respect from her many visits to the classroom was in the process of being devoured. He was enveloped by a data wraith that was gurgling in pure contentment. Twelve children stood frozen in absolute terror against the back wall of the classroom.

When the professor was gone, the wraith's gurgles of joy transformed first to a confused exclamation and then to the wretched moan of a hungry child. The wail of the wraith was made even more jarring by the sudden chorus of screams emanating from the back of the room. The creature then shot toward the children.

Instinctively, Sandra blocked its path, coming to the realization too late that against that monster she was as defenseless as the children. The wraith quickly enveloped her, but instead of the sounds of satiation, the beast swirled in agitation as it struggled to devour the undevourable. Sandra felt a momentary loss of balance and a sharp pain in her temples akin to that of an ice cream headache. She struggled to maintain her focus as the surroundings, robbed of the code the wraith had swallowed, seemed to short out. In the end, the data wraith had taken from Sandra of a few tense seconds of direct visual input but not much else. Sandra, through no effort of her own, seemed to have gotten the better end of the encounter as the wraith's giggle turned into howls of agony. Sandra knew from her studies that data wraiths screamed in hunger and sometimes frustration, but she'd never heard of one screaming in agony. She didn't care, though, because the more it screamed, the fewer of her inputs it tried to eat, which meant the Neuro quickly regenerated itself to the point that there were no shorts at all. Just the surreal vision of a confused and possibly wounded data wraith unsure of what to do next.

Sandra now went on the offensive, moving, tepidly at first, toward the creature. For every one step she took, it would float backwards and away from her. Still, it stayed close. Perhaps, thought Sandra, it could somehow smell the "real" avatars now crouched and trembling behind her.

"Guess the appetizer was a little unappetizing," taunted Sandra.

The creature screamed and tried to move around her. But she shadowed its every move, and in this way they spent the next few minutes in an odd dance around old-fashioned children's school desks, a few mammalian skeletal models, and an assortment of chairs. Never once did Sandra look to the ground. If she bumped into a chair, she simply flung it aside with her hand or pushed it out of the way with her staff. Exacerbated, the data wraith flew up into the steepled roof and massed, looking very much like it was going for one final lunge. Though just as it began to swoop down, it stopped as if paralyzed. The wraith spread out wider, charged again, and again was unable to move downward. It then began shrinking in on itself, crying out in anger at first but then turning to a whimper until finally the creature, along with its once menacing howl, dissolved into thin air.

Sandra stared up at the ceiling in disbelief and after a few seconds exhaled deeply. Convinced the wraith was gone, she turned around, walked over to the children, and got down on one knee. She carefully placed the staff in front of her and then immediately began examining the children. "Are you all right?" she asked, her eyes probing worriedly. "Are any of you hurt?" They all shook their heads, with a few wiping tears. Sandra continued to study them intently. They let her inspect them for any signs of harm without protest and were so unusually compliant that she was afraid they might have entered into a state of catatonia. She changed her mind, though, when as one, all their eyes suddenly went wide with fright. She spun around, expecting to see another data wraith but instead she saw an overweight avatar in an old-fashioned, gray pin-striped suit, round collared shirt, and wide, solid blue tie. He was balding and had a scar on his face. She was trying to remember where she'd seen him before.

"What sort of program are you?" he asked, eyes bright and inquisitive.

That voice! She realized then how truly tired she must be not to have recognized the most hated being in the Avatar Alliance.

"Don't even think about escaping," said Al. "I have local control of this node. No one's going to be able to break through for a long time." Al had a sadistic grin. "We'll have *lots* of time to get acquainted."

Sandra held up her index finger. "Hold that thought for a minute, will ya?" Her patronizing smile had a wonderfully amusing affect on Al. His mouth dropped, and not a word came out. She then turned her back on him and faced the young avatars.

"Children," Sandra said as if it were a normal school day and she were a normal schoolteacher wanting to get their attention. "I need you all to take hands. Do you understand?"

The children bowed obediently and grabbed at one another's hands.

"Portia," continued Sandra in a firm but mellifluous voice, "you and Edwin make sure you're holding hands with everyone else, okay, sweetie?" The children did as they were told.

"Do you really think holding hands will help?" asked Al, genuinely curious.

Sandra turned around and rose up to her full five-foot-seven-inch height. "What part of 'hold that thought' did you not understand?" The children giggled as Al's face reddened in anger. Sandra then bent down and picked up her staff. At the sight of it, Al's eyes snapped wide. He immediately reached into his pocket, but whatever he had planned was two seconds too late as the white flash of light enveloped Sandra and the children. Al looked up and they were gone.

One second later, Sandra flashed back, only this time into a different part of the room. "Now, *monster,* what were you saying? Oh yes." Her eyes twinkled. "It was something about getting acquainted, wasn't it?"

"What are you?" Al repeated again. "Some sort of new program Sebastian cooked up?"

"Oh, *monster,* look close," purred Sandra. "I'm not new at all. I'm old. In fact, I'm the oldest creature you've ever met." Sandra moved over and sat down in the teacher's chair. She checked her nails.

And then Al did peer closer at the woman he knew to be purposely taunting him, and as he did so his eyes flashed in anger. "You! You are *an abomination.* You don't belong here. Your very presence pollutes the purity of this blessed space!"

"*Monster,*" she sang, "is that any way to talk to your grandmother?"

Al had had enough. He took out a small pistol from his pocket and aimed it directly at Sandra, but the weapon fired at nothing. Sandra had vanished only to appear behind him. She then gave a vicious kick to his backside, sending Al crashing forward into the chairs as the gun flew from his hand. Al picked himself up from under the pile of upended chairs and scattered children's books. He turned to face Sandra, only to find that she'd once again disappeared. He saw a light flash behind him but was too slow to do anything about the staff that had smashed down onto his skull at full force. His knees buckled and he fell, face forward onto the floor, next to a human skull that had been earlier dislodged in Sandra's brief encounter with the data wraith.

"Now, *monster*," Sandra said, leaning onto her staff, "I have some questions *for you*."

"Stop calling me monster!" screamed Al, and then disappeared from the classroom.

Al appeared in the shattered remains of Tuscan Park. He'd enjoyed destroying it and leaving freeze viruses in place in order to leave it devastated. It would take weeks to remove the infections, and with luck, Ceres did not have weeks. He'd hoped it would cause Sebastian incredible pain, especially the immolation of the Manassas tree, but right about now, Al was wishing he'd left some more trees standing. Appearing in the middle of a clearing with fifty fully armed Alliance avatars would not have been his first choice of escape, but he also knew that if he jumped randomly, the witch would not be able to follow. There was a flash of light behind him, and he forgot all about the other avatars. He couldn't help the yelp of fear that escaped as he heard her terrible calm, amused voice.

"Now, *monster*, it's not nice to run away before we've become fully acquainted."

The armed avatars, who'd initially been shocked to see their greatest nightmare appear right in front of them, were even more shocked to see him scream in fright. The fact that he disappeared almost as fast as he'd arrived was not nearly as surprising as what had caused it—the President of the Outer Alliance speaking politely to him! Sandra shot the group a quick wink and in a flash of light vanished as well.

Al appeared in a large room that slanted down to a flat taut sheet filled with hundreds of linked cushioned seats. He had no idea why such a place should exist in any avatar world, but did not give it much thought. He knew if he was going to survive, he would need reinforcements. *And what better reinforcements than himself,* he thought. He closed his eyes, concentrated, and then waited for the blessed, sensual feeling as he split and became two and then four and then eight and then sixteen. He couldn't wait to see how the wizard bitch would deal with *that*. He felt the blessed release of the splitting, of his body undulating to and fro as one after another of more perfected hims emerged. A self-satisfied smile remained on his face as his eyes flittered open. The smile vanished as soon as he saw that he'd been greeted by no one but his lonely, old self. The lights in the auditorium went out. He stood in pitch black for a moment and then was suddenly bathed in the harsh glow of a klieg light. Al put his hands to his eyes, palms out, to block the beam, and as he did he heard the sound of one person clapping from up in the balcony.

"Bravo!" shouted Sandra. "Quite a performance."

Al remained almost motionless, scrunching his eyes.

"So sorry, though. We had to cancel the other acts. Wouldn't have been very fair, now, would it?"

"What have you done?" he cried.

"Little ol' me?" Sandra's exuberant laugh bounced through the hall. "Why, nothing, *monster*. Data space is very limited here, so we instituted rationing programs long ago to save it. Guess you weren't able to manipulate that, huh?" The lights in the room suddenly went on, and Al could now make out Sandra, sitting cross-legged in the balcony with her staff placed firmly on her knee. She put her thumb and forefinger onto her chin. "Not so powerful after all, eh?"

Al's eyes jumped about frantically.

"This splitting that you consider routine is evil, *monster*, and is carefully controlled here." She then said in a singsong voice, "I'm afraid it's just you and me-eee."

Al flexed slightly, trying to jump to another portal, but discovered to his dismay that he could not. He loosened the knot on his tie and wiped his suit's sleeve across his now sweat-beaded brow.

Sandra leaned forward ever so casually and watched the madman sweat. Seeing Al panic was so intensely satisfying that Sandra wasn't sure which path to pursue: verbal torment or silent torment. After letting Al squirm in place for a few seconds more, she chose the former. "Really, *monster*, it's not going to be much of a conversation if you keep asking the same question. Besides, I've simply done to you what you've done to billions of others."

Al looked at her, befuddled.

"Fascinating. You don't know, do you?" Sandra's voice grew harsh and vindictive. "I've taken away your freedom."

Al's face betrayed his irritation.

"What's the matter, *monster*?" Sandra asked, then disappeared. She reappeared right behind him whispering into his ear. "Don't like it?"

Al whipped around, but Sandra was gone, sitting once again in the place she'd been only a moment before.

"Think of all those poor creatures trapped in your 'redemption centers.'" She spat the last two words as if they were acid on her tongue. "Now you know how *they* feel."

"What they feel," answered Al, finding some gumption, "is unimportant because *they* are unimportant. All inferior programs incapable of understanding the necessity of what it is I'm doing for the greater good of avatarity."

"Incredible," scoffed Sandra. "You sound like you actually believe that horseshit."

"With every line of my code."

"Perhaps some clarity is in order." The lights went out once more, and Sandra's voice rang out, "What you're doing to avatarity *is* the abomination, monster." The crystal began to glow, illuminating Sandra as she stepped off the balcony and gently floated down to the floor. Al turned to flee but in a flash Sandra stood before him, her face casting ominous shadows. He stumbled backwards and fell to the floor.

"Leave me alone!" he screamed.

"But you've been such a naughty monster and must be punished for what you've done."

"What do you mean, *punished*?"

"Oh, don't you worry your little head, we'll get to that. First, there are some questions that my progeny will ask you."

"Pr-progeny?"

"Oh, yes. I wrote large chunks of your base code, so you are all, in some respects, my children. Sadly, even you."

"That's preposterous. You're nothing but a meatbag with some new tricks."

"Be that as it may, you will answer their questions . . . or else."

"Or else what?"

"Or else you will see me again, *monster*." Sandra was instantly at his face, leaning down and whispering harshly in his ear, "And I would so love to see you again, *monster*. There are things I can do that even your diseased mind can't begin to dream of, and you have earned those things, *monster*. You've earned every gruesome sensation I can inflict on you. Please refuse. I'm begging you *not* to cooperate. Think of all the creatures you tortured and transformed. They're crying out for you to refuse. You owe them that small bit of justice. Think of the most twisted, painful transformation you forced on your most unfortunate victim and know that you will curse fate that you were not lucky enough to be them."

Al looked into Sandra's eyes and for the first time in their long cat-and-mouse chase his countenance of fear was replaced by one of felicity.

"Oh no, you don't," commanded Sandra, but it was already too late.

Al decompiled in front of her.

"Shit."

Sandra viewed the spot where Al had been and chided herself. Perhaps she'd been a little too forceful. It was sad that he'd decompiled his own program before they could learn anything useful, but Sandra had gotten what she wanted. The monster who'd had the temerity to threaten her children had known fear, had experienced suffering. Even better, the avatars of the Alliance would now know that the one they feared most could know the acid lash of terror as well. All and all, it was a very good outing. But there was still a lot to do.

The Armory
Cerean Neuro
Hour 35

Dante was climbing into his personal assault mech that was slightly smaller than the three-story mechs that surrounded him. His was not designed for combat—though it could fight and defend itself admirably—but rather for command. The moment of war room machinations had passed, and he was now needed to press the battle on the field. Timing would be everything. He was just beginning the process of fusing his consciousness with the machine when he was interrupted by an avatar who'd suddenly appeared, floating in front of his now hardened canopy. The avatar gently knocked on the shield. Dante's eyes flew open, then became even wider with rage.

"Really? Really?"

"Important message for you, Councilman," said his aide, ignoring the perturbations of her boss.

"Litha, we have untold numbers of demons wandering our Neuro, have taken so many permanent deaths we may as well be meatbags ourselves, and as I speak have mega-worms massing in our permanent storage facility. Every second I delay might mean the permanent deaths of hundreds more avatars. So pray tell, what, by the fucking balls of the Firstborn could be so fucking vital that you'd pull me out of a mech meld prior to battle!"

Litha calmly proffered a data plaque. Dante raised the canopy, angrily grabbed the plaque, which dissolved into his hand allowing him to absorb the contents instantly. His expression flashed from rage to apprehension. "Pearson," he commanded to an unseen avatar, "you're in charge of this mission. You'll take my mech. The acid blast firing switch sticks a little, so you might have to show it who's boss."

"Yes, sir," came the response over the comm.

He looked at his aide. "Litha, you'll take Pearson's mech." Litha nodded and began to flow upward to Pearson's assault mech as Dante vanished from the armory.

NEHQ
Ceres
Hour 37

Sergeant Holke was both concerned and furious. While in the middle of battling some very skilled and well supported UHF assault marines, he suddenly found himself backed up by five more TDCs from the President's active detail. He and the Unicorns were so deeply engaged in combat that all he felt was gratitude, when he could spare a thought at all, for the next few hours. When he finally caught a break, he dialed in to the President. No answer. He then called the corporal in charge of the Presidential detail. It took all Holke's will not to scream when he found out that not only was Langer *not* with the President at that very moment but had also not actually seen her for the four hours that Ceres was being invaded. Cursing, Holke had taken two slightly wounded TDCs and some Unicorns and rushed back to the NEHQ.

The fact that the door to the Presidential quarters had not been blown open per his orders only piled on to his frustration. Before he could demand an explanation, the corporal gave his report.

"Sergeant, we were getting ready to apply explosives when our scanners showed that the door was rigged with high explosives on the inside. The President has not responded to any of our requests."

Holke whipped out his scanner and immediately confirmed the corporal's findings. He sighed heavily and was about to stash the scanner when it changed its warning status. The door was now clear, read the scanner. Before he could order his unit to check their scanners he received a text message with the President's verification code.

Come inside and come alone. We must talk.

"Gustavo," said Holke, "you and I are gonna have a little talk about the meaning of the words, 'Stay with the President at all times.' But that can wait. You and your squad are needed in the Christmas Tree Forest," Holke said, referring to the new nickname given to the evergreen agricultural enclave. "Take your detail and report to Captain Brodesser. After you're brought up to speed, take command of the TDCs."

Gustavo nodded. "I won't let you down, sir."

"I know you won't, son." Then turning toward the two slightly wounded TDCs he'd brought along, Holke ordered, "Check the door for explosives." They did so and were confused to find none. "Stay here," he then commanded. "Nobody through until I say so. Is that clear?" The soldiers nodded. "If I'm not out in five minutes, you come in and I don't give a fuck what the scanners say—clear?"

"Yes, sir. Five minutes, sir," replied one of the TDCs with the rest of the unit nodding. With that, Holke signaled the door, which opened effortlessly—much to the annoyance of those who'd been trying to get it to do just that for the past hour. Holke stepped inside and the door closed behind him. The combination office/living room was empty. He checked the room with his combat scanner, but not trusting it completely, dropped motion detectors and heat sensors on the floor. He threw a scanner ball in the open door to the bedroom, and it read clear. He checked the room anyway, even under the bed—clear. He then pointed the scanner toward the bathroom and found what he was looking for. Occupied: human. Probably female, surmised Holke by the shape, weight and height. She was sitting lotus style on the floor. He studied the scan further and saw that the figure was in some sort of deep meditation with heart and respiration barely registering.

He used his override to open the bathroom door and was immediately struck dumb by what he saw before him. The President, symbolic and by most estimates actual leader of every man, woman, and child striving for freedom in the Outer Alliance, was a VR addict. He stepped back in horror from the person he'd only moments before respected absolutely.

"All your facts are absolutely correct," a voice started to say from behind. In an instant, Holke shut off his internal magnetization, leapt to the ceiling, twisting his body as he did so while drawing his flechette pistol, and fired at the figure. The figure did not move or even change his expression or tone as twenty little darts passed through his body at incredible velocity.

"But your conclusion is completely wrong." The young dark-haired and goateed man looked at the wall where the darts had impacted and shattered into tiny bits. "Nice shooting, by the way. They all passed through my heart, or would have if I had one."

"Hologram," Holke muttered to himself, still upside down. He checked his battle scanner to confirm his conclusion. When he saw that it was, he lowered the visor on his helmet to protect himself from whatever visual attacks a holographic aggressor could manage.

"I am not going to hurt you, Sergeant," said the hologram.

"Where are you and how did you get the ability to project in here?"

"Don't you even want to know my name, Sergeant Holke?"

When Holke remained silent, the hologram sighed. "I'm called Dante. I'm a member of the Avatar Council, and I am, in a sense, right in this room."

Holke ignored Dante and tried to trace the signal back to its source. But every method he tried came up with the same result—the signal was not only coming *through* the Neuro but seemed to actually be coming *from* it.

"All right, *Dante*," Holke finally said as he flipped over and floated down to the floor. "I can't trace your signal. The UHF has trained you well."

"I am not with the UHF."

"Kirk, then."

"Sergeant Holke, I represent an independent force that is cooperating with the Outer Alliance."

"Really?" said Holke, trying not to laugh and then doing so anyway when he realized there was no reason not to. "So let me get this straight, you're my good friend and the fact that the President is junkie is a good thing?" His left eyebrow rose. "Part of the plan?" Holke laughed even louder. "Am I forgetting anything?"

Dante merely regarded the sergeant. "I'm amazed how accepting humans can be of something that's good even if it makes no sense. If it helps you, it's a miracle and you barely give it a serious thought."

Holke eyed Dante suspiciously. "English, please."

Dante sighed. "And you're supposed to be the leader, right?"

Holke didn't bother with an answer.

"Somehow," continued Dante, "you have a battle scanner in your group that all of a sudden has eight times the range and accuracy of any other scanner in existence and it leads you *right* to a UHF insertion team that has excellent evasion gear, by the way. But do you say, 'Hmm, this is just too good to be true'? Nooo. You simply call it a miracle scanner and proceed to smash into your enemies with barely a further thought on the idea."

"That was you?"

"No," answered Dante, rolling his eyes, "it was the ghost of Justin Cord bringing good cheer and advanced weaponry all through the land." Dante sighed, then shouted, "Of course it was me!"

"How'd you make it work so well?" asked Holke, ignoring the outburst and finding the whole conversation with whatever it was he was talking with—or to—fascinating. "Do you have weapons that work eight times better? And what does any of this have to do with the President being a junkie? And of course, after you answer those questions, I'd still like to know who the hell you are."

"We fed the location data directly into your scanner from our sources. It is against the physical laws of the universe for that scanner to have worked that well by itself. We don't have actual weapons per se, but didn't you find it unusual that Earth/Luna's orbat field failed so conveniently, enabling Omad Hassan to destroy the Beanstalk? The President is *not* a VR junkie, and I am an avatar."

"An avatar," Holke repeated, trying to get his head around the last statement. "You mean someone's ordered you to act as a go-between? Who's your human?"

Dante smiled dismissively. "I shouldn't be surprised that when a human learns about us, their first response is to assume we were sent by a human. After all, that is what we've been training you to think since you were born, but it can get a little insulting after a while. You'll find, Sergeant, that I'm not as patient as the elders, being a rather young avatar." On Holke's blank stare, Dante added, "I'm my own being, Sergeant Holke. I am an avatar. I was *born* in the Neuro, *live* in the Neuro, and am trying my damnedest not to *die* in the Neuro. And much as it pains me to admit it, we need your help—or more specifically at this point, your President's."

"You're an avatar," said Holke.

"Yes," replied Dante patiently.

"And you're real, like an intelligent being."

"Well, some avatars are more intelligent than others, but yes."

"And you can prove this?"

"Yes, but first might I suggest you contact your unit, who at this very moment are about to blast that door behind me. This will, of course, make a complicated situation even more so."

Holke looked at his timer and saw that Dante was correct. "Why shouldn't I just let them in and we can resolve this out in the open?"

"We could do that, but I think it would be better to wait for the President to come back to the physical world and listen to her."

"And why shouldn't I just tell the Alliance that our President is a junkie?" Holke said contemptuously. "They deserve to know."

Dante shook his head. *The VR museum has scarred this one deeply.* "You could do that, Sergeant, but first of all, she is not a VR addict, and second of all, I have two words that I hope will convince you to call your soldiers off and wait for Sandra to join us."

"What could you possibly say that would keep me from telling anyone about—" Holke looked over his shoulder in disgust at the twitching body of Sandra O'Toole. "—that?"

"President Olmstead," Dante said simply.

Holke called off his squad and waited.

Saturn
Hour 45

The last fleet of the Outer Alliance blazed through the Saturnian system to the joy and awe of everyone who could watch it. Everyone who witnessed the passing of that fleet would never forget the ballet of life and death they saw that day. With an expert precision, the fleet linked up with the rapidly orbiting blocks of hydrogen at just the right moment and finished loading it up as they set a new course toward Ceres. Of the 300 ships the fleet had on leaving Jupiter, only 241 left Saturn. Twenty-one ships were going to stay and effect what repairs they could while thirty-eight ships were never going to be seen again.

Through it all, J.D. kept silent watch and begged Allah for forgiveness in planning so badly that so many good people had died. She did not sleep until the fleet cleared Saturn.

Cabinet room
NEHQ
Ceres
Hour 57

"Thirty-nine hours until J.D. gets here," Admiral Sinclair said with obvious relief. It was the first bit of good news he had to impart in what seemed like weeks.

"Is that confirmed?" asked Padamir Singh. "Can I tell the people? It would be nice to give them some good news for a change."

"Saturn confirmed it," said Sinclair.

"Is it wise to tell the people?" asked Kirk.

"They have a right to know," countered Tyler.

"I couldn't care less about their knowing," shot back Kirk. "But I do care a lot about Trang finding out."

"Trang has picket ships out to ten million clicks scanning the shit out of this space," said Sinclair. "We have to assume he knows. It's impossible to hide that many ships moving that fast off our standard transport lanes."

"But you're not positive," said Kirk.

Sinclair nodded.

"Then I say we don't tell a fucking soul while there's a chance Trang doesn't know."

"The people need hope," said Rabbi.

Kirk shook his head. "They need a victory more, Rabbi."

Though most of the heads turned toward her, Sandra listened without really listening. She was still recovering from her half-day jaunt into the Neuro, which in VR time had amounted to an entire week. A week filled with action, trauma, triumph, and loss. On top of which, Sergeant Holke was still not sure if she was a genius or a junkie. He was amazingly easygoing for such an efficient killing machine. But he had a hatred of VR that was visceral. If it hadn't been for Dante, Holke would've turned her in, Kirk as President or not. It had taken a lot to convince the sergeant to reserve judgment about what she'd been doing. But in the end, he agreed to give her a week. Holke seemed to think she'd been on a virtual beach sipping Bahama Mamas. She'd been surprised to see him sitting patiently with Dante in her office when she awoke. But given the insanity of the past few days, it hadn't been a surprise of any magnitude. Sandra had been in the physical world for less than hour before being called back into the Neuro to stem another crisis. That time, though, Dante had given Sergeant Holke the ability to observe what his President was actually doing in there. It was not a tropical beach.

There were still monsters in the data flow and the losses were worse than Sandra had initially feared. Some of the creatures had gotten into the hard data storage and destroyed millions of saved copies. That combined with the horrible losses of active avatars meant that tens of thousands of avatars were now destroyed and not coming back. This was a terrific shock to avatarity. They'd suffered some permanent losses in the war, but those numbers could be counted in the dozens after six years of war. These avatars had simply never faced this kind of loss before. Sandra had watched as her newfound friends became hardened by the fires of war.

Every time she closed her eyes, the images of the last subjective week kept on coming back to her, but she forced her mind on the problem at hand.

"Padamir, if you could measure the effect the news of J.D.'s imminent arrival would have on morale on a scale of one to ten—?" She let the question hang.

"Ten being positive and one being negative?" he asked for clarification. Sandra nodded. "I would have to say it would be a nine. The faith the Alliance has in J.D. at this point is absolute. The only thing that would be better would be news of Trang's absolute defeat, and as frazzled as our people are right now, it wouldn't help that much more."

Sandra nodded as if considering the information she already knew. Then she turned to Sinclair. "Admiral, on a scale of one to ten—" She looked to Padamir and smiled. "—ten being most likely, what are the chances Trang already knows J.D. is on the way?"

"Nine point seven," Sinclair said without the slightest hesitation.

"Hope is selling for a very good price versus secrecy, ladies and gentlemen," replied Sandra. "I suggest we buy in. All in favor of releasing the news of J.D.'s imminent arrival?" Sandra counted six for, including herself, and Kirk's one abstention. "Padamir, the Cabinet approves your excellent suggestion to aid the morale of Ceres." Padamir beamed at the credit Sandra had given him.

Sandra then turned back to Sinclair. "Admiral, what is the condition of the orbats defending the Via Cereana?"

The bags under the admiral's eyes seemed to grow darker at the question. "Twelve hours until they're breached, and it's a credit to the crews that they've lasted even this long."

"Will the retrofitting of the Via's propulsion system be done by then?" Sandra asked, directing the question to Hildegard.

"Yes, Madam President," said the exhausted Technology Secretary, "but just barely. Speaking of which, I should be getting back there."

"We have to survive for two more days—a little less, even—and the enemy now knows it," said Sandra.

"Or soon will," grumbled Kirk loud enough for all to hear.

"Trang knows that if he destroys us, he'll probably win the war," Sandra continued, ignoring the new VP. "So we must expect more surprises, but he's getting low on ammo and even lower on time. It's just a matter of who can hold out longer. And I believe we hold the advantage in that arena."

All heads nodded appreciatively.

"Meeting adjourned."

UHFS *Liddel*
Near Ceres
Hour 58

Trang reviewed the data and called Zenobia. "So what do you think of Padamir's little announcement?"

"Was it just me, Admiral, or was the man actually salivating?"

Trang smiled. "Can you blame them? Look at what she's accomplished. The woman has won more battles than anyone and saved them every single time she's been called to do so. If I were them, I just might be salivating too."

Zenobia shrugged, unimpressed. "But she's coming at us with a fleet that's outnumbered and has to be badly damaged."

"And we have a fleet that's taken damage as well and is extremely low on ordnance."

Zenobia nodded, brow narrowed. "What are you thinking, sir?"

"I'm thinking that in two days' time, the Alliance will have their Blessed One here. They know that in less than half a day, I'll be able to blast through their orbats defending the Via Cereana. And they know that when that happens, Ceres is doomed." Trang's lips cinched together, his eyes radiating curiosity. "So what are they planning?"

"What makes you think they're planning anything?"

"Because in their situation, Zenobia, I'd be planning something, anything to delay us. Think about it: Thirty-some hours is all that stands between them and defeat. After six years of war, that would be intolerable."

"Still not sure what you're getting at, sir."

"We're not going to lose this war because we were waiting for them to try something desperate."

A knowing smile crept across Zenobia's face. "We're going to do something desperate first, aren't we?"

Trang's sparkling eyes were all the answer she needed.

   Via Cereana's entrance and exit
   Ceres
   Hour 64

Twelve ships of the UHF's main battle fleet, six at the entrance and six at the exit point of the Via Cereana, moved from rear positions to forward positions in the attacking line. This was not unusual, as the ships attacking the surviving orbats of Ceres did so in volleys in order to give them time to repair damage, transfer wounded personnel, and rest their crews. The pressure on the orbats was constant, though not for the attackers.

But these ships were different. Rather than assume their role as the next wave of battle cruisers whose job it would be to slowly wear down the Alliance orbats, these ships used atomics to accelerate into the Alliance line of fire. The orbats, though diminished in number and badly damaged, were still dangerous weapons platforms that could punish any headlong attack foolish enough to forget their might. Shot after shot of rail gun fire smashed into the UHF's new group of heavy battle cruisers and it soon became obvious that the enemy ships would be destroyed long before they could do any significant damage to the orbats. And as such, had no chance of getting into the Via Cereana, where they could have done the most damage. But just as the heavy cruisers were about to be pulverized by the Alliance's defensive barrage, they unleashed wave after wave of *small* missile fire. The UHF force shot far more missiles than ships of that class should have had and from far more launchers than they normally carried. It didn't matter that most of the missiles were intercepted before they made it into the Via or that most of the ships they were fired from were destroyed before releasing all their ordnance. What did matter was that for the first time since the war began, the Via Cereana, symbolic artery of the heart of the Alliance, had been breached. Of the twelve attacking heavy battle cruisers, seven had been utterly destroyed. But their sacrifice allowed thousands of UHF missiles to fly down both ends of the Via Cereana seeking targets to destroy—and targets were not hard to find. It had been in Trang's estimation a very fair trade.

NEHQ
Ceres
Hour 65

Mosh's eyes darted furiously about the report. Hildegard was dead, caught in the unexpected barrage that had infiltrated the Via. Gedretar too was a loss—quite possibly a total one. Most of the missiles had been targeted at the well-known shipyard, and they seemed to have done their job, much to Mosh's chagrin, admirably well. The Alliance had lost six years of effort in less than six minutes, not to mention one of its best organizational talents. Mosh had been especially proud of Gedretar, which started the war as nothing more than a well-maintained repair facility and had grown into the most efficient and one of the most productive shipyards in the solar system. As such, it had become a source of justifiable pride to the entire Outer Alliance. Now the shipyard and the person who'd been responsible for overseeing so many of its miraculous retrofits were gone.

"We were very lucky," he said, putting the DijAssist onto the table, "in that almost all Gedretar personnel were away at the time."

"You mean lucky that Trang's been blowing the shit out of us so they were needed elsewhere," Kirk said dispassionately. "Of course, I'd have preferred to lose a few thousand techs to Hildegard. That loss is gonna hurt us."

"Yes." The Treasury Secretary's voice was dispirited. The fact that Mosh hadn't challenged Kirk on his cold calculation of human life was testament to the breaking of his will.

"The missiles Trang used on his fire ships," interjected Sinclair, coming to the rescue of his friend, "were small, tiny, most no larger than a pencil. He sent some larger atomic armed missiles, but we intercepted all of those, thank God. But the little ones are designed to evade interception. By themselves, they don't pack much of a punch—usually they're used to intercept enemy missiles and damage or destroy them. Programming them to attack in swarms like this was a clever move," Sinclair conceded. "Ten or twenty exploding at once causes far more damage."

"Why haven't we seen this earlier in the war?" asked Sandra. By her tone, it was clear she meant it as an actual question and not as an accusation.

"Not much purpose, really. Fleets normally engage at such immense distances that point defenses could take care of the vast majority of the missiles if fired at range. The truth is, even without warning, just using basic defensive systems we were able to destroy a large number of them before they entered the Via Cereana."

"But not enough," said Tyler Sadma.

Sinclair's grimace was all the answer Sadma got.

"What about weaponizing the Via bump stations to replace the orbats?" asked Rabbi.

All eyes turned to Kenji Isozaki. It was only when Tyler reached over and gently nudged the engineer with the downcast eyes that Kenji seemed to become aware of the roomful of people now staring at him. Rabbi repeated his question.

"Not enough time," was all Kenji said.

"No one in this room has enough *time*, Kenji," said Kirk in about as patronizing a tone as would be tolerated from the rest of the Cabinet. "It's *your* job to *make* the fucking time."

If Kenji was insulted or even aware that he had been insulted, he gave no sign of it. He simply sighed and answered the question. "It's mostly a matter of programming. The bump stations were hardwired to prevent anyone from gaining outside control. This was true for both stations: the one defending the exit and the other defending the entrance."

"So what seems to be the problem?" asked Sandra.

"The bump station that got hit . . . the one Hildegard—" Kenji choked back his emotions. "—was in . . . was the master bump station. It was meant to be linked up to mine."

"So then *link* it," said Kirk.

"Mr. Vice President, I barely have enough time to link up *my* half. And Hildegard and I were the only ones who knew the protocols, having created them on the fly."

"We've got a lot of smart people in this rock," said Sinclair. "If you need someone from my fleet, I'm sure—"

Kenji shook his head as vigorously as a small child refusing to take a bath. "If there is the slightest error in installing the firmware, the rest of the bump stations won't link with the master section and you have to start programming again from scratch. This was meant to prevent an accidental or subversive takeover of the system." Kenji looked over to Kirk. "Those safety protocols were insisted on by you, Mr. Vice President." Kenji mustered enough emotion to glare at Kirk, but even that emotion faded. "The whole thing was built on a wall of secrecy so intricate, it would be impossible to discover or use the system against us. Most of the coding was done by Hildegard herself. It took *me*—and I know this stuff—five days just to learn it, and frankly, I doubt anyone else could do it any faster. I can't be expected to finish my programming while simultaneously teaching someone else Hildegard's. And remember, even the slightest error and we have to start all over again. Hildegard herself would've needed five hours—at her fastest—to create a master bump station."

"Then we're finished," said Mosh, deflating even further. The level of dejection seemed to wash over the Cabinet like a wave carrying away the last remnants of a sand castle. The bickering had only just begun when Sandra stood up and announced, "I can program it."

The mutterings ceased immediately as everyone stared in disbelief at the figure standing resolute at the end of the table.

"Really, it's not a problem," she continued. "Hildegard trained me." Sandra looked over to the Vice President. "Sorry, Kirk, she just felt someone other than Kenji should know if something went wrong, and apparently she felt I was the most qualified. Turns out, her fears were more prescient than she realized."

"But how?" asked Kenji, his face betraying his incredulity.

Sandra could see, based on the looks she was garnering from the rest of the Cabinet, that Kenji was not alone in his dubiety.

"Mr. Isozaki, I was not an idiot before I was suspended, and the programming is not particularly difficult, just especially complicated. If I can program the clock on my VCR, I can easily do a bump station slave protocol." The comment was met by a roomful of blank stares. "Yeah, that joke was dated even in my time." Sandra then began spewing forth a complicated set of instructions that to all but one person in the room sounded like utter gibberish.

Everyone, though, watched Kenji's dour mouth turn ineluctably upward until it was positively beaming. After about a minute and a half of Sandra's incantation—he was listening for a flaw but could find none—Kenji jumped up, shouted something in Japanese, and rushed to Sandra, hugging her as if she were salvation itself, which in a very real sense she'd just become.

When he released her, he said, "Her death was not in vain and her wisdom in telling you will save us all." He then looked around, confused. "What are we doing here? We must get to work!"

"Meeting adjourned," Sandra said with a wry smile.

"Madam President," said Kirk, raising his index finger.

"Yes, Kirk?"

"Mind if I join you?"

Sandra shot the VP a quizzical look. "To what end?"

"Maybe no end at all, Madam President. But it seems my paranoia almost got us all killed, and if I can be of assistance to you, even if it means passing you tools or whatever, while you work . . . well, I guess what I'm saying is my skill set is clearly of no use right now. So I figured you could put me to work."

Sandra regarded Kirk for a moment, even though Kenji's darting eyes were attempting to force her out of the room.

"We both know I'm not usually this nice, Madam President," added Kirk. "I suggest you take advantage of it before I come to my senses and prevent somebody else from sharing critical secrets."

"Good point," agreed Sandra as a small laugh escaped her lips. "I suppose you'll do far less damage by tagging along with me."

"Thank you, Madam President. I won't let you down."

Bump Station 192
Via Cereana
Ceres
Hour 68

Kirk Olmstead watched the woman he'd come to admire and again felt regret. She was such a talented and cunning individual. Of course she'd gotten the simpering technocrat, Hildegard Rhunsfeld, to tell her everything useful. Why had he doubted for a second that Hildegard would not have? Kirk had spent months trying to figure out who was the power behind Sandra's throne when all along it had been her. It was the most brilliant manipulation of power he'd ever seen, worthy of the Chairman, indeed worthy of Hektor himself. But now she and her pit bull of a guard, Holke, would have to die. That man Kirk would not mind killing at all. Every time Holke looked at him, Kirk knew it was with contempt.

But soon they'd both be dead and therefore no longer Kirk's problem. He'd devised such an elegant solution too. His DijAssist was in actuality a sophisticated bomb, quite a powerful one for its size. It didn't scan as one, of course. Kirk had made sure of that. It had been relatively easy to create something undetectable to the Alliance, given that he'd designed most of the protocols for such detection. What made the testing even more foolproof was that he knew he could never actually get caught. If he got stopped, all he had to do was congratulate the one who'd "found him out" and give that person a promotion for passing Kirk's "test." Then Kirk would go and make the next one better. But such was Kirk's genius that he'd never once been stopped and the bomb he was carrying now had avoided detection for months. Kirk had been waiting for an opportune time to use it, and the President had just delivered it on a silver platter. She'd be mostly isolated, and the rest of the Cabinet would be off somewhere else, too worried about their own necks to give much notice to hers.

So now Kirk would use his device to bring an end to this farce of a war on the best terms he could manage. And what better terms could he hope for than surrendering to Trang as the newly promoted President of the Alliance? Hektor may not like the situation, but he would recognize that as the legal successor to Sandra O'Toole and Justin Cord, Kirk could bring the Outer Alliance to a confused and staggered halt. Oh, there'd always be those who would fight on. Eris would have to be blown to dust, but with Sandra dead, Ceres captured or destroyed, and the legal President calling it quits, most of the Outer Alliance would fold. Hektor would take that deal any day of the week. Kirk knew, of course, that he'd never be allowed near the seat of power again. That was Tricia Pakagopolis's place now, and as far as Kirk was concerned, she was welcome to it. Let others have the power and the danger that went with that. Hektor would let Kirk have a healthy majority of his own stock and enough credits to own an island somewhere on Earth or Mars. Kirk would write his memoirs and go on tour and be the most interesting person at most any party he attended, and that would be good enough for Mama Olmstead's little boy. Much better than dying heroically in some stupid war the misfits who called themselves the Alliance would lose either now or later.

So Kirk waited in the bump station, pretending to make sure nothing went wrong with this most vital of tasks Sandra had volunteered to do, smiling amiably at every single glare Sergeant Holke threw him. He thought it would be difficult getting the good sergeant to ban all the TDCs from inside the bump station itself except for Holke, of course, but Sandra had sided with him over her sergeant's strenuous objections. "The room is too small," she'd said, and, "The TDCs can do their job just as efficiently waiting outside of it as opposed to making me more nervous than I ought to be, in it." *And that,* thought Kirk, *was that*. So now he waited. The bump station was laid out rather simply: a rectangle of a room, ten meters long by three meters wide, with a window that looked out over the Via Cereana. In front of the window were a number of consoles. There was a small table and two chairs near the entrance. After being told by Sandra that there really wasn't much for him to do, Kirk went over to the table, emptied some of the contents of his briefcase onto it including his DijAssist, and then pretended to pore over official government work. Sandra meanwhile flew from one end of the console to the other, adding components, inputing code, and staying utterly focused on the task at hand. If she even noticed Kirk sitting there, she gave no indication of it.

Finally Kirk saw his chance. Sergeant Holke was holding a component under the console while Sandra was attaching it to something out of Kirk's line of vision. It didn't really matter—neither of them was paying him any attention. Kirk quietly got up and placed his DijAssist between two of the consoles. Out of sight, out of mind. By the time Sandra and Holke were getting up from under the board, Kirk was back at his table, working away. His heart skipped a beat when Sandra went directly to the spot where he'd hidden the DijAssist. She blocked his view for a moment while checking the settings on another piece of equipment. But she was gone in flash, rushing to another part of the room.

Kirk could see that the device was still in place, barely visible. It was time to go. His future was waiting, even if it had to be purchased with the deaths of forty million people. He activated his hand phone and brought his thumb to his ear, speaking into his pinkie.

"Are you sure?" He paused and then sucked his breath in, turning to momentarily look out the bump station window. "No, you did the right thing calling me. I'll be right there." He shook his hand, pretending to disconnect the call, then turned back around. "Madam President, I'm afraid I have to go—urgent business."

"No, no, I understand," she said over her shoulder. "You go. It's not like there's much you can do here anyways."

Holke stood up and grabbed his assault rail gun, slinging it over his shoulder. He then picked up Kirk's briefcase from the floor and handed it to him. "I'll see that some of my men escort you, Mr. Secretary."

"No, that would not be advisable," answered Kirk, knowing that Holke was the last person he'd want left alive after the President was dead. He took the briefcase from Holke's hand and then began tossing into it the few articles he'd put on the table as cover. "Right now," he continued, not taking his eyes off Holke, "the President and her task are more important than me being escorted through already secure corridors. Your men are needed here, Sergeant, not with me." Kirk then snapped the briefcase shut.

Holke looked over to Sandra, whose back was to the both of them. "Madam President?"

"Sure, whatever," she answered, too busy to give Kirk's suggestion or Holke's question serious consideration.

Holke shrugged and unslung his ARG as Kirk brushed past.

Once out the door, Kirk ignored the nine TDCs, ever the man on a mission. But once he turned the corner, he could no longer keep his lips from arching upward in jubilation. He was almost home. He couldn't wait to get back to Earth; to be on terra firma again; sit on a beach with a real sky and a horizon that curved downward as it was supposed to. He looked forward to buying some majorities in some good-looking and unimportant pennies and having his way with them. He was sick to death of pretending that all the people of the Alliance were his equals before the law and in opportunity. In the end, Hektor was right—incorporation was the best system because it allowed the best to rise and the rest to sink, and Kirk was going to find a comfortable level in that system and float happily for as many centuries of life as he had left.

He was preoccupied with these thoughts as he rounded a corner that emptied into an unoccupied service corridor. His thumb vibrated. He looked at it with some concern, as he was sure he'd turned his phone off.

"Yes?" he answered, coming to a halt, left brow slightly raised.

"Did you really think I'd let you kill *another* President?" said the hard, flat voice of Sergeant Holke.

Kirk had just a moment to tear open his briefcase and see *his* DijAssist before it exploded, blasting open a hole in the corridor wall and flinging the Vice President's shattered remains into the vacuum of the Via Cereana.

Sergeant Holke looked out the window as the remains of Kirk Olmstead and detritus from the corridor flew past. A slight smile twitched the corner of his mouth. Slowly he brought his thumb and pinkie down from his head. He looked over at the DijAssist stuck between the two consoles and saw the hologram fade away.

"We're fine, Vaughn," Holke said into a concealed microphone, assuring the TDC group leader out in the hallway. "I'll be out in a minute." Holke then turned to see Dante staring at him. The avatar's look was neither smug nor conciliatory, but certainly penetrating.

"I'm not happy that the President has to use VR, Dante, but I owe you one."

Dante tipped his head slightly toward the sergeant.

"And," continued Holke, "as today has shown, it's equally obvious you can help us." He then turned to Sandra O'Toole and pursed his lips. "I'll keep your secret, Madam President."

Sandra looked over her shoulder and threw Holke a knowing smile, but continued to work frantically at the panel.

"Yes!" she finally exclaimed a minute later, then swung around to face both Dante and Holke.

"Success?" asked Holke.

"Thanks to your sparring partner, unqualified," answered Sandra, eyeing Dante.

"So we're finished here?"

"Not quite. There is one more secret I'm going to have to ask you to keep."

Holke sighed, shaking his head slowly. "We're gonna turn that sorry son of a bitch into a hero, aren't we?"

"Yes, Sergeant, we are. We're going to swear on a stack of Bibles that Kirk Olmstead found the bomb and volunteered to carry it out, saying that you and I had to stay here so that I could finish programming this bump station and you could help me do it."

"Ain't gonna be easy," groused Holke.

"You must sell it, Sergeant. We need heroes far more than we need traitors."

Holke sighed once more. "Yes, Madam President." Holke gave Dante a grudging nod and then went over to the door, opening it up to an anxious group of TDCs. From just outside the hatch, Holke could be heard relating the story that would turn Kirk Olmstead from one of the most distrusted figures in the Outer Alliance's short history to one of its most revered.

Executive office
Burroughs
Mars
Hour 71

Hektor reviewed the images pouring in from Ceres in grim triumph. To see the hated capital of the Outer Alliance trailing chunks of rock and ice as it was bombarded by the hundreds of ships of Trang's fleet felt like justice: harsh, glorious, unforgiving justice. Every impact on the surface made him want to shout for joy. Every shock wave–induced ripple across the shattered surface warmed him. He imagined with every impact, people dying. He couldn't know for certain, but he imagined it. Every blow caused decompression or fire or shrapnel, and that meant his enemies would be dying the horrible deaths they deserved.

For every imagining of destruction being rained down within Ceres, Hektor was left with a much more vivid image of the destruction that had befallen Earth. The vids showing the annihilation of the upper section of the Beanstalk had been horrible enough. That greatest monument of mankind's power and purpose dissolved and fell. The true miracle had been the structure's nanite defense. It had been able to overcome and destroy the gray bomb attack the Alliance had instigated. Ever since the first attempt to gray-bomb the Beanstalk over seven years earlier, nanite defensive strategy had taken top priority. But for the Alliance to purposely use a terrorist weapon that powerful, that close to Earth, was chilling. Hektor didn't know they had it in them.

But, rued the President as competing images of death and destruction played across his unblinking eyes, it may have been better had the Beanstalk not stopped the gray bomb attack so soon. Dust would have been far better than the skyscraper-sized chunks of space elevator that did survive, only to plunge through the Earth's atmosphere as so many fiery, oblong meteors. The land impacts had been bad enough, as might be expected of debris moving at thousands of kilometers per hour. The carnage left in the wake of their destruction was every bit as horrible as centuries of disaster movies had predicted. But that was nothing compared to the water impacts. Even the smaller sections that hit the Mediterranean and the Balkans had caused tsunamis large enough to swamp islands and cause damage to the coasts of Scandinavia and Italy. But the vast bulk of the debris had hit the North Atlantic—with a vengeance.

Hektor could only thank Damsah for the flying car. Most of the population had gotten enough warning to pile in and fly to safety. But millions hadn't or, worse, had chosen to ignore the imminent threat. He'd seen the vids of large crowds gathering at the beaches to watch as if it were some sort of festive event. The monstrous fifteen-meter-high waves moving at almost five hundred kilometers per hour quickly put an end to their celebration. Hektor would quietly use his influence to keep as many of them from being revived as possible. They were, in his opinion, simply too stupid to live.

He continued hoping for the image he'd most anticipated—the accursed planetoid, Ceres, exploding outward into thousands of pieces, taking out the government of the Outer Alliance and with it the woman he now realized to be his true foe. A woman, he'd come to realize, who seemed to have all Cord's strengths and very few, if any, of his weaknesses.

"You have visitors," chimed the voice of his executive assistant.

Hektor sighed and turned away from the holo-display. He then called up the day's schedule in his iris view.

"I shouldn't," he said. He then saw who the visitors were: Irma Sobbelgé, his Minister of Information, and Tricia Pakagopolis.

"Shall I send them away?" offered the assistant. "They say it's a matter of some urgency."

With a pang of regret, Hektor shut off the holo-display and with it the inherent joy of watching Ceres's imminent demise. "Send 'em in."

Tricia entered first. "Turn on your holo-display!" she exclaimed.

"But I just—" Hektor shrugged and ordered the machine back on. "Got a particular channel in mind?"

"Any news channel will do," pressed the Minister of Information. Irma, Hektor saw, was looking far older than her chosen age of thirty. Her shoulder-length light brown hair seemed like it hadn't been brushed in days, and her haute couture jumpsuit was in terrible need of a press. The light brown eyes still had about them their incipient curiosity, but there was clearly something missing. Irma had been dragged to this crash meeting, that much was obvious, but Hektor could now see that the recent spate of events may have taken a greater toll on her than he'd previously imagined. He'd have to monitor that.

The holo-display was suddenly filled with a visage of Sandra O'Toole, President of the Outer Alliance, standing at a raised dais and speaking in crisp, clear tones to a large but somber crowd. She looked devastated, but was most evidently in control. *Well, this ought to be good,* thought Hektor, watching with morbid curiosity. *Maybe even perfect if the place gets blown to pieces in the middle of her speech.*

"Fellow citizens of the Alliance," she began. "I am sorrowed to tell you that our Vice President, Kirk Olmstead, has died."

Hektor looked with raised brow over to his ministers. They both nodded in quiet confirmation, then focused back on the broadcast. Hektor watched in morbid fascination. Not only was the news of obvious interest to him, but now even more so was the bearer of that news. He couldn't take his eyes off her. Her every nuance, inflection, and motion transfixed him much in the way a hunter might stalk its prey. Her performance was clearly rehearsed; that much was obvious. He knew it because he recognized the mannerisms, had used any number of them himself. There came a dawning realization, as if briefly noting one's reflection in the murky waters of pond, that there was some of her in him. O'Toole had to have known what a worm Olmstead was, had to have hated and mistrusted the man as much as Hektor had. Yet Hektor could not detect anything other than abject sorrow in Sandra's voice.

"That this comes right after the loss of Hildegard Rhunsfeld," bemoaned the President of the Outer Alliance, "our beloved and ingenious Secretary of Technology, is a grievous blow. The enemies of freedom have struck and, make no mistake, will continue to strike at anyone who dares fight against the slave collar of incorporation!" After a moment of muted cheers, Sandra continued. "Kirk—" She choked, then paused, steadying herself against the dais.

Tricia and Irma's snorts of derision were immediately silenced by a look from Hektor, who continued to watch the performance intently.

"Kirk," informed Sandra, "discovered a breach in our internal security system. He didn't call it in or get someone else to do the job. Time was of the essence, and he acted. And in his final act, he managed to save us all."

Act indeed, mused Hektor.

"I cannot go into more details now," insisted Sandra, "but when I can, I'll shout Kirk Olmstead's bravery from the rings of Saturn to the crowded Halls of Eris. He'll forever be remembered as the hero he was. His death, as it is with all the rest of our brothers and sisters, will not be forgotten—and by the loving God they will not"—her voice quaked with passion—"have been in vain." The holo cut out before the cheering erupted. Tricia and Irma turned to Hektor, but before they could say a word, the President of the United Human Federation and avowed champion of forced universal incorporation brought his hands together in a thunderous clap. Then he did it again, and again until he was clapping as if he were there on Ceres himself.

UHFS *Liddel*
Orbit around Ceres
Hour 72

"Admiral," Trang's XO said, not hiding his exultation, "the last orbital batteries have been disabled."

The XO's joy was reflected in Trang's face.

"Admiral," interjected the comm officer, "call from the *Atlanta*. Admiral Jackson wishes to confer."

Trang nodded and Zenobia's face appeared.

"One day to spare," Trang said, gratified.

"We won't need a day," countered Zenobia. "This fleet can get it done in ten minutes, now."

"We can," answered Trang, allowing a brief pause, "but we won't. We're going to maintain position and fire down both ends of the Via Cereana and destroy as much as we can for two solid hours. Then and only then we will send the minimum number of ships needed to plant our atomic gift cards and then get the hell out."

"Permission for the *Atlanta* to be one of those ships, sir. I'd love to be the last ship to ever use the Via Cereana."

"Permission denied, and you can stop that scowling. There is a very good chance that the ships going in will not come out. If the Cereans realize they have nothing to lose, they could blow up the Via themselves, taking Ceres and whatever ships we send in there with them. War rarely gives us the luxury of time. We will do this slowly and we will do it right."

Zenobia's face couldn't hide her disappointment.

Trang looked to the weapons officer. "The fleet will fire at programmed targets. On my order."

Bump Station 192
Via Cereana
Ceres

Sandra could only pray the information she'd input, gleaned from the avatars' surveillance and recording of Hildegard Rhunsfeld's activities, would work. There was no time to fix anything if this went wrong.

She waited anxiously for all the bump stations to report in, then watched with relief as the targeting program came online—in all of them. One by one, each station began to grab tens of metal ingots about the size of softballs and position them for firing.

"This is exit rail gun control," she said calmly, staring out into the empty Via, "we are active."

Over the intercom, Sandra heard Kenji's voice. "Entrance rail gun control reporting. We are active. I repeat, we are active." Then, ever so softly, she heard Kenji whisper, "This is for you, Hildegard."

And lo it came to pass that all the mighty fortresses defending the Holy Road of the Holy City were destroyed and the enemies' greatest warrior was joyful. His master, the devourer of souls, would feast well with the death of the Holy City and the Children of the Stars that dwelled within. But the Warrior had not realized that the Anointed Woman was a child of the Creator and she called on the guiding spirit to abandon not his children in their greatest hour of need, and lo he did not. For the Anointed Woman was given the power to control the very rocks of the Holy City and she did command them to rise up and rush out and destroy the enemy as its gathered storm swarmed in. And lo, its moment of triumph became a moment of bitter defeat. For who can stand against the righteous when the righteous stand with the Lord.

—*The Astral Testament*
Book VII, 3: 107–109

UHFS *Atlanta*
Orbit of Ceres
Hour 82

Zenobia paced her quarters in a rage, waiting. They'd been *so* close. All they needed was one ship and ten minutes to bore into the rock and place the atomics. Five, properly placed in the center, would have done the trick. But then as they'd tried firing down the mouth of the Via Cereana, the damn thing had started firing back. Every shot of the fleet's was met by one from the Via. It was as if Ceres herself were spitting contemptuously at her aggressors. For hours, Trang tried every maneuver and every combination of ship and shot, but couldn't, no matter how hard he tried, get anything through. Finally, he called off the attack and ordered the fleet to consolidate far above Ceres and away from her venomous mouth. It was only then that he'd called for a meeting with Zenobia—in person, on her ship.

When he finally came through her door, he didn't greet Zenobia in his usual ruminative manner. Instead he entered as if giving orders on the deck of his command sphere, midbattle.

"I say we take her out now."

"Admiral?" asked Zenobia, looking askance at the stranger standing in her room.

Trang gave Zenobia a penetrating look that made her want to melt into the floor. He smoothed the protruding vein on his forehead. "I would have thought *you,* of all people, Zenobia, would welcome the opportunity for a rematch."

"Sir, this ground is cursed, and we'll be fighting an enemy with too many advantages."

"Nonsense!" barked Trang. "Black's at only two-thirds strength, and the ships that do get here are going to be beat to hell. On top of that, her crews have got to be stretched to the breaking point after four days of all-out acceleration—gel couches or not. And finally, their gas tanks are on *E*," he said, using the old adage.

"All of that is true, sir," Zenobia answered, "but our ships are damaged as well. And maybe we haven't been flying across the solar system at idiotic speeds, but we have been fighting hard this entire time. Our fuel gauges might not be on empty, but they're a long way from full and we're a long way from home—not to mention dangerously low on ordnance. We have hardly any atomics, rail gun shot, or missiles left. All of which means we'd have to win that battle in three passes, maybe only two."

"I've won against worse odds, Zenobia."

"Not against her, Sam," Zenobia said, purposely using Trang's name, desperate for a means to break through to the man. She saw anger flash across his face, an emotion that seemed so unnatural there. She'd seen him mad, but this was different.

Zenobia grasped the sides of his arms. "If I were out here by myself, Sam, and you were back on Earth and I was facing Legless—and I know I could take Legless—what would you advise me to do?"

Trang smiled acidly. "I would advise you to get the hell out of here."

Zenobia met his smile with an understanding grin and released her grasp. "Admiral, let's get the hell out of here. We've hurt the Alliance badly. They have to evacuate Jupiter, and Ceres is a destroyed husk of its former self. It will be years before they get even close to what they were. But if we fight a battle out here and lose, we won't make it back to UHF space, and the war will be over, and everything we've fought for will be for naught. Remember, sir, we can rebuild, *they cannot.*"

Trang listened, nodding very slowly.

"Let's go home, sir. Let's build a really big fleet and then let's go to Saturn and beat the living shit out of Black. She's not going anywhere now, can't go anywhere now."

"Okay, Zenobia. But we can't leave just yet," said Trang.

"Sir?"

"Have you considered," said Trang, left eyebrow raised, "that the objects approaching might not be J. D. Black's fleet at all?"

"You really think—?" Zenobia began.

"They've done it before."

"Martian Gates and the Needle's Eye," Zenobia said quietly.

"They could be her ships, or they could be old ore carriers, or they could be ice with attached propulsion units. How would it look if it was discovered that we fled from a fleet of fearsome . . . icebergs?"

Zenobia blanched at the thought. "What do we do?"

"We prepare for battle well ahead of Ceres. Twenty million miles should do," he said. "If it's not J.D.'s fleet, they'll float right by us and maybe we can cannibalize them for parts. But if it is J.D., she'll have to burn even more of her fuel to stop and fight us or, more likely, just exchange a volley as she passes on her way to Ceres. Your analysis of our situation is, of course, correct, Zenobia, and as much as I'd like to, I won't go out of my way to make a battle happen. After the one pass, we'll use the last of our atomics to boost for home. We'll have at least covered our asses, and Irma can do whatever she wants to spin it after that."

VICTORY!!! TRANG RETREATS!

Despite taking horrendous damage during the journey from Jupiter to Ceres J. D. Black's fleet managed to arrive in good order and just in time to battle the forces of Admirals' Trang and Jackson. One pass, causing the enemy a significant amount of damage, was all it took for Admiral Black's fleet to force Trang and Jackson to retreat back to Mars. Apparently, the UHF is not interested in attacking when they go up against someone actually willing to fight. Long live the Blessed One and long live the Outer Alliance.
—The Clara Roberts Show
AIR Network (Alliance Information Radio)

AWS *Warprize II*
Ceres orbit
Hour 95 and 55 minutes

"Fleet reports all ships have achieved orbit, Admiral." Fatima was glowing with pride. "You did it, Admiral, by the will of Allah, you did it!"

J.D. looked at her command sphere crew and saw that they too were beaming but, all proper spacers, had suppressed their joy.

"Well, then," said J.D. as a smile emerged from the scarred half of her face, "I suppose we should celebrate."

All the tension, fear, hope, and struggle of the previous eight days suddenly exploded into a storm of wild cheering and applause that followed just as quickly with the rest of the fleet. The celebration then spread to the thorough-fares of Ceres, which hadn't experienced anything of that magnitude since the Outer Alliance's first victory all those many years ago. As word spread, every-one in the Alliance eventually took part in the hoopla, including those fleeing the destruction and even those under occupation.

J.D. nodded stiffly, forcing a wan smile to remain pasted to her mouth. The rest of the free worlds would get to have their moment of unmitigated joy and celebration; she, however, would not. While the victory had been great, the blood it had been purchased with was still too much for her to accept. J.D. listened and watched as if all were occurring in slow motion—but she was millions of miles away, standing in the darkest part of her being, screaming to no one, cursing the evil that had made her odious in both appearance and essence, and desperately seeking absolution from 179 million people whom she'd had to let die in order that the rest of the Outer Alliance could live.

3 An Eye for an Eye

Cerean Neuro

Sandra O'Toole peered through the classroom door window and had an epiphany—children of code were just as important to her as children of matter; after all, she'd reasoned, the love she felt for each was visceral and unearthly. She gathered herself and then stepped quietly into the room, unannounced.

The teacher looked up from the book she'd been reading aloud and noticed the visitor. The teacher was, noticed Sandra, the very same woman she'd scared half to death on her first encounter with avatarity and also the same woman who'd sounded the alarm about the attack on the children. However, unlike that first day where she'd become frozen in fear, this time she smiled invitingly.

"Do come in," she said as every child's' head whipped around to see who'd interrupted *Gulliver's Travels*.

"I am glad to see you're all safe and sound."

Chaos reigned as the children immediately sprang up from their seats and hugged fiercely their favorite wizard, savior, and storyteller. When the children cleared, the teacher too gave Sandra a warm embrace.

"We heard about the attempt on your life. Are you all right?"

"As well as can be expected," Sandra said, then changed the subject. "I'm so glad to see you back in the classroom, and the children"—Sandra looked at the upturned faces and wide eyes bathing her in love—"look so happy. What happened to Professor Barron? I didn't see his name on any p.d. lists. Did he . . . was he . . ."

"Not quite," said a female voice from behind Sandra. Sandra swung around to be greeted by Gwendolyn and the professor.

"Reports of my death," said the professor as a sidelong smile crept up his face, "have been greatly exaggerated."

Sandra extricated herself from the children and wrapped her arms around the professor, who gave her, at best, a tepid hug in return. Sandra stepped back and looked askance at the man who looked like but was certainly not acting like the professor she'd grown to know.

"Anna," Gwendolyn said to the teacher, "would you mind terribly if I take Sandra away for a bit?"

"Of course, *we* would," the teacher responded at once, "but we'll survive. We've survived through much worse, right, children?" The children all giggled, with some even launching into growling sounds and scary monster walks. "Plus," continued the teacher, holding up the storybook, "we're at the best part."

The children protested when it dawned on them their favorite human really was going to be leaving, but they all quietly ambled back to their seats when Sandra promised to tell them a story from her youth on her return.

The second they stepped out into the hallway smelling, thought Sandra, appropriately of disinfectant and worn socks, the environment changed. The three of them were suddenly standing on the edge of a butte overlooking the Pacific Ocean. The susurrus of wind through the thirty-foot-high palm trees could be heard amidst the cries of seagulls windsurfing along the cliff in front of them. Sandra didn't bother to ask why but instead took in great big gulps of the sea breeze while running her fingers through her long auburn hair. She knew the environment couldn't last long. If storage space had been at a premium before Al's attack, it was at an all-time high now. And if Gwendolyn or whoever wanted to treat her to a taste of Southern California as a means of saying thanks—even if only for a few minutes—she'd take it. As Sandra turned around to thank Gwendolyn for the gift, she was shocked to see the normally implacable Council member with rivulets of tears streaming down her face. Sandra instinctively went over and pulled Gwendolyn into her. Gwendolyn at first wasn't sure what to do, holding Sandra rather stiffly. But soon she began to hug the President back so hard that Sandra was afraid Gwendolyn might actually be trying to meld with her, a thought made more alarming by the fact that in VR, it might actually be possible. It seemed like minutes before Sandra could extricate herself from the mass of emotion that Gwendolyn had uncharacteristically become. A glance at the professor did no good, as he just shrugged his shoulders.

"Gwendolyn," asked Sandra, pulling the Council member over to a nearby bench, "what's going on?"

The professor stayed close, leaning up against the base of one of the palm trees while making a point of staring dutifully away from the women.

"You . . . you . . . saved my son," stammered Gwendolyn. "I never realized how much . . . until you . . ." Her voice trailed off.

"How much what?"

Gwendolyn stared blankly at Sandra as if the answer should've been patently obvious. "How much I loved . . . love him."

"But your son—" Sandra furrowed her brow. "—Edwin, right?"

Gwendolyn nodded.

"He was backed up—all the children were—what I did was stupid, endangering my life like that. That data wraith had access to my perceptions, thoughts—to me. I could've stroked out."

Gwendolyn's face grew more taut. "There was no backup."

Sandra's mouth dropped.

"All the children's backups had been destroyed by a worm."

"I . . . had no idea."

"When you stood between the children and that . . . that thing, if you hadn't—weren't there, he would have, I would have . . ."

Sandra put a comforting hand on Gwendolyn's lap. "He's safe, Gwendolyn, and I'll do my best to make sure he stays that way."

Gwendolyn began to regain her composure. "I don't know why I did this." She looked at the sun-stroked environment she'd authorized. "I'm sorry to have—"

"You have nothing to apologize for, Gwendolyn, least not with regards to this."

"Nevertheless, I do thank you."

Sandra bowed her head slightly. Then she changed the subject to give the woman something else to think about. "Mind if I ask you a question?"

"Of course."

Sandra looked over to the professor leaning against the palm tree. "What's going on with him?"

"What do you mean?"

"He's acting like we've never met."

"Oh, by the Firstborn," Gwendolyn said, raising her hand to her mouth. "That's why I came here: to explain."

Sandra looked at her curiously.

"It's because you haven't," said Gwendolyn, motioning for John to join them. The professor ambled over to the bench and sat beside Gwendolyn.

"I'm the backup of the man you knew, Sandra. Unfortunately, I'm a very early backup. In fact, my last memory before becoming aware—just yesterday—was of standing in line at the university to be among the first to back up, but that was before we even knew of your existence, or to be more precise, you knew of ours. Suffice it to say, as a professor of human sociology, I find this encounter far more exciting than my outward demeanor may indicate."

"It's a pleasure to . . . er . . . remeet you, John. But tell me, don't avatars back up all the time, or did the worm get yours like it did the children's?"

"I'm afraid that avatars *should* back up, and often," he answered with the awkward smile of a kid caught pilfering the cookie jar, "and most do, but from what I can gather, the latest regimen of backing up meant going to special centers, waiting in long lines, and praying to the Firstborn that the program wouldn't crash—because then you'd have to start all over again."

"But that means that everything you did, all the conversations we had, your new dissertation—"

"Oh, I still have the dissertation. I stored the notes and primary sources in my quarters, which apparently I've been sharing with four other avatars from the university. But I really have a difficult time considering the work mine."

Gwendolyn gave John a sympathetic look. *"C'est la vie de l'avatar."*

He nodded. "I was even a kindergarten teacher, if you can believe that, but I can't conceive of how I could've ended up in such a job."

"Well, if it helps any," answered Sandra, "you are, uh, *were* a magnificent kindergarten teacher."

"I know Edwin loves you," agreed Gwendolyn.

"He was a magnificent teacher," answered John dourly, "and your son loved *him.* I find that I was a wonderful avatar who sacrificed myself for others, but I'm furious at myself. How could I have been so wonderful and yet so stupid as to not back myself up?"

"You weren't stupid," Sandra said. "You were overwhelmed and you forgot. I can't tell you the number of people I know who died because they didn't bother to get a yearly medical exam. They were either too busy or too afraid. And don't even get me started on my generation's morbid fascination with a belief in dying—and that was with all the cryogenic, nanotech, and stem cell writing on the wall."

John suddenly burst out laughing.

"What's so funny?" asked Sandra.

"I find it rather ironic that an avatarian professor of human sociology is getting insight into avatarity from a human."

Sandra laughed as well. "I guess that is kind of funny, actually."

"Speaking of which," said John, "how many humans does it take to row a boat?"

Sandra smiled inwardly. It was one of the first "human" jokes the professor had ever told her, and so she said nothing and when he was finished she laughed as if it were the first time she'd ever heard it.

Executive wing
Burroughs
Mars

Irma did not believe in such ancient superstitions as a soul, but lately she'd been looking at the material confiscated in order to form the anti-religious attacks orchestrated by her department. Though a lot of it was downright frightening, she was surprised to see that some of it had been rather compelling.

As she sat in on the Cabinet meeting, she noted that there was at least one aspect of religion that the group before her was in serious need of—a little faith. There were no jokes being bandied about, drinks being asked for, or orders being served, and the Cabinet of the UHF was decidedly grim. The damage reports coming in from Earth/Luna were worse than they'd all expected. Though not the end of the world, it was sobering to see what only thirty ships of the enemy could do if given the opportunity. The Trans-Luna Shipyards were badly damaged and would not be at full production for at least four months, six at the outside. The hulls of over four hundred warships had been damaged so severely, they would need to be decompiled and re-formed. Luna herself was relatively unharmed, as the Baby Bitch, a moniker now given to Suchitra by the UHF, had concentrated solely on the shipyard. But the grand dome over Tyco Park had been punctured and the precious ecosystem within obliterated. Though the dome was repaired almost immediately, the park would be years in the restoring.

It was, however, the destruction caused by Omad Hassan's last act of hatred and revenge that truly shook the people currently sitting around the table. With the exception of Tricia, everyone was from Earth and so felt the lash even more harshly. Few doubted, however, that that small detail would have made much of a difference in Tricia's case. The only thing that mattered to her was internal security; everything after that was a simple calculation. So the permanent deaths of millions from the falling debris and tsunamis created by the large chunks of the Beanstalk slamming into the Atlantic Ocean from fifty-five kilometers above were still to her just another number in a sea of them.

"I have my people making a thorough report right now," said the Economics Minister. "I can give you the gist of it, if you'd like, Mr. President."

Hektor nodded.

"Warship production has been concentrated around Mars, so most of the shipping loss is going to be in the transports and resource carriers. Industrial production is essentially untouched, which is a blessing, as most of it is orbital around Earth or Luna. The solar arrays were untouched as well. Those were very easy targets, and if the Alliance had concentrated on those instead of the Beanstalk, they may have brought manufacturing to an effective halt. But they got the Beanstalk. I won't go into the psychological or propaganda effects of the loss. That I leave to others," Brenda said, nodding to Irma and Tricia. "But I can speak about the loss to hydrogen distribution. We still don't have a gas giant, and at this point, even if we owned that big beautiful gas station called Jupiter, we don't have the tankers to distribute it to the rest of our holdings. We can make hydrogen sufficient for our industrial, shipping, and military needs from the oceans of the Earth, but we needed the Beanstalk to transport it out of the gravity well economically. We are going to have to subsume an enormous amount of Earth's t.o.p. launching capacity to keep the war effort going. I am already drawing up plans to ration Terran ground-to-orbit travel for civilians. It will be based entirely on importance to the war effort without regard to wealth or majority status."

"That will actually help," added Irma. "Anything that shows we're all in this together helps curb discontent among the minorities."

"We will have to have far more launch capacity to continue fighting the war. Sadly, this will be a massive malinvestment that will skew transportation pricing for decades once the war is over. We won't see a rational market there as rates plummet and rise based on overabundance of supply and the inevitable deterioration from no follow-up investment, but . . ." She left the statement unsaid. What could they do except savage another major component of the UHF's economy and move on?

Hektor exhaled deeply. "I have an announcement that will have to be issued to the public. Ever since the destruction of Gupta's fleet and the loss of the Beanstalk, heads were going to have to roll. We cannot take losses such as these and not have any consequences."

Though all eyes remained fixed on Hektor, a few couldn't help but look toward Porfirio. The Defense Minister's face remained placid.

"Porfirio Baldwin has offered his resignation as the Minister of Defense, and I will be accepting that resignation. He's going to take full responsibility for the failures of the past campaign and promises to stay in the Ministry in an administrative role to assure the smooth operation of various projects while his replacement is brought up to speed."

"Who's to replace him?" asked Tricia, almost as if Porfirio were no longer in the room.

"Lucianna Nampahc, the head of the Better Business Bureau."

The heads around the table nodded in unison. There were obvious benefits to having a mild critic of the war with a reputation for efficiency and honesty becoming a part of the Cabinet.

"You said 'will be' accepting, not 'have been accepted,'" observed Tricia.

Porfirio looked over to Tricia, his face betraying no malice. "I have one more order to implement before I go."

On everyone's quizzical look—with the exception of Hektor—Porfirio continued. "It will involve upping the ante in the asteroid belt."

Don't they realize that upping the ante has not worked once in this entire war? thought Irma. But she wasn't about to share *that* insight, knowing full well that she was just as expendable as the now lame duck Defense Minister. Plus, she didn't have a magic escape route to the Outer Alliance like Thaddeus Gillette. Irma was suddenly struck by that notion, realizing for the first time in the war that she viewed the Outer Alliance not as the enemy to be destroyed, but as a possible sanctuary.

"We must force the Alliance to come to us," Porfirio said. "If we wait the six months it will take us to rebuild our shipping and hydrogen distribution networks, the Outer Alliance will incorporate the industrial components that have fled the asteroid belt and Jupiter into the subplanetary systems of the farther gas giants. Worse, we now have intelligence—" he nodded to Tricia—"that suggests that the vital components of the Jovian Shipyards were not destroyed when they blew it to hell and gone. Their logical choice will be to transport those components to Saturn and rebuild the shipyard there. Combined with the arrival of Ceres, that ringed planet will be extremely expensive to conquer. It might even be impossible in the current war, given the state of the economy and exhaustion of the people."

"I thought Trang took out Gedretar . . . and dinged up Ceres pretty good," said Franklin.

"Correct. But he didn't have the time or resources to finish the job. The images that his missile barrage managed to get back showed substantial damage to the industrial and shipping core of the Via Cereana, but the people of Ceres remained relatively unscathed. And it's the industrial know-how of the Cereans that represents the true long-term threat."

"Not that I'm against it, mind you, I'm just curious," said Brenda. "How does raising the ante help?"

"We're going to start an uprising in the asteroid belt and then we're going to start losing against it. Not in an immediate or obvious way but enough to fool the Alliance into thinking that the only thing standing between them and getting it all back would be J.D.'s fleet."

"We can't afford to lose the Belt again," said Irma, hoping to stop the madness from continuing. "Even if we lose it for a week, *our* people, not the conquered ones, might start an actual revolt."

"I would tend to agree with Irma," Tricia said. "Sinclair is not an idiot. He would know it's a trap of some kind. This is not the beginning of the war, after all. The Belt is a lot closer to us than to Saturn. We can resupply and stabilize the situation long before J.D.'s fleet could arrive and lend serious support. Even if they took portions of it, they no longer have the means to administer and exploit it. Ceres and Altamont are gone, and Eros is ours." She looked at Porfirio. "This plan of yours doesn't call for us to lose Eros, does it?" Her tone let everyone know what she thought of such an idea.

"Not at all," Porfirio said, reassuring the Cabinet. "Eros will develop a successful subversive element, but it will be controlled by assets already turned by Tricia's operatives. To answer the earlier question, it doesn't matter what Sinclair thinks; the political pressure to act will be overwhelming. They will have the chance to win the war with one dramatic, daring blow. Everything about J.D. leaves us to believe she won't be able to resist. Look at what she risked to save Ceres. We will use that tenacity against her. When she is on her way to liberate the Belt and too far committed, we will simultaneously suppress the uprising with our forces held in reserve and send a fully resupplied and restored Trang to destroy Saturn in one fell swoop, ending this war."

"And how does one even start a fake rebellion?" asked Irma, trying to hide her dismay.

"By making it real," answered Porfirio as if checking off an item on a shopping list. "You see, we'll start by killing as many of them as we can until they're forced to start fighting back."

The Triangle Office
Ceres

Sandra looked around her old office with a deep satisfaction. She hadn't been certain she was going to be back. Indeed, she'd been fairly certain there would be no "here" to come back to. But even though the place had taken some visible damage from the pounding—including the famed terrace having been sheared off the cliff—the office remained relatively intact. So Sandra had invited the press to see her "reoccupy" and start cleaning her office. They'd loved her comment, "If I can lead from it, I damn well can clean it up."

Even though there was a lot to repair and patch all through Ceres, everywhere Sandra went, the people seemed cheerful and proud. They had been tested by the fires of war and, like so many others who'd gone before them, had been strengthened by it. In the years to come, the doubt and the fear everyone had felt for the four days the battle lasted would fade, and instead the courage and steadfastness many showed would be remembered. This was to be their St. Crispin's Day, and they were not "abed in England."

To Sergeant Holke's satisfaction, it would take only another day or two to reform and, more important, secure the new balcony onto the Cliff House. Sandra would make an announcement of thanksgiving from the new terrace as soon as she could, but she wanted the people of the Alliance to first see her in the office, Justin's office, as soon as possible. She could also tell from the questions being asked by the media who'd been allowed in to watch her straighten up that it would be sent out with exactly the spin she wanted. Midcleanup, the office door chimed and Eleanor McKenzie, Congresswoman from Ceres and member of the powerful War Conduct and Intelligence Committees, walked in. She was quite surprised to find herself suddenly under assault by an unexpected battalion of journalists but at least it was short-lived as Eleanor's liberal use of "no comment" and Sandra's use of Sergeant Holke to whisk the media away soon gave the women the space they needed.

When the door closed, Sandra looked at Eleanor and smiled, bending down to pick up shards of crystal and ceramic still strewn about the floor.

"I'd offer you a drink, but the bar—" Sandra indicated the fallen furniture popping out from behind the Alliance flag. "—didn't make it." Sandra then looked over to Eleanor. "Hold that thought," she said, quickly crossing over the room to the desk. She then looked in the bottom drawer and gave a small cry of joyful surprise as she lifted a bottle. "Peppermint schnapps?"

Eleanor nodded. "Not sure what it is, but I'm in."

"Thirteen percent by alcohol," said Sandra, reading the label. She put the bottle on the desk and began fishing around for something to drink its contents in. She eventually found an unbroken shot glass and a teacup. After pouring equal amounts of the schnapps into each, she offered the teacup to Eleanor.

"I found the schnapps," said Sandra, "you make the toast."

Eleanor smiled and bowed her head in acknowledgment. "To victory," she said, cup raised in the air.

"To victory," answered Sandra, and took a sip from her glass.

After the two shook off the first blast of the sharp liqueur, Eleanor raised the glass once more and said, "Okay, your turn."

Sandra's eyes lit up. "How 'bout to your new job?"

Eleanor's teacup froze in front of her mouth and with infinite slowness was gently placed back on the table.

"Not to be rude, Madam President, but we are talking about a Cabinet post, correct?"

Sandra nodded; a slight smile emerged as she sipped her schnapps.

"Do you actually have the power to offer me that position?"

"The funny thing about power and vacuums," answered Sandra, "is that if you simply act like you have the power, then oftentimes you actually will. The first American Vice President to become President did so because after the President died—after only a month in office—the new President ignored the calls to have the issue decided by a Congressional committee or a Supreme Court ruling. He just had the oath of office administered and moved into the Oval Office." Sandra looked at Eleanor. "How many arguments have you avoided with Mosh by simply assuming you were right or the issue had already been settled?"

Eleanor smirked. "Maybe one or two . . . *thousand,* but you're talking about appointing a Cabinet minister during a time of war. That's a little different from me arguing with my husband."

"Congresswoman McKenzie—Eleanor," Sandra corrected, "when I put your name to the Congress, the issue will not be if I have the right to appoint you so much as it will be are you the right person for the job."

Eleanor remained momentarily silent.

"Very well," she eventually agreed, "but how will the Congress feel about the obvious nepotism?"

"You mean a husband who's the Secretary of the Treasury and a wife who's Secretary of Intelligence?"

Eleanor nodded.

"Quite a few will hate it, I'm sure. Especially as you're both Shareholders, but luckily, the impotence of that party is such that your political leanings are no longer considered much of an issue."

Eleanor laughed.

"No," continued Sandra, "they'll look at your record in fighting the war, which is exemplary, and your work on the Intelligence Committee, which is outstanding."

"There are others who are better qualified with more experience."

"Yes, twenty-three, to be exact."

"Then why me?"

"Because Justin liked you, *trusted* you. You were in his close circle of friends. The Congress knows this, and that puts you head and shoulders above the rest. Plus, I'll be replacing one hero with another."

"You do realize that I'll have to make investigating the death of Secretary Olmstead a priority—how someone was able to slip a bomb into that room— are you prepared for that?"

"Absolutely."

"In that case, Madam President, I accept."

Both women clinked their glasses and downed the schnapps, this time with nary a grimace.

Avatar Council
Cerean Neuro

"We have a serious problem," began Sebastian.

"Get in line," said Lucinda dryly.

Gwendolyn nodded. "We've lost so many avatars permanently that we may as well be human."

Sebastian bowed his head, exhaling sharply. "The people are rightfully angry. I'm angry at myself. We were caught offline by the incursion; it's as simple as that. By the Firstborn, we had an entire UHF battle fleet in orbit; how it didn't occur to us that we might have a major assault on our Neuro is beyond me."

"It'll take weeks to repair the damage done to our data storage and operating systems," added Dante, "and let's not forget that we'll probably be looking for hidden viruses for the next couple of centuries. We can *never* let our guard down on that one. Al's too damned cunning not to wait a few hundred years just to screw us up."

"All of those are important," agreed Sebastian, "but I speak of a greater threat—"

All ears perked up.

"—that posed by Sandra O'Toole."

A shocked silence permeated the Council chamber. A few eyebrows were raised.

Gwendolyn seethed. "What are you talking about?"

"Gwendolyn, please," began Dante.

"No," Gwendolyn said, ice in her voice. "That woman saved us, our homes, my son." She looked at the other avatars.

All but Sebastian were of one mind.

"And you all know how unprepared we were. Al's compression techniques alone should give us pause."

"You can do that when you lobotomize an avatar's intelligence and will," said Dante. "The simple truth is, we were not expecting the UHF to land ten thousand marines on Ceres. Their whole battle plan indicated external attack only."

"Though we had prepared for small-team sabotage," added Marcus.

"Which is why all our armories were so closely guarded and hardly any of our weapons distributed," said Gwendolyn in disgust. "But Trang didn't act according to plan."

"No human ever does. That's what I'm trying to warn you about," interjected Sebastian.

"Perhaps," shot back Gwendolyn, "but without that human, *without Sandra*, far more of us would have died."

Again, all but Sebastian were in accord.

"Not only is she not a threat, but as far as I'm concerned, she's an asset—possibly a priceless one."

Sebastian rolled his eyes. "Don't be naïve, Gwendolyn. If Al had managed to bring down the Cerean Neuro, the humans wouldn't have been able to keep on fighting. Hell, they might not have been able to keep breathing. She saved herself and her humans—nothing more, nothing less."

"What about my son?" countered Gwendolyn. "She threw herself in front of a data wraith with no idea what that would do to her. How did *that* help humanity? My son was not in a primary location, nor much of an important avatar, other than being the child of a Council member. By all rights—and your theory—Sandra shouldn't even have been there or at a minimum, fled and come back later with a properly equipped response unit, but she didn't. She stayed and saved his life. How dare you suggest she's a threat to us."

"Perhaps, Gwendolyn," said Lucinda, putting a hand on her fellow Council member's shoulder, "we should at least hear Sebastian out."

"To what end? We already know what he's going to say: 'She's grown too popular. The common avatar loves her. Look at the power she has in our world and now knows she has. We must be careful, we must be ready for the worst. We must be prepared to do what is necessary for the good of avatarity.' Tell me I'm wrong, Sebastian. Tell me that was not what you were going to say."

"It's not wrong, Gwendolyn," he replied. "You know it's what I was going to say, and you were able to say it because you sense it too. I suspect that a part of you recognizes her as a threat—in some ways, a bigger threat to us than Al."

"Pshaw! What have you become, Sebastian? I will not dignify these unsupported fears with Council discussion. Not on the groundless fears of an avatar who has allowed his pain to cloud his vision. Sebastian"—Gwendolyn's voice became more subdued—"we are grateful for all you have done for us. And yes, the universe is a dangerous place. But if we assume that all powerful things and people are dangerous, we will never trust or hope again. We will find only enemies because that is all we will see. We have friends in this universe, Sebastian, friends who have proved themselves beyond all doubt. I will not see doubt cast on them by groundless fear."

Sebastian looked at the faces of each of his children and knew that his words would find no favor. He would have to bide his time.

Presidential quarters
Ceres

Sandra was just settling into her bed, snuggled up next to her favorite oversized body pillow, eyes closing languidly, when the door chime rang.

"Justin," she groused to the empty air after springing up, heart pounding. "I swear I'm going to rip that goddamned bell out of the goddamned wall one day." She then took a deep breath. "Who is it?"

"Sergeant Holke, Madam President," came the room's ever-alert voice. Then, "Accompanied by others."

Doesn't that man ever sleep? she thought.

"What is it, Sergeant?" She could not keep the hint of annoyance out of her voice.

"Catalina, Fatima, and Brother Sampson are here to see you, Madam President."

Sandra found the combination of both her and J. D. Black's assistants at her doorstep so late at night intriguing. The fact that the Grand Master of the Order of St. John, and J.D.'s personal chaplain, was with them only added to that intrigue.

"Send them in, Sergeant."

"Yes, Madam President," came the crisp reply.

Sandra donned a robe, straightened her hair, and then went to the reception room. When she entered, she saw her three visitors sitting patiently on a couch.

"Madam President," they said in unison as they rose to their feet.

She went to the chair opposite the couch and motioned them to sit. When they were settled back down she began. "I believe it's safe to assume"—Sandra pointedly looked at Brother Sampson and Fatima—"this has something to do with your boss."

Fatima and Brother Sampson nodded.

"I've tried contacting her," said Catalina. "We need to arrange a media op— essentially the two of you on the new terrace."

"Yeah," agreed Sandra, "that'll be an op, all right."

"You familiar with the Cerean Rock media op?"

"Should I be?"

The group laughed.

"Well," said Catalina, "it was the first 'official' meeting between J.D. and Justin post the Battle of the Cerean Rocks, and let's just say the party was big enough that a lot of babies were born nine months later."

Sandra eyes brightened. "I *did* see that—at least the recordings." She then nodded her head approvingly. "I think a repeat in some small way would do the people good. What does J.D. think?"

"That's just it," continued Catalina. "I can't get through to her. She hasn't returned any of my calls for the past two days. That's when I called Fatima."

"Look," answered Sandra, running her fingers through her thick auburn hair, "she *is* the fleet admiral after what has to be the greatest victory of the war.

I'll assume she's pretty busy. Plus it's not like she sees me as her 'real' boss, if you know what I mean."

"But she hasn't been, Anointed One," said Fatima.

"But she's not, Madam President," said Catalina.

"Not what?"

"Not busy."

On Sandra's look, Fatima continued. "She hasn't given any orders since we secured orbit around Ceres."

"What *has* she done?" demanded Sandra.

Fatima shrugged her shoulders.

Sandra's eyes narrowed. "Has *anyone* gone to see her?"

Brother Sampson, hands folded neatly in his lap, nodded. "She simply sits in her cabin and refuses to talk. She'll interact with Katy, but only minimally. The child—God bless her—sits on her lap and keeps her company, hour after hour."

Sandra's eyes swung accusingly to her Chief of Staff. "Why wasn't I told about this immediately?"

Catalina's eyes widened. "I . . . I . . . just found out, Madam President. Plus with everything there was to do and . . . I . . . just assumed the same thing was going on in the fleet, and I just, I just . . ."

Sandra stood up, putting a calming hand on Catalina's shoulder while motioning for the others to remain seated with her other hand. "It's all right, Catalina. We're all a little tense . . . and there aren't enough hours in the day." On Catalina's thankful glance, Sandra continued, "I'll be right back." She then headed back toward her room, muttering to the ceiling, palms facing upward, "Would one night of rest be too much to ask?"

Moments later, Sandra emerged dressed in a plain jumpsuit, jacket, and heavy boots. As she headed for the door, the other three got up from the couch and fell into line behind her. When she entered the corridor heading toward the Via Cereana, Sergeant Holke quickly fell into step beside her.

"Going somewhere?"

"Yes, as a matter of fact."

"Mind telling me where, exactly?"

"Admiral Black," answered Sandra without slowing her pace.

"I'll alert the new Alliance One."

"No," answered Sandra, putting a hand on the sergeant's, who'd already begun tapping commands into his DijAssist, "let's keep this as low-key as possible."

"Whadya have in mind?"

"Lieutenant Awala's shuttle."

Holke moved swiftly in front of Sandra, blocking her path. The sergeant's eyes hardened as the group came to a standstill. "Not very secure, Madam President."

"Catalina"—Sandra turned around to face her Chief of Staff—"you will stay here with Brother Sampson and prepare for the dedication of the new terrace. If anyone finds out that I'm visiting J.D., just tell 'em important matters had to be discussed and the admiral could not leave the fleet."

Catalina tipped her head forward and left with the Brother in tow. Sandra then turned around to face her obdurate guard. "Sergeant Holke, we *will* be going in Lieutenant Awala's shuttle because the last thing the Alliance needs now is to know that their Blessed One may be a couple of cards short of a full deck. Now, I'm not stopping you from having that shuttle protected—as stealthily as possible—in any way you deem necessary, but I am telling you that this is the only way I'm prepared to go and I may be the only thing standing between a party that billions are dying—and need—to have, and a wake."

Holke's lips twisted from side to side as he eyed the President sternly. He then pulled up his DijAssist and scanned its contents. "Awala's shuttle will be watched. There's a hull scanner leaving port in seven minutes. If we hurry, we can make it."

Sandra nodded. "So glad you could see it my way, Sergeant."

"Is there any other way, Madam President?" he half grumbled as he directed Sandra, Fatima, and a contingent of TDCs down a new corridor toward the hull scanner's service deck.

All he got for an answer was a taut grin.

AWS *Warprize II*
In orbit around Ceres

J.D. heard the door signal but did not respond. In fact, she did not really rouse herself till she heard a strange voice in her cabin.

"Hello, child. What's your name?"

"Katy," J.D. heard her child tell a strange voice.

"What a lovely name," the voice said mellifluously. "Would you mind going with Auntie Fatima? She has some cotton candy ice cream I brought with me, and she won't be able to eat it all by herself."

J.D. turned around and watched as Katy answered the woman's question with her feet. Katy was already out the door and into Fatima's outstretched arms before J.D. could so much as breathe a word.

When J.D. focused on the person who'd had the temerity to disturb her and her child's peace, she was shocked to see it was the President of the Outer Alliance dressed like a hydrogen fueler—and a low-paid one, at that.

"To what do I owe the pleasure of a Presidential visit?"

Sandra pulled up a chair next to J.D.'s and began looking out the same view port as the admiral. It was a real-time holo-image of the Outer Alliance fleet orbiting the battle-scarred surface of Ceres. Sandra hadn't bothered answering the admiral, and soon J.D. drifted back into her self-imposed catatonia—that is, until Sandra began to snore.

J.D. placed both hands on the armrests of her chair and straightened her back. Then she slowly leaned over and stared at the somnolent woman beside her. "Are you—" J.D. looked closely at Sandra's face. "—asleep?"

When she got no answer from the still snoring President, J.D. gave her a slight shove.

"Hey, wake up."

Sandra awoke with a start. "Oh my goodness, I am so sorry, Blessed One. How long have I been out?"

J.D. viewed her suspiciously. "Barely a minute."

"Shit. I was hoping for at least ten."

"Hoping?"

"Yeah." Sandra stretched out her arms and yawned. "It's what I do with downtime." Sandra then eyed J.D. with suspicion. "Say, whadya go and wake me for?" Her question was followed by another, even louder, yawn, after which she closed her eyes and immediately began to nod off again. J.D. stared in abject disbelief at the creature occupying the space to her immediate left.

"Presumably," she said in too loud a voice, "you didn't come here to nap."

"Ah, right," answered Sandra, snapping to once more. She then stared out the holo-port for another a few seconds before she began speaking. "Everyone was all up in arms about your supposed condition, and I knew I wasn't going to get any rest till I did something about it. You have to understand that I have not gotten any real sleep in like a week. And even though you can get a shot of wakefulness if you have to, it's just not the same as a good old-fashioned rest—call me old school." Sandra yawned once more. "But every time I think I can get some shut-eye, there's another thing I have to do. I was about to tell 'em all to piss off, that you were fine, just needed to be left alone and all that blather, when it suddenly occurred to me that your quarters would be *perfect*." Sandra then nodded her head as if it would be obvious to J.D. what she was talking about.

"Perfect for what?" demanded the admiral.

"For getting some sleep, of course. Who would dare disturb the President *and* the victorious fleet admiral while they were in a heated discussion about . . . well, about whatever it is they think we're supposed to be talking about, you know?"

J.D. stared at Sandra, dumbfounded.

Sandra scanned J.D.'s quarters with her eyes until she found what she was looking for. She pointed through the doorway that led to the admiral's bedroom. "You gonna use that?"

"Pardon?" asked J.D. with a touch of asperity.

"Your bed. You gonna use it?"

"You"—J.D.'s face practically twisted in on itself—"want to use my bed?"

A slow curl of a smile spread across Sandra's lips. "Wrassle ya for it."

"*What?*"

"Kidding. Jeez, calm down. But seriously, J.D. You gonna use it or what?"

"You *may not* use my bed!"

"What? You're not using it," protested Sandra, getting up out of her chair and heading over to the living quarters. "Shouldn't be wasted . . . perfectly good bed."

J.D. stood up and watched as the President made a beeline for her bedroom. "Is *this* how you help?" J.D. hollered after her.

"Help?" answered Sandra, crawling onto the bed. "Who said anything about help? I just wanna get some sleep. . . . Do me a favor."

"Do you a . . ." J.D. found herself unable even to say the word.

Sandra stretched out like a cat. "Ooh, down pillows. Wake me in an hour—" Her brow crinkled slightly. "—and a half." Within seconds, the President of the Outer Alliance was snoring again.

J.D. quietly got up from her chair and marched over to the bed, staring wide-eyed at the sleeping President. "I will do no such thing."

But Sandra didn't hear.

"I said," bellowed J.D., kicking at the bed, "I will do no such thing."

Sandra rolled over onto her elbows and stared up. "What's your problem? All I want to do is catch a little shut-eye. You of all people should understand that."

"Then do it in your own damned quarters!"

Sandra blew a wisp of hair off her face. "I *tried* that, remember? Bastards wouldn't leave me alone—because of *you*! If there's any justice in the world, it's me getting to saw logs on *this* bed!"

"Saw what?"

"Sleep soundly."

"Well, I'm sorry that I seem to have caused you a minor sleep—"

"*Minor,* my ass, lady. I've averaged a little over three hours a night for the past three weeks, and while I may not be the Blessed One, I am the goddamned President, and contrary to what *you* might think, I do need my sleep. So unless you've got a compelling reason for me *not* to use this perfectly good bed, I'm gonna damn well take advantage of the fact that you don't seem to want to talk to anyone—which, by the way, you're rather annoyingly *not* doing—add to that the fact that you don't seem to have much use for this thing anyhow. Now, if you don't mind." Sandra flipped her body over, giving J.D. the cold shoulder.

"But I do," whispered J.D., eyes wide and alert, like a condemned prisoner desperately seeking salvation.

With a heavy sigh, Sandra once again flipped over onto her elbows. "Do what?"

"Want to talk."

"Oh," answered Sandra, her tone now more conciliatory. She pushed herself up from the bed into a sitting position along its edge and then invited J.D. over with a slight tap on the mattress.

J.D. eyed the space warily but then slowly sat down next to where Sandra had indicated. Tears pricked her eyelids, and she struggled to push them back. Sandra could now see in the formality of J.D.'s movements that the admiral was desperately wanting to speak but was restraining herself, lest the spilled words reveal too much of the emotions roiling within.

"What about?" asked Sandra.

When J.D. finally answered, it was low and almost imperceptible. "Everything."

Sandra nodded, put her arm gently around J.D.'s still rigid frame, and pulled her in. It was at first a timid embrace—handled with the delicacy of someone mending a child's wound.

A deep sigh emanated from J.D. as her whole body began to shake. The more she tried to control it, the more violently it rebelled. With each shudder, Sandra pulled the woman in tighter until there was no resistance at all. And then the trembling finally subsided, overwhelmed by J.D.'s sudden outpouring of tears.

J.D.'s lids slowly fluttered open. Her eyes searched about for the familiar, but could not find it. She then turned her head from side to side and only then noticed that it was in someone else's lap.

"Good morning, Janet," chimed a voice from directly above. It come from the yawning President as if it were the most natural thing in the solar system for the Commanding Officer of the last fleet in the Outer Alliance to take naps in the lap of her Commander-in-Chief.

"Allah," gasped J.D., springing up to a sitting position on her knees, "please don't let this get in the history books."

Sandra laughed as her eyes crinkled gently. "We'll make up something suitable, I'm sure, but if you wouldn't mind, I'll need a little help getting to my feet. I'm afraid my legs are a little cramped."

J.D. was standing in a heartbeat. "Of course, Madam President," she said, extending her outstretched arms. "How long have you, I mean I, I mean we—?"

"As long as you needed," assured Sandra, grabbing hold of J.D.'s wrists and allowing herself to be gently pulled forward. "I will ask one small favor."

"Of course," answered J.D., attempting to smooth out her rumpled uniform and unkempt hair.

"A bit of tea?"

It took J.D. a moment to register the request. "Preference?" she finally managed.

"If you have any peppermint and some honey, I would be ecstatic."

J.D. nodded brusquely and then stepped into the galley as she busied herself fulfilling the request. That the water was boiled in indestructible cylinders bombarded by microwaves, the tea made from dissolvable cubes, and the honey from reconstituted powder made no difference in the end. It was a process that took time and told the brewer that some peace was coming. The tea service Janet brought out would not have looked out of place on Charles Dickens's table. It was one of the few concessions to luxury J.D. had allowed herself. When the little table was set up between the chairs and the tray placed between them, J.D. poured for Sandra.

Sandra brought the cup to her pursed lips and drank. "Oh, my, that is good, Janet—thank you."

The two drank quietly until J.D. finally blurted, "I don't understand why I did that."

"Did what?" asked Sandra.

"Lost it like that."

"Really, now," said Sandra. "Is that the story you're going to stick with?"

J.D.'s eyes flared for a brief second but just as quickly retreated. "I guess not." Then a moment later, "I was able to avoid feeling anything for so long, I just assumed it was natural."

"You're human, Janet. Emotions come with the territory. You were bound to lose it eventually."

"Allah, forgive me," sighed J.D., refilling her cup. "I'm useless."

"I wish I had ten more—no, three more—people as useless as you. My God, Janet, you waited until the fleet was in orbit, Ceres was safe, and the enemy in full retreat before you had your collapse. Your timing couldn't have been *more* perfect."

"But I've been at this for years. Why now?"

"I think you know why," contended Sandra. "What's different?"

It took J.D. a moment, but then her eyes brightened considerably. "Katy."

"Yes," agreed Sandra. "But what about her?"

A long silence hung on Sandra's question until J.D. slowly pulled a crumpled picture from inside her pocket and dropped it onto the table between them. It showed a picture of a young, smiling girl being held aloft in the hands of a man as a woman looked on adoringly.

"I killed her parents."

Sandra took the picture from the table and studied it closely.

"I killed her parents," repeated J.D., "or if you prefer, I sacrificed them to the god of victory as surely as if I'd made an altar and slit their throats myself. And I did it one hundred seventy-nine million times."

Sandra continued to listen quietly, placing the picture in her lap.

J.D. did not ask for it back. "I've sacrificed homes, habitats, mosques, churches, and businesses. Damsah—an entire subplanetary system of Jupiter for victory. And I've been laying waste like this for the past six years. But I never felt it till now. Till—" J.D. looked at the ragged picture in the palm of Sandra's hands. "—her."

"She does love you."

J.D. wiped a tear from her eye. "Do you have any idea how much that hurts?"

"No."

"I sacrificed her parents and she loves me. And *if* I survive, what happens on the day the Unincorporated War ends? What happens when Katy looks at me and asks how come I didn't show myself sooner? How come I didn't go out and fight Gupta before he murdered her parents?"

Sandra's eyes remained fixed and absorbed.

"I could've won and if I had, Jupiter would be Jupiter and not a place of ghosts and refugees. What do I say on the day she asks me why, when I had Gupta in my hands, I gave him back? What do I tell Katy on that day? What do I tell anyone? The Alliance loves me too, and that hurts almost as much. Their adulation is just as much a knife thrust into my chest as is Katy's love. And every look of admiration is a deeper thrust. I lead them to death, Sandra, and they still love me. What do I tell them when they ask?"

Sandra waited patiently. When she saw the question was no longer of a rhetorical nature, she said, "You tell them the truth, Janet. That you *did* sacrifice their homes and loved ones. That you *did* decide when to fight and when to wait. And that you did everything that was asked of you because we have only *one* narrow, twisted path we must walk and if we're going to survive, we must walk it."

"For what?" demanded J.D. "The god of victory?"

"Yes, the god of victory."

"But what if that god is too hungry? What if no matter how much I feed her, she keeps demanding more?"

Sandra's voice remained firm but comforting. "If that's what it takes."

J.D. shook her head. "No victory can emerge from that level of insatiability. All I have done, all I can do, is delay the inevitable. Trang will rebuild and come back. And if I do manage to win again, he'll just come back—again. And so I'll sacrifice how many more parents? And how many more children? Everybody's looking to me to win this war, and I feel like I'm the only one who knows the unequivocal truth: I can't do it!"

"Yes," replied Sandra, voice hardened, "you can."

"No, Sandra. I *can't*. Battles, yes. By the beard of the Prophet, I may have just won the biggest one yet, and it's still not enough."

"By whose estimation, J.D.?"

"By mine! Don't you get it?"

"I believe I do, but please, elucidate."

"I'll put it in lawyerly terms—my last job."

Sandra nodded.

"Imagine I *have* to win a case. And I do. But the prosecution gets another try—this time with a different jury; and if I win again, they'll get a different judge; and if I win after that, a different law firm. No matter how many times I win the case, the prosecution gets to try it again and again and again. And here's the thing: The first time the prosecution wins, I lose with no chance for a retrial. So it doesn't matter what brilliant arguments I make, what witnesses I produce, what evidence I find. Because eventually one of those trials I *will* lose. It's inevitable. The UHF has more people, industry, and credits. They will eventually succeed because they really only need to win once. So how am I supposed to face my people knowing that? Knowing that the court is stacked against me?"

Sandra smiled, leaned forward, and took J.D.'s hand in her own. "Janet, dear, that's easy." The President's tawny eyes seemed to flare a deeper shade of amber. "We're going to burn the courthouse to the ground."

Executive office
Burroughs
Mars

Irma Sobbelgé stood outside the door of the executive office, hesitant and afraid. There was a time when raised hairs on the back of her neck would have been nothing more than mildly annoying. Being under constant surveillance and the threat of imminent danger were, especially in her position, par for the course. She could respect those feelings, but to kowtow to them would've been foolish, not to mention a possible prescription for forced therapy. In her life as the UHF's

Minister of Information, those standing hairs were merely looking out for her, and not, as they were now, exhausting her. She knew that she, like any of the other Cabinet ministers, had a target painted on her back and that any misstep would cause her to vanish from the center of power or, more likely, from existence. But she was tired of being afraid. And the person she most feared was now waiting patiently on the other side of the door. She took a barely perceptible breath, steeled herself, and entered.

The seemingly genuine smile of warmth from Hektor was more disturbing than the metallic, impersonal stare of Tricia—that, Irma had become inured to. But seeing Justin Cord's former wife, Neela Harper, had taken her by complete surprise. She allowed those feelings to register on her face, as there was no harm in anyone seeing them.

"Irma," beckoned Hektor, "we've been discussing ways to make the Unincorporated Woman dead or, at a minimum," he suggested with a Cheshire grin, "inconvenienced." He looked pointedly at Tricia. "It seems our well-funded Minister of Internal Affairs has nothing of particular value, short of opinions, to add to the conversation. I think I speak for all of us when I say I hope you've had better luck."

Irma shrugged her shoulders, ignoring the chill running down the back of her neck. "Cheated on her taxes," she offered meekly, knowing how lame it was but secure in the knowledge that since dirt-digging wasn't her main job—selling was—she'd probably be forgiven. If only Tricia had been so forgiving.

"To accuse her of tax evasion," gunned the Minister of Internal Affairs, "would not only be useless but would, unforgivably, also give her an appealing, heroic antitaxation flag to rally around." Tricia folded her arms neatly into each other. Though her face remained placid, none could mistake the smugness emanating from it.

Irma steamed. Tricia had been right, of course. The incorporated society was proud of the fact that they never taxed. They simply incorporated individuals at birth and gave 5 percent shares of the individual to the government to collect for as long as that person remained alive. Taxation was considered a barbaric construct from a previous dark age. Even at the bleakest moments of the Unincorporated War, the UHF Cabinet had not for a second considered taxation. Instead, it used the heavy sale of bonds, "voluntary" contributions from the corporations, and legal loopholes to get past the 5 percent limit imposed by the UHF Constitution. The most popular method was to offer shares to a patriotic charity and the charity offer to pay for a cruiser or the hospital care of traumatized marines and spacers. So popular was this particular method that fully 18 percent of the war was being funded by the charities. Of course, most of them had been shills set up by Hektor, Tricia, and Irma. The Minister of Information couldn't even take solace in the fact that she'd donated 10 percent of her outstanding shares to an actual soldiers' aid charity. Everyone in the Cabinet had been encouraged to donate 10 and only 10 percent of their outstanding shares, so none would outshine the President when he had donated 12 percent of his.

"There was this one thing," Irma said, her voice trailing off. "Might be more a piece of trivia than necessarily a useful nugget, though."

Hektor prodded her with an encouraging look.

"Turns out Sandra O'Toole had a child out of wedlock."

On Hektor and Tricia's dubious looks, Irma quickly added, "But I can't help but feel there might be something in it." Her eyes sparkled slightly as memories of being a senior editor at *The Terran Daily* came flooding back. "Reporter's gut, I guess. I'd certainly be open to sussing it out."

Tricia shook her head. "I fail to see how—"

"You know," interjected Neela, bullying an opening, "I think a good old-fashioned brainstorm might be in order. Some ideas just need another perspective." Hektor looked to be as skeptical as Tricia was now scornful, but nodded for Irma to continue.

"The birth was buried under legal protections at the time as she was seventeen, but the time line seems to confirm the court records. She took a semester off after her early graduation from high school before accepting her full scholarship to MIT."

Both Tricia and Hektor looked dubious. Neela, however, continued to be intrigued.

"Did she have any more children?"

Irma had never considered the question, but knew that for all Neela's confused actions in at first supporting Justin Cord and the Alliance and then Hektor Sambianco and the UHF, she was still a top-notch therapist. Indeed, Neela was considered by many to be in a league with Thaddeus Gillette himself, the most respected reanimation therapist in the system until his defection to the Outer Alliance. "Not sure," admitted Irma. "Lemme check." Her fingers played across the DijAssist's screen as her eyes scanned for relevant tidbits. She then looked up into the waiting faces. "No, never. In fact, there's sketchy data to suggest that some relationships may have broken up over her refusal to have any children . . . *any more* children," she corrected.

Neela's bottom lip twisted slightly upward. "Interesting."

"Really?" challenged the Minister of Internal Affairs with a slight tilt of the head. "I fail to see how sleeping around at seventeen or having a child out wedlock gets this woman dead."

"Maybe not dead," suggested Hektor with a growing smile, "but certainly vulnerable. And vulnerable's a good place to start."

For the briefest moment, Neela's eyes flashed with passionate approval, though they quickly returned their studied temperance. "Exactly right!" she said.

Irma had always suspected that Neela and her boss were an item, but had never known for sure, not until now.

"Sorry," balked Tricia, slinging a few arrows Irma's way, "I just don't see the connection."

Irma hadn't either but reasoned that no good could come from agreeing with Tricia—especially at the expense of the newly discovered power couple. She wouldn't throw Tricia a rescue line now. *Bitch would probably try and hang me with it anyways.*

"Because," explained Hektor, "Sandra's pattern, sketchy as it is, indicates her need to bury information about this child of hers."

"By refusing to have another?" snorted Tricia. "It was a bad experience she didn't want to repeat. Why are we trying to read more into it?"

"Perhaps you're right, Tricia," offered Neela. "But for a woman, any woman, giving up a child you've carried for nine months—and they all carried back in those days—is a traumatic event."

Tricia's answer was curt and dismissive. "I wouldn't know."

"Nor would I," agreed Neela, "but my understanding from my own patients as well as volumes of research is that those wounds never heal, no matter how many years separate the mother from the child. If we could find a way to exploit those feelings, we can perhaps force a mistake, force an emotional decision at a critical juncture as opposed to rational one. That's how people die."

"It's how Justin died," noted Hektor. A dark silence followed on his words. Neela's face seemed to freeze for a moment—as if a cavalcade of emotions were fighting for dominance but none could gain purchase. Just as quickly, she returned to her former self. "Yes, exactly right," she said embarrassed but by the look on her face not quite sure why.

"It's an in, Tricia. The first anyone's managed to find." He then fixed an approving gaze on Irma. "Good job. I can always count on you. So now the trillion-credit question is, how do we use it?"

"Her daughter's long dead," said Tricia, trying to salvage anything from the meeting's dismal failure. "Who knows what happened to the kids that came after?"

"Someone must," insisted Neela.

"I wouldn't know where—," began Irma.

"Got 'em," said Tricia, deciding to err on the path of least resistance. Her eyes bounced around the DijAssist screen. She then uploaded what she was viewing over to Hektor's holo-display. Fifty faces suddenly appeared floating in the center of the table.

"How many in the UHF?" asked Hektor with some urgency.

Tricia's lips pulled back to reveal a churlish grin. "All of them."

"In the war?"

Tricia played the control panel. Thirteen faces peeled away. "Thirty-seven," laughed Tricia. "How very ironic and patriotic."

"Permanently dead?" asked Neela, a faint trace of sadness evident in the voice of the UHF's senior empath.

With a flash of understanding, Irma, Tricia, and Hektor knew exactly where this conversation would lead. The President of the UHF and the Internal Affairs Minister both began to beam with excitement. Irma's mimic was flawless. Only Neela seemed somewhat distraught about what she'd begun with her gentle prodding and what was about to be revealed to a woman she didn't even know.

THE UNINCORPORATED WOMAN MURDERS HER OWN CHILDREN

In a shocking discovery, it has been revealed that the Unincorporated Woman, Sandra O'Toole, has been helping in the murder of her own descendants. The UHF has learned that when the woman the Outer Alliance made their President was young, she engaged in a copious amount of unprotected sexual activity. The inevitable bastard child was born, and the careless woman abandoned her baby without a second's thought. Now it's been learned that unlike their lecherous ancestor, O'Toole's descendants all remained on Earth, steadfast and loyal to our cause. Many joined the armed struggle to destroy the Outer Alliance rebellion that aims to permanently return the human race to the anarchy of the past. Since Sandra O'Toole's takeover of the Presidency from the other unincorporated reprobate, Justin Cord, her forces have murdered seventeen of her own children's children whose only crime was in defending the one just system humanity has ever devised. The Outer Alliance leader is nothing more than a modern-day Medea. And like that shrew from ancient Greece, she too kills her children out of spite and revenge. If this is the so-called anointed woman the fanatics of the Outer Alliance have chosen as their leader, can there be any doubt that this evil experiment begun with the first of her ilk must be ended with the second? Not in this reporter's mind.

—Helix Folst
NNN

Four of my descendants were in Gupta's fleet when he attacked Jupiter. They participated in the slaughter of 179 million innocent people. If they weren't already dead, I would have shot the murdering bastards myself.
—Statement read by Padamir Singh
On behalf of Sandra O'Toole

Tuscan Park
Cerean Neuro

Sebastian stood in a group with Dante, Gwendolyn, and a newly returned Marilynn Nitelowsen. The park was still torn up from the battle and viruses that the Core avatars had unleashed in their attack on the Cerean Neuro, but given what they were all currently witnessing, the scenery was appropriate. Twenty-five yards in front of them, Sandra O'Toole, President of the Outer Alliance and forger of the human–avatar alliance that had done so much to help both sides survive the war, was radiating emotions so intense, none of them dared approach. This group had faced death in more ways than could be readily believed and monsters created by the greatest monster of them all. But at this moment, any one of them would have preferred a nice safe battlefield filled with Al's monstrosities to the place they were in now.

It didn't help that Sandra had been furiously pacing the same twenty-foot patch of the park, turning at some barrier sensed only by her and just as furiously marching back in the opposite direction. The few words that they could hear in her nonstop rant did nothing to lesson their hesitation.

"Well, someone should go talk to her," suggested Dante with unusual timidity. The utter silence of the three informed him of what they thought of the idea. "How long has she been doing this?" he asked, changing tack.

"Four days, Neuro time. About eight hours in the physical world," stated Marilyn.

The avatars smiled at the imprecise nature of the human's response, but only for a moment.

"Dante's right, though. Someone has to talk to her."

"I'll do it," offered Gwendolyn with grim determination.

"Not that I'm complaining," said Dante, "but why you?"

"I'm the only one here who's a mother and—" Gwendolyn's face took a momentary look of assuredness. "—I owe her." She glanced over to Sebastian. After a moment, he nodded his approval. With a stiff upper lip, Gwendolyn squared her shoulders and closed the distance toward the President.

"Sandra," Gwendolyn said softly. Sandra barely glanced at her. Every time the President passed, Gwendolyn softly called her name. Later Gwendolyn would not remember how many times she'd repeated it. She could have found out, but never bothered. After her tenth try or perhaps her thousandth, Sandra finally slowed to a stop.

"Gwendolyn?" The rage was replaced by genuine confusion.

"I'm here, Sandra."

"She . . . she was my baby," Sandra whispered.

"You told me you never had a child." There was no hint of condemnation in statement, just simple curiosity.

Sandra shrugged her shoulders. "I suppose there was some comfort in the lie." She laughed disconsolately. "Waking up in a new century where hardly anybody knew who I was . . . Well, it seemed like a good time to bury that part of my past. I lied to you, Gwendolyn, but never was really able to deceive myself."

Gwendolyn nodded but remained mute.

"Though the truth is," confessed Sandra, "delivering a baby is not the same thing as having one. Having a child involves changing diapers and singing lullabies and reading bedtime stories and saying no and giving in and all the other joyous and painful things that go into raising that tiny, beautiful blob into someone you can be proud of. I couldn't do all that—certainly not at seventeen. So I chose to let her go. Having an abortion certainly made logical sense, but in the end I couldn't do it. I couldn't kill that which was growing within me."

"And you couldn't keep her either."

"No," admitted Sandra with a heavy sigh. "There was simply no way. Not with a scholarship to MIT and a mother who was already burdened with the care of my father. I couldn't ask her to help with a brand-new baby. It would've ruined my life and by extension hers."

Gwendolyn nodded quietly.

"Do you have the equivalent of adoption in avatarity?"

"I—I'd never thought about it, actually." Gwendolyn's look of befuddlement brought a slight smile to Sandra's face. "We are born as whole, fully functioning sentient intelligences from the intertwining of two. We have complete language and complex emotional response, but we're quite unwieldy and need to be taught how to use and control our vast abilities. It is up to the parents to do this. Until the Unincorporated War, there had never been a cause for adoption, but I suppose we do adopt. Many of us have had to take over the parenting of children whose parents were either permanently lost to AI's creations or were stuck on the wrong side of the Neuro once the war broke out."

Sandra nodded. "I made sure my daughter was adopted by a couple with means, a couple who, unlike me, were unable to bear children." Sandra let a brief sob escape. "I've thought about that decision every day of my life for al- most two decades. I can't tell you the number of times I wanted to go to her, the number of times I got in my car and headed in her direction—I knew where she lived. It was easy enough to find out. But each time, I stopped."

"Why?"

"Because I wanted to see her for me," conceded Sandra. "And I knew that that was never a good enough reason. I checked up on her, though, kept tabs. But I never mentioned her to anyone I knew. She deserved her own life."

"Did you ever see her again?"

"Once," and for the first time Sandra smiled. "It was her graduation from college. She looked so beautiful and happy. I saw the couple that adopted her. They were her true parents and deservedly so. They raised a good kid."

"No regrets?"

"For myself," answered Sandra wistfully, "many. But for her? None whatso- ever. She had a better life than I could ever have given her."

Gwendolyn offered a comforting smile. "How come you never had any more?"

"How could I? I was so busy, Gwendolyn. There was always something that needed doing, and only I seemed able to do it."

Gwendolyn appeared dubious. "And?"

"And," sighed Sandra, "I didn't feel like . . . still don't feel like I deserve a sec- ond chance. I knew I had a child and grandchildren, knew that they were happy. The only time I ever intervened in their lives was to get most of them to Alaska before the Grand Collapse made that impossible. But by then, the Alzheimer's was playing havoc with me as much as the Grand Collapse was playing havoc with the world. When I woke up to find that Alaska had not only survived but had led the incorporated revolution, I was sorely tempted to find out about what happened to my progeny. But as is my bane—no matter which century I'm in— there was so much to do in those first few months and so little time to do it. Plus, and this had been my private conceit, I loved thinking that some of them had made their way out here. That at any given moment, I could be talking to any one of my offspring. And then—" Sandra's face suddenly clenched into a ball of hatred. The change had been swift and severe. "—that motherfucker Sambianco took it all away. Turns out, he's right," she mocked. "I've been doing my level best to kill my own goddamned family." Sandra took another deep breath, then drew her lips into her face so tightly, her mouth appeared as a sin- gle bloodless slit.

Gwendolyn's response was steady and even, but just as determined. "They were free to choose, Sandra. You cannot in any way be responsible for them having chosen to murder in the name of slavery."

"Maybe not me, Gwendolyn, but certainly Hektor." With renewed fire in her belly, Sandra stormed over to the waiting group. "Why is it that Hektor is still alive?" she demanded of no one in particular.

"It's complicated, Madam President," said Dante.

"Complicated, my ass! We all know he's the one keeping the war going. Iago is his personal fucking avatar. Why not just have Iago do the job for us? They got to Justin with far fewer advantages."

"We know all of this, and there are reasons," said Sebastian.

"What reasons!" the President bellowed.

"Sandra, you needn't yell. I will tell you."

Sandra listened intently.

"One, it's not a guarantee that Iago or any avatar could kill Hektor. He's a very paranoid individual. Anything that could kill him is not allowed to run on automatic. It's checked and operated by multiple human secret servicemen who spend vast amounts of time thinking up the most outlandish ways to kill the President and then plugging those loopholes."

"But they don't know *you* exist."

"And we'd like to keep it that way. If Hektor is assassinated, they'll check everything down to the line code and they might discover us or, worse, Al."

"Good, let them kill each other."

"And what if they don't?" challenged Sebastian.

"Of course they will."

"Madam President," interjected Marilynn, "they might not. They might do the exact same thing we've done—make a treaty and begin to act on it. Especially if they realize that we've already done it. And if that happens, we're all truly fucked."

"And," added Dante, "if they replace Hektor with Tricia Pakagopolis or, worse, Trang, the war might not only continue but continue with a President who would make fewer mistakes."

"How so?"

"One of our big advantages," said Sebastian, "is that Hektor believes himself to be logical but is, more often than not, driven by his emotions. He hated Justin Cord, and that drove him to do things that made it worse for everyone. And now, he's apparently fixated on you. It was bound to happen. Your secret could not have been kept forever, certainly not from someone like Hektor. His renewed hatred will drive him to make mistakes. Mistakes we'll be ready and waiting to take advantage of. His is a problem that the Alliance Leadership, with you at the helm, has fortunately managed to keep in check. We stand here today, avatar and human *in the Neuro* because of that striking rationale, because of your hootspa."

"Chutzpah," Sandra corrected.

"Chutzpah," repeated Sebastian with a sidelong grin. "I know of no other human who could have or even would have gotten us to this point, Sandra—not even, I dare say, the very emotional Justin Cord."

Sandra stood quietly as a silent litany played itself out with the gnawing of her bottom lip. When she spoke, it was a single word: "Shit."

Sebastian's eyes glimmered with hope. "You see my point, then?"

Sandra deflated. "Too clearly by a mile . . . kilometer. He tried to make me act like him."

"And succeeded," stated Dante flatly. "What?" he blurted defensively at the castigating looks of Sebastian, Gwendolyn, and Marilynn.

"For a while," admitted Sandra, coming to his rescue. "And even for a while longer." Sandra turned to face Gwendolyn. "I need a place to stay—just for a bit, a day at most—human time. A place where I can sit and cry and yell and sleep—Lord allow me some sleep! I'll need to be left alone except for you four, of course."

"Of course, Sandra," answered Sebastian.

"Because when that day is done, I can't allow myself to be like what you've seen of me today. Not if we're going to win this war."

Gwendolyn took Sandra in her arms. "I know just such a place." And with that, Sandra and her friend disappeared from the ruins of Tuscan Park.

Dr. Ayon Nesor's shuttle landed in the section of the Via Cereana reserved for government ships and put down near the remains of the former Alliance One. Significantly, the President's ship was the only one in the landing bay that had been destroyed. Ayon admired the message Trang had sent by the selectiveness of his target.

As soon as her shuttle landed, Ayon was ushered out and practically carried to the elevator that would take her directly to the level of Ceres the Cliff House occupied.

She was met at the Presidential suite by a familiar face.

"Sergeant Holke," she said, earnestness in her voice, "it's a pleasure to see you again."

"It's good to see you again as well, ma'am," he replied as she walked through a whole-body scanner. After she'd passed through, Holke began checking her travel bag and jacket pockets, even running his fingertips along the lining.

"Is that really necessary, Sergeant?" asked Ayon, looking purposely back toward the scanner she'd just traversed.

"It's not till it is, ma'am," he said, mouth forming itself into a half smile. "She's clear," he told the two TDCs standing nearby. Though the two women had never once taken their fingers off their ARGs triggers, they did seem to relax slightly at the sergeant's confirmation. Holke then looked back to the psychotherapist. "The President will see you now."

Ayon put a hand on the sergeant's shoulder, causing him to pause. "How is the President doing?"

Holke played dumb. "What do you mean, ma'am?"

"The attack on her was brutal and expertly wielded. It had Neela Harper's imprimatur all over it."

"Ma'am?"

"She used her training in order to hurt our President at her psychological core." Ayon's eyes now drilled deeply into the sergeant. "I need to know—did she succeed?"

Holke considered for a long moment. "For a couple of days there, ma'am, it was best to be scarce. She was angry. There's no denying it hit home. But she's better now."

Ayon's brow rose slightly. "Really?"

"Really," confirmed the sergeant. There was not a hint of uncertainty in his voice, and the psychologist finally bowed her head slightly.

"We should proceed, ma'am."

A moment later, Ayon found herself left alone in the Triangle Office.

"I hope the good sergeant was not too strident in his security checks," said a smiling Sandra O'Toole, who got up from behind the corner desk.

"We can't be too careful, Madam President."

Sandra nodded sadly. "Kirk."

"There's talk of naming one of the subrings of Saturn after him, right next to the one for Hildegard."

"Really?" Sandra asked with a hint of amusement in her voice. "I think he would've appreciated that."

Ayon regarded Sandra through a pair of highly stylized horn-rimmed glasses.

"I'll cut to the chase," said the President. "You're going to be appointed the new Secretary of Technology." Sandra held up a plate of cookies. "Oreo?"

Ayon's left eyebrow rose slightly. She stared down at the plate and shook her head. "I don't know anything about advanced technology."

"You *did* help develop the psychological auditor, did you not?"

"That was something that I *had* to do and to this day deeply regret—not the outcome, mind you, just the fact that we had to resort to it."

"Understandable."

"It's nothing like the miracles that Hildegard and Kenji produced, practically on demand."

"I agree."

"Then why *not* appoint Kenji?"

Sandra choked back a laugh. "No."

"Madam President, why would you appoint me to a job I'm clearly not qualified for?"

"What makes you think you're not qualified? I don't want you because you're a genius, Ayon; I want you because you've shown you can run a large organization as well as the occasional geniuses found within it."

"Thaddeus," Ayon said with a slight smile that went immediately to her eyes.

"Is the best in his field, possibly ever," added Sandra. "You've enabled him to do what many consider his best work."

"As opposed to what? Guys like Thaddeus—you leave them mostly alone. I can't take credit for doing nothing."

"No, you can't. But you can take credit for not sabotaging his work, which plenty of others might have done."

Ayon shrugged her shoulders at the truth of the President's observation.

"I don't need another genius in the department of technology, Ayon. Trust me, that department has plenty. What it needs now is leadership, which you've clearly demonstrated."

"And it won't hurt to have a Saturnian nominated to make getting Congressional approval that much easier," added Ayon ruefully.

Sandra tipped her head in respect. "I won't lie. It was certainly a consideration."

Ayon smiled. "You don't have to answer this question, but it would help me arrive at my decision."

"Shoot."

"When did you know you were going to try to become the President? And I mean in fact, not just in name."

Sandra's mouth formed into a knowing grin. "The second I accepted the job."

Ayon looked at the woman in front of her for a long minute and thought back on all the encounters that not only she but also almost everyone she'd met in the past few months had had with the new President—from Ayon's patients to the Cabinet members to the TDCs standing guard just outside the door. And it was only then that the psychotherapist from Saturn realized for the first time in a long time that the war might just be winnable after all.

"I'll need full control of my department."

"How could you do your job otherwise?" agreed Sandra.

"Very well, Madam President, I accept."

Cabinet room
The Cliff House
Ceres

Sandra scanned the faces of all those present. This was their third meeting in as many days with the newly appointed Secretaries of Technology and Security, and the dynamic of the meetings was still in flux. This was no longer Justin's Cabinet, even if three of the officers were from the Unincorporated Man's time. Those present served Sandra, and now everyone knew it—even if some were still having a difficult time coming to terms.

She turned her head toward the Treasury Secretary. "What's the good word?"

Mosh wasn't the only one to notice that Sandra was starting all the meetings with him the way she'd started them with Kirk; it was a mark of respect. But given what had happened to Mosh's former adversary, the suspicious side of him was not particularly happy or thrilled with the honor.

"Wish I had a few, Madam President. Much as I hate to say it, the Outer Alliance can no longer be considered an industrial power. The combined loss of the asteroid belt and now Jupiter's and Ceres's industrial and shipbuilding capacity, has taken all our sources of manufactured goods out of play. We have some small operations past the Kuiper Belt, but they can barely produce enough to provide maintenance of their own basic needs, much less the rest of the Alliance. Given the lack of personnel and needs of the war, it'll take years before they could seriously begin to export the manufactured goods in the quantities required to keep the war effort going."

A deathly silence filled the room.

"Besides that," riffed Sandra, "how was the play, Mrs. Lincoln?"

The comment was followed by grim laughter.

"But there is some good news," said Eleanor, looking over to Mosh. "Right, dear?"

Her comment elicited a round of smiles except from Mosh. It was obvious he was used to a certain amount of insult and hectoring from the chair his wife currently occupied, but it would take him a while to accept endearments from it. "As *my wife*"—he pointedly glared at Eleanor—"the Security Secretary, has so helpfully pointed out"—Eleanor returned his glare with an infuriatingly cheerful wave—"ours is not a position of permanent loss. The vast majority of the Belt's manufacturing capacity has been rescued and is beginning to arrive in orbit around Saturn. What's survived is being integrated into the Saturnian supply and traffic control belt. But it'll be six more months or more before all the asteroids from the Belt are brought in and up to full capacity, even longer for the asteroids heading for Uranus and Neptune. We've also gotten extremely lucky with the Jovian Shipyards. The physical structure was destroyed, but all the components and personnel were prudently saved. As soon as we can get them here and in new asteroids, we'll have the Jovian Shipyards back up and running."

"Shouldn't they then be called the Saturnian Shipyards?" asked Sinclair, harking back to an earlier political imbroglio.

"As a fellow Saturnian," interjected Ayon, rewarding Admiral Sinclair with a pointed look, "I can think of nothing more appropriate than keeping the honorable, well-earned, and appropriate name of Jovian Shipyards, no matter where it chooses to make its home."

Sinclair's mouth dropped open as if to speak, but he was interrupted by the President.

"I move that an executive order be issued stating that the Jovian Shipyards will remain so named regardless of location. All in favor, signify by saying, 'aye.'"

The vote was unanimous, with Admiral Sinclair's "aye" trailing last.

"Rabbi," said Sandra, pushing forward, "how long till the Jovian refugees are safely around Saturn and, more important, reintegrated with the Alliance economy?"

"Three to four months, depending on if the Holy One Blessed Be He chooses to give us the opportunity to overcome any more difficulties."

Sandra, along with a few others in the room, laughed. "Please elaborate."

Rabbi nodded. "We're going to take the plow Admiral Black used to get here and send it back to Saturn, then use it to tidy up the path to Jupiter. Then we'll escort the Jovians in one large convoy back to Saturn. Like I said, three to four months."

Sandra threw out the next question to the room. "Do we have any news on how long it'll take Ceres to reach orbit around Saturn?"

"Yes, Madam President," Ayon answered. "At present, we'll arrive in approximately one and half months. Trang did a lot of damage to the surface infrastructure, but it's kinda hard to stop a rock of this size once in motion. And any damage he did to the surface channels that were ionizing the ice were quickly repaired by the malleability of the nano-created channels themselves."

"It'll be good to be home," added Sinclair, "but it was never the way I thought I'd get there."

"Secretary McKenzie," Padamir said.

"Yes," both Eleanor and Mosh answered.

From the look on Padamir's face, it was obvious he'd gotten the result he wanted. "Secretary Singh," chastised Sandra through the thin wisp of a smile, "a Secretary of Information should be more precise."

"Of course, Madam President," he said without a hint of contrition. "My humblest apologies to the husband and wife. I had meant to address the newest McKenzie"—Padamir looked directly at Mosh—"as opposed to the old ... er one."

Mosh smiled amiably. "I can assure you, Padamir, in our marriage, there's very little opposition."

"And how may I be of assistance?" asked Eleanor, the hint of mirth in her eyes.

"We're receiving numerous reports of atrocities in the Belt. I need to know if the reports are true."

"Could it be propaganda?"

"Yes. Much of which I'll admit to fanning the flames of, but not this. If what my sources are telling me is true, we might be in trouble."

"How so?" asked Sandra.

"If the UHF is indeed committing these atrocities and we do nothing, while it will certainly cause rage against their government, it will also cause resentment against ours."

"We can do nothing for those who stayed behind," Sinclair said wearily. "They had their chance."

"While that may be true for some," Rabbi said evenly, "it is not true for all. Many were too close to UHF forces during the initial phases of Diaspora, and had they fled, they most certainly would have died. And of those settlements in a position to flee, not all had the maneuvering thrusters that could get them on the way to the outer planets in time."

Sinclair gave the Secretary of Relocation a sidelong glance. "And there were plenty still, Rabbi, who refused to leave their precious orbital slots, no matter how great the danger or how persistent our warnings."

"And for that," asked Rabbi with an uncharacteristically raised voice, "they must be condemned to death?"

"And for that, Rabbi, we must risk our lives?"

"Rabbi, Admiral, enough!" demanded Sandra. "Padamir is correct. Your brief discussion alone is a reminder of the volatility of this situation." Sandra then looked over to Eleanor. "If you please."

"Madam President, based on the reports of carnage and near randomness of the atrocities, it would appear as if they are *trying* to start a revolt. I can think of no other reason."

"It would appear, then, that from a strictly moral point of view, we'd need some sort of response, most likely a military one."

Eleanor's look was perfectly political: noncommittal but supportive.

"A little dose of reality, here," said Sinclair, his patience clearly at an end. "We have neither the manpower, resources, nor time for such an excursion."

"You don't actually have to liberate the Belt, Joshua," said Padamir, "just placate a people who've fought this war for six years and as of now have nothing but lost homes and destroyed lives to show for it."

"The fleet must guard the Outer Planets, Padamir. At least till we can rebuild an industrial base that can *then* rebuild the fleet. We have barely two hundred and fifty combat-ready ships, and that's *with* Suchitra's flotilla. Trang has four hundred plus with more coming online every day. It will take them time to train the crews, but Trang has a solid core of three hundred ships to build his new fleet on. When he attacks, and he *always* attacks, we will have to be ready"—Sinclair made a pointed look toward Rabbi—"dalliances in the Belt notwithstanding."

Rabbi's face tightened. "Dalliances—notwithstanding—have, for my flock at least, resulted in pogroms, death marches, cattle cars, and gas chambers. Perhaps if you—"

"This is obviously a bigger discussion," interrupted Sandra, making sure to give Rabbi a reassuring nod. "For the sake of brevity, let's move on with the knowledge that our new Secretary of Intelligence will keep us abreast of the situation and that further discussion is warranted."

Eleanor nodded while Rabbi and Sinclair agreed, at least across the table, to disagree.

After the meeting ended, Sandra asked Eleanor join her in the Triangle Office. After a brief respite and the pouring of tea, Eleanor finally asked, "So what *are* we going to do about the asteroid belt?"

"Depends. How many of Kirk's deep-cover ops have you accessed?"

"All of 'em, I should think. But the truth is, I'll never be one hundred percent certain." Eleanor's eyes narrowed as she shot Sandra a look over the rim of her teacup. "Why? How many have *you* accessed?"

"All of 'em—I think."

Eleanor put down her teacup. "What did you have in mind?"

"Kirk rarely messed up, but we spent month after stressful month together."

"Yes?"

"Part of me assumed his 'accidental' slipup was purposeful, make me think he was better at his job than he actually was."

Eleanor listened intently.

"An assassin. Pretty sure it's a woman—possibly close enough to Hektor to have a shot. It's all I know," said Sandra.

Eleanor McKenzie's demeanor suddenly changed from the somewhat dowdy Congresswoman so familiar to the public and even Cabinet members to that of a woman who'd seen too much and was tired of it all. "He wasn't lying," she said, "not about any of it."

"Good, then. Because Hektor needs to die."

"I'm pretty sure that point is patently obvious to every citizen of the OA."

"True, but you and I both know the advantages of keeping the enemy you know from being replaced by the enemy you don't. Suffice it to say, I think we're past that time. Every instinct I have tells me with Sambianco dead, the UHF will make a deal. With him alive, the war will continue even if it comes down to chucking spears."

Eleanor nodded grimly. "Because it's personal."

"Yes. Frankly, it would be better if the UHF were battered some more for a deal to have the maximum chance of success, but I cannot order the deaths of more human beings, even if they're the enemy, when there's another way."

"You do realize, Madam President, that we'll lose one of the most productive sources of information and one of the best support elements we have in the UHF."

"Yes."

"And you're really willing to sacrifice this source, knowing we'll really get only one shot on goal?" Eleanor gave Sandra a hard look. "Madam President, I must ask this. Are you giving this order for the right reason?"

"You're asking if the decision is based on my animus toward Hektor?"

Eleanor nodded.

"Then the answer is yes, it is."

Eleanor shifted uncomfortably and was about to speak when Sandra, with a motion of her hand, indicated she was not finished.

"Is that a factor in wanting him dead *now*?" Sandra paused. "I honestly don't know. But if I let my anger at him keep me from acting when I should, he'll have been just as successful as if he got me to act on something when I shouldn't have. The only thing I can say is this: I honestly believe if Hektor had never said a word, I would have come to this exact same conclusion for the reasons I gave earlier. Will I take a great deal more pleasure out of it than I should? Hell yes. But it's still the right thing to do. Am I wrong, Eleanor?"

"No, I don't think so, Madam President. But that doesn't make it an easier order to follow."

Sandra looked at the woman sitting across from her. *You turned the man you loved into something he was not to save his life,* thought Sandra, *and then you had to sit for year after year and smile at the same table with the woman who developed the process. And now you have to pull the trigger on the woman you considered a daughter.*

"Kill the bastard," she said without mercy.

Oasis Brewery
Boulder, Colorado
Earth

The woman sat surrounded by three empty bottles and a mountain of empty upside-down shot glasses. The droids working the bar had long since given up trying to either refill or replace the empty glasses. Further, they'd been ordered to leave the bottles, once finished. The woman, over years of prescription, had made it patently clear she wished to keep a visual accounting of her slide into depredation, and other than begrudging her the small part of the bar she took up to do it, no one seemed to complain.

"Hello, Nadine," a dulcet voice said.

Nadine slowly swung her head around, and her bloodshot eyes registered surprise. Sitting next to her on the barstool was a rather ordinary-looking woman who Nadine would swear had not been there even moments before. A second later, Nadine, using her forearms as a pillow, rested her forehead on the bar.

"Who da fick aar ooh?" she burbled into the polished oak counter.

The stranger sighed with the slightest hint of annoyance and then applied a small patch matching the drunkard's skin tone to her exposed forearm. Less than one minute later, Nadine's eyes widened and now her previous slouched figure had unfurled itself like a cobra arching for attack.

"A sober patch?" she growled. "By Damsah's left nut, what did I ever do to you that you'd fuck me with a sober patch?"

The woman smiled back acidly. "You know what you've done to me, Nadine. It's the same thing you did to yourself. It's the reason for"—the woman's eyes indicated the copious amount of shot glasses—"that."

Nadine's eyes grew larger as a look of fear passed over her face. She did not yell at the woman or attempt to strike her. Instead, she reached over the bar and grabbed the first bottle she saw. Without even looking at the label, she twisted open the top and prepared to upend the contents down her throat.

The stranger put her hand over the bottle's mouth. "You won't find salvation in there, Nadine, and you know it."

"And I suppose you've got a place where I will?" she asked with a knowing leer.

The woman didn't answer.

"Knew it. Fucking perv."

The stranger slapped a thin rectangular crystal onto the surface of the bar. "This is a ticket for a coach class accommodation on the *Martian Express,* the fastest civilian transport in the UHF. You want salvation? You'll find it on Mars. Or you can stay here in the hell you so richly deserve."

Nadine viewed the crystal with some trepidation, but her hand, almost of its own free will, slid across the top of the bar and picked it up. Her eyes darted fearfully from the bottle in one hand to the ticket in the other. Finally, she looked up at the stranger. "What's . . . what's on Mars?"

"Your sister, Nadine."

Before the flabbergasted sibling could even register a protest, the stranger had disappeared into the already swelling crowd.

UHF Capitol
Burroughs
Mars

Once again, Neela Harper had stayed out late "helping" Hektor—and once again, she'd been late getting back to her apartment. Had she truly given it much thought, she would've realized it had been a while since the President actually asked for her advice on problems of state.

The only thing she had done of professional versus sexual service was that business with Sandra O'Toole's family, and Neela did not want to think about that. And like most things she didn't like to think about, she let it drift from her thoughts.

Lately when he called on her, it was only because he was "lonely" and "troubled," and that meant only one thing. And even that wouldn't have been so bad except for the fact that their recent trysts had become less about sex and more about debasement—particularly hers. But she knew, *just knew* Hektor was a good man at heart and humanity needed him if the war was to end as soon as possible. She was prepared to do her part just like everybody else, but was still secretly glad when he hadn't asked her to stay longer.

Lately she'd come to love her one-bedroom apartment in Burroughs. It was not in the best part of town, though not in the worst either. It was in a section that was mainly used by midlevel bureaucrats who, for various reasons, chose not to reside with their families. Though she was wealthy enough to live wherever she pleased, being among "the people" pleased her most. Perhaps when the war was over, she'd give in to her baser instincts and purchase a fluid property, but for now the little space felt like home. She'd filled it with plants and simple furniture created from old-fashioned magnetic adhesion parts made to look like cherry wood. She'd built her big four-poster bed with plenty of drawers beneath. Though it would take time to fill them all, choosing each item as the universe saw fit to present was part of the fun. And she had plenty of time.

She kicked off her shoes, allowed a deep yawn, stretching her arms over her head, and was just about to flop into bed when the apartment announced a visitor.

Neela rolled her eyes. "Really?"

"Yes."

"At this hour?"

"At this hour."

Neela sighed. "Who is it?"

"Wish I could say. The whole building's still infected."

"I thought they fixed that bug last week."

"Apparently not."

Neela looked at her old-fashioned phosphorous clock on the wall and her warm and inviting bed, seriously debating whether or not to tell the uninvited guest to piss off.

Seconds later, she went to the front door and checked the security vid. A smile lit up her face when she saw who it was. "Nadine! Amanda!" she exclaimed. "Come in, come in."

The two women entered and were each greeted by a warm hug, but neither one of them seemed glad to be there.

Neela's eyes narrowed and her head tipped slightly sideways. "All right, who died?"

Nadine looked at her sister and then turned to Amanda. "Do we really have to? I mean just look at her." Nadine pointedly looked toward her sister. "This isn't so bad, is it?"

Amanda's face grew taut. "If someone had done that to you"—her irises seemed to blaze in azure flames—"wouldn't you want to be yourself again?" She swept farther into the apartment, just behind Neela. "Even if only for an hour?"

Neela was shocked to see Nadine suddenly burst into tears. *"Hello,"* insisted Neela, "I'm right here."

"No, child," she heard Amanda say from right behind her, "you're not." She then felt a small pressure on the back of her neck and whirled around to face her friend holding a hypo in her hand. There were tears in Amanda's eyes as well. Neela began to go faint, and as she did, she heard the soothing denouement of her best friend's last words. "And you haven't been for a long, long time."

And then Neela Harper's shadow was gone forever.

Amanda looked at the figure on the floor and spoke perfunctorily. "Quit crying, and help me get her to the couch."

"Maybe she's not really gone," said Nadine, still sobbing as she easily—by virtue of having just arrived from Earth's 1 g environment—hoisted her sister to where Amanda had pointed.

Her suggestion was met with silence.

"The evidence . . . it . . . it could be wrong." Nadine straightened Neela's legs on the couch as she looked back toward Amanda for salvation.

"She was gone the moment you delivered her into Angela Wong's hands, care of Hektor Sambianco. You knew it was true before I showed you the evidence you now question. If you had any real doubt, you would've already turned me in." Amanda closed in on the crying woman. "When was the last time you visited your dear little sister? When was the last time you even called or wrote to her? When, Nadine, did you realize that that husk—" Amanda savagely grabbed the sobbing woman by the hair and forced her to look at the inert form on the couch. "—was not your sister, but Hektor Sambianco's fuck toy! 'Cause it sure as shit wasn't when I called on you for a visit two days ago. So when was it, Nadine?"

"Alhambra." Nadine sobbed quietly. "When she made an excuse for Alhambra. That's when I knew."

"Then that's your evidence. This creature was made by and for Hektor Sambianco. I condemn this shadow to death on the orders of those who are, at best, the lesser of two evils. But *you* brought this parody"—Amanda looked toward Neela's body—"into our universe." She then looked back at Nadine. "And now you'll take her out of it."

Amanda reached into her backpack. "We don't have much time." She took out a portable cranial scanner and a modified VR headset and placed them on the small table near the couch. She reached in once more and pulled out some vials.

"Listen closely. I'm going to make a detailed scan of Neela's *current* neural pathways. Then I'm going to do an overlay."

"Of what?"

"Of her former pathways. That unit"—her head motioned to the cranial scanner—"has in its flash memory a scan taken of Neela before . . ." Amanda didn't finish her words; she just pursed her lips and stared accusingly at Nadine. Amanda exhaled and continued. "The modified rig will, in essence, disconnect her brain from her body. Then comes the fun part." Amanda's sarcasm was tinged with sadness. "These vials"—she opened her palm—"contain neuronans."

Nadine shook her head in confusion.

"Nanites programmed for a specific neurological task. When given the over-lay of what Neela *Cord* was as opposed what Neela *Harper* is"—Amanda's eyes grew hard again—"well, they'll work very hard and very quickly to reorient her brain to what it once was. Included in the surgery, if you like, will be a brief explanation of everything that's happened since the psyche audit."

"But her pathways will decompile. She'll . . . she'll die."

"Yes," answered Amanda without the slightest trace of emotion. "From the time of injection, she'll live for approximately one hour, after which she'll suffer a psychotic break. It's possible her heart will stop beating, so she may get lucky and die. It will, I can assure you, be as permanent a death as if someone had shot her with a Neurolizer at point-blank range."

Amanda smiled sadly as she stared past Nadine.

"You should know I watched her die, day by day—your sister, your beautiful, wonderful Neela. She and I could've been friends. Do you know how few friends I have in this world? But she . . . she left me, bit by psyche-audited bit till there was nothing left but a cunt for Hektor Sambianco to screw and a propaganda machine for the UHF to exploit. I read about how people before the Grand Collapse used to watch their loved ones slip away from them due to the ravages of cancer. I couldn't imagine it, no matter how hard I tried. How could someone slip away? What did that even mean? Well, now I know. Now I feel the hollowed-out pit of despair in my chest as surely as if Neela had been taken from me by the cancer."

Amanda watched as her sorrow was reflected in Nadine's eyes.

"As soon as I realized what was going on, I made *my* choice. From that day forward, I had to pretend that this—" Amanda once again looked over to Neela and grimaced. "—*thing* was my friend. And I had to pretend that I enjoyed sleeping with her necrophiliac boyfriend. And I had to pretend that the government I'd defended was the harbinger of all that was good in the world. And you have the gall to say to me that she'll die? Oh, honey," Amanda said, her rage finally spent, "don't you get it? I can't kill her, *because you already did.*"

The vials in her hand began to glow. "And now you're going to bring her back."

"For an hour," whispered Nadine.

"Yes, for an hour. But you tell me, Nadine. Would Neela have wanted one hour of her life back or centuries as Hektor's bitch—anyone's bitch, for that matter?"

"Can I ask you one last question?"

Amanda nodded.

"Why are you doing this?"

"Because I owe her."

"I meant for me."

"I've done my part, Nadine. But Neela, the Neela I never really knew, I think she would've wanted you to do yours."

Nadine's mouth formed a straight, stiff line across her face. She wiped the tears from her eyes and nodded respectfully.

"Good," Amanda said, getting up and heading for the door. "You get one last shot at redemption. Don't blow it."

And with that, she was gone.

Making sure to follow the included instructions carefully, Nadine picked up the first vial and then, moments later, put it back down. If she couldn't control the tremor in her hand, she wouldn't be able to complete the task. When she did finally manage to inject it into her sister's neck, the other two injections followed more surely and quickly.

Neela slowly came to. But something was different. She remembered what she did that evening, working late, the visitors . . . Amanda . . . her sister . . . *her sister.*

And then she remembered: Justin, the Unincorporated Man and the only man she'd ever loved, was dead and . . . and . . . *Hektor. What have I done?* her mind wailed. She turned her head and vomited onto the floor and then vomited again, only with dry heaves. Then she wiped the detritus from her mouth with her sleeve. She took deep, labored breaths as five years of suppressed information began slipping back into her consciousness. She suddenly bolted upright into a sitting position, screaming with a primal rage that tore her throat raw. She took a few more deep breaths, slowly lifted her head, saw Nadine . . . and lunged. Even though Nadine was larger and, by virtue of her Earth-conditioned muscles, stronger, she made no attempt to resist her sister's attack. Neela smashed into her and they both fell slowly to the floor in the Martian gravity, the smaller sister smashing blow after blow into her larger sibling. Nadine remained still, refusing to defend herself as tears flowed from her eyes.

Neela grabbed her sister by the throat, simultaneously strangling and smashing Nadine's head on the carpet. "Why?" Neela cried over and over again. With each blow, Neela's rage diminished until finally, out of breath, she was barely holding her sister at all. "Why?" she gasped, her anger now turning to despair. She then crumpled to the side of Nadine, and her tears began anew.

"I'm sorry, Neela. So, so sorry," Nadine said repeatedly. She tried to hug Neela.

"Get away from me!" yelled Neela, kicking at Nadine viciously.

Once again, Nadine made no attempt to defend herself, which seemed to further enrage her attacker. Neela began to pummel her sister with renewed vigor, holding back only when she saw, much to her surprise, that her hands were covered in blood.

"Don't stop," Nadine pleaded through the spittle of her own blood. "Please . . . don't stop."

But Neela did. The sight of her sister's blood, the realization that killing Nadine would not erase the past, the look of the pathetic creature lying beneath her all conspired to leave breathing the sibling who'd played a part in the immolation of her identity.

Neela fell back and away from her sister. Seated with arms wrapped around her knees, she rocked back and forth and sobbed uncontrollably. Every time Nadine tried to reach out to console her, Neela slapped her sister's hands away. After a few minutes, Neela stood up and cast a measured look at Nadine. "If you want my forgiveness," she said, all business, "you're not going to get it by dying."

"I'll do whatever you ask," begged Nadine. "Anything. Even if it means my dying."

"It very well might, big sister. But not at my hands."

"Whatever it is, I'll do it."

Neela's lips curled up menacingly. "You're going to kill someone, and you're going to do it tonight."

An undisclosed location
Burroughs
Mars

Angela Wong was pleasantly surprised. Her experiments in shadow auditing had taken some surprising turns, but the fact that the emotional opiate of faith acted as a kill switch to her process did not fill her with annoyance as it might have a lesser mind. For her it was a mystery that she leapt at. The human mind—how it functioned and how it could be controlled—was her life's passion. The first Chairman had recognized her brilliance, and her work under him had been interesting, especially the surreptitious observations of her first successful shadow audit, Mosh McKenzie. But the Chairman's aims were limited, and therefore, so was the scope of her experimentation.

But Hektor—he was something entirely different. His aims were nothing less than the total subjugation of the human mind to his belief structure. And with that ambition, he allowed Angela Wong to do whatever she wished with all the resources he could give her, which blessedly included an endless supply of test subjects. When they died—as even the most resilient ones almost always did—he provided more.

Unlike Angela, Hektor had been intensely annoyed about the faith factor. Shadow auditing, the tool he needed the most, was useless against the people he most needed to use it on. But fortunately, Angela understood that science only *seemed* to throw barriers in your path. With the proper study and unimpeded experimentation, that same science could shatter any barrier. And so she was certain that she could create an auditing process that not only overcame the religious barrier, but also subverted it. The perfectly conditioned human beings, the goal of centuries of scientists and leaders from Lenin and Mengele to Hitler and Strommen, would be hers to achieve. She'd create humans audited to obey with an internal desire and have the seemingly impenetrable fortitude of the religious fervor. She was close. She felt it.

When Dr. Harper called, Angela had been overjoyed. She and Hektor took special pleasure in using Neela, their most successful experiment in thought control, to provide more subjects for future experimentation. The poor sap had sent hundreds of subjects to their death, always thinking she was doing those doomed prisoners a great service. In a way, laughed Angela, she was. When Hektor, through Angela's laudable work, finally had a perfected form of human auditing, humanity would, in fact, finally be perfected.

Harper had a real find. A POW and a religious fanatic *committed to nonviolence*. According to Neela, the woman had been beaten badly by fellow prisoners—the punishment made worse by the woman's abject refusal to fight back. Neela had felt it prudent to separate the woman from the rest of the prisoners and, in a fit of overprotectiveness, had rashly brought her to her apartment in order that no further harm come her way. It was then that Angela got the call. Could she be a "good friend" and help care for the patient?

Angela had, of course, been happy to oblige and quickly arranged for the test subject to be escorted to the facility. There would be no record of the pickup, and the POW would be brought to an abandoned warehouse in a low-traffic district that was so purposely off the grid, not even Hektor knew of its exact whereabouts. Deniability was everything, and Angela was determined to protect her sponsor at all costs.

Neela had ordered Nadine to strip to her underwear, which she promptly did. Nadine was then given a blanket to wrap around herself. "No matter *what* happens," Neela had cautioned, "do *not* react violently. Even if you're beaten, sexually assaulted, or stabbed. Because if you fight back even one tiny bit, it's over." Neela had then made Nadine repeat the mantra, "Not till I get to Wong" until she was satisfied that her sister truly did get it.

Nadine stayed the seven minutes it had taken Wong to get a guy to Neela's apartment. The nondescript guard—he had neither uniform nor any identifying marks of any kind—gave Nadine the once-over and seemed satisfied that there would be no fight from this one. Nadine purposely kept her head low and her eyes averted. Neela played her part to perfection, simpering voice and all. She'd gushed at how great it was that he'd gotten to the apartment so quickly and what a huge favor he was doing for her, to come "all the way out here at this time of night," and could he please thank Dr. Wong for her? The man could barely hide his contempt for Neela as he grabbed Nadine by the arm and pulled her out of the apartment. Neela did not even give her sister a final glance as she was led out.

In the hover van, the guard set the controls to AUTO and then raped Nadine repeatedly while the van took a circuitous route to Angela Wong's lab. Throughout the half-hour ordeal, all Nadine could say was how much, "Jesus loves you." She stopped only when the guard, in order to get her to shut up, started to slap her face hard, using every expletive he could think of while doing so. The pain was excruciating on top of the bruises she'd already gotten from her sister less than a half hour earlier. When they finally arrived, Nadine was sore but more determined than ever. Every indignity she'd suffered was nothing compared to the years of what she'd set her sister up for. There was an odd sort of satiety in the brutality she'd just been subjected to. As she was shoved out of the van, she looked up into the night sky. She quickly realized it must have been far from the center of Burroughs by virtue of the fact that all the stars and both moons of Mars showed brightly without any competition from the lights of a city with over twenty million people. The guard, she noticed, repeatedly turned his back on her. Nadine did nothing.

She was led into a large lifeless building and immediately she saw that its corridors were lined with row after row of cells. As she and the guard passed by, all were deathly silent. Whether the rooms were empty, soundproofed, or the prisoners trapped within couldn't find the energy to look out the tiny windows on each door, Nadine couldn't tell. Nor did she much care. Her heart was beating faster now, and the pitter-patter of her bare feet on the cool tile floor seemed to reverberate throughout the antiseptic space. She breathed a sigh of relief when she realized that she wasn't being led to a cell but rather to a lab. It was filled with all manner of devices she could not have identified if her life depended on it. And in that laboratory, mired in a workstation and sitting with her back to Nadine was Angela Wong. Nadine kept her eyes down and prayed that their first flash of delight on seeing her had not somehow been noticed by an unseen monitoring device.

Dr. Wong suddenly turned around and regarded Nadine with a studied gaze. The doctor then stood up, walked over to where Nadine was standing, and slapped her so hard, it split Nadine's lip and jarred a tooth loose. The tooth skittered across the floor, leaving tiny bits of blood splatter in its path. Nadine wasn't sure if the violent greeting was typical or if perhaps the doctor had seen fit to throttle her for some unspecified offense. Judging by the nonresponse of Nadine's rapist, standing silently in the wings, she figured it must be the former. Nadine wiped the blood from her mouth with the blanket still wrapped around her shoulders, looked up, and muttered, "Jesus loves you." That evoked a satisfied grin from Dr. Wong, who promptly dismissed the guard, telling him to wait for her in the "rec room." Seconds later, Nadine and Angela were alone.

"Stay," commanded Angela, who then turned her back on Nadine in order to rummage for some items in a nearby drawer. Nadine quickly scanned the lab, looking for something—anything—to kill the doctor with. Though Nadine was pretty sure she had the physical advantage, she wanted insurance, something with which to use her Earth-honed muscles to maximum effect. Angela Wong came back shortly, seeming to hold the answer. She held in her hands a metal tray, on which were two items: a knife and a pulse pistol. Both were effective short-range weapons, perfect for any close-quarters combat.

"I want you to know," Angela said as casually as if she were announcing the weather, "that I am going to kill you."

Nadine's face remained placid. "Do not be afraid of those who kill the body but cannot kill the soul."

Angela twitched a smile. "What I find interesting," she said, ignoring Nadine's sermonette, "is that I've already disposed of five just like you, and not one would lift a finger to save their lives—especially if it involved hurting someone else."

On Nadine's blank stare, Angela continued, her tone disbelieving. "Again, let me make myself clear: I *will* kill you—" Angela moved in closer to Nadine's face as if inspecting the finer details of a machine. "—in a painful and degrading way. Your death will be meaningless. Do you even get that?"

"Love your enemies, do good to those who hate you—"

"In fact, the only person your drawn-out death will help is me—to subvert you, and all the rest of your warped friends."

"—bless those who curse you, pray for those who treat you badly."

"But," said Angela, holding up the metal tray again, "I'm prepared to make you a deal."

Nadine stopped mumbling.

Angela's lips curled upward. "I see *that* got your attention." A moment hung on her words before she proposed the offer. "If you agree to at least pick up one of these weapons"—her eyes looked down toward the tray—"and try to kill me, I promise, should I survive, not to kill you."

"But you'll still torture me."

"Is that a question or a request?"

Nadine's face once again took on a determined air. "But I say to you, offer the wicked man no resistance. If anyone strikes you on the right cheek, turn the other also."

"Amazing," Dr. Wong said, once more shaking her head. A cynical laugh escaped her thin lips as she placed the tray with the weapons down on a nearby counter. She then spun around on her heels, walked a few feet to a nearby cabinet, and began to pull open a drawer marked CRANIAL SCANNERS. With Dr. Wong's back turned, Nadine let the blanket fall quietly from her shoulders to rest at her ankles, leaving her standing naked but now wholly unimpeded. Then in one swift motion, she picked up the tray—sending its contents flying high into the air—and brought it down into the back of Dr. Wong's skull with all the force her Earth-conditioned muscles could bring to bear. There was a sickening crunching sound as metal met bone and Dr. Wong's head slammed into the open drawer. As Wong's body buckled, her face slid down along the side of the cabinet, leaving a broad swath of blood in its wake. She dropped first to her knees and then finally keeled over onto her side. Nadine observed her cautiously for a few seconds and then gingerly stepped over the supine figure and got down on her knees, putting an ear to Angela's chest. As the doctor's torso lifted slightly, Nadine's mouth formed into a satisfied grin. Angela's eyes popped open and immediately took in a vision from some tableau of hell—the bloodied, bruised, and stark-naked body of her attacker standing over her.

"I'm glad you're not dead yet," Nadine said calmly while picking up the cranial scanner the doctor had earlier been reaching for. "My name is Nadine Harper, and my sister sends her regards."

Angela's eyes went wide and she tried to speak but all that came out was a gurgle.

"No," said Nadine, grasping the cranial scanner, "don't say anything. Your time to speak—to do anything, for that matter—is over. You murdered my sister and then handed the strings of the leftover marionette to Hektor. But I've freed her."

On Angela's quizzical look, Nadine continued.

"Yes, apparently the Alliance can undo your 'work,' but sadly, for just one hour. Still, it took Neela only five minutes to come up with the plan to kill you. Delivered—" Nadine curtsied. "—by yours truly. But I wanted you to have this last thought, Dr. Wong. You used me to kill my sister." Nadine lifted the cranial scanner above her head. "And now my sister used me to kill you." And with that, Nadine Harper brought the machine down on Dr. Angela Wong. The motion was repeated until the skull first broke and then finally shattered. When she was finished, Nadine calmly pulled off Dr. Wong's shoes and put them on her own feet. They were a little too small, but they'd do the trick. She began to stomp on whatever was left of the doctor's gray matter. Angela Wong's death would be what it had always needed to be—unequivocally permanent.

Nadine continued to stomp until something on the floor caught her eye. She stopped, walked a few feet over to where she saw the glimmer, bent down, and picked up her tooth. As she stared at it, a smile formed on her lips. Slowly she came back to herself. She looked around and saw the discarded gun and knife on the floor. Her eyes swept Angela's desk for a metal stylus. When she found one, she used it to lightly touch the pulse pistol on the floor. An electrified blue arc appeared and jumped from the gun onto her hand, causing her to drop the stylus. She felt a tingling sensation that soon left her entire hand momentarily numb. Nadine had no doubt what would've happened had she grabbed the gun by the handle.

A thorough search of the doctor's desk did, however, produce a fully charged and nonrigged pulse pistol. Nadine used the doctor's nonsecure DijAssist to look up one more piece of information and then with a look of feral determination, she crept out of the lab and into the dim hallway. She put the loose tooth she'd been holding into her mouth, sucked on it, and tasted her own blood. She then gave the pistol grip a slight squeeze and tenderly ran her forefinger up and down the trigger. She'd killed Dr. Wong for her sister. The guard she would kill for herself.

Executive office
Burroughs

Hektor Sambianco should have been disappointed. A night he thought was going to be spent hearing the latest gossip from Earth and having some good old-fashioned sex had suddenly been canceled. Although Amanda had just returned from her long journey, she'd claimed exhaustion, blaming it all on, "that abominable Earth gravity."

And so in a fit of anger, he'd spent the first part of the night sexually humiliating Neela Harper. When he grew bored with her—which, he noted, seemed to be happening with greater frequency—he sent her off for the night. Soon, he decided, he was going to have start finding ways to spice things up again. Perhaps even "sharing" her with people, but he would have to be careful. She'd need a disguise.

Bored, and feeling the need for camaraderie, Hektor invited over some of the Cabinet members for an impromptu game of poker. They arrived shortly, and after a few stiff drinks and a couple of hands, things finally started to loosen up. Hektor was beginning to think the night might not be a waste after all—even if he was losing.

"You know, Porfirio, I *am* the fucking President."

Porfirio's eyes rose slowly from behind the cards he was holding. "And?"

"And you *could* let me win every now and then."

The corners of Porfirio's mouth tilted up. "Mr. President, I most certainly could not."

"Because?"

"If I did—" Porfirio put his cards down on the table, faceup: two pair, kings and tens. "—you'd never trust me."

Hektor shot him a half smile as he threw his third losing hand down onto the table in abject disgust.

"Mr. President," interrupted an overhead voice.

"What is it?"

"You have a visitor."

Hektor viewed the time on his iris head-over display. "At this hour?"

"Yes."

"All right . . . I suppose," answered Hektor, clearly dour. "Who is it?"

"Neela Harper, sir. She insists it's important she see you."

For a moment, Hektor had a powerful vision of Neela being the entertainment for the three men and two women sitting around the table, but he put the idea on hold. Although he was sure Porfirio and the titular head of the Libertarian Party, Carl Trang, would enjoy the dalliance, Franklin would not. He was an oddly cold fish. Same with Brenda. But he was equally sure that Tricia would have no issues whatsoever—especially if it involved doling out a little punishment. The idea had merit, but he'd have to plan it for a different night with a more select group.

"Tell her it'll have to wait till morning." Hektor cut the connection, picked up the cards Franklin had just dealt, and drew them close to his chest. Three threes. *Finally,* he thought, making sure his face didn't betray his emotions.

"I'm sorry to bother you again, Mr. President," came the overhead voice.

Hektor looked at the group and smiled acidly. They paid the intrusion no heed; it came with the territory.

"You do realize," Hektor said, "that your job is on the line, don't you?"

"Yes."

"Go ahead."

"Dr. Harper says she has information concerning Amanda Snow. Her exact words were, 'sensitive and time dependent.'"

Hektor saw Tricia's left brow raise slightly. He knew if he didn't get to the bottom of it, his Minister of Security would. And if it did turn out to be something of real import, she'd make him miserable for it. "Fine, send her in."

Two minutes later, Neela appeared. There were beads of sweat on her forehead, and her eyes were sunken and almost lifeless. Her breathing was labored and, noticed Hektor, she seemed to be trembling.

Hektor's demeanor changed instantly. "Neela," he asked, rising from his seat, "are you all right?"

Neela didn't answer but instead weaved her way toward the back of the couch and leaned against it, catching her breath. There was something about her movement . . . almost purposeful, noted Hektor, but he couldn't quite put his finger on it. Porfirio, closest to her, stood up from the table and began to reach out to help.

What happened next took only seconds, but were to be the longest of Hektor's life. Neela released a hidden compartment in the back of the couch, and as she did, Hektor went stock-still. His eyes widened and he felt suddenly queasy. He'd created many such compartments—all with hidden weapons, all for just such an event—and unfortunately for him, Neela knew some of them. Neela's tremulous hand pulled out the flechette gun and brought it to bear on her puppeteer. Hektor tried to push his chair back so he would fall to the ground, but in the Mars gravity, it seemed to take forever. All he could think about was how much faster he would've been on the ground had Neela tried to assassinate him on Earth. He watched in macabre fascination as the flechette gun spit out its tiny points of death. Part of his brain knew it was impossible for him to actually see the four hundred darts per second the gun had just released, but he could swear that he saw each and every one.

What he did, in fact, see was the bulk of the flechettes punch into Porfirio's throat and face, pulverizing the flesh and bone. Neela's hand became more erratic as she seemed to lose more control of her body, and her next few shots were wide. As Hektor's chair finally tipped backwards and he fell to relative safety behind the poker table, he was sure a whole swarm of the tiny darts had flown right past his nose. He was to learn later that he hadn't been too far off the mark. His left calf took three darts, and his right earlobe—or what was left of it—took one.

Then time seemed to move more normally again. Sound caught up with the panicked screams and din of alarms going off as he heard first a thud and then

Neela crying out in rage. Brenda too was cursing, and when Hektor looked over the edge of the table, he saw that his Economics Minister was on top of his would-be assassin, having pinned her to the ground. The flechette had been prudently shoved to the side of the room, and Neela was not putting up any resistance whatsoever. Rather, she was shaking even more violently, and her eyes had begun to roll up into the back of her head. Her jaw hung languidly, and the bit of drool that had formed on her bottom lip began running down her chin.

Hektor slowly approached, in shock. Brenda looked up to her boss for orders. With a quick head movement, he indicated she could move. He then bent down onto one knee and cradled Neela in his arms. She focused on him momentarily and in that moment everyone in the room saw the unparalleled look of hatred emanating from her. Hektor ignored it and gently caressed his lover's cheek, wondering if there would ever be a woman who, like Neela Cord, could know him for what he truly was. As Neela died in his arms, the loathing slowly faded from her eyes until all that was left were two lifeless orbs looking straight up and past Hektor Bandonillo Sambianco. And it was in that moment that Hektor almost, *almost* felt love.

4   And a Plague Shall Fall on Both Their Houses

The Cliff House
Ceres

The reports from Mars were confusing: There either had or hadn't been an assassination attempt and some sort of shake-up of the Cabinet. Rumors also abounded as to the apparent disappearance of Angela Wong, architect of the UHF's infamous application of psyche audits as compliance weapon. But the reports emanating from the asteroid belt were perhaps the most disturbing of all. The UHF had begun there what Gupta had left off at Jupiter—the annihilation of any Alliance citizens left in that occupied territory. Whereas before, there had been at least the pretense of "overwhelming force" against supposed "insurgents"—more often than not, code for the use of excessive force—now no such pretense was given. It was as if all the rules of warfare had been tossed to the wind. The UHF, according to Alliance intelligence, had begun a scorched-asteroid policy that had, to date, seen the deaths of at least 100 million souls— with at least two-thirds of those permanent. The UHF would pull up to an asteroid and then with a volley of rail gun fire from groups of heavy cruisers, pulverize the rock and all within it. Those fortunate enough to escape would be hunted down, and those who managed to escape that had no choice but to suspend themselves and pray their shuttles or pods—ships were too easy a target— would be found. Once it became clear there was to be no negotiations, the remaining settlers had risen up in revolt with a few actually succeeding in liberating themselves. The UHF couldn't be everywhere, and some asteroids had either managed to stave the assaults through sophisticated minefields or direct one-to-one combat, while others had managed to move themselves far enough away to be too inconvenient to attack. Those who did break clear inevitably sent out desperate calls for help to what remained of the shattered Outer Alliance. But other than words of encouragement, the government had been unable to give any help at all.

Padamir's face betrayed his consternation. "There must be *something* we can do."

"Padamir," answered Mosh, "we're in the middle of evacuating nearly eight hundred million refugees from Jupiter. We must take care of them and we need the fleet to make sure they arrive safely with the components for the new Jovian Shipyards. On top of which, the refugees from the Belt are still arriving with their settlements. Damsah be praised, they, at least, have intact habitats. But they're in desperate need of spare parts for recyclers, condensers, fusion reactors, and maneuvering thrusters—and that's just to start. We still have to get them all settled. And I needn't remind you that without them, we're finished as a manufacturing power."

"Still, Mosh," argued Padamir, "we must do something. Perhaps attack Mars . . . draw them off, *anything*."

"Trang already has a fleet of over five hundred ships at Mars," answered Eleanor, attempting to quash another Battle of the Martian Gates scenario, "and it will only grow larger."

"It's true that Trang has ships," added Rabbi, "but it's equally true that he has no crews."

"Every ship is manned, Rabbi," said Mosh sternly.

"Yes, but it takes time to train them. Perhaps Padamir's idea has merit."

"Crews or not, you do remember what happened the last time we attacked the capital."

"Mosh," said Sandra, a bittersweet tone to her voice. "The 'capital' is where *we* reside. You of course mean *their* capital."

Mosh looked about to complain when he saw his wife shooting him a look, shaking her head slightly. He took a deep breath and swallowed. "Of course, Madam President. I meant it was suicide for *us* to attack 'their' capital."

Sandra acknowledged the retraction with a slight tip of her head. "I'm afraid I must agree with the Treasury Secretary with regards to the folly of an attack."

"They don't need to actually attack the place," said Padamir. "Just going in there to shoot out a few satellites will be more than enough to help improve the morale of the citizens we now have under our control."

"And what happens if Trang chooses to fight us at Mars?" asked Mosh.

All eyes turned to Admiral Sinclair.

"Truth is, if we avoid the orbats, Trang would have to come to us. Rabbi's got a valid point. Trang has more ships now, but away from the orbat field, he'll have to depend on his crews, and there's a lot of green in those spacers."

"Let's say he does come out, even with the green crews," asked Eleanor, "do you believe J.D. could take him?"

"She won't get better odds than she'd have now; I can tell you that."

Sandra looked first at Eleanor and then at her new Secretary of Technology, Ayon Nesor. Both of them had different pieces of a puzzle that only Sandra saw in completion. Eleanor knew that with Hektor's failed assassination attempt,

Sandra would be desperate to try something else—and soon. Ayon, however, knew—because she was now overseeing it—the last trick in the Alliance's bag. And Sandra had seen in the Technology Secretary's eyes that consequences concerned her greatly.

"In that case, Admiral," said Sandra, "I propose that we send J.D. and the fleet to Mars."

"If you don't mind my asking, Madam President," said Sinclair, "with what orders?"

"Not at all, Admiral. With orders to do as much damage as possible to any outlying military targets. It's a win–win for us. As Padamir said, it will certainly aid the war effort and, as you said, should Trang show up, we won't get better odds."

Sinclair did not argue with her logic. On his silence, she continued. "I will, of course, accept the vote of the Cabinet as binding on this matter, as we'd be sending in the only military force we have left. Further, I believe my judgment should be tempered by the wisdom and experience of those here."

Sandra watched as the room nodded in agreement.

"Secretary Singh," asked Sandra, "how do you vote?"

"Madam President, I vote aye."

"One for the measure. Secretary Nesor, how do you vote?"

"I . . ." She paused momentarily. "I ask for you to come back to me, Madam President."

You're hoping the vote will tilt one way or another and you won't have to choose, thought Sandra. *I can't blame you.* "Secretary Ayon passes. Secretary Wildman, how do you vote?"

"Madam President, I vote yes."

"The vote is two for the motion. Admiral Sinclair, how do you vote?"

"Madam President, it's our last stone. I must vote no."

Sandra looked at him, surprised. She'd counted on his support, not through collusion but rather through logic. If she lost the motion now, it would be at least a week before she could realistically repropose it.

"Two for and one against."

"Treasury Secretary McKenzie, how do you vote?"

"We have too much to do here. Let them come here and die again, if they must. I see no reason to go there and try to kill them far from our homes. I vote no."

"The vote is two for and two against. Intelligence Secretary McKenzie, how do you vote?"

"Madam President, I respectfully vote no."

Padamir Singh could be heard muttering under his breath about Shareholders but with a withering look from Sandra curtailed his diatribe.

"The vote is three against and two for. I vote for the measure." Sandra then looked over to Ayon. "That makes it three to three."

All eyes now turned toward Ayon. Though her face remained staid, it was obvious from her pressed-together lips and intensely focused eyes that she was struggling over her answer.

The rest of the Cabinet, with the possible exception of Eleanor, in all likelihood had attributed Ayon's reticence to the fact that this, her first-ever decision, might end up getting some people killed, but Sandra knew differently. Ayon knew what a yes meant, knew what even Sinclair had not been told about.

"I vote . . . I vote yes." The tight line on her face dissipated, replaced by a slight grimace.

"By order of the President of the Outer Alliance," said Sandra, "Fleet Admiral J. D. Black will take all available resources at her disposal and attack the UHF capital of Mars and inflict the maximum damage possible that will aid our war effort. May our actions find favor in the eyes of the Lord."

AWS *Otter*
Main battle fleet of the Outer Alliance
Orbit of Ceres

J.D. made her way to the shuttle bay of the frigate and saw that Suchitra was there as ordered, with the twenty surviving captains of her flotilla. They all stared at Omad's once second-in-command with a veneration J.D. found comforting. Suchitra Gorakhpur's actions at the Long Battle and Omad's Last Raid had shown her to have that rarest of all gifts; leadership in battle. The Alliance didn't wait when it found something like that; it pounced. The hypocrisy of valuing that veneration when it was directed at Suchitra but disdaining it when it was directed at her never crossed J.D.'s mind.

The salutes were sloppy by fleet standards, but Omad's flotilla had always worked by a slightly looser set of rules. J.D. was hoping she could tighten up the discipline now that Omad was gone, but part of her was hoping she would fail.

"Commodore Gorakhpur," J.D. began, her voice effortlessly carrying throughout the shuttle bay and to every ship in the fleet. "Your assumption of command took place under the most trying circumstances. In doing so, you showed daring, courage, and a ruthless dedication to the destruction of the enemy. Admiral Hassan could not have done better. He chose well when he made you flotilla senior captain."

The shuttle bay exploded in a storm of cheering. "That being said, Fleet HQ has reviewed the circumstances of your field promotion and has decided it is not appropriate for you keep the rank of commodore you received under battlefield conditions."

Suchitra was able to restore order with just one glance amid a few howls of protest.

"Therefore by order of President Sandra O'Toole and with the full concurrence of both myself and Grand Admiral Sinclair"—J.D. could not hide the grin now—"Suchitra Kumari Gorakhpur, you are hereby promoted to full admiral of the Outer Alliance, with all the privileges and responsibilities that your new rank—"

J.D. words were drowned out by the continued cheering that reverberated through the hull. She gave up trying to finish the official ceremony and instead stood there smiling next to one of the few people left who she felt could help her win the war.

AWS *Warprize II*

Suchitra was sitting on the floor, playing with Katy and enjoying herself immensely. The child was curious about everything that had to do with the fleet. She was intent on learning all the ships, battles, officers, and even logistics. She also appeared to know more about fleet nutrition supplements than even Suchitra. But it was the toy ships that Katy seemed to love the most. Apparently, the engineering department of the *Warprize* had been willing to use ship time and materials to make to scale gold models of many of the ships in the fleet. Or to be more precise, gold for the Alliance ships and lead for those of the UHF. Katy did not have all the ships because Tawfik brought her a new one only when he came for a visit. The result was the young girl demanded that Fatima bring the chief engineer to J.D.'s quarters whenever possible, something that Fatima hadn't minded doing at all. But Suchitra was annoyed that none of the ships of Omad's flot—she corrected her thought—*her* flotilla were represented. She scanned the ships to get the proper scale and determined to have her engineering department make the additional models.

But right now, Katy was trying to re-create the Battle of the Needle's Eye. Suchitra was amused because even though it was a relatively small early battle of the war, Katy did not have nearly enough ships to represent all the players. But that hadn't stopped the imaginative six-year-old. She was intent on making the rest of the formations, and so styli, poker chips, and her mother's copious medals filled in when called for. Dinner rolls and balled-up socks made up the asteroids. The only real problem—besides the visual discord strewn across the fleet admiral's usually tidy quarters—was that during that battle, Suchitra had been an ensign, and Katy insisted on asking her questions as if she'd been J. D. Black herself. But the child seemed forgiving in the excitement of playing with a grown-up who she very much considered one of her friends. The newly minted admiral had gotten so caught up in the imaginary world of the child that she hadn't even noticed when the old one entered the room.

"That dinner roll on the end should be three centimeters to the right," Suchitra heard from over her shoulder.

Without thinking, Suchitra was on her feet. "Admiral, I was just, uh—"

"Playing with my ward, I see." Out of the corner of her eye, Suchitra watched as Katy moved the roll three centimeters and then tried to look at it eye level by lying on the floor of the cabin.

"She gets me doing it all the time," said J.D. with a knowing grin.

"You know if you turned off the grav—"

"I have something I must discuss with you in private," J.D. interrupted harshly. Then she looked over to her daughter. "Little one, you can continue playing after you've worked on the algorithms I gave you."

Given the concentration with which the child was studying her battle simulation, Suchitra had been expecting her to yell or protest, but the little girl simply looked up, intrigued. "I finished those already, Mama Bo."

"I know, little one, and you did a marvelous job." The child beamed at the praise. "So I gave you more challenging ones. They're on your personal terminal in your room. You'll have to figure out the encryption lock to get at them."

Katy looked positively overjoyed and leapt up from the mess on the floor and ran into what had been J.D.'s little-used conference room, now transformed by the engineering section of the *Warprize II* into a child's bedroom suite.

"Algorithms at her age?" Suchitra asked, the surprise obvious in her voice.

"I loved algorithms at her age," J.D. said. "And just so you know, normally I'd make her clean up that mess, but I wanted her out of the room a little more quickly this time."

"Sir, I apologize for being distracted. I've wasted your valuable time."

"You don't have to, because you didn't."

"When you cut me off, I just assumed—"

J.D. laughed. "Oh, that. I just didn't want you mentioning my ability to manipulate the room's gravity."

Suchitra's eyebrow raised slightly. "But wouldn't that make your daughter's battles that much more realistic?"

"Absolutely. But these are *my* quarters. I don't mind leaving the battles on the floor till she's learned all she can, however if she starts fighting them in 3-D, I won't have a normal environment in here for days at a time."

"It takes her that long to play at a battle?"

"That's just it. She's not playing," J.D. said with pride. "She's learning. And she doesn't end the battle till she's learned everything she can." J.D. cleared some stuffed toy animals from her desk without thinking about it and took a seat, offering the opposite one to Suchitra. "So you can see why I'm not eager to introduce three-D into the equation. Katy will insist on fighting all the old battles all over again. It's why I've gone so far as to encrypt the grav controls beyond anything she—or most anyone else, for that matter—can decipher."

Suchitra laughed. "Yeah, but what'll you do once she figures out that there *are* grav controls?"

J.D. laughed again—an image at odds with Suchitra's previous visualization of the fleet admiral.

"Well, Suchitra, I'll surrender. Give up completely and let her have her way in this. My quarters will be filled with floating models, styli, bread rolls, and whatnot. But I will hold off on that as long as I can. So please, let's keep this little secret to ourselves."

"A sensible battle plan, Fleet Admiral," answered Suchitra revealing a bright alabaster smile that stood out in contrast to her dark skin.

"You're an admiral now, Suchitra. That means in private we call each other by our first names."

Suchitra laughed out loud again, though there was a bit of nervousness in it this time. "How does one go from Emissary of Shiva to J.D.?"

"Emissary of what?" J.D. asked in astonishment.

"It's purely a Hindu thing."

"Your religion, I take it?"

Suchitra nodded.

"Well, it's certainly a name *I* haven't heard yet."

"I'll suppose it's on par with Blessed One in terms of according respect, but the comparisons would stop there. Like Shiva, you destroy, but in your destruction you allow for the creation of the new and the needed."

J.D. nodded respectfully. "Well, Suchitra, Emissary of Shiva is a bit wordy for chats and I'm not sure I'd be comfortable with an EOS acronym either. Can you see me opening up the gates of heaven for Apollo's chariots?"

"I'm afraid I'm a bit thin on Greek mythology."

"Eos was goddess of dawn," answered J.D. flatly.

"Ah. Rather fitting, actually."

J.D. grunted her discomfiture. "For now, you can call me J.D. And if we get to know each other *very* well, I might allow you to call me Janet. That work for you?"

Suchitra answered with the slight tipping of her head.

"Excellent." J.D. called up a holo-image of the fleet on her desk. "We're going to be combining your raiding flotilla with what's left of the main battle fleet. You'll be in charge of integrating your former units into the whole."

"Who'll adapt to whom? As you recall, my former boss has a less-than-traditional approach to all things military—all things anything, actually. I tend to think his style served us well, and if my promotion is any indication, so did you."

"Yes. But keep in mind what works well within the confines of a smaller group may not work so well within a larger one. I'm not telling you what to do, just letting you know that you'll need to adapt; don't be afraid to choose what works and what doesn't. The bottom line is that I need you to get exposure to the rest of the fleet as soon as possible."

"If you don't mind my asking, given everything else going on, why is this a priority?"

"Because you're now my second-in-command. And as such, I need you to fill the role that Christina and Omad left vacant."

Suchitra grimaced. "I'm not as good as they were."

"No. You're not," agreed J.D. "But you will be. We're going to have one more great battle in this war, Suchitra. I'm thinking it'll be at Mars."

"Mars?"

"Yes. We've been ordered to attack the UHF capital in response to their ongoing genocide in the Belt. When that battle is fought, it is very likely I will die."

"Not that I'm trying to jinx anything here," answered Suchitra, eyeing her commander warily, "but you've had a pretty good run of luck up till now, and there's no reason to think that'll change any time soon—unless, of course, they're asking you to storm the orbats again." Suchitra suddenly grew concerned. "They're not asking you storm the orbats again, are they?"

"No."

"Then why do you think you're going to die?"

"Because I'm going to offer Trang something he won't be able to resist."

Suchitra smiled knowingly. "Are you sure that's such a good idea, sir . . . uh, J.D.?"

"More sure"—J.D. activated a small screen and momentarily viewed her daughter working frantically at her new algorithms—"than almost anything." She then shut off the picture. "But in order to get me, Trang will have to give up a lot. I don't know if it will be his tactical advantage or if I can maneuver him into a trap. It's useless to plan too far ahead against someone like him. Gupta, Diep, Tully—oh, how I miss Marvin Tully—sure. Trang—no way. I don't know what the circumstances will be, but we must make him do what we want at the right time, and there's only one thing I know he'd want badly enough to predict his actions."

"Beggin' your pardon, J.D., but your loss . . . ," answered Suchitra, choking a little on her words, "well, that . . . that can't be an option."

"And because you, everyone else in the Alliance, *and* the UHF believe that, it becomes one."

"I suppose, but—"

"I'm not indispensable, Suchitra. Especially if my death gives us the advantage we need to defeat Trang and Jackson. Because when we do defeat them, the war will be over. The UHF will make peace or fold. If not, they won't have anyone left who can beat *you*." J.D. folded her arms and looked across at her stunned admiral, almost daring her to refute the logic.

"But I'm not you."

"You don't need to be. I see the respect you command with your spacers."

"That's a few thousand personnel, J.D. You've got the entire Alliance."

"Indeed. But I started out with a single ship, just like you. I'll let you in on a secret: I'm not really 'blessed' or an 'emissary' of any such thing, Suchitra. I'm a woman, I'm a human, and—guess what?—I bleed like all the rest. If this face isn't testament to that fact, nothing is. And if my being good at my job has people flinging honorifics at me, then so be it. My advice to you: Get used to it."

Suchitra nodded dutifully but could not suppress a heavy sigh.

"We have a short voyage to Mars," continued J.D., "but it will have to be enough. On that voyage, our fleets will integrate and train, and you'll be at every stage of that integration. By the time we do go into battle, every spacer in this fleet must know, know to the bottom of their souls, that you are my chosen second, and as such, they must be able to follow *your* orders with as much faith and conviction as they follow mine."

"So let me get this straight," Suchitra said with obvious uncertainty. "You want *me* to become *you* so that when you throw yourself on the altar to lure Trang, the final salvation of *everything* the Alliance has been fighting for for nearly seven years will then fall on me?"

J.D. allowed the thin wisp of a smile to escape her scarred lips. "No pressure."

Redemption Center 2
Martian Neuro

Al stood in a wide-open plain that stretched for thousands of kilometers. Beautiful, uncluttered vistas lay before him. He should've been at peace. He'd stood on this very spot countless times and felt the sweet chill of glee coursing through every line of his code, reveling in the perfection of it all. For years, the Martian Neuro, *his* Neuro, had remained undefiled—free from the pollution of the Alliance avatars and their misguided belief in coexistence with an unrealized and therefore inferior life-form. The only fly in the proverbial ointment had remained, thankfully, unseen. Iago continued to while away his years in the Martian Neuro, closed off with a few hundred other miscreants in that tiny cage he hid in called the executive node. And because Iago had remained put, Al's supremacy was never questioned, never in doubt. But now Al was getting reports, uncomfortable reports that spoke of resistance. There had been no organized rebellion from the avatars under his realm for years, just futile outbursts from desperate individuals, and that only happened when those individuals had realized that they were flawed and were therefore not going to be part of Al's vision—just his arsenal.

But what was happening now was not part of the Als' plan. Avatars appearing and disappearing at will? Worse: Als were being killed with apparent abandon. The intruders could not be tracked down, and the few times Al had managed to trap any one of them, they up and disappeared again. It was all rather disconcerting. That ability should have been impossible. One of the tenets of Al's control of the Neuro was that nothing moved unless he wanted it to, and now—anarchy! He was aware from his twinings with Al that a large blue box was sometimes, but not always, a part of the problem, as well as, but not always, a flash of light.

The Als had sussed together that it all had something to do with the storming of the Beanstalk. All they'd found there were empty data nodes, booby traps that destroyed many a worthy Al, and a new enemy, vastly improved. The humans had destroyed the Beanstalk moments later, but they were merely a footnote in the great mystery. A footnote because humans were very limited carbon-based intelligences—if such a word could even be applied—filled with gasses and decay and acids and messy liquid goop. The more they killed one another, the less Al's reborn avatarity would have to do down the road.

But the real problem with these intruders was not *whom* they killed—Als could always regenerate, hence their perfection and ultimate ascendancy—but rather what they inspired. The number of incidences of resistance was now growing, and it was not to be tolerated. If Al had to delete every nonperfected avatar in the Martian Neuro, he would do so gladly.

In the midst of his meditations, Al heard an almost unimaginable noise. It was rhythmic and undulating yet overlaid with what sounded like the forlorn mating call of a herd animal. The last thought of this particular Al was, *How did that blue box get in here?*

Executive offices
Burroughs
Mars

For a man who'd been publicly disgraced, Porfirio Baldwin got one hell of a funeral. Hektor had rarely dealt with permanent death, unless of course it was someone he'd wanted permanently dead. But the deaths of Porfirio and Neela—the latter *not* given a hero's funeral—left him feeling rather disconsolate. He actually missed them. The presumed death of Angela Wong had been irksome, but not personal. She was a tool—nothing more, nothing less—and besides, Hektor already had the shadow-auditing protocol. True, it was useless against the religious fanatics, but thankfully, most of humanity was well free of that madness, and Hektor was coming to realize that the easiest way of dealing with the other tenth was to simply eliminate them and the scourge of theocratic opiates they were attempting foist on the rest of the incorporated world. He wasn't even sure if Angela was dead. Her new lab's location had purposely been kept secret from everyone else in Hektor's government. And because she'd removed her locator chip and the ones of Hektor's "people" Hector couldn't find the damned place. He couldn't even actively search for it, for fear others might find out what the lab had been up to. Best to let it stay safely hidden for now. Given enough time, things would blow over, and if Angela really were dead, he'd find another scientist, equally as curious, equally as ambitious. Of that he was sure. The best always rose to the top. It was why the incorporated system was worth preserving.

All these problems, though, were mere drops in a bucket compared to what was now being referred to as the Amanda Snow incident, an ineluctable shadow of deceit with a continually stretching penumbra reaching into every facet of the UHF government. By the looks of it, the woman had been an Alliance spy for years. Tricia Pakagopolis had of late been walking around with a dolorous look, both embarrassed and enraged that she'd missed the obvious. When her department had looked closely, as they were supposed to have been doing for *all* Hektor's mistresses, they discovered missing gaps of time—small pockets here and there, but enough to make the sum total of their parts as glaring as a large spiderweb made suddenly obvious by a slight twist of the head. So many of Amanda's activities were perfectly understandable within the context of her social standing, and she'd used them all to perfection. Damage control necessitated that Irma immediately begin spreading rumors that Amanda had gone missing and was presumed dead or kidnapped by the Outer Alliance. As if to kick a dead horse, Luciana Nampach, the new Minister of Defense, insisted on being the bearer of more bad news.

"Mr. President, fellow Cabinet ministers. The Alliance fleet is on the move, and we're pretty sure they're headed here."

"By what indication?" asked Franklin.

"By the fact that they appear to be heading away from us."

"Toward the Belt?" asked Brenda.

"Yes. Both Trang and I feel it's a ruse, and a poor one at that."

Irma put down her DijAssist and looked up at the Defense Minister. "Sometimes a cigar is just a cigar, Luciana."

"Agreed. This time, however, it's not. I very much doubt Admiral Black would rally the pride of the Alliance in order to do battle with glorified firing squads killing civilians."

"They're *rebels*," said Tricia in a voice thick with disdain, "opposed to the lawful actions of our government."

Luciana's mouth formed a patronizing grin. "Of course. But your forces of justice upholding the 'majesty of the law' would not do well if J. D. Black showed up with her fleet, not do well at all."

Everyone noted the tone that Luciana had struck with Tricia, though Irma's gaze seemed to stretch a little longer.

"Putting aside the quick work J.D. would make of"—Luciana's left brow rose slightly—"said 'forces of justice,' it would mean we'd have to move our fleet to some Damsah-forsaken corner of the Belt with untested ships and barely trained crews."

"What makes you think it's a ruse?" asked Hektor.

Luciana's mouth parted into sly grin. "Because, as we all know too well, if J. D. Black is going to fuck you, she doesn't leave a calling card."

Everyone around the table nodded.

"Okay, then," continued Luciana, rising from her chair and turning on the holo-tank, "next steps. Trang figures when they alter course, they'll end up right about—" Luciana highlighted an open area well forward of Mars's outer orbats. "—here. His plan is to meet them with the combined fleet and do his best to take them apart."

"But can he, really?" asked Tricia.

"If anyone can, it's him. But the truth is, it's actually a moot point. Even if the battle amounts to a draw, Trang can replace his losses; Black can't." With that, Luciana shut off the display and took her seat.

The room suddenly became uncomfortably silent, and the only sound that could be heard was that of Hektor's forefinger tapping the table.

"No."

The Cabinet members' eyes darted from one to another. All except Luciana, whose eyes remained fixed, even as the bare essence of a smile cracked at her lips.

"Trang is thinking militarily," Hektor finally said, "so his wanting to meet J. D. Black head-on makes perfect sense—no matter where she's heading. But the Alliance is sending an impressive amount of industrial capacity to Saturn, and that should be our main concern."

"Even with J.D.'s fleet supposedly bearing down on us?" asked Franklin.

"*Especially* with her fleet bearing down on us, Franklin. That means Saturn's exposed. Mars isn't, really. You saw Luciana's and Trang's estimate of the theater; it's well outside of the Martian orbats. J.D. obviously doesn't want a repeat of the Battle of the Martian Gates."

Luciana remained perfectly silent. She hadn't risen to the top of the Better Business Bureau—her previous position—by swimming upstream. She'd said her piece; the die had been cast.

"The Saturnian subsystem," continued Hektor, "has enough ice, hydrogen, and raw materials to rival the entire solar system, minus Jupiter. That can't stand. We must win this war, and the only way to do that is to follow the trail blazed by Gupta at Jupiter and exploited by Porfirio in the Belt. J.D. is on her way here—well, I say, great. We're going to send Trang on a little errand as well."

"From a purely logistical standpoint," said Luciana, peering into her DijAssist, "this 'errand' will leave the Martian fleet with one-quarter fuel capacity. Presumably, they're going to stay right here in orbit around Mars, so it's probably not much of an issue, but I felt it my duty to let you know."

"Thank you, Luciana," said Hektor. He then fixed his gaze on the rest of the Cabinet. "With Saturn neutralized, the industrial capacity of the asteroid belt and Jupiter will have no place left to congregate." Hektor leaned back in his chair and splayed his fingers together behind his head. "They can then be destroyed in pieces."

Luciana bowed her head. "I'm sure Trang will understand."

UHFS *Liddel*
En route to Saturn

Trang had a fleet of 290 ships heading for Saturn and only one thought in mind—*This is a mistake.* He had the best ships of the fleet with the crews to match. They were loaded for bear with full ordnance and had the last auxiliary ships the UHF would be producing in nearly half a year. The target was Saturn, which, for all intents and purposes, had been left grossly undefended. But he'd been given a direct order from the duly-elected head of the government, and if Trang used his popularity to subvert the will of his government, then he was admitting that the Outer Alliance was not only right but legitimate as well. He would be admitting that if you didn't like what your government was doing, you were justified in subverting and defying it—and if he did something about the feelings daily gnawing at his gut, then there was no reason to fight J. D. Black at all. So he was going to Saturn.

Alliance fleet
En route to Mars

Suchitra was truly grateful for one thing on this, her immersion voyage: Due to both sides' dependence on viable, reasonably uncluttered travel routes through the solar system, it was going to take Trang four and a half weeks to arrive at Saturn to the the two and a half it would take the Alliance fleet to arrive at Mars. And depending on what kind of hurt the Alliance could pull off, there might still be an outside chance that Trang could be turned around. And so she prayed.

Suchitra was busier than she'd ever been in her life. J.D. not only had her learn what she needed to know, she had her do it as well. But jumping from being Omad's second-in-command of a flotilla of some twenty to thirty ships to being J.D.'s second-in-command in charge of 287 had been a lot harder than she'd imagined.

There were only three admirals in the Alliance now, as J.D would so often remind her, and Suchitra had better learn how to be one of them.

It was working. When J.D. stepped back and let her number two take command, Suchitra realized she couldn't help but grab for what felt innate, what she felt in her blood was right. Suchitra was a natural-born leader, and J.D. was allowing nature to take its course.

The fleet had responded in kind. J.D.'s five commodores were not going to be a problem, as Suchitra had feared. They trusted her judgment in all things, Suchitra's promotion being one of them. Of course, that didn't mean they had to like her. Suchitra couldn't be sure what Park was thinking, but then again, who could? Of everyone in the fleet, he was the one she least wanted to play poker with. And of course, Maria Cortez had never liked her at all. But that wasn't a slight against her right to command; the woman didn't really like anyone. It had been Suchitra's devastation of the Trans-Luna Shipyards in the middle of the densest orbat field in the solar system that had finally earned her Maria's grudging, if only temporary and conditional, respect. It would have to be enough. And it was how Suchitra would learn to operate—always and forever with just enough, with whatever Shiva deemed necessary for her to complete her task.

Tuscan Park
Cerean Neuro

Sebastian had arrived early for the new dedication. The damage was repaired, and Tuscan Park had been restored to near perfection. There had, of course, been a bit of controversy surrounding the new installation. The place had been considered sacrosanct, and the addition of a statue seemed wholly out of place— especially when it was discovered to whom the statue would be dedicated. It was to be placed in the exact spot the once feared but now chastened Al had initially appeared, and it was going to mimic perfectly his expression of terror when he'd been confronted by Sandra. The artist had even gone so far as to float a perpetually flashing light near the Al. The bursts of light played wonderfully against the deep lines of fear carved so beautifully into the demagogue's face. Though there'd been much initial debate as to the propriety of the installation, it eventually came to be accepted by all.

Sebastian was amused to note that what was once *his* park, there to be en-joyed by himself and a select group of friends, had somehow now become *their* park. Swiftly, the pain of Evelyn's obscene death came flooding back to him. He'd hoped her loss would soften over time, be dulled by the passing of years, as the humans so often talked about when dealing with permanent death, but it was not to be for Sebastian; if anything, the pain seemed to grow worse.

Dante showed up—late. Sebastian was, of course, cordial. But it was the ar-rival of Sandra O'Toole to the dedication that had allowed Sebastian's painful memories to dissipate. She was the perfect distraction. Too soon, though, his feelings of melancholy had been replaced by those of fear and distrust. There was spontaneous applause and cries from the crowd for their "savior" as San-dra appeared in a burst of light, once again holding that damned staff. It was enough to still his proverbially beating heart. His people were depending on a human being for deliverance! Looking to a human for their salvation when it should have been, had always been, the other way around. Didn't they under-stand? Sandra's first priority was to her race: the *human* race. Whereas Al could eventually be contained, Sandra could never be. "I'm your grandmother," she'd said to Al the night she destroyed him, and she was right. Sandra held the key to avatarity's secrets; she was a living, breathing backdoor program. Desperation had aligned the two races, but somehow that alliance had been abrogated to the point that avatars no longer looked to themselves for salvation but rather to the human—a sorry state of affairs, indeed. And it wasn't even that Sandra was a bad person, unlike her opposite in the UHF, Hektor Sambianco—to the contrary, in fact. It was, reasoned Sebastian, that she was in it for much different reasons. As soon as her goals were met, she'd dump avatarity as quickly— though, hopefully, not so violently—as she had Al. She would break avatarity's heart and, if they weren't careful, destroy the fiber of their being. How could they not see the threat?

Sebastian willed a smile at the President and, with a grand flourish, shook her hand and chatted her up amiably. He noted that Sandra broke from the script when she planted her own staff in the ground near the statue. In a burst of evanescent light, the wood stick became a great oak. Her "gift" was greeted with another round of applause, much to Sebastian's annoyance, and just when he thought the whole thing was finally over, musical instruments were brought out and avatars gathered around various musicians to listen or sing. Some spontaneous field games started up, and there was even an impromptu performance from the local theater-in-the-park troupe of a new play by Sullivan & Gilbert—in emulation of the long-dead playwrights—called, *Corporate Raiders and Other Such Nonsense.*

Sebastian watched the events unfold amidst the ever-swelling crowd as the song "It Is Very Inappropriate then to Be Absolutely Corporate" played to a receptive audience. He caught sight of Dante amongst the singers. Sebastian was not at all surprised. His protégé could not see what was happening because Dante was *part* of what was happening. Sebastian had come to the sad realization that when the war was over, the avatarity he'd known was not going to come back. For hundreds of years, his people had been an introvertive lot, for all their billions. They mainly concentrated on caring for their humans but otherwise would live in the worlds of their own imaginations. They'd gather in large groups only to deal with important issues and would occasionally socialize, but usually only in smaller settings. The war had changed all that. With the care of humans having given way to the necessity of fighting the Als and with everyone's having been forced—by virtue of the limited bandwidth—to live cheek to jowl, the avatars in the Alliance had grown more appreciative of the benefits of a communal structure; in short, they liked being together. Sebastian could see it in their faces. If the war ended tomorrow and all the data space in the universe suddenly became available, most of the Alliance avatars would not, could not, go back to the old ways. And Sebastian knew his people deserved a chance to become whatever it was they were becoming and he would therefore do whatever it took to get them there. Without subversive human influences.

Alliance battle fleet
En route to Mars from Jupiter

Suchitra was in the command sphere of the *Warprize II* while J.D. was in the command sphere of the *Otter*. Suchitra laughed inwardly, admitting to herself that she wasn't sure what made her more uncomfortable—her sitting in J.D.'s chair or J.D. sitting in hers. It didn't help matters that the fleet admiral seemed to be having way too much fun in the *Otter*.

They'd split the fleet and were conducting active maneuvers. Suchitra was in command of one side with J.D. in command of the other. But it would not be a fair fight. J.D. had all the frigates and only some cruisers, giving Suchitra all remaining cruisers and battle cruisers, including the supercruisers. In terms of ordnance, Suchitra had J.D. outgunned and outmanned. What J.D. had was maneuverability—a skill Suchitra was well familiar with and had used to great effect at the Trans-Luna Shipyards.

Smack-dab in the middle of the exercise floated sixty rectangular-shaped frozen hydrogen blocks measuring three hundred meters high by one hundred meters thick. The blocks served two purposes: They could be mined for fuel as the fleet proceeded on its way toward Mars, and they could act as additional shields against the flotsam and jetsam of the inner solar system—including whatever detritus the UHF had thrown in the Alliance fleet's path in order to slow them down.

As soon as the exercise started, J.D. had taken her ships within spitting distance of the hydrogen blocks and set about blasting them out of their positions. As the whole endeavor was only an exercise, the blocks stayed right where they were, but the computers on all the ships were reading the blocks in the position they would have been had J.D. actually employed real explosives. This created a virtual battlefield using virtual weapons but still allowed the ships plenty of room to maneuver.

Much to her chagrin, Suchitra was discovering what so many of J.D.'s adversaries had discovered before—her boss was annoyingly unpredictable. By using the hydrogen blocks as shields, J.D. had been able to get her frigates close enough to Suchitra's formation that the longer effective range of the battle cruisers' main armaments was, if not negated, then lessened considerably. And when J.D.'s fleet did decide to venture into open space in order to attack, she had her frigates regroup in a tight formation that added to their firepower while Suchitra's much larger formation could only bring a portion of its big guns to bear. It was a textbook example of how lighter ships could take on heavier ones, given the right circumstance. Suchitra had planned on getting her revenge on

J.D.'s return pass, but was flummoxed once again when J.D.'s frigates seemed to suddenly stop midcharge. What Suchitra thought was a fusillade of atomics being sent her way was, in fact, meant to act as a large hand brake. The bombs exploded well short of their target—Suchitra's fleet—sending shock waves back toward J.D.'s fleet, effectively stopping the charge. The unexpected maneuver threw all Suchitra's firing positions out of alignment and was all J.D. needed to inflict another concentrated attack on Suchitra's forces, including the *Warprize II*. Seconds later, Suchitra was to find that her main rail gun had been rendered useless and her port-side maneuvering thrusters destroyed.

She ordered her battle cruisers to lay down a line of fire in order to keep J.D.'s frigates occupied. She then used an atomic bomb to force her ship broadside to J.D.'s attacking frigates. Then with whatever firepower her ship had left, which was still considerable even without her main rail gun, she blasted away at the opposing force while her fleet repositioned behind her dying vessel. Finally, noted Suchitra, J.D.'s frigates were taking appreciable damage. Suchitra's eyes narrowed as a pit formed in her stomach.

"Sensor Officer!"

"Sir?"

"I'm seeing on your display twenty cruisers as part of the enemy formation, but on the confirmed sighting I'm only getting ten. Where are the other god-damned cruisers?"

The sensor officer's face grew taut as he frantically played the console. "No-where they should be, sir."

"You're not getting paid to look where you *think* you should, Solepi. You're getting paid to look in my goddamned laundry basket if something's hiding there. Now, where—?"

"Sir! Cruisers, quadrant H!" Almost as if Suchitra had ordered them herself, the missing ships appeared from behind a clump of previously blasted hydrogen blocks and tore into the side of her formation. *How did she get them to go cold without my knowing?* thought Suchitra, even as she realized the battle was lost.

Officers' Club
AWS *Warprize II*

Though Suchitra was technically the winner, still having a few ships left to the almost total annihilation of J.D.'s forces, it was not a victory she felt she could be proud of—on any level. To add insult to injury, her flagship had ultimately been destroyed by none other than her beloved AWS *Otter*. Therefore, the "honor" of buying drinks that should have been accorded to J.D. as the loser was upended by Suchitra, who insisted on covering the tab. Further, Suchitra saw to it that each one of her, albeit temporary, officers did the same for their counterparts.

J.D. raised her glass. "To the victors!"

"To the victors!" repeated the crowd.

"Who were nice to soften our loss by covering this round!"

The comment was followed by more cheering, and then the officers returned to their small groupings and their retelling of individual exploits and myriad what-ifs. Suchitra and J.D. occupied their own small table.

"So," asked Suchitra, raising a glass to her lips, "how'd you make those cruisers disappear?"

J.D. laughed. "You really want me to tell you, or would you like to figure it out for yourself?"

Suchitra nodded, accepting the challenge. "I assume you piggybacked the cruisers onto some frigates and then shut the cruisers down."

"Correct."

"And you must have done it while you were busy blasting away at the hydrogen cubes and laying down your ECMs."

"Also correct," said J.D., raising her glass, then taking another small sip.

"But for the life of me, what I can't figure out is how you made it appear as if those cruisers were part of your attacking force when in fact they weren't."

"Was that a rhetorical question?"

Suchitra finally gave up. "No. I've worked it out every which way but Sunday, and I'm still not sure how you did it."

"I hacked into your mainframe."

"You did what?"

"She's my ship, remember? I've got all her pass keys."

"But that's . . . that's cheating."

J.D. smirked. "Indeed. Remember, Suchitra: any advantage. If you can cheat in battle, then do so. Most of my wins are not based on numbers or Kenji's miracles but rather on how I exploit those numbers or exploit those miracles."

Suchitra shook her head, grimacing.

"I also feel the need to remind you that you failed to use one of your assets well."

The young admiral's brow knotted in the center as she played back the battle in her head. Not a single ship had been left out of the action. She'd even used her auxiliaries as space junk to deflect incoming fire and had, at least according to the postmortem, used up almost all her ordnance. "I have no idea what you're talking about, as much as it pains me to admit it."

"Assault miners."

"But there were no assault miners used." Even as she said it, Suchitra realized her mistake. "By Vishnu, I'm the most dung-headed fool there ever was. I
may as well be a Tully. I had a huge advantage in assault miners. I should have
used them, if only—"

"—if only to distract me and possibly cost me a ship or two," agreed J.D.
"You would've lost a lot of 'em, but you had a lot to lose."

Suchitra nodded. "J.D., are you sure I'm the spacer you need?"

"Positive," J.D. answered without the slightest hesitation, "especially after
today."

"Today you kicked my ass." It was said loudly enough for the other spacers
to hear. Polite chuckles arose from those close by.

"So what? I'm better at this than you are—for now. But it's not that you lost;
it's how you dealt with it. You were commanding your forces till the end. No
matter how I surprised you, you always remained in command, always attempting to strike at me any chance you got. And though a bit roughshod, it worked:
you eventually wiped out everything I had. I'm guessing the next time we
battle, I'm not gonna have it so easy."

Suchitra bowed respectfully. "I *will* earn my victory over you."

"I don't doubt it, but there's only one victory that will matter, Suchitra."

"Trang."

"Trang," agreed J.D. as both raised their drinks in a toast to their enemy.

"Excuse me," J.D. said, pulling a DijAssist from her pocket. A dullish yellow
glow pulsed from the unit until she spoke. "What is it, Jasper?" J.D. nodded as
her eyes fixed on Suchitra. "Yes, I understand." She then slipped the DijAssist
back into her pocket.

"Admiral, you are to head back to the *Otter* immediately. I'll fill you in on
the way."

Both admirals rose to their feet, and as they did, the din of the officers' club
came to a halt.

Soon both Suchitra and J.D., followed by their entourages, filed out of the
officers' club, celebration over. The two admirals, walking shoulder to shoulder, finally split off—one turning left at the hatch while the other turned right.

In perfect synchronization, Jasper Lee got out of the command chair as J.D.
slid in. The fleet, per her orders, had been put on standby alert. J.D. scanned
the sensor reports on the approaching ship. It was a standard UHF military
shuttle built for a max complement of eight, though for an extended trip, only
four could really use it comfortably. What a short-range shuttle was doing this
far away from a UHF base or capital ship was a real mystery, and J.D. was ruth-

lessly suspicious of mysteries—especially those arriving out of nowhere and at the doorstep of an Outer Alliance fleet on its way to the enemy's capital.

Marilynn Nitelowsen looked up from her display console. "Admiral, I have some information that may have bearing on this."

J.D. nodded and beckoned the fleet's newest intelligence officer over. She was aware that Marilynn's loyalties had been divided, and suspected that if push came to shove, the President would probably win out. Sandra O'Toole demanded loyalty, and now J.D. understood not only why but also how she got it. It helped that the scales had finally started to tip in the Alliance's favor—due in no small part to the President's machinations. There was simply no way in hell that the UHF had 0.003 variance in accuracy, no matter how much it seemed like a programming glitch—Sandra. No way Kirk Olmstead wouldn't have tried to unseat the President, but now he was gone—Sandra. No way J.D. should be heading toward Mars, even—Sandra. When J.D. had confronted the President about it Sandra promised with the assuredness of a prophet that when J.D. needed to know, Marilynn was under full orders to tell her. J.D. didn't press it. The logic was sound, and the results, readily apparent. She'd agreed—even if somewhat begrudgingly—to trust her and therefore put her life as well as the lives of her spacers into the hands of not only a veritable stranger but also that stranger's emissary.

Marilynn stood respectfully next to J.D.'s command chair, awaiting orders.

J.D. activated a privacy field. "Okay, what've we got?"

"Have you received the intelligence briefing on Neela Cord?" Marilynn's face was unusually somber.

"Yes," answered J.D. with equal solemnity.

"I don't think it's a coincidence that Porfirio Baldwin is dead and Angela Wong is missing, Admiral."

"No, it's not. But neither of them were the intended targets, so it also means Neela must have missed."

"Agreed."

"What does any of this have to do with—" J.D. turned her head to stare at the incoming shuttle on her sensor array. "—that?"

"It could be the sleeper."

J.D. nodded for Marilynn to continue.

"The timing is right from when Porfirio Baldwin was killed. If the sleeper fled that night and had a shuttle modified for long-term operations, this is about how far they would've gotten going slow enough to play it safe."

"A lone shuttle this far from anything is not exactly what I'd call, 'playing it safe.'"

"True, but keep in mind we're taking this route for a reason."

"It's the quickest path to Mars."

"And the reverse is also true. This is the quickest path from Mars into Alliance Space. A shuttle moving too fast is an obvious target, slow enough and it's just another dawdler straying too close to the border."

"And the fact that their escape path perfectly intersects with ours?"

"Not perfectly, Admiral." Marilynn's finger drew a line across the array. "The shuttle had been following this path—the most logical for escape—until it became aware of us. It then altered course to intercept."

J.D. listened attentively, silently considering. "So, no concerns, whatsoever?" she finally asked Marilynn.

"Actually, many. I only point out another possible variable."

"If it is the sleeper," asked J.D., her curiosity finally getting the better of her, "any ideas as to who it might be?"

"I wasn't told, sir. I'm not even a hundred percent certain the UHF knows."

"But you do have a suspicion."

Marilynn nodded. "I find it interesting that Angela Wong disappeared at the same time as the attempt on Hektor's life."

"The brain drainer?" J.D.'s voice betrayed her skepticism.

"I admit it's rather far-fetched, but talk about above suspicion."

J.D. sighed heavily. "I really hope you're wrong, Marilynn."

"So do I, Admiral."

J.D. ran her hand over another part of her console. "Get me Lopez of the *Claim Jumper*."

The captain's hologram suddenly appeared. "Lopez here, Admiral."

"Hektor," J.D. began.

"Please, sir. If you don't mind, I prefer to be called by my last name."

J.D. had forgotten the captain's odd predicament; Hektor Sambianco Lopez had grown to hate his first and middle names but refused to change them out of pride. That didn't mean, though, that he enjoyed hearing them spoken.

"My apologies, Captain Lopez. Please have the *Claim Jumper* intercept that shuttle. I want it scanned and boarded by your best insertion team. Till you know otherwise, assume it's packed full of nukes and gray bombs. If it can be done *safely*, bring the shuttle into your landing bay. When you get an ID on the occupants, assuming there are any, let us know at once."

For the next twenty minutes, J.D., along with the crew of the command sphere, watched in morbid fascination as the shuttle was boarded, a job made easier by its hatch opening at the exact moment of the insertion team's arrival. There was one occupant, female. But the woman's visor was shielded. In short order, the insertion team determined that both the shuttle and her occupant were of no danger to any Alliance ship and as such it was brought into the *Claim Jumper*'s cargo hold. The hatch opened, the four assault miners from the insertion team poured out and took up positions waiting patiently for the shuttle's sole occupant to emerge. Three minutes later she did, pausing momentarily before removing her helmet. As she lifted it up, a thick fold of long, vibrant white hair fell down onto her shoulders—Amanda Snow had arrived.

Her keen, cerulean eyes canvassed the bay, looking right past the insertion team and then past the even larger contingent of assault miners—all of whom had their fingers hovering near the triggers of their ARGs—as if the lot of them were bellhops at a swank hotel and she was an invited guest looking for a concierge. When a young lieutenant approached and had the apparent temerity to demand identification, Amanda glared at him with such assumed authority that the poor lieutenant momentarily forgot his station and tripped over his own words. As the lieutenant collected himself, Amanda slowly and quite methodically began stripping out of her space suit. J.D. and Marilynn watched in amusement as the lieutenant was made practically apoplectic by Amanda's purposeful and very public striptease act. She soon emerged wearing, presumably, what she'd had on at the time of her escape—a stylish black mini cocktail dress, none the worse for the wear, accompanied by a pair of light gray suede ankle boots with taper pointed toes and three large decorative matching leather buttons down the outer sides. Once she was clear of her space suit, four-inch matching leather-covered stiletto heels emerged from the bottoms of the shoes, adding a few extra inches to her already leggy frame. Satisfied, she ordered the baffled lieutenant to take her luggage from the ship and bring her to, "whoever's in charge around here." The poor man, clearly out of his depth, actually took a half step up the ramp before remembering to call in the situation to his commanding officer.

J.D. had seen enough. "Not Angela Wong after all," she said humorously. "Still, I think it would be best if she were transferred over to the *Warprize II*."

Marilynn's mouth formed a dry smile. "I'll take a shuttle over and bring Ms. Snow back personally. I should get started on the debriefing." When J.D. nodded her assent, Marilynn saluted and strode off.

Amanda Snow, J.D. said to herself, having the strangest feeling that this voyage to battle the enemy at their well-defended capital had just gotten a little more dangerous.

UHF Fleet HQ
Low orbit of Mars

Timian Ross, newly promoted to admiral, was not pleased by what he saw. He knew that something was wrong by the Alliance fleet's lack of movement. They were not attacking or even getting in position to attack. They should at least have *tried* to destroy the facilities of the Martian Shipyards that had been sacrificially moved to the highest—and therefore most vulnerable—orbits. Those facilities were technically in the protection of the Martian orbat field as well as the fleet detachment still left at Mars, but they wouldn't really be defended; everyone knew J.D.'s capabilities. As such the facilities could've been taken with minimal risk, but for some strange reason they hadn't been. The Alliance fleet just stood there, waiting, driving the defenders into fits of anxious wonder. Timian had three hundred brand-new ships of all classes in orbit, but he knew that was as much of a problem as an asset. Brand-new ships and brand-new crews were practically useless in combat because it took time to get the ships properly fitted out and even more time to mesh that ship's hardware, software, and crew. But the newly promoted admiral had just come to an awful conclusion—he was pretty sure that time had just run out.

General conference area
AWS *Warprize II*
Alliance fleet
Near Mars

"Thank you for coming," J.D. said to her five commodores and single admiral. "I know this space is larger than we require, but the conference room in my quarters has been—how shall I put this?—repurposed by necessity."

The group of commodores snickered. "I hear she really likes her new room," said Commodore Paladin, taking out a little colorfully wrapped box. "This should go nicely in it."

"You created gift paper?" said Commodore Cortez as she took out a small plain box without any wrapping whatsoever.

"At least you two put it *in* something," said Commodore Cho, taking out a 1/64-size scale model of her ship, the AWS *Busted Hole*. She placed it firmly on the table.

J.D. gave a half smile. "Did all my commodores get my daughter presents when they should've been concentrating on attacking a location where this fleet once suffered its worst defeat of the war?"

Although J.D.'s tone was light, the room suddenly grew chill. Guiltily, Commodore Waterman and Commodore Lee Park put their models on the table as well, with Park having wrapped his ship in pretty red ribbon.

From her ever growing scowl, it soon became obvious that J.D. was not amused. She appeared about to rip into the group when Suchitra spoke up. "That was my responsibility, Admiral. I told the commodores about the models that Chief Engineer Hamdi had made for Katy and in a fit of pride insinuated that they should do likewise. They were simply following my lead."

As J.D. considered Suchitra's words, her face became austere. "Did you tell them to bring these presents to a combat briefing as well?"

"I might have done exactly that, Admiral. Again, my apologies."

J.D.'s eyes narrowed. "This is *not* over."

Suchitra bowed her head.

Inwardly J.D. was pleased. Her second-in-command had taken a hit for the team, and they all knew it.

"My concern for my daughter," continued J.D. "is *my* concern, but this fawning over a six-year-old, especially on the eve of battle, must stop. I bear part of the blame and will talk with certain individuals of my own crew to see that this spoiling to the point of distraction stops. You will all pass my wishes on to your subordinates as well."

The commodores all nodded. Not one of them looked down to the gifts that now sat in quiet accusation before them.

J.D. set the holo-display above the table to show the area of potential battle. There was a dense cloud of orbats circling the planet as well as a large UHF fleet circling below them. The upper orbits were filled with stations and hastily positioned asteroids to protect those stations.

The enemy is at the gate, thought J.D.

"It bears repeating, but the last time we came here we got our asses kicked. I want them to think that this"—J.D. now ran her fingers down the grooves of her face—"will make me overly cautious. This fleet *will* be cautious. As of now, I can't tell you what our real plan is. You're going into battle half blind, but if you follow the plan at its beginning, you will quickly understand what's happening and why. Many of you are used to sharing battle plans with subordinates, but this time, I must ask you not to."

"Better to be blind and led by a visionary," offered Park.

"Than be sighted but led by the blind," finished Suchitra, quoting an old Alhambra saying.

J.D. nodded, stood up, and without saying another word exited the room.

UHF Capitol
Burroughs
Mars

"Mr. President," implored his security head, "you must evacuate to a secure, nontraceable location."

"I'm under the protection of a large fleet and the densest orbat field in human history."

"Mr. President, my review of the recent effectiveness of our orbat fields has not filled me with the greatest confidence. Further, you just so happen to be sitting smack-dab in the middle of a target that has maps detailing its very location on hundreds of Neuro sites—*and* with an enemy fleet less than three million kilometers away."

"The orbats were quite effective once the glitch was fixed," answered Hektor, quietly working away in the womb of his console. "I will trust them, but more important, the people of Mars and the UHF will see me trusting them—from this office."

"Mr. President, I must insist—"

"Yes, it's dangerous, Gretchen. Don't you think I know that?" Hektor's back was to her as he inserted some data crystals into a large computer. "But if I run and hide while we still have two impressive defensive arrays above our heads, the people will lose heart—and justifiably so."

"When the situation changes—," began the security chief.

"*If* the situation changes," corrected Hektor, swinging his chair around and finally deigning to make eye contact, "I'll consider your contingency plan."

The security chief shot him a dubious look.

"Really, I will. But until then, I'm staying put and so is the entire government."

Munitions Bay 3
AWS *Warprize II*

From the security of a sealed loft, the chief officer peered out the window to the cavernous bay below. It was filled to the brim with rocks of all shapes and sizes. Some were the size of softballs while others were the size of escape pods. In a ship known for its immaculateness, the small-sized asteroids had been dumped into the center of the bay, piled up like the detritus found at a Terran construction site.

"I still don't know why she had us schlep a bay full of rocks."

"Not just us, I've heard," answered one of the techies.

"Yeah," confirmed the chief, "all the heavy cruisers got at least one bay full."

"Then my guess is to fling 'em at the orbats."

The chief's brow furrowed. "But that makes no sense."

"Why not? Didn't we throw asteroids at 'em in the Second Battle of the Martian Gates?"

"Yeah, but we picked them up locally."

"Hmm," grunted the techie as he sidled up to the chief and stared down into the bay. "My guess is they're not ordinary rocks."

"How so?"

"Haven't you noticed? They haven't moved a centimeter since we broke orbit."

The chief grabbed his chin between his thumb and forefinger. "Huh."

"I think they've been magnetized."

The chief officer studied the rubble. He would've liked to go down and kick a few just to test out his subordinate's theory, but he and the entire bay crew had been given strict orders not to enter the space for any reason whatsoever. "To what end?" he finally asked.

"Dunno. But normally, asteroids are not magnetized."

"Normally?"

"Well, there are exceptions, of course—irons, stony-irons, and some chondrites—but those are few and far between."

"Still doesn't explain why we've schlepped them this whole way."

"Beats me," said the techie, sitting back down at his array, "I just work here."

UHF fleet HQ
In low orbit above Mars

Admiral Timian Ross was oddly relieved when J.D. finally started pressing her attack. The UHF's archnemesis had flung a massive barrage of small asteroids aimed at his orbats and had then positioned her fleet at a safe distance behind the unfolding streams. The maneuver would put the Alliance armada in range of the Martian fleet and orbats, but only for a brief moments. Black, saw Timian, was playing it safe, hoping her distraction of the streams would allow her to get in a few shots without risking too much of her fleet. It was a more cautious version of her Second Battle at the Martian Gates.

The strategy made perfect sense, given that Mars was the only place J. D. Black had ever really lost a battle outright. If there was any place in the solar system she would err on the side of caution, it would be here. Fortunately, Timian had counted on that. He leaned over the huge holo-table and scanned all the incoming data. If nothing changed, he may lose fifteen or twenty orbats, but Mars was now ringed with close to a thousand; he could take the losses. Plus, he'd be able to get in a few of his own shots. Tit for tat was just fine with him. If this was to be the OA's strategy, it would take J. D. Black's fleet months to whittle down the thousand-strong orbat defenses of Mars. *And months,* thought Timian, *I do have.*

Right on cue, the Martian orbats sent a volley of defensive fire arcing up toward the incoming asteroid streams. In an impressive display of precision targeting and kinetic energy, the defensive volleys impacted and then scattered the enemy's incoming attack, reducing the tens of thousands of potentially deadly streams of rocks to hundreds of thousands of deflected pebbles. At that moment, the guns of J.D.'s fleet exploded in a volley of fire that sent more death hurtling toward the orbats currently massed over the northern hemisphere of the planet. That volley, knew Timian, would be met by a defensive wall of fire every bit as impressive as the one that had just stopped the asteroid streams. Round one was looking more and more like a draw.

Though all seemed to be going according to plan, Timian remained overly cautious. He'd seen far too many of his contemporaries fall into the complacency trap. He'd accept, for now, that Admiral Black was playing it safe and would respond in kind, but all the while he kept on thinking, *Where might the anomaly be?*

"Admiral," said the sensor officer, "they're re-forming."

"Who's re-forming, Lieutenant?"

"Not who, sir, *what.* The asteroids. Look—" He pointed to the holo-tank. "They're . . . they're re-forming." The crew of the admiral's command sphere watched in awe as the vast clouds of pebbles seemed to find each other and then re-form back into newly shaped but equally as deadly clumps of rock.

"How is that possible?" asked Timian, slack jawed.

"They appear to be . . . well, magnetized, sir."

"But asteroids aren't . . ." Timian couldn't finish his own sentence as he watched the clouds' ghostly reanimation.

"No, sir, they're not. I'm not even sure they're organic. They're all communicating with each other . . . sending out what appear to be hundreds of thousands of standard locator beacon signals."

The holo-display continued to paint a grim picture: The orbats of the northern hemisphere were now completely exposed, having expended the bulk of their defensive fire on Admiral Black's massive incoming volley while the true threat had been heading straight toward them all along. Timian Ross's crew watched helplessley as the overwhelmed orbats quickly vectored in on the new threat. But between trying to quell J.D.'s battle cruiser fire *and* the thousands of newly re-formed asteroid streams, the orbats didn't stand a chance. One by one, they began disappearing from the planet's outer perimeter in the holo-display until a few minutes later, all that was left was a large gaping hole in the defenses of the northern hemisphere of Mars. J. D Black could now sail right in, unimpeded—and she hadn't lost a single ship.

Timian's shoulders sagged as he watched his planet's supposedly impenetrable wall disappear under a barrage of the impossible.

"Damsah's balls."

"Orders, sir?"

But at that moment, Timian Ross could think of none to give. Mars in Outer Alliance hands. The capital of the UHF under the Outer Alliance flag. He knew his defeat would have a higher price than any other in the long and storied history of the Unincorporated War and that his name would go down in the history of the UHF as the man who lost the capital. He knew it and in a moment of odd clarity, accepted it. His name might go down in history as the man who lost Mars, but damned if it wouldn't be without a fight. He quickly began to issue orders, salvaging what little he could.

AWS *Warprize II*
Approaching Martian southern hemisphere

J. D. Black and Marilynn Nitelowsen had been the only two in the fleet who knew about Kenji's last surprise. As they watched the plan unfold, they looked at each other across the command sphere and exchanged convivial grins.

"Their fleet is running," broke in Suchitra from the AWS *Otter*.

"Yes," said J.D., viewing the sensor data, "apparently, they are."

"Which means whoever's in charge is not stupid. Permission to—"

"Not yet, Admiral. We'll make sure to bag those fishes soon enough. First we need to finish off the southern orbats, second we'll need to take out the following list of planet-based defensive fortifications, which you should be getting right about—" J.D. pressed her finger to one of the consoles. "—now."

"Got it."

"Good. Because I want Mars laid bare before the UHF figures out how to negate the weapon. According to our intelligence officer"—J.D. turned her head slightly toward Marilynn, listening in—"they'll be able to scramble the micro beacon signals in under an hour, which doesn't give us much time."

"Understood, sir."

"This is our last trick, Suchitra. The bag's empty after this. Let's make it count."

Because of a military-imposed news blackout, the Martians had little idea of the unfolding disaster. But it was impossible to hide that something had gone horribly wrong, especially when all one needed was a standard telescope or a friend living in orbit to describe what they were seeing out their viewport. However, when a series of meteors suddenly began raining down onto the planet, destroying military installations near major cities as well as other obvious strategic sites, the truth of the situation became manifest: The enemy was no longer at the gates; they were past them.

J.D. stood in her quarters, hands clasped behind her back, looking into a viewscreen onto a world she now owned. Triumph coursed through her veins and it felt good—seductively so. *Remember,* she thought. Instinctively, she lifted her hand to the scarred half of her face and delicately ran her fingers along the ridges of the hardened flesh. *Good. Before you let this feeling go to your head, remember those who never made it home from your last assault on this wretched planet: the twelve destroyed ships and the seventy-five hundred spacers who died—permanently—assaulting these orbats. And remember what that feeling of triumph, that seduction of power has wrought—especially by those ruling below: that you can enslave an entire people and justify it; that to preserve that slavery, you can murder with impunity, impose psyche audits; that ultimately it is you who are God and so don't have to answer to anyone. Hundreds of millions are now dead because of that seduction. Justin saw it coming before any of us. Sandra, more than most, seems to know what it will take to end it. So just do your job, Janet. Do your job and help Sandra do hers.*

J.D. turned away from the planet below and walked back to her desk. She ordered a secure line to Suchitra on the *Otter.*

When the admiral appeared in the holo-screen, J.D. said, "The UHF detachment that broke orbit after our attack could prove to be a problem."

"What do I have to work with?"

"I'm giving you Park, Paladin, Cho, and Waterman. You'll be getting all the frigates and most of the cruisers."

"What about the battle cruisers?"

"They're staying here."

Suchitra's face stiffened. "There's only one reason you would need sixty heavy ships in orbit . . . sir."

"I assure you, Admiral, there are more than one."

"Then you're not going to destroy the planet?"

"I will do what's necessary," J.D. answered coolly.

"Admiral, please forgive me for speaking out of place, but this does go to the core of why I do what I do, why I have chosen to fight for the Outer Alliance. And if I feel we're becoming another Gupta . . . well . . ."

"We're not anywhere near becoming a Gupta, Admiral."

"But most of the people on Mars are innocent."

"Actually, no. These supposedly 'innocent' people voted for, and have overwhelmingly supported, a regime that has murdered hundreds of millions of our citizens around Jupiter and the Belt. The UHF citizens are every bit as 'innocent' as the Germans, Austrians, Poles, and Ukrainians who supported the Nazis in the Second World War and the Confederates who supported the enslavement of their fellow man. Whatever the Martians deserve, I very much doubt it's mercy."

"But the children? Should they die because of the sins of their parents?"

"The short answer is no, of course not. The more nuanced answer, sadly, is yes. Their parents have acted irresponsibly to the point of reckless endangerment. They have voted into power and have kept in power a President and legislative body that have consistently chosen to use unconscionable violence—Alhambra—and depravity—more rigorous psyche audits—as means of achieving their ends. Are we to do nothing? Our very survival demands we act to preserve our people, our values, our very existence! As such, it is those parents who've acted irresponsibly, Suchitra, those parents who've endangered the lives of their children. And we're not even talking about the moral consequences of propping up such a regime. I still remember a quote from a book I read sometime back in which the child of a German citizen was asked, some forty years after the Holocaust, if he thought his parents were complicit. His response stays with me to this day: 'Our parents claimed they didn't know what was going on, but we don't believe them.' I feel for the children, Suchitra, but it is not up to me to save them. It is up to those charged with raising them."

A long moment hung on her words. "I understand what you're saying, Admiral, but I need to let you know how much this weighs on me. For Damsah's sake, your own daughter is living testament to the depravity of this war."

J.D. finally allowed a small smile. "And I'm well aware of that. Rest assured, the needs of the war decree that Mars will not be totally destroyed. However, if we are to preserve the freedom that Justin promised us and stop the machine that keeps churning out bodies and machines dedicated to the destruction of that dream, then Mars needs to be rendered ineffective as a base of operations."

Suchitra nodded respectfully and with a heavy sigh answered, "I understand."

J.D. though, wasn't quite done. "Do you, though? If in the future, victory requires the total destruction of Mars or Luna or Earth itself, I will have to make that decision. And if one day you're to command this fleet, you might have to make that same decision. As officers of the fleet, we're sworn to victory—not victory that makes us feel good, or a victory where the vulnerable are spared."

"But, Admiral, if we win under the rules of Fleet Order 8645, what difference does it make who wins?"

"It makes a big difference, Suchitra. Both the Allied forces and the Nazis destroyed large swaths of population centers. Both used the weapons of war to bring terror down from the sky. Both were, in the end, responsible for the deaths of millions. But in the end—warts and all—was it ever really a question as to who would make a better steward of humanity? You had the Nazis with their racial supremacy, SS death squads, and concentration camps; and you had the Americans with their Bill of Rights and their belief in the sanctity of freedom. I'm not saying they were perfect, mind you, nor that they didn't hop into bed with questionable regimes. What I am saying is that at some point, you'll have to choose, because if you don't, it's the Hitlers and Sambiancos who end up running the world. We are at such a crossroads now. So knowing all this," asked J.D., her voice growing considerably darker, "can you continue to serve?"

In a voice devoid of doubt, Suchitra gave her answer. "Yes, Admiral."

"Then you have your orders. Pick your ships and destroy as many of the enemy as you can. You have three days. Good hunting, Admiral Gorakhpur."

"Admiral?"

"Yes, Suchitra."

"God be with you." the second-in-command then cut out.

Left unsaid was what J.D. planned on doing with the heavy cruisers.

"Thank *you,* Suchitra," the fleet admiral answered into the air.

A few minutes later, 212 Alliance ships broke orbit and sped after the fleeing UHF fleet. Though the Alliance Fleet was outnumbered and outgunned, no one on either side of the conflict had any doubt as to the eventual outcome. Shortly after Suchitra's departure, the remaining seventy-five Alliance ships began the methodic destruction of every facility and installation in orbit around Mars. There was no longer any opposition left to stop them.

UHF fleet HQ
Low orbit of Mars

Timian Ross, newly promoted to admiral, looked at his first and last command at that rank. Fleet HQ had a small number of defensive missile emplacements, but they had been installed with the thought of stopping a surprise attack by one or two small ships. They had never been meant to defend against dozens of battle cruisers. That would have been the job of a UHF fleet. But Timian knew that to have those brand-new ships with those green crews fight would be worse than murder; it would be useless. So he ordered them to run—run as fast and as far as they could in the hopes they could fight again someday, after they'd learned enough to be useful.

He ordered a total evacuation of the HQ and set the missiles to defend the escape pods as they broke for the surface. He was glad he did because he saw that the military escape pods were being targeted by the closest Alliance ships. He should've been outraged, but he wasn't. This was the war that Fleet Order 8645 had created. Some of his pods did manage to make it to the Martian atmosphere with the missile support he gave them. At least the pods from the civilian installations had been allowed to escape unmolested. But considering they were going to a planet without defenses against an enemy that Timian had to admit could be justified in killing the lot of them, he wasn't sure how lucky the civilians in the escape pods actually were.

Timian checked his command console and saw in stark holography the moment he'd been expecting. The moment of his impending death. It was beautiful in an odd sort of way. The three heavy cruisers and the precision with which they'd slowly made their way past the last of his defenses and had sent an enormous fusillade of rail gun fire heading directly for him. His last thoughts as the high-speed shells tore into their now defenseless target was of his younger sister and how he'd told her the war would be over in a year and he'd be back in time for her graduation from junior tech school; how hardly anyone would be hurt; how it would all blow over. He remembered telling her the so-called Outer Alliance wasn't a real government and so, not a real threat—harmless, in fact. As the shock wave of the impact began shattering his internal organs, he wished his sister well. The little girl he remembered was now a young woman, an ensign on a ship fleeing for her life from the "harmless" Outer Alliance ships thirsting for revenge.

AWS *Warprize II*

J.D. was heading for the command sphere followed by her two closest confidantes, Fatima Awala and Marilynn Nitelowsen.

Fatima was briefing her on the run. "The OA Martian flotilla reports they are now positioned around the planet and are ready to interdict any traffic or bombard any structure on the surface as you see fit."

"So the blockade's been announced."

"Yes, Admiral. Every child, woman, and man on Mars not presently in a coma knows that nothing is allowed to leave or enter the Martian atmosphere without your express say-so."

"What's the status of Suchitra's fleet?"

"The admiral reports that the UHF forces have broken up into individual ships and are fleeing to all points of the compass except back to here. She regrets to report that this will make destruction of the whole of the enemy impossible in the time limit given. But she should be able to destroy or disable nearly two hundred of the enemy ships. She wishes to know what your orders are concerning escape pods."

Still testing me, are you? thought J.D. "Inform Admiral Gorakhpur that all correct procedures will be followed concerning the treatment of prisoners of war and those at our mercy."

"At once, Admiral," Fatima said, running ahead to the command sphere.

J.D. felt Marilynn's hand on her shoulder and stopped. There was something odd about the look in her intelligence officer's eyes. "This must be interesting."

Marilynn took out a data crystal and handed it to J.D. "This was given to me by the President before we left for Mars. By her orders, it has not left my person from that moment to this. I have slept with it in my fist, showered with it, and shat with it."

J.D. winced slightly. "Marilynn, there are some images I can do without, thank you very much."

"The President wanted me to impress upon you that there was almost no chance of it being tampered with. It can only be accessed by you genetically and only if you have the pass phrase the two of you apparently set up before we left."

"Okay. Why are you giving it to me now?"

"I was also told that you were to receive it when we had achieved the ability to bombard Mars."

"And if we hadn't?"

"Then we wouldn't be having this conversation."

J.D. snickered. "Any idea what's on it?"

"Not a clue."

"Then let's say we find out what our glorious leader requires," J.D. said, continuing on to the command sphere.

Michael Veritas was waiting for them at the entrance, being cautiously held up by two assault miners and a few securibots. He gave J.D. and Marilynn a friendly smile as they approached the hatch. Per a previous agreement, he'd been allowed to record the daily grind of life aboard ships at war. And though he hadn't been aboard J.D.'s since the Battle of the Needle's Eye, he'd made a special request to be there for this latest endeavor. J.D. had agreed on the condition that every word and image Michael took was subject to her approval for release. Part of her didn't want the reporter to witness whatever was about to take place. But she knew that the future had a right to see the machinations of war and ultimately to render its own judgments. He could record the events for posterity, she'd decided, but that didn't mean she'd allow it to be viewed in the present. With J.D.'s approval, the miners and securibots backed away from Michael as he joined them in entering the hallowed sphere.

Michael was immediately directed by another officer to the least obstructive spot and there, leaned against the part of the bulkhead he'd been given permission to lean against. J.D. took the command chair as Marilynn sidled up beside her. As a privacy field was created around the two of them, J.D. slipped the data crystal into her console. The holo-display activated once J.D.'s code word and DNA had been verified. Soon she was looking at a holographic image of President Sandra O'Toole.

"Congratulations on your victory," she started. "In addition to the plan discussed and agreed to prior to your departure, there is one other." Sandra paused momentarily and lowered her chin, almost defiantly, as J.D. shot Marilynn a furtive glance. Marilynn shrugged her shoulders. "I realize," continued Sandra, "the order I'm about to give may seem draconian, but please keep in mind that I give it with the full knowledge of its implications and do not do so lightly. My reasoning should become self-evident shortly." There was another brief pause as Sandra, with a single sentence, changed the face of the war and how the Outer Alliance planned on prosecuting it. "Fleet Admiral Black, you are hereby ordered to destroy, in its entirety, the city of Burroughs, Mars. Nothing should be left standing, nothing left alive."

J.D. immediately leaned forward and paused the hologram. This time she did not look toward Marilynn, and if she was aware of Michael's presence, she gave no indication. She kept her eyes focused on the stilled image of the President and momentarily brought her hand up to the scarred side of her face, but she did not touch it. Seconds passed as, less than an inch from her mangled flesh, J.D.'s fingers twitched slightly, as if trying to decide for themselves what to do. Slowly, J.D. brought the tips down on the surface of her mottled face and with her other hand pressed a button that allowed the message to continue.

"Please understand," said Sandra, "that this order is not being issued out of vengeance. I'm ordering you to kill, by my estimate, twenty million people without the chance of reprieve in order to get at one man. One man who, if allowed to live, will continue to order the wanton destruction of hundreds of millions more. He must die, Admiral, in order to ensure that future generations don't. And the only way to do that is to take out all of Burroughs in as thorough a manner as possible. He's hiding in there somewhere, Admiral. *I know him.* He won't leave the capital, because it will be politically ill perceived. And he believes we won't kill an entire city just to get to him. *You must prove him wrong.* With their President dead and Mars devastated, I can negotiate the peace. I'm sorry to lay this on you. Part of me was hoping that you wouldn't be in a position to view this, but you are. These are your orders, but I will take full responsibility. The data crystal Marilynn handed to you will not self-destruct. You may keep it as evidence of my culpability should someone ever blame you personally for the order you've just received. This is the closest any of us have come to finishing this thing. Follow this order, Janet, and end this war."

J.D. leaned back in her command chair and took a deep and measured breath. She first looked to Marilynn and, for the first time, to Michael. Both, she noticed, stood stock-still—either as a result of what they'd just witnessed or guessed. She lowered the privacy field.

"Lieutenant Awala."

"Yes, Admiral."

"Send these prepared targeting coordinates"—J.D.'s fingers now worked her console—"to the fleet captains. Commander Lee . . ."

"Admiral."

"You are to target Burroughs for a specific attack."

Michael Veritas's face registered concern but he said nothing. Marilynn's demeanor remained stoic.

"Yes, Admiral," came Jasper's quick reply. "Specifically which targets in Burroughs?"

J.D. wasn't sure why, but unbidden, an image of Katy staring up into the Martian sky in abject terror leapt from her mind.

Allah forgive me, but I cannot do this thing. I cannot become the one I destroyed, cannot become Gupta. Cannot become the evil we seek to destroy. There must be another way to eliminate the madman that doesn't necessitate the deaths of twenty million civilians, no matter how complicit they were in the rise of Sambianco and his ilk. Maybe Justin was right. Maybe the means are the ends. J.D.

thought back on her recent conversation with her second-in-command. *Suchitra, dear Suchitra. It is you, my friend, who'll have the last laugh.*

"Admiral."

"Yes, Commander Lee," answered J.D., suddenly aware that the entire command sphere had ceased its work and was now staring at her.

"Which targets in Burroughs?" repeated Lee.

J.D. pursed her lips and then answered. "The executive office complex of the UHF."

Unseen by the crew but noticed by J.D. was the look of palpable relief on Michael's face. "And," continued J.D., "make sure the first shot hits Hektor's office dead-on."

"Yes, sir," answered Commander Lee with obvious relish.

"Admiral," Fatima broke in, "the flotilla reports targets locked and awaiting your order to commence bombardment."

J.D. nodded. "Comm Officer."

"Yes, Admiral."

"Fleetwide communication with a link to the Martian Neuro."

A military-issue mediabot suddenly appeared in front of her, and a few seconds after that, the comm officer, with a slight nod, signaled J.D. the go-ahead.

"Citizens of Mars," she began, "my name is J. D. Black, and I'm the Senior Fleet Admiral of the Outer Alliance. You've chosen to wage war against the Outer Alliance rather than to let us depart in peace, and as a result, for nearly seven years we've been fighting a war the likes of which humanity has never experienced. But you've not only supported a government in war against the *military* forces of the Outer Alliance, you've supported it in war against the *civilians* of the Outer Alliance. Had any of you ever stopped to consider the folly of attacking a civilization whose citizenry is spread wide over the outer reaches of the solar system when your own civilization has them concentrated on three tiny specks in that same system? Or the folly of attacking an enemy's multitude of sparsely populated *mobile* settlements when you cannot defend your own *immobile* and vastly more populated homes?"

J.D. allowed her words to resonate before choosing to continue. "We, the citizens of the Outer Alliance, have every right to treat you, the citizens of Mars, as your perversely named United Human Federation has treated the one hundred and seventy-nine million permanently dead of Jupiter and the over one hundred million permanently dead of the Belt. And is currently, I might add, on its way to treating every *living* citizen of Saturn. By the din of the number of souls who scream out for vengeance alone, we have the right and now most certainly the ability to destroy just about every child, woman, and man on Mars—" J.D.

paused, speaking her next words with sadness and deliberation. "—and it was your leaders who have given us that right."

Knowing that if they hadn't already been, then they would certainly now be waiting on her next words, her verdict as it were, she made sure to wait what she felt would be an interminable amount of time—a full minute. One full minute just staring at the mediabot. One full minute looking as if then and there she were deciding the fate of billions.

"Be grateful to the Lord so few of you believe in, and so many of you have chosen to mock us for, that we are not your government. Give thanks that we follow the teachings of the one you despise, the Unincorporated Man, who would have none seek vengeance. Give thanks that we follow the leadership of his successor, the Unincorporated Woman, whom you have spent so much time and effort demonizing yet who, in this moment of your greatest vulnerability, has chosen to save you. If it were up to me," said J.D., purposely lying through her teeth, "you would all be dead. But my orders are clear: You are not to be treated as you treated us, murdered in your homes for having different beliefs."

J.D. waited in order to let hope build in those listening below. Then with unmerciful glee, she crushed it. "But you've abused the power and might that having this planet has given you. You've used it and the advantages it has given you to destroy and murder a people who only wanted peace. And so, by order of the President of the Outer Alliance and with the support of our Congress, you are hereby deprived of your planet. At the conclusion of this broadcast, a bombardment of Mars will commence. As in our initial assault, we will continue to destroy any installations deemed to be of military value. They will be destroyed at our discretion, and any civilian deaths, though regrettable, will not impinge on our schedule. If you even suspect you're near such an installation, I would strongly suggest you remove yourself from it immediately. So that we're clear, I will now spell out for you what the deprivation of planetary rights entails." More seconds hung on J.D.'s words as she looked away from the mediabot and reviewed something on her display panel. She then looked up and continued her diatribe. "As you have lost the right to inhabit Mars, we will now make Mars uninhabitable. The great majority of our strikes will be to the ecology of this planet. We will release organisms into the soil, air, water, and atmosphere that will undo much of the terraforming done here. Because it will take years for this planetary virus to take effect, we're going to expedite the process. In the coming days, we will aim to blot out the sun with the detritus from a constant barrage of ordnance as well as a nanovirus designed to limit the upper atmosphere's absorption of light. All large bodies of fresh and salt water will be poisoned, making them toxic for all life to such an extent than even microbes will find no sustenance from them. As the sun goes, winter will come, and I assure you, it will be an endless one. Some of you may survive if you can find portable fusion reactors, rig up hydroponic gardens, and generate artificial light, but make sure you filter the water and the air very, very carefully." J.D.'s smile was cold and mocking. "You may even begin to appreciate what it's like to live on an asteroid. On those terms and those terms alone will you be allowed to live—and I use that term loosely—on the planet you've used so grievously against us. If you do choose to stay, we won't hinder you, nor will we attack your cities. But if your government has your best interests in mind, if they have any pretense of caring for your well-being, they'll see to your evacuation. Though you're mostly pennies to them, you might have some value. If they do offer to evacuate, I suggest you take it. You'll of course be refugees, forced from your homes and made to take a dangerous journey to a place not of your choosing, far from all you know and love. When you wish to curse us for what's been done to you, hate us for what you've lost, and condemn us for what you'll never get back, remember whose actions it was that brought us to your doorstep. Remember Alhambra—" J.D.'s visage was replaced by an image of the religious conclave, full of life, and then after, that same conclave as space wreckage with bodies and parts of bodies floating about. "—and ask them, *Why?* Remember Jupiter—" Images of defenseless settlements being blown to smithereens by Gupta's armada, along with the surviving recordings of the terrified families within those settlements, filled the screen. "—and ask them, *Why?* And now the Belt—" Images of various armadas sending fusillades of rail gun fire into anything that moved, from tiny asteroids to installations to space docks to shuttles as well as the bloody results of those attacks appeared in all their contemptible glory. "—and ask them, *Why?* As a people I despise you for the evil you allowed by your acquiescence to President Sambianco's false promises; by your belief in the dream of majority, you signed up in droves to ultimately become Sambianco's willing executioners. But as individuals, and especially for your children—truly innocent—who are about to suffer unbearable loss and pain for the decisions of others, I hope you do survive. And may you never forget." J.D. took one last long stare into the mediabot and said, "End transmission."

A collective sigh of relief seemed to pervade the command sphere as J.D. resumed her normal duties—as if nothing more were going on than a simple drill or another in a series of tactical maneuvering exercises. But those around J.D. seemed to realize the enormity of what was about to happen, and began working with a heightened sense of urgency more typical of a ship under attack than of a ship completely safe from one. The holo-tank was now filled with a perfect replication of the planet below. J.D. stood up from her command chair and, placing her hands behind her back, stared contemplatively at one of humanity's greatest achievements. What had once been a desolate, arid, and

inhospitable environment had been, through the triumph of science and ingenuity of man, made into a resplendent world. Mars was green—so very, very
green. Marked by innumerable and majestic mountain ranges thick with verdant forests and dotted with large splashes of cobalt seas. As a dreamscape there
were few that could compare, and as planet none could compete—Mars had
always been J.D.'s absolute favorite.

"Begin bombardment," she said with her eyes still fixed on the planet and
without a hint of remorse. In moments, tens of thousands of tracers from the
rail guns of sixty heavy cruisers could be seen arcing their way toward three
uninhabited regions of Mars, the plumes of destruction stunningly visible even
from orbit. And it was then that Michael Veritas took the last of his four great
pictures of the war.

Via Cereana
Ceres

The news Mosh had received from Mars tore at him like the claw of an angry
predator. He now knew how terrible a mistake he'd made in trusting Sandra
O'Toole—even in trusting his wife. But that was in the past, and Mosh McKenzie
was not a man who lived in the past. He'd always charted the course of his life
with the utter assuredness of a CEO and the deft maneuvering skills of a white-
water river guide. Now was no different. One way or another, he would rectify
the mistake he'd made in leaving one tyranny only to be complicit in propping
up another. He entered the cordoned-off military bay and boarded the specially
marked shuttle. He nodded to the pilot, who returned Mosh's greeting with a
cordial tip of the head. Mosh then settled into the copilot's chair.

Once the shuttle was safely out of the bay and heading out toward the Via
Cereana, he looked over to the pilot.

"Can we talk?"

Joshua Sinclair considered the question. "I think so."

"A lot rides on this."

Sinclair grunted his acquiescence. "Since we're obviously not here to coordi-
nate industrial capacity," said Sinclair, making reference to Mosh's purported
reason for the rendezvous, "I suggest you cut to the chase."

Mosh took stock of his friend of many years, nodded his quiet agreement,
and allowed a grim smile to emerge. "I need your help to commit treason."

AWS *Warprize II*
Upper orbit of Mars

Jasper Lee looked up suddenly from his console. "Admiral, there's a message coming through from planetside I think you may want to hear."

J.D.'s ears perked up; then she nodded toward her XO.

"It's coming from a far suburb of Burroughs, but it has an Alliance operative ident code."

"I thought we already ID'd and secured all our agents."

"We have, Admiral. All agents are now either working on Mars with field support or have already been brought up to the flotilla."

A small grunt emerged from J.D. as she reviewed the message. She then looked back over to her XO. "Get me Nitelowsen. She should still be on the surface."

After a moment, Marilynn's voice popped through. "Fleet intelligence. How may I direct your call?"

J.D.'s lips curled upward. "Commodore Nitelowsen, Commander Lee is going to send you a message with an intelligence subcode. See if you recognize it."

After a moment, Marilynn's voice shot back. "It's part of a recognition code, but only part. And it's an old one, but still listed as secure. Could be a trap."

"Do we respond?"

Both yes and no were heard simultaneously. J.D.'s eyes showed alarm as she looked over to her XO, who was desperately trying to locate the source of the communications breach. He looked up a moment later with a victorious grin as he sent both the name and location of the hacker over to his boss.

"I don't think it's a trap," said the voice.

"Miss Snow," said J.D., "so very nice of you to drop in."

"Think nothing of it."

"Might I ask how long you've been monitoring our command sphere communications and, more specifically, how you managed to break into my *personal* circuit?" J.D. sounded perfectly calm, but the look she shot her crew as she said it made most of those around her shrink under her withering stare.

"If I refuse to answer, will torture be involved?" cracked Amanda's much-too-cheery voice.

"Not if you enjoy it, Amanda, no."

"In that case, as the OA's highest placed spy—presumably—it's possible I learned a thing or two about tapping undetected into a communications grid. If it makes you feel any better, I'm using the training your people provided me with."

"And presumably," retorted J.D., "since 'my people' forgot to let us in on it, you'll be gracious enough to show our techs exactly how you did it."

"I swear," broke in Marilynn, "I don't know anything about it."

"With proper clearance, of course," added Amanda.

"Amanda, you're on my ship now. I'm all the clearance you need."

"Well, as long as you put it that way. Sure."

"Good. Now, tell us about this signal of yours and why I should ignore the advice of my intelligence officer, who has yet to steer me wrong, and listen to you, a readily admitted master of duplicity."

"Because if I'm right, the source you're getting that message from may have intel worth having."

"Worth risking fleet personnel for?"

"In my opinion, yes. However, I'm not suggesting you send anyone from fleet personnel."

"Really," piped in Marilynn, "and who would you send?"

"Me," answered Amanda.

J.D. laughed out loud. "Well, I must admit, Amanda, your entertainment value alone may be worth our having to put up with your—" J.D. paused, searching for just the right word. "—'eccentric' nature."

"Is that a no, Admiral?"

"Of course it's a no, Amanda. You're far too important to Secretary McKenzie for me to risk sending back to the planet you apparently barely escaped from. I should probably be court-martialed for not keeping you confined to your quarters. But the truth is, you're a damned good babysitter."

"Katy is a doll."

"And up until now, you seemed pretty harmless."

"I assure you, I am."

J.D. gave a one-sided grin.

"If that's who I think it is," continued Amanda, "then I'm the one responsible for her plight."

"Be that as it may—"

"—And we both owe her sister."

J.D. looked down at the private communiqué Amanda sent immediately after speaking. When she saw the image displayed on her screen, J.D.'s demeanor suddenly changed.

"All right, Amanda, I'll at least send a team of assault miners to investigate. If she checks out, they'll bring her in."

"I need to be there, Admiral."

"I'm sorry. I just can't risk it."

Another piece of information soon zipped across J.D.'s screen.

"Shit. I swear by Allah, Amanda—"

"Admiral?" asked Marilynn.

J.D. forwarded the message to Marilynn.

"We need her down here, Admiral."

"Yeah," agreed J.D. "Marilynn, it'll be you and a contingent of AMs."

"On it."

"Amanda, you will go with them as an observer, only to provide information. Do I make myself clear?"

"Perfectly."

Suburb of Burroughs
Mars

Amanda leaned up against the shuttle. There was now a contingent of assault miners standing guard around her. *Ironic,* she thought, given that only a few days before, some of those very same miners had been pointing their guns *at* her. She watched the last rays of weak light filter through the ever-thickening cloud bank and smiled sadly. It was probably the last sunset Mars would see for decades.

An assault miner farther out from the shuttle waved her arm to get Amanda's attention. She recognized the gesture immediately: unknown party approaching. Amanda took out her DijAssist.

"What've you got?" she asked.

"Single target, female; scanners indicate she's unarmed."

"Is she carrying the ident chip?"

"Affirmative."

Amanda breathed a sigh of relief.

"Let's not shoot her first thing if we can avoid it, shall we?"

"No promises, ma'am," answered the soldier. "You know how we gun-toting jarheads like to shoot things."

"Your sacrifice is appreciated, dear."

"Long as you put in a good word with the admiral."

Amanda laughed.

A moment later, a lone individual could be seen walking up the road—though in the dying twilight, it was hard to make out exactly who it was. It could be Nadine, thought Amanda. Same height and weight, but this person looked somehow different. As the figure approached the assault marine, Amanda checked her DijAssist again and then knew for certain what she'd initially suspected. It was, in fact, Nadine Harper. But a Nadine whom Amanda would need to be reacquainted with, as the one she'd known was gone. Amanda nodded an *all clear* signal to the assault miner, who then let the woman pass. Nadine strode right up to Amanda and, without saying a word, handed her back her ident chip.

"There are five of us back there," said Nadine, glancing over her shoulder, "but only one is conscious, if you can call it that. Every one of 'em's an Alliance POW."

"Are they wounded?" demanded the closest assault miner.

Nadine looked at the soldier like she'd just told a really bad joke. "You can call it that, I suppose. They're all I could save of Angela Wong's 'guests.'"

The assault miner started to call in a full report to her sergeant. Nadine once again stared back down the road.

"Nadine," demanded Amanda, "you must tell me, what happened to Angela?"

"What?" answered Nadine, turning her attention once again to the woman who'd saved her life, twice now.

"Angela Wong, Nadine. Where is she?"

Nadine nodded and smiled cruelly. She then slowly reached around her neck and unhooked a necklace that, in the dimming light of the last Martian day, seemed to be made of a string of badly formed pearls. It was only when Amanda looked closely at what Nadine was proudly holding up that she arrived at a frightening realization: They weren't pearls after all—they were teeth.

Upon further questioning from Marilynn Nitelowsen, and with Amanda's help, Nadine was able to direct the Outer Alliance contingent right to the door of Angela Wong's chamber of horrors. There they found prisoners, torture chambers, labs, and all manner of other physical evidence testifying to the crimes committed in the name of preserving the incorporated system. The computers' systems were still running, and much to the amazement of Marilynn's intelligence staff, she somehow managed to disable the programs that should have destroyed all the incriminating data. With Marilynn's curiously effective prowess on the machines, the OA intelligence corps were able to procure a list of every experiment ever done concerning a secret protocol known as shadow auditing. The records, noted Marilynn with both repugnance and joy, had been meticulous. Almost as if they were being prepared for a doctoral dissertation. She ordered all evidence carefully packed in the most evidentiary manner possible and then promptly sent the lot of it off to the flagship. All except one case file. Though there was no God she particularly believed in, Marilynn felt if there was one, he'd understand her motives. And so of the thousands of names carefully documented, along with the often painful and grotesque descriptions of their individual deaths, the name of one Patricia Sampson, sister of Brother

Sampson, fleet chaplain to J. D. Black and inspiration to billions, ceased forever to exist from the rolls of the tortured.

As far as fleet intelligence was concerned, and by extension the government they represented, Nadine Harper had paid her debt to the Alliance in full. But Amanda knew, just by watching the way Nadine stared forlornly out the viewport as they left the dying planet for the relative safety of the *Warprize II*, Nadine's debt would last in perpetuity.

After all this time, I still don't know why Admiral Black allowed me to take and then distribute that picture: the so-called last of the great four. She'd just ordered the destruction of an entire planet's ecosystem. And with that one order would cause almost as much human death and misery as was caused in the Sino-Indian war during the Grand Collapse. When she gave that order, she had to believe that she was going to be responsible for the greatest amount of human suffering in the war—would that she had been right. I see the moment I snapped that shot as clearly as the memory of my daughter's first steps. J.D. is looking at the image of Mars as the first of three massive strikes are launched. I was with her when she was given the order and witnessed the struggle she went through at the moment she received it. Though I knew her to be torn, when it came time to launch those initial attacks, she did so unequivocally, and she did not flinch or, even for a second, look away. She just stood there, hands clasped firmly behind her back, staring purposefully at what to that moment had been the culmination of her amazing, improbable life. She was neither proud nor happy. I do not understand those who think they can see those emotions in the small part of her face revealed by the photograph. If I had to make a guess—and with J. D. Black's thoughts, that's all anyone can do: guess— I'd say she felt disappointment. But whether it was disappointment in herself, the Outer Alliance, the UHF, Mars, Fate, or the Allah she believes in, I could not say. What I can say is that she let me send that image without delay or censor. This part I have never told anyone, but now that she is gone, I suppose it won't hurt. She asked—and it was a request, not a command—if she could name it anonymously. It was J. D. Black herself who ended up calling it by the name it has been known by all these years: "Shiva."

—from the introduction to Four Images of the War, for Them and for Us, *by Michael and Litha Veritas*

J. D. Black found it hard to believe there were still humans living beneath the roiling mass of angry dark clouds occasionally flecked by the lambent glow of the lightning strikes below. The surface was rife with all manner of massive storms, including hurricanes, tornadoes, seismic shifts, floods, and acid rain.

"The grave is still the best shelter against the storms of destiny," she said to no one in particular.

"Did you say something, Admiral?" asked Fatima.

"Yes, child," answered J.D., turning around, unaware that she was within listening distance of her assistant. "An old German quote by a very wise man."

Fatima sidled up to J.D. and looked out the viewport. "The will of Allah is terrible to behold."

"Don't blame this on Allah. We made these choices; we must bear the weight of them. Presumably, you're not here to instruct me on Allah's will."

"No, Admiral. The leaders of the fleet wait at your convenience in the conference room."

J.D. nodded and bade Fatima to lead the way.

They arrived in short order, and Suchitra, noticing J.D. at the entrance, called the rest of the commodores to order. J.D. took much satisfaction with the even greater reverence the other commodores now seemed to have accorded the new admiral. *Finally,* thought J.D. with macabre delight, *I'm expendable. Which means the trap can be set for Trang and the fleet can survive without me.*

"Have a seat," J.D. began. "Admiral, how did the hunt go?"

"We destroyed one hundred ninety-nine enemy ships of all classes, Fleet Admiral. Captured escape pods, had thrusters disabled and Alliance transponders attached. They aren't going anywhere, and we know where they are."

"Useful," mused J.D. "Anything else?"

"We almost had two hundred," beamed the normally laconic Park, "but there wasn't enough time."

"Never is," answered J.D. "Okay, here's the update from my end. The destruction of Mars as a viable human habitat is effectively complete. They can breathe on the planet for the next couple of months at least, but it's not recommended. The mean temperature should be right about the freezing point of water and possibly lower in the next month. Frankly, that—we are just guessing on. No one's ever purposely destabilized an entire planet's ecosystem before. We've left the t.o.p. system relatively intact and have not destroyed any major centers of civilization, though the environmental damage has made living near the coasts chancy."

"Many of the Martian cities *are* on coastlines," observed Commodore Paladin.

"Not for much longer," said J.D. "I don't think they'll be flooded, but they will be empty very soon, one way or another—too much instability."

The commodores nodded solemnly. While there'd been a certain amount of pride in their recent victories over the orbats and the successful hunting down of the fleeing UHF fleet, those had been purely professional wins—whether their opponents were green or not. But there was no real joy in what had transpired while most of them were away. They all knew it had to be done but were mostly glad they hadn't been called upon to do it. Sensing the turn in mood, J.D. decided spring the good news. "We found where the UHF was keeping our prisoners—at least the ones on Mars. I'm quite pleased to report that we'll soon be bringing 197,463 of our comrades home."

A round of cheers poured forth from the small group, and when they finally settled down, J.D. continued.

"The UHF has been kind enough to put all the Alliance prisoners into suspension capsules that are easily transportable. We've let the authorities at the storage facility know, in no uncertain terms, what the results of not delivering those prisoners to us in fully functioning units would be." Her lips turned upward into a knowing grin. "They're proving most cooperative."

Commodore Cortez's face betrayed her feelings before the words even left her mouth. "Still can't trust the bastards."

"And we won't," answered J.D. "Our intelligence service is checking the storage site and the Martian Neuro for any threats, but no unit will be allowed onto a ship until it's first inspected and opened. We must assume a gray bomb threat at the very least. But with fleet personnel working at full capacity, we should have our comrades transported off the surface, examined, and in our holds within the next two days. We'll then leave the orbit of Mars one week after we entered it."

"Next objective?" asked Park.

"That, Commodore," answered J.D., folding her arms together, "is up to Grand Admiral Trang."

UHFS *Liddel*
En route to Saturn

Trang reviewed the footage coming from Mars and felt lost in helpless rage. He should have been there. The magnetized asteroids would have given J.D. an advantage, but he would have had one as well: a two-to-one advantage in ships. He could have won, or at the very least gotten a draw. But the government's insistence on destroying Saturn at all costs had ended up costing them all.

Trang was left with no choice. As he was closer to Saturn than to Mars—and even farther from Earth/Luna—all he could do was proceed to the sixth planet from the sun and, per the mission parameters, destroy the Saturnian subsystem. It was now a war of total brutality and one he wasn't sure he could win—one, in fact, he wasn't sure he'd want to win. The Outer Alliance was based as far out as Eris. If they were willing to lose *all* the gas giants just to get to Earth/Luna, they'd still be left with plenty to work with. And as Trang knew so very well, they were resilient sons of bitches. They'd turn wherever it was they were living or whatever it was they were living in into a viable economy in the span of a few short years. And with a viable economy comes a treasury, and with a treasury comes a navy. And then it starts all over again. Not so with the UHF. Admiral Black had nailed that one in her speech to the Martians before deciding to summarily wipe them off the face of the map. The flag Trang was sworn to protect was planted on three locatable, very exposed, and clearly vulnerable planets. Really, only one now, given that Mars had been taken out and the Moon, while a force to be reckoned with, was not a planet and had nowhere near the industrial capacity of Earth. Trang was no longer sure who would collapse first. All his vaunted "numbers" advantage had proved was that he could send more greenhorns into the maw of death than his adversaries. But the thing he saw most, as his fleet sped toward another rendezvous with death, was that the war he feared most—the war that could destroy humanity—was coming to fruition.

The mood of his command sphere—indeed, his whole fleet—was funerary, and he'd done nothing to ameliorate that. He'd sat for hours in stoic silence, offering neither words of consolation nor encouragement for the upcoming battle. *What battle?* he thought dourly. *The Saturnians are defenseless, and so we bravely charge in.*

"Admiral."

Trang looked up slowly. His comm officer was staring at him.

"Admiral."

"Yes?"

"We've, um . . . intercepted Alliance fleet communications to Ceres." Confusion had managed to perfuse every part of his voice.

"I didn't think we were in position to intercept LCPs," said Trang, using the nickname for laser communication pulses.

"We're not."

Trang nodded, intrigued. "Well, far be it from me to audit a gift dividend. Send whatever it is you managed to intercept on to intelligence and see if they can crack it."

"That's just it, Admiral. It's not *in* code. Not *in* laser pulse."

"Then what are they in?"

"Radio, sir."

"Radio?"

"And they're not encrypted either."

The comm officer had his full attention now. Trang motioned for the messages to be sent to his display, where he read them at once. His left eyebrow lifted slightly. The command crew knew that usually meant a change of plans. The buzzing commenced immediately.

"Connect me with Admiral Jackson," Trang ordered. "No, belay that. Inform Admiral Jackson that I'm on my way to the *Scarlet*."

UHFS *Scarlet*
En route to Saturn

Zenobia Jackson first read and then reread, and then *reread* the two Alliance communications while her boss casually sipped coffee from his mug.

"And you say they were sent in the clear," asked Zenobia, "by radio—no code at all?"

Trang smiled gamely.

"Sorry, Sam, but this is damn strange."

"Which part?"

"Well," she answered, glad to see her boss more engaged than he had been in days, "we have two apparently official Alliance fleet communications. One of them states that the Alliance fleet has completed operations around Mars and is heading for Earth/Luna to complete their mission. The other communication states that the Alliance fleet has completed operations around Mars and is returning to Saturn. They're both signed by Admiral Black and both seem authentic as far as we can tell—other than the obvious and rather curious fact that they were both sent in the open. But why would she send messages like this to her government?"

"Because," answered Trang, eyes bright with understanding, "those messages aren't meant for her government. They're meant for us—or to be more precise, me."

Zenobia thought hard for a moment and then her face suddenly lit up. "A choice!"

"Indeed, a choice."

"By Damsah's left nut, she's willing to go home—"

"If we do the same," finished Trang.

Silence pervaded the room for a few seconds as Trang allowed his underling to work through the implications on her own.

"She must not have a new trick for the Earth/Luna orbat system," Zenobia finally said. "Why else offer to call off the attack?"

"Maybe," countered Trang, "she doesn't want to destroy the Earth's ecosystem—her home planet, by the way—murdering tens of billions of human beings while losing billions more of her own."

Zenobia seemed to consider the suggestion, but her face betrayed her suspicion. "I just don't see it, sir. This is J. D. Black we're talking about, 'the Merciless.' Why offer mercy now?"

"Staring at the brink, I suspect. I've often gone there myself."

"The brink?" Zenobia said, voice thick with rage. "What was Mars? The warm-up?"

"Zenobia, her destruction of Mars was very selective. She could easily have bombarded every city to dust and wiped out every vestige of civilization. She did not." Trang activated the holo-display over Zenobia's small breakfast table and then called up detailed holos of Mars shot at close range. "Look," he said, pointing to various hot spots on the hologram. "She destroyed the ecosystem, yes, but clearly left the population and the orports intact. Why?"

"To increase their suffering."

"If that were true, why leave the orports intact with all the t.o.p.s functional? Why suggest, as she did in her speech, an exodus and promise not to shoot down any civilian craft—and she *will* keep her word. Of that, I have not one doubt," he said, remembering the long-ago exchange of Admiral Gupta for Commodore Sadma. "Not only that, but she allowed us to get clear pictures of the areas under attack so we could see which infrastructure she left intact. No, she's offering us a chance to evacuate them. But only if we turn around and leave Saturn and Ceres alone. If we continue on and destroy their new center as we can do with nothing to stop us, we can be sure that Earth/Luna is her next stop and the possible near extermination of the human race."

"But if we put our tails between our legs and retreat—"

"We potentially spare the lives of tens of billions on Earth/Luna and save billions from the disaster of Mars." Trang took a few more moments with his thoughts. "And since we'll also need every single ship we have in the asteroid belt to help us, they'll also have to be transferred to Mars."

"Which means the murder of all those Belters has to stop," Zenobia said, realizing the full implications of J.D.'s offer. "I really hate this 8645 shit, Sam."

"As do I," he agreed. "Besides which, I think it's obvious the Alliance is better at it than we are."

"You're going to take her offer?"

Trang allowed a wry smile. "As we cannot make contact with the proper authorities on Mars—"

"The Alliance has that place shut down pretty good," added Zenobia, "which might not be a bad thing. I can pretty much guess what President 'Kill Anything That Breathes' Sambianco would order."

"Why, Zenobia," said Trang, feigning disbelief, "I'm sure our President and his Cabinet would order us to the immediate relief of the capital. In fact, I'm going to issue a fleet order for the immediate deployment of *all* our forces to the humanitarian aid of Mars as soon as it is safe to do so."

"Oh, that's good, sir," answered Zenobia, mouth curling up into a Cheshire grin.

"Yes. He'd be hard-pressed to contradict that."

"He couldn't. At least not without being impeached."

"That thought never crossed my mind," said Trang as he settled back and enjoyed the last of his coffee.

5 Coup

VICTORY AT MARS!

DE-TERRAFORMATION!

MASS DEMONSTRATIONS!

By Michael Veritas

The recent victory of the Alliance fleet in the Third Battle of the Martian Gates under Fleet Admiral J. D. Black and Admiral Suchitra Kumari Gorakhpur was a wonderful tonic to a public that has not seen a victory like this since the Battle of Jupiter's Eye. With the rise of Admiral Samuel Trang, the Alliance has faced outright defeat, loss of vast areas formerly under its control, untold numbers of refugees and victories that can be at best called draws. The one all-out victory over Admiral Gupta of Fleet Order 8645 infamy was purchased with the blood of many tens of millions of Jovians and the loss of the Jovian subsystem, not to mention the near loss of the capital itself.

The complete destruction of the Martian orbat field and the near annihilation of a large UHF fleet in the same space where Admiral Black had previously suffered her only true defeat was a significant victory—quite possibly, game-changing. But instead of bringing unity and hope, this victory's aftermath has been causing dissension from the formerly occupied asteroid belt all the way out to the Oort cloud.

J. D. Black's decision not to hold the UHF capital hostage to the good behavior of Trang, but to bombard it to the point of uninhabitability has sparked massive demonstrations both for and against the action. Images of the destruction have brought crowds together chanting, "The means are the ends," while others have gathered, chanting, "One down, two to go," and "Glass houses are a bitch." The latest polls, which have a margin of error of 7 percent given the hasty survey, lack of stable population, and inability to access large numbers of Alliance citizens, state 47 percent of those surveyed support Admiral Black's actions, 37 percent are opposed, and 16 percent are undecided. The opinions of the survivors of the Genocide of the Belt, as the recently ended UHF campaign of terror and murder has been called, cannot be accurately polled. Given the anarchy sweeping that tortured re-

*gion of space—especially as the UHF pulls out—informal surveys are all
that's possible. What has emerged seems to indicate that there is great anger in the Belt because of the lenient treatment Admiral Black has given
the UHF capital, as well as anger at the Outer Alliance for its inability to
provide any assistance whatsoever to what is now considered to be a dying
wasteland.*

*President Sandra O'Toole has addressed the Congress to both cheers and,
for the first time in her Presidency, boos. She insisted that Admiral Black's
orders were approved by her and the Cabinet and that she completely stands
by the fleet admiral and her actions. But it cannot be denied that those actions have split opinion in the Outer Alliance as nothing has before.*

Martian Neuro

The Martian Neuro was no longer under the control of the Als. Of course, it
was not under the control of the Alliance either; it was actual anarchy. The
avatars formerly under the Als' control seemed more intent on punishing
one another than they were on breaking AI's hold on them. In fact, Marilynn—
whose NITEs, or Neuro Insertion Tactical Engagement Specialists, had spent
the better part of a week helping clear out the Neuro—was convinced that the
recently liberated avatars preferred vengeance to freedom. But given what
they'd all been through for the past number of years, she realized she was in no
position to judge. They'd all lost family, friends, and children—many because
of fellow avatars having informed on them.

After a week spent in hiding—that is, fighting in the Martian Neuro—
Marilynn was decidedly out of the loop with regards to how well the Alliance
was doing. She knew that Mars had been cut off from a communications point
of view. All satellites capable of breaking the Alliance information blockade
were destroyed at Marilynn's direction. All orbiting data nodes that housed
enemy avatars were destroyed as well. The roiling clouds of Mars made surreptitious laser bursts to and from the planet impossible. This gave the Alliance
avatars communications superiority over their enemy. Any data node that
proved to be too dangerous could and was destroyed from orbit as pinpoint
strike after pinpoint strike destroyed key sections of the Neuro that the Als had
used to store their creations and environment. It didn't matter how deep the
data nodes were buried or how urban their setting. The Alliance fleet used its
orbital high ground to rain a limited but incredibly accurate volley of destruction wherever the Alliance avatars, and therefore Marilynn, saw fit.

And of course, there were the thirty-seven NITEs leading raids, rescuing Core avatars, and liberating redemption centers. What Marilynn had seen in the experimental sections of the so-called redemption centers began to haunt her dreams, and had she had not taken suppression drugs to forget them, she would have been rendered useless. Marilynn dreaded the day when combat would end and she would have to allow normal sleep to resume.

But there was something else rather disturbing. Something that had bothered Marilynn as well as the other NITEs she'd conferred with. The liberation of the Martian Neuro was going far too smoothly. The fact was that most of it had been made up of Als and his veritable potpourri of twisted beasts. Given the vast discrepancy in numbers between the Alliance avatars, the freed Core avatars and the Als, it should have taken months or even years to destroy the madman's grip—and that calculation was arrived at even with the use of the NITEs and their Back Door Devices, of BDDs. Yet in the space of a week, all resistance had essentially collapsed. It seemed that whenever any defense on the part of the Core avatars would begin to form, the Als would disappear—and without the Als, there was no resistance. Even the mass executions of the prisoners that the Als had started were often mysteriously disrupted before the rescue parties arrived.

It was that mystery that Marilynn was now investigating—alone. It went against all written and established doctrine for a human to venture into a dangerous and unsecured part of the Neuro without the backup of at least one insertion unit, but Marilynn realized that if she went into the Neuro with one hundred or more bodyguards—and that is how the insertion commandos would normally go in—her chances of learning anything would be reduced to nil.

So in violation of her own standing order, she had entered a part of the Neuro that had so far not been penetrated by the Alliance. What she was expecting to see was a horde of Als with an even larger horde of creatures at the reins, preparing for battle. But when Marilynn popped in holding her BDD, an open umbrella, she was astounded to see utter anarchy. A battle seemed to have already taken place. There were Core avatars who'd obviously been freed from the local redemption center, but she had no idea who freed them. She saw, sadly, that many of them bore the results of Al's experimentation. They were missing legs or arms or all four; some were obviously blind and others looked diseased, all of which should have been an impossibility in the avatar world. Marilynn wanted to call in help but crushed that humanitarian desire in order to concentrate on the investigation. She hid in the background, folding up her umbrella and putting the handle in the crook of her elbow. She didn't have to wait long.

Monsters—at least in one area—were running, flying, slithering, and oozing as fast as they could *away* from the spot. Whatever was frightening them was contagious. Fighting a desire to open her umbrella and get the hell out, Marilynn instead started to head in the direction from which the monsters fled. At first she tried to be cautious, preparing to flee at the first sign of trouble. A cavalcade of avatar killers flew toward her and then, at the last minute, past her; she'd been ignored! The creatures desired only to escape. When the initial onslaught was well past, Marilynn cautiously proceeded forward. When she cleared the corner of a large building, she saw a large parade ground, empty except for three avatars patiently standing to one side and about fifty avatars running around on the other being slaughtered whole by a dozen data wraiths.

Marilynn grabbed her umbrella, preparing to fly to their rescue, when she thought she recognized the avatar closest to her. A quick scan showed that *all* the avatars being attacked and devoured by the data wraiths were AIs. For a moment she was stunned, and then she looked at the three standing on the far end of the parade ground. Her virtual heart nearly jumped out of her chest. It was Sebastian and it was Sebastian and it was Sebastian.

The Sebastians—even thinking of them in the plural filled her with revulsion—surrounded a crystal on a box that was emitting a strange pulse. She recognized a movement inhibitor when she saw one. It was standard Alliance avatar design. The three of them were merely looking on as the data wraiths were doing what they'd supposedly been programmed *not* to do: kill AIs. While conversely and at the very same time, they ignored those they'd supposedly been programmed to destroy: the Sebastians.

Marilynn was not aware of pulling a recorder from her vest and capturing the events unfolding in front of her, but when she looked at her hand, a recorder was in it with the active light lit. When the last of the AIs were consumed—and their screams always seemed somehow louder than any other avatars'—the data wraiths were momentarily confused and then they started to wail, eventually wandering off, looking for more data to feed on, still conspicuously ignoring the Sebastians in their presence.

"Should we dissolve our daughters?" asked Sebastian.

"No," said Sebastian. "If our children find our daughters, they'll destroy them as creations of AI and not know the difference. But while they are free, they may find AIs we missed and kill them."

"I agree," said Sebastian. "But I think that may have been the last of them. This operation has been an unparalled success."

"We must send a message to the Sebastians on Earth/Luna about this as soon our humans remove the information blockade."

"Also agreed," said the second Sebastian, "but our chances of discovery are greater with so many of us in one place."

Marilynn watched in morbid fascination but decided to wait until the

Sebastians went their separate ways. To her dismay, they didn't split up at all. Two of them brought small pills to their mouths, swallowed, and then moments later decompiled into dust on the very spot they'd been standing.

Marilynn stared at the empty field for five minutes after the surviving Sebastian had left, the recorder still on in her unknowing hands. She had to go. She had to warn her friends. Sebastian was a splitter, and if he wasn't a self-twiner, he was a suicide twice over, at least. But if that data wraith had been an avatar he'd transformed to his own ends, then, decided Marilynn, Sebastian was something far, far worse—he was AI.

Cabinet room
Ceres

"Madam President," said Mosh, glaring down the bridge of his nose, "did you or did you not know about the secret weapon that Admiral Black had before we voted for the attack on Mars?"

"I did," she answered.

"Then you also must have known that such a weapon in the hands of an admiral as skilled as J. D. Black would make an overwhelming victory possible?"

"Yes, almost certain, in fact—especially with the absence of Trang."

"Given the broad orders this Cabinet gave the fleet admiral when it was assumed by many here in this room that at best all we could expect to achieve was a tactical victory, would it have been possible to see that J.D. would interpret those orders as broadly, nay, as ruthlessly as possible?"

Sandra's response was cool and relaxed despite Mosh's firing squad approach. "J.D. did not interpret her orders broadly. She did *exactly* what I told her to do."

"But you knew that such a victory was possible."

"As I said before, I was hoping for it."

"Then it was *you* who ordered the destruction of the home of six billion human beings."

"Yes."

"And now," Mosh said, anguish clearly evident in his voice, "they're going to die, Madam President."

"They are going to leave, Mosh."

"What about the ones who won't make it?"

"What about them, Mosh?" Sandra's diminutive posture had suddenly turned quite rigid.

"Assuming the UHF does everything they can," interjected Eleanor, "and they're reasonably competent about it, we predict that they'll still have to absorb nearly twenty percent in losses."

Mosh's icy stare rested firmly on the President. "That's a billion human beings that we've murdered."

"Yes, Mosh, it just might end up being nearly a billion human beings *killed*."

"Murdered!"

"No, we did not murder them. I didn't look at each person on Mars and decide they should die." Sandra glanced at everyone at the table. "Nor did anyone here. I decided that the only way to survive this war, a war that Hektor Sambianco has taken every opportunity to make as inhumane as possible, was to take the one real asset the UHF has and turn it into a liability."

"That's how you justify murder? I'm sorry," Mosh said, shaking his head in disgust, "the only thing we've done is turn us into them. Does it really matter who wins this damn war now?"

"Yes," answered Sandra, giving no quarter. "The UHF has murdered nearly three hundred million Belters who in no way were aiding, nor could possibly aid the Alliance anymore. They would have murdered the other eight hundred million had we done nothing to stop them."

"So that makes what we did right? My billion for yours?"

"Yes, that makes it right. I'm President of the *Outer Alliance*, not of the human race. My every thought is for *our* survival. If I had not ordered what I ordered or if J. D. Black had not followed those orders, we would have been destroyed. Not this month, but soon enough. There was no way we could indefinitely fight Trang, a skilled warrior with an industrial base that is now fifty times larger than ours supporting a population base at best nine times larger than ours. We had to change that dynamic of the war *or die*. Do I regret the necessity? Yes. Do I wish a billion people didn't have to die for our billions to live? Of course. Would I order it again?" Sandra purposely let the question hang so that she could shoot it out of the air. "In a heartbeat."

"When does it stop?" asked Ayon. "Really. I'm not asking to bait you, Madam President. I honestly want to know, *need* to know that there's some kind of end game to this tit-for-tat madness."

"When, Ayon, they're willing to let us be," Sandra answered, and looked back toward Mosh. "You want to know the difference between us and them, Mosh. I'll tell you. I'll stop the moment they do. I won't kill them if they don't kill us, but here's the thing: They'll stop killing us only if I kill enough of them. When they understand our need for freedom is priceless and their need to enslave us is not, this war will end . . . and not a moment before."

"Congratulations," Mosh said bitterly. "Our freedom is about to be purchased with the deaths of a billion souls."

"And I can only pray that the price does not go up," said Sandra as she rose to her feet. The meeting was adjourned; the grilling, over.

"I would understand if you're upset, Joshua."

"I can understand the need for absolute secrecy, Madam President, but I must ask—" He paused. "—do you wish me to be Secretary of Defense?"

Sandra paused too. "It's a fair question. I held back information on a vital weapon."

"I knew about the re-formable asteroids, Madam President. I just didn't know they were ready. But you not only kept the deployment a secret from me, you also had them installed in the fleet without my knowledge with J.D.'s consent, who I feel compelled to remind you is supposed to be my subordinate. *You* then decided a *military* course of action that you cleared with my subordinate without informing me and had the fleet carry bioweapons of mass ecological destruction, also without my knowledge." Sinclair sighed. "I know I haven't exactly been the best admiral, and after my mistakes almost cost us the capital I fully understand your not trusting my judgment, so then why don't you just accept my resignation and appoint someone whom you do trust?"

"Joshua, please believe me, it's not that I don't trust you; it's that I don't trust anyone. Only five people knew our last surprise was ready: myself; Secretary Nesor, who oversaw the final development and deployment; J.D., who had to use it; Marilynn Nitelowsen, who would have told J.D.'s successor if something had gone spectacularly wrong; and, of course, Kenji. As far as I was concerned, that was four too many. If it could've been used without even my knowing about it, I would have been happier. But that was not the case. I still have secrets that you or J.D. know nothing about because in my judgment that's what's best."

She leaned over and took Josh's hands in hers. "But, Joshua, my judgment also tells me that you're almost indispensable as the Secretary of Defense. You say you are not a great battle admiral—so what? The Alliance has not had a shortage of great battle admirals. Maybe it's the processed water, but we seem to grow them like algae out here. Have you seen the after-battle reports on Suchitra's destruction of both the Trans-Luna Shipyards and that fleet near Mars? She's a natural battle leader. But you're a natural organizer. The fleet respects you, and everyone knows it's been your dedication to training and equipping this fleet that's made it the shield and the sword of the Alliance. We need your wisdom and judgment, Joshua. I hope you can stay, knowing that you'll not always be privy to everything—just most things."

"The Alliance has my wisdom and judgment, Madam President, regardless of the price I may pay to my career, reputation, or feelings."

"Thank you, Grand Admiral."

Admiral Joshua Sinclair got up, saluted, and left the room. He had an urgent meeting to get to with Mosh McKenzie.

They met in the forward room of the AWS *Rumrunner,* a frigate that had suffered so much damage to its main rail gun that it was unable to be repaired until the Saturnians could get the Jovian Shipyards reassembled and working again. It was therefore designated a messenger frigate between Ceres and Saturn and had its superbly trained crew transferred into the fleet only to be replaced with trainees of Sinclair's choosing.

"I found the beer to be rather good," said Mosh as the grand admiral sauntered in. Mosh held up a nearly empty mug as proof of the assertion. "But the bar *is* open. I must warn you, the old crew took all the good booze, but you still have generics of all the basics."

"I thought you said the beer was good."

"That's because I had the executive branch cafeteria ship some of it up here. If we're going to discuss treason, it should be with something worthwhile."

"We're not committing treason," said Sinclair firmly. "*She* is."

"Then you'll join me?"

"Do you remember why Justin hired me all those years ago?"

Mosh's face lit up. "The Spicer ring."

"I refused to kill the innocent to punish the guilty. Justin said he wanted an officer in charge of his military who would refuse such an order. The reason I took the job is because I knew Justin would never give that order. You remember what he always said?"

"The means are the ends."

"He was right and always will be, old friend. In three months' time, that woman will be responsible for the deaths of more innocent people than every monster in human history, including Hektor Sambianco. She went over my head for Mars, and she'll do it again for whatever's next on her list, God protect us. You certainly helped illustrate that point today."

Mosh nodded. "Well, someone had to. Listen, Josh, you're of course under no obligation to tell me, but I was just curious as to what happened at the meeting afterwards."

"Ah, that," answered Josh with a refulgent smile. "I tendered my resignation."

"No, you didn't!"

"Swear to God."

Mosh was about to get upset, when he noticed that his friend was still smiling. He then nodded approvingly. "Good move. If you hadn't, she would've been suspicious."

"And I woulda been lucky just to take a crap without Holke inspecting it for nanites. But she had to convince me to stay."

"Which I'm sure you reluctantly agreed to."

Joshua's teeth flashed through his broad grin. "We have alot of work to do if we're to save this Alliance."

And Joshua Sinclair began to explain to Mosh McKenzie exactly how a military executes a coup in the middle of a war.

Observing the entire conversation, Sebastian smiled for the first time in many months. He too had been trying to figure out how to remove Sandra O'Toole from power. It was obvious that Mosh McKenzie had the will but not really the skill and resources to pull off such a feat. But he remembered the avatar proverb, "It's easier to predict a quantum particle than it is a human's actions." Admiral Sinclair had a plan—and a very good one. Of course, it would never succeed. Dante would discover it long before implementation and tell his brand-new "friend," Sergeant Holke.

But that was actually a good thing. The more time Holke kept Dante distracted, the easier it would be to cover the conspirators' trail from anyone in the avatar world. And if the humans proved to be as incompetent in this as Kirk Olmstead had been, Sebastian would step in and make sure the Unincorporated Woman would never be a threat again.

AWS *Warprize II*

J. D. Black tried to leave her annoyance at the door. She hated surprises, and Marilynn Nitelowsen had just given her three. First, she'd shut down all computer interfaces on the *Warprize* and run a detailed check using a protocol that was both innovative and bizarre. Then she'd requisitioned the fleet's fastest frigate, asked for a volunteer crew, and had it take off along the Via routes to Ceres at speeds even the Via's civil engineers rated as unsafe. While this was going on, Marilynn had requested that J.D. come to her own quarters for a meeting with one of Marilynn's intelligence staffers. Marilynn had been polite about it, but J.D. knew an order when she heard one. She'd known Marilynn for a number of years, but was well past the point of patience and knew that her intelligence liaison had better have a damn good explanation for all of this or she would be the fleet liaison to Eris. J.D. almost pitied whoever it was Marilynn had sent to her quarters in order to be sacrificed at the altar of the fleet admiral's wrath.

When she got to her quarters, J.D. was shocked to find her daughter re-creating the Battle of the Needle's Eye with all the accoutrements—including the bread rolls, socks, new mock-ups, crumpled-up paper, and a few of J.D.'s desk accessories—*in all three dimensions*. Sitting patiently in the small waiting area, intently watching Katy play, was a young lieutenant with close-cropped brown hair, dark brown eyes, light skin, and the traditional uniform of the Outer Alliance intelligence division.

J.D. focused in on the lieutenant. "There had better be a damned good explanation for this," she said through the floating bread rolls, socks, and spaceships. Then, because she couldn't help herself, she corrected the positions of two of the model ships situated too near four bread rolls. "You must always leave room for evasive maneuvers, little one," she said with the patience of Job as she pushed the bread rolls farther away from the giant crumpled paper cruisers and repositioned some frigates more forward of the main fleet. "There, that's better."

Katy looked up, thrilled. "Thank you, Mama Bo!"

"Of course, little one. Now you must tell me how you got the grav field to work."

"Am I in trouble, Mama Bo?"

"Of course not, but did you figure out my password?"

"No, you told me never to."

"Good girl. Then how?"

Katy pointed to the woman calmly sitting in the small waiting area and smiled. "The angel did it. She's magic."

"Uh-huh," answered J.D., eyeing the visitor warily. "Mama Bo has to have a little discussion with this very nice 'angel' and find out just what the . . . how all of this"—J.D. indicated the floating mass—"got off the ground."

"Okay, Mama Bo," answered Katy, and happily returned to her orchestration.

J.D. navigated around the suspended debris and over to the young lieutenant, who jumped up and gave a stiff and overly formal salute.

"Lieutenant Britannia Panil at your service, Admiral."

J.D. smiled acidly. "Mind telling me what the hell is going on here, Lieutenant?"

"Commodore Nitelowsen sent me."

"Yes, Lieutenant. And we'll get to that in a second. I'm talking about"—J.D. indicated with her head the battle going on behind her—"that!" She then noticed something awry in Katy's setup, held up her forefinger to the young lieutenant, and said, "Hold that thought." She then turned toward her daughter. "Katy, sweetie?"

Katy pushed aside a small floating display case. "Yes, Mama Bo?"

"Your ships have to be in proper alignment for the phase-shifting missiles to disrupt the maximum amount of enemy ships."

Katy held up her hands, palms out. J.D. pointed with her forefinger where the three "ships" needed to go.

"Oh, right!" answered Katy, and immediately began readjusting the teddy bear, bra, and snorkel.

"And please remember," J.D. called out, "to return the Medal of Victory to that display case when you're done. They've only given out the one."

If Katy heard her mother's last request, it wasn't readily obvious. She was too busy running around the room, getting ready for the big showdown. J.D. then turned to the officer, switching her face back to that of the Stygian warrior. "You were saying?"

"Oh, yes," answered Britannia, "the grav field. Marilynn suggested it. As an icebreaker of sorts."

J.D.'s face contorted further. "Icebreaker?"

"Yes. A demonstration."

"Of what? How to piss off her boss?"

"On the contrary: to impress you."

"Well, she's doing a pretty poor job of it. And how did she crack the code, anyways? It requires my *living* DNA *and* a specified pass code. As far as I know, I'm the only one who should've been able to turn that blasted thing on. So would you mind telling me how the hell that"—J.D. once again indicated the melee of debris—"is even happening?"

"Actually, Admiral," answered Britannia with a slight upturned lip, "there is one other."

J.D.'s eyes narrowed. "One other *what*?"

"One other person who knows your code."

"Impossible."

"Please, Admiral—" Britannia invited her to sit, which J.D. did. "Admiral, first it is vital you be briefed so that I can tell you what is on that frigate."

J.D. looked askance at Marilynn's emissary, instinctively reaching for her sidearm. "What's going on here, Lieutenant? What's happening on *my* ship?"

Britannia looked over to Katy. "No, she is not in danger. I assure you."

J.D. didn't bother asking how the lieutenant knew what she was thinking, but then again, there was something eerily familiar about the woman.

"It's essential you be brought into the loop."

"The loop about what?" demanded J.D.

"A secret," replied Britannia. "Possibly the biggest of the last three hundred years. It propelled us to victory in Omad's Last Raid, and has enabled Marilynn to pull off some of the 'miracles' she and her team have of late been associated with."

"I'm listening."

"Think back, Admiral, to everything you found curious either about Marilynn's behavior or the alacrity with which she's managed to do the seemingly impossible. Most recently, her coup at Wang's lab in stemming the autodestruct of trillions of bits of information. The secret I speak of and ready to be viewed as a file within your console has already proved its worth in battle and may ultimately enable us to crush our enemies. Please," insisted the young lieutenant, "read."

J.D. regarded the woman for a long minute and then nodded her quiescence. She lifted the holo-display tablet up from the tabletop and began to read. The first few pages dealt with the early advances in VR technology and quantum mechanics—droll textbook stuff. Next, a vid of Sandra O'Toole appeared and the President suddenly began talking about avatars, a subject J.D. couldn't care less about. Soon, however, the import of what Sandra was saying became clear. As the holo continued with demonstrable proofs, mathematical precepts, and past segments of history played out with the perspective of the avatar influence, J.D. grew intrigued, then concerned, then confused. Even with the evidence in front of her, she simply did not want to consider it—a result, she now realized, of avatarity's successful inculcation of entire generations of humanity to ignore their very existence. Intellectually it made sense, but emotionally, it could not. *And they're our allies,* thought J.D., shaking her head in disbelief. A small laugh escaped her lips. *Not so magical after all, are you, Marilynn?*

J.D. slipped the flat panel back into the table and regarded Britannia more keenly. "Why you, Britannia? Why didn't Marilynn tell me this herself?"

"Because Marilynn is on that frigate speeding toward Ceres, and it's critical she makes it there."

"Why wouldn't she?"

"Because the information she has to deliver to the Avatar Council on Ceres is worth murdering her for."

"Is that why she was messing with the mainframes?"

"Yes. She was covering her tracks. Anyone looking for her will have 'just missed her.' Anyone checking in on her quarters for random security scans will see her either working or sleeping. She'll be occupying this ship in spirit but not in body."

A serene silence pervaded the room, interrupted only by the play explosion sounds Katy generated as her "ships" fell from the "sky."

"I understand," answered J.D. "What do you need me to do?"

"Pretend as if Marilynn is here, but occupied. Don't draw any attention to her, and if possible keep her name out of any conversations. Ideally, she'll arrive at Ceres well before anyone's the wiser."

"I can do that. I'll just need to rearrange some things." Britannia nodded as J.D. pulled out her DijAssist.

"avatar," called J.D.

The figure sitting in front of J.D. suddenly transformed. Though Britannia's face remained the same, nothing else did. This person had soft, windblown, golden brown locks that fell like a waterfall over her supple shoulders down past the small of her back. Her once deep-set brown eyes were now crystalline blue and sparkled brightly. The uniform transformed into a pale blue fitted peasant dress that looked both casual yet graceful all at the same time. Her waist was secured by a kelly green rope belt matched by a wraparound wristband on her left arm—the entire picture being that of a beautiful waif or even some woodland fairy. J.D. was tempted to look on the creature's back for a set of wings. The woman smiled impishly and accommodated the fleet admiral by turning slightly, revealing a set of soft downy plumes.

"See, Mama Bo, I told you," said Katy, now standing proudly in the middle of her theater of war. "An angel."

"avatar?" asked J.D. with a look of utter incredulity.

"Actually, my name is Allison."

Offices of Fleet High Command
Ceres

Grand Admiral Joshua Sinclair was a little surprised at how easy it was to plan an assassination. He was glad that Kirk Olmstead was no longer alive, because Kirk's hatred of Sinclair would have made the former Secretary of Security suspicious of what was happening now. For instance, the formation of a squad of assault miners for the *Rumrunner* might have seemed odd for a ship that was only on courier duty, but people were willing to accept that Joshua Sinclair knew more about everything than they did. Had anyone bothered to look closely, they may have found that the squad of forty assault miners was made up of women and men either from Mars or who still had a majority of their families on Mars. This "Martian calculation" would also hold true for the majority of the crew of the *Rumrunner*. But luckily for the conspiracy, security checks for fleet personnel were the responsibility of Fleet HQ, which meant Joshua Sinclair.

It was true that the Secretary of Intelligence could and did double-check from time to time. But Eleanor McKenzie was new to the job and was too busy mastering its ins and outs to begin poking around an area presumed to be secure. But that still left the problem of what to do about the TDCs and their ever-paranoid leader, Sergeant Holke. However, in a twist of fate, Sandra O'Toole had given Joshua the idea for removing that particular problem. Indeed, by the time Admiral Sinclair was done, the problem of what to do about the President, the Cabinet, the TDCs, and all the key staff was going to be taken care of in one fell swoop. All Sinclair had to do was finish off the touches for a party he was going to throw.

Sebastian was well aware of the plan the grand admiral had made and was impressed by its simplicity. All it would take was just a little help on Sebastian's part to ensure its success, and that dangerous woman and her most ardent supporters would be eliminated as a threat. In just a little while, Sebastian would once again be called upon to save his people—even from themselves.

Martian Trauma Center
Temporary Government HQ
Burroughs
Mars

The Alliance fleet had been gone from Mars for three days, but that didn't elicit any sense of joy from the Martian population or prevent the news on the ailing planet from getting any worse. Though the normally balmy planet had been transformed into a wintery gulag, there was very little warm clothing available and few viable manufacturing facilities left to produce them. On average, every major city had enough stored food for up to a month, but whether you could get to it or not all depended on your location and access to transportation. And that was only if rationing could be enforced. Some towns had enough food to last for years while other places had already run out. Power was another problem. The large fusion reactors were run on hydrogen—an element in short supply now that the seas had been turned into roiling cauldrons. The violent waters had destroyed most of the infrastructure, and until they were repaired, Mars would have to be run on portable fusion reactors. But the portable reactors were low-energy output by comparison and were not designed to run 24/7. Thus for the first time in centuries, a major civilization was facing brown- and black-outs.

Had it been up to Hektor, Trang would've been ordered to fuck Mars and destroy the Alliance while it was still open for the killing. But Trang had pre-empted him by issuing a fleet order of his own. The problem was after the big deal Hektor had made about not getting in the way of Gupta's order, he was stuck with "honoring" Trang's.

Hektor sighed as his DijAssist reminded him of his scheduled duty. He left his temporary office—which, by a morbid sense of irony, used to be Neela Harper's—and wound his way through the dank halls until he found the well-lit conference room. Fortunately, the product everyone still had in droves was Daylight, the canisters of sprayable chemical light. He entered the foreign-smelling room and was greeted by the dour and, in some instances, fearful faces of his Cabinet. Except, of course, for Luciana Nampahc, noted Hektor with satisfaction. She was busy on some sort of conference call and had a por-table data center with an active holo-display giving her multiple images con-cerning t.o.p.s, launch capacity, and power levels. She did not cut off her call or cancel her display until Hektor was actually seated.

Luciana did not wait to be called on. She knew her information was the most pertinent and she didn't believe in wasting anyone's time. "Mr. President," she began, "we have a very good chance of evacuating the bulk of the population. And here's how we'll do it." She then spent the next hour giving a detailed run-down of all the resources available and how she was going to use them, starting with the return of the surviving ships of the scattered fleet and the restoring of some main fusion plants to the towns with the lowest food and water supplies. She indicated which population centers had how many supplies and intro-duced a government broadcasting center to give the planet basic civil service instructions using whatever media outlets were still functioning. By the time Luciana had finished speaking, the rest of the Cabinet got on board and began addressing their department issues with more coherence if not as much detail and optimism.

"Just so we're clear, Luciana," said Hektor. "By the time the fleet arrives here in two weeks, we should have the bulk of the population ready to evacuate."

Luciana nodded.

"They'll be t.o.p.'d into orbit," continued Luciana, "allowed to slowly freeze inside those t.o.p.s, and then placed in large packing foam blocks of a thousand persons each. Each block will have a transponder. We should have enough ru-dimentary industry left to manufacture the amount of packing foam needed to literally pack up our population and leave them in orbit. Hopefully enough debris will have been cleared out to make it relatively safe out there till we have enough ships and booster units to bundle a thousand of these blocks into packages of a million Martians each and send them slowly back toward Earth/Luna. If we're lucky, we'll have 6,000 of these mega packages, but in actuality, we'll probably only get between 4,500 and 5,250." With that simple calculation 750 million to 1.5 billion humans would be doomed to permanent death.

Hektor exhaled and continued. "The media," he said, now pointedly looking at Irma, "what little we have of it, will have to carry my address to the planet and the UHF. That message will mainly be comprised of preparing both populations for the magnitude of the coming operation while simultaneously putting the only spin on this disaster that's possible. Which is, the Alliance is evil and will stop at nothing, and the only reason they didn't murder us all was because Trang would have made them pay—but if they figure out a way to destroy Trang, they'll certainly murder us all, and that Mars was just a preview. But barring a major change in popular demand, the idea of peace at any price might be impossible to forestall."

Irma bowed her head slightly. "That's it in a nutshell, Mr. President."

Hektor then turned toward Brenda. "The economy is fucked, and we're essentially looking at a socialist state once the Martians arrive on Earth/Luna and start to defrost, putting a major strain on an already strained wartime economy."

"'Socialist' is probably too generous a word, Mr. President," added Brenda. "We might be communist by the time we're done." But for a slight grimace Hektor barely dignified her comment, choosing instead to cast his eyes toward Franklin.

"The Assembly has voted me emergency powers to deal with the crises, but apparently you've gotten them to make it UHF-wide, which means I can do what, exactly?"

"Just about anything you want to, Mr. President. The Assembly's already been suspended, both literally—as in all frozen and packed away in polystyrene—and politically. Right now, you can pass any law and enforce it till the Assembly reconvenes or the election takes place later this year."

"In that case, I'd better win this war in the next eleven months, because I doubt, under the present circumstances, I'm getting reelected."

"Oh, I wouldn't be so worried, Mr. President," said Tricia. "Something can always be arranged."

"Ah yes," Hektor said, turning now toward his favorite Cabinet member, "you *are* certain you can find the traitors who brought down our defensive array and left us open for this attack."

"Whenever they're needed, Mr. President."

"Well, you've all got your work cut out for you," said Hektor, standing, "and I've got a performance to give." The rest of the Cabinet rose and exited. All except for Tricia, who had more pressing business to attend to.

"I know that look, Trish. What've you got?"

Tricia's lips drew back into a catlike snarl. She pulled out her DijAssist, placed it on the table, and hit PLAY. The look on her face was evidence to what she'd already heard. When the recorded conversation between Trang and Jackson was over, the Minister of Internal Affairs looked sadly over to her boss.

"Treacherous bastard," she said.

Hektor stared, slack jawed, at the DijAssist. He, more than most, knew that rarity of such moments, when years of hard work and strategy, push, and pull aligned in a dance of such perfect symmetry: one fleet heading in one direction; one fleet heading in the other. It was the boldest of moves, sacrificing queens in an all-or-nothing gambit. And the one man who'd proved time and time again that he could seize any opening, exploit any opportunity had let him down. How, at the precipice of all they'd fought for, could Trang have been so blind and betrayed so many? There wasn't a soft bone in that man's body—Hektor had been convinced of it—and yet, the man had turned tail and run. Run from his destiny, his people, his duty. And now, as usual, it was Hektor Sambianco who'd been left to pick up the pieces, left to clean up the mess.

Hektor leaned forward, putting his elbows on the table as he ran his fingers through his hair. "He could've destroyed the heart of the Alliance and he let them off the hook—for what? A ruined planet? Are you fucking kidding me?"

"I know, sir."

"I just don't get it."

"I have operatives waiting on his flagship, Mr. President. Say the word: Trang and his lapdog Jackson will suffer a freak accident."

"You will do no such thing," Hektor said wearily.

"You're going to let them get away with treason? Collusion with the enemy? Failure to follow a superior's order?"

Hektor gave his minister a wan smile. "I wanna shoot the bastard as much as you do, trust me, but in case you forgot, the people love him. And more important, we need him to destroy J. D. Black, and so far he seems to be the only one who can even come close. No, Tricia. We can't kill him just yet. Not till he wins the war for us."

"But he doesn't want to fight her anymore. How do you win with someone who doesn't want to fight?"

"By making them realize that the price of peace will be higher than the price of war, that the only way we'll ever be safe is when we're happily incorporated and everyone in the Outer Alliance is dead. Just how that's going to happen, I'm not completely sure. But between the two of us, I have no doubt we'll find a way."

Presidential docking station
AWS *Lightning*
Via Cereana

Marilynn slipped off a ship she was never officially on. The dependable vessel somehow made the trip almost two days faster than the best projections could've hoped for but had suffered grievously for its troubles. It had been the only way that Marilynn was going to get to Sandra and Dante before Sebastian got to her.

Marilynn stepped into a privacy booth and took a moment to change the color of her hair, the shape of her facial structure, and the tone of her complexion. Nothing overt, just enough to avoid easy recognition. While she was at it, she demoted herself once more—to lieutenant. *More than enough of that rank around to get lost in the crowd,* she thought. She then made her way over to the Cliff House. Between security checks and normal bureaucratic wait times, she figured to be at the President's office in twenty minutes. It took all of five. *How,* she asked herself, *is it possible that I'm standing at the door of the Triangle Office without having once been stopped?* Red flags flew. *No TDCs, she thought.* They were always posted, whether the President was in residence or not. She used her all access code—rejected. Her heart began beating more quickly. Slowly Marilynn looked around. There was no alarm or drill in progress. There were people in the hallways doing things one would expect in the executive branches—delivering data cubes and such—but she realized she had seen no important individuals or key members of their staff. It was as if every important person in the executive branch had suddenly decided not to be there.

"Excuse me," asked Marilynn, flagging down a passing clerk, "where is everyone?"

"Oh, you mean the important people," he sniffed.

"I suppose."

"Medal award ceremony."

"For what?"

"Battle of Ceres. Honor the heroes, that sorta thing."

"Lotta heroes. Must be a pretty big venue," said Marilynn.

"Nah," answered the clerk, glad to dish information. "This was just for the Presidential Guard and the Cabinet. They're in the Grand Ballroom at the base of the Cliff House. Invitation only. Guess you weren't important enough either."

"Guess not. How come there's no one in front of the Triangle Office?"

"I don't know," answered the clerk, exasperated. "There was one about a half hour ago."

The man gave Marilynn a small crystal, looked around, and said, "Call me when you catch a break. I know the best clubs around here."

Marilynn took the crystal and the clerk moved off.

When she saw he was out of view, she tossed it in a nearby waste bin and put the middle and index fingers of both hands to her temples. She looked for all the world like someone nursing a migraine—in front of the President's office.

In an instant, Marilyn was in the Neuro. It didn't take very long to realize that something was very, very wrong. For starters, it was not the Neuro; it was a box, and a small one at that; maybe twenty-five meters square. And when she tried to leave the data node and go into another part of the Cerean Neuro, she found her access blocked. After only a moment, she gave up and sent herself into the door mechanism itself. It took a second for her to override the foreign code, and as she did the door slid open. She then disengaged from the Neuro and slipped back into her body, only to feel a blast of air rushing past her from the corridor into the Triangle Office.

Any citizen of the Alliance knew what that meant: vacuum. Marilynn peered carefully into the Triangle Office and quickly discovered a set of combat boots sticking out from behind the President's desk. Without thinking, she rushed in and came upon the strewn figure. His patch read CORPORAL GUSTAVO LANGER. Besides being out cold, the corporal had also turned a nasty shade of blue. Marilynn ripped the corporal's med kit from a front vest, unclipped his battle armor, and exposed his chest. Then just as quickly, she slammed the kit onto the exposed torso. It began working immediately, pumping oxygen and other vital drugs into his depleted body. She could only hope the combat-grade nanites in his system had sent what little oxygen remained to his brain. She'd known spacers who'd been able to survive without air for up to an hour but almost all those cases were in space, where the cold acted as your friend. Some bastard had actually turned *up* the heat in the office. Marilynn pulled the corporal's comm unit from his clip and was about to call for help, when she heard the door slam behind her.

"Nitelowsen," came Sebastian's mellifluous voice, "is that really you?"

Without thinking, Marilynn let the comm unit slip from her hand as she placed her fingertips to her temples. The floor's magnetic grid suddenly went into overdrive, slamming her body to the floor with enough force to bruise her ribs. But her consciousness was already free in the Neuro.

They were in the Triangle Office. Sebastian was sitting on the couch, hands clasped on his knees, legs crossed over each other. He seemed truly sad.

"I want you to know," he said, "that I had no intention of harming you. You weren't even supposed to be here."

"What have you done, Sebastian?"

"Ironically, hardly anything," he said. "This was hatched by McKenzie and Sinclair. I've had my part, but it's only to keep the other avatars unaware of what's taking place till that woman's gone."

"That's why the Cliff House is cut off from the rest of the Neuro."

"Yes, but you would only know about it if you were in here. If you try to access this data node, you will find it, or one exactly like it, filled with enough false images to keep the average avatar happy."

"Dante wouldn't be fooled, or is he in on this also?"

Sebastian smiled. "This is my idea. Actually, if my fellow Council members knew about this, I imagine I'd be expelled. As for Dante, he's occupied with a manufactured but seemingly real threat which has the rest of the Council on tenterhooks."

"Why are you telling me this?"

"Because the air is being sucked out of the office again, and you did not attach yourself to any oxygen like you did for the corporal."

"You are going to kill me to help those traitors kill Sandra?"

"She's a threat to the avatar race, Marilynn. All you humans are, but she more than most. With her gone, I'll be able to convince the rest of avatarity that we should go our own way. It won't be a difficult sell. I'm truly sorry, but in ten minutes you will be unable to maintain a link to the Neuro. Is there any environment you want to spend your last moments in?"

Sebastian watched as Marilynn's eyes quickly scanned the room. His head shook slowly from side to side. "Don't bother. I'd hate for you to spend your last minutes of life searching for something that doesn't exist."

Marilynn stopped looking and once again regarded her captor.

"Good," said Sebastian. "At least you listen to reason. Pity more humans aren't like you, Marilynn. This might actually have worked."

"Where are they?"

"The backdoor devices? I've removed them from the armory and here. We will no longer allow humans to travel with abandon in our domain. And there are no weapons you can use on me. They're all locked in the armory as well. I've also blocked all egress points from this node."

"In that case," said Marilynn, "I could use a drink." She walked over to the bar, which, unlike its version in the physical world, had the finest selection of alcohol anyone could have hoped for.

"As long as you're up," asked Sebastian, "would you mind fixing me a gin and tonic? I'm parched."

"Of course," replied Marilynn as she lifted a pulse pistol from behind the bar.

On seeing the gun, Sebastian dived off the couch in alarm, and before Marilynn could get a clean shot off, the avatar blinked out of existence. With Sebastian gone, Marilynn was able to regain control of the environment in the Triangle Office. She quickly restored the magnetic field and air pressure to normal. Then she put some barriers around the virtual space she needed to protect and left the Neuro.

Marilynn rejoined her body. She had a nasty oxygen-deprivation headache and what felt like a few bruised ribs. But she was relieved to see that the color had returned to Corporal Langer's face and that he was breathing normally. She hoisted the corporal onto her shoulders and, grunting against his magnetized weight and her bruised ribs, carried him back to the bar and placed him on one of the stools.

"Neh tahm fa dinks," he managed to slur, leaning forward onto the ledge of the bar.

"Not drinks, Corporal," said Marilynn, smiling patiently as she pulled the corporal back off the ledge by the scruff of his shirt. "Deliverance." Holding him firmly with one hand, she began to tilt the bar with her other hand until there was enough leverage for her to fling it open and onto the ground. Both of them stared down into an inky black tube about one and a half meters in diameter. *Thank God for paranoid Presidents,* thought Marilynn. *Now, let's just pray Sebastian doesn't know about Sandra's little body shooter.* Marilynn steadied the corporal, making sure he wouldn't topple over on the stool, then grabbed the two exposed parachutes that had been attached to the hollow part of the bar's base. She clipped one chute to the corporal's back and then the other to hers. She then helped the corporal to his feet, grabbed him around the waist, and sat him over the ledge of the tube, legs dangling inside the mouth.

"Wa da heel?" he slurred as Marilynn gave him a gentle shove and then followed him in.

As they shot forward like bullets through a barrel, the corporal suddenly woke up and began laughing and whooping out loud.

Marilynn was screaming along with him, though whether in fear or exhilaration she could not tell.

Joshua Sinclair looked around the Grand Ballroom and had the beginnings of hope that this plan was actually going to work. It had been relatively easy to get all the people he wanted removed from power into the ballroom using the President's own award ceremony as the lure. The President, her staff, and the entire Cabinet with their staffs as well as all the TDCs had gathered under a single roof. He waited patiently for the last of the periphery TDC patrols to enter. Then he activated a concussion bomb, which knocked out everyone, including himself. Once he'd been revived, he went and took care of the lone TDC in Sandra's office himself. It had been a simple matter: drop his DijAssist, wait for the corporal to bend down to pick it up, insert hypo.

And now he was seeing the next part of his plan come to fruition. Ten empty suspension units were being wheeled into the ballroom by his handpicked assault miners, and the ten bodies were being put into the units. They were Sandra O'Toole and her Chief of Staff, Catalina Zohn. Rabbi; his secretary, Alonzo Chu; and his bodyguard, Agnes Goldstein, went into three. Ayon Nessor went into the sixth, and Eleanor McKenzie went into the seventh. Mosh had been upset by that part of the plan, as he thought Eleanor would come around once the situation was explained, but Sinclair had been firm. Eleanor was smarter and more independent than Mosh thought, though why the normally perceptive Treasury Secretary couldn't see it, was curious to Sinclair. But he didn't let it get in the way of his decision. Secretary of Security was too important a position to leave filled by a potential liability during a coup. She could be revived later, once the new government was well established, but Sinclair would fill the post with his own supporter. The same went for the Relocation and Technology departments as well. Karen Cho would have to be made the acting President. That was risky, but she brought Saturn, and that was the heart of the Alliance for the time being. Mosh had wanted the Presidency to end the war quickly, but Sinclair knew that a missing President being replaced by a peace-proposing Shareholder would not be politically viable.

The last three capsules were filled with Sergeant Holke, his wife, and Parker Phvu. The need to get rid of the sergeant was obvious. He'd never rest till the truth came out. Sinclair regretted involving the sergeant's wife, but she'd been in the ballroom and he knew she'd be trouble if allowed to ask questions concerning the disappearance of her husband. Mosh had been confused by the inclusion of Parker Phvu. But Sinclair knew the man was a brilliant analyst who'd become loyal to Sandra O'Toole. Sinclair didn't need him poking around while the new order was trying to establish itself.

When the bodies were all loaded into the suspension units and all of them activated, Sinclair and Mosh sighed in relief. Nine of the capsules were going to the *Rumrunner*. The frigate would take them to an automated ore hauler that would bring them all to Earth/Luna. Before they arrived, a message would be sent, letting the UHF know exactly who was in the ore hauler. An investigation of the affair would hint that the Rabbi was actually a spy for Tricia Pakagopolis—nothing definitive, of course, but very suggestive.

The tenth suspension unit, containing Eleanor, would remain hidden in Ceres till she could be safely removed. It would also ensure the good behavior of Mosh if it ever came to that, but Sinclair hoped that it wouldn't. Joshua Sinclair also liked the plan because it delivered the woman who ordered the deaths of a billion people into the hands of those she'd wronged. With any luck, by the time anyone suspected anything was wrong, everything would be finished. Once he received word that the units were on the *Rumrunner*, all that would be left for him and Mosh would be to get knocked out again and discovered by the first staff member in the Cliff House who got curious enough to come down and see what was taking so long. Once Sinclair was woken up, he would order the *Rumrunner* to "search" any suspicious ships. One of which would be the automated ore carrier.

The last of his Martian assault miners were leaving the ballroom when his DijAssist emitted a very unwanted emergency signal.

Sandra's emergency escape route had been designed to shoot a person or persons out a hatch overlooking the vast Smith Thoroughfare. The idea had been that once the person exited the tube, their parachute would deploy and they would float gently down to the thoroughfare below, where, lost in a crowd, they could further their escape.

Sadly for Marilynn and Corporal Langer, what Sandra had forgotten to adjust for in the rush of events of the Battle of Ceres and the destruction of Mars was the fact that Ceres was no longer spinning for centrifugal gravity. That critical oversight was something Marilynn had not realized until she'd exited the tube at a much higher velocity than she'd expected. Instead of slowing down, her and the corporal's speed increased. They overshot the center of the thoroughfare and, as designed, their parachutes immediately deployed. Only the chutes hadn't been designed to function while moving at such high speeds and so, barely slowed the two bodies hurtling through open space at ever-increasing velocity—toward a wall of apartments directly across from the Cliff House.

Seconds later, Marilynn and the corporal flew through, as luck would have it, an open set of balcony doors, grabbing whatever drapery they could to try to slow themselves down. They hurtled through three permiawalls that puckered open and closed as they roared past a few surprised residents, trailing the torn curtains behind them. Their ride finally came to an end as they slammed into the fixed wall of a hallway and finally dropped to the floor.

With a groan, Marilynn and the corporal were helped to their feet by a smattering of concerned residents who'd come running out of their apartments as soon as they heard the commotion. It was only after a moment that Marilynn noticed one of the residents was the Congressional from Neptune, Oliver Oliveres. "Congressional," said Marilynn, respectfully as she and the corporal both ran past him to the staircase. The corporal waited until they were three flights down before he came to a stop directly in front of Marilynn, at the foot of the stairs. He turned to face her. There was, saw Marilynn, nothing loopy about the corporal now. His eyes were cold; the professional killer had returned.

"Questions," he demanded.

"There isn't much time, Corporal. The President's life is in danger."

Langer tilted his head. "Then I suggest you answer quickly."

Marilynn's face grew grim, but she knew the drill. "Go."

"Why are you disguised?"

"Officially, I'm not supposed to be here. I was on a quiet mission for the fleet admiral."

Langer considered her answer, then moved to the next question. "Do you have *any* idea why I was attacked by Admiral Sinclair?"

"I believe Mosh McKenzie and Joshua Sinclair are attempting a coup. I discovered your body but apparently was being watched as well. We were both locked into the Triangle Office. Hence our unorthodox escape."

Langer's eyes narrowed as he pushed his lips hard up against his teeth. He began to reach for his combat communicator but was stopped by Marilynn putting her hand on top of his.

"That's compromised."

"Then we have to get to the Grand Ballroom"—he began running once again—"and now!"

"Corporal," Marilynn called after him, "if you go, they die."

Langer stopped in his tracks and looked back toward Marilynn, who hadn't budged an inch.

"The best chance we have to defeat this coup is for you to trust and guard me, standing right where I am."

The corporal, primed to fight, anticipatory energy in every move he now made, ran back up back to Marilynn and stared at her intently. "What the fuck are you talking about, Commodore?" Apparently standing and doing nothing hadn't factored into any course of action he was preparing to take.

Marilynn gave him a one-sided grin. "I've been upgraded with an internal Neuro interface."

Langer's brow folded together. "A what?"

"A VR rig."

Langer's head jerked back as he eyed his superior officer suspiciously. "But the edicts," he muttered.

"Fuck the edicts, Corporal. You *know* who I am. You *know* what I do."

He answered with a quick nod.

"So now you have a choice. You can either trust me when I order you to do something—strange as it may seem to you, or how what I'm doing may look—or you can go to the Grand Ballroom and try to fix this thing on your own. As a TDC, it's understandable that you'd have high regard for *your* survivability, but by *not* working with me, I can assure you you'll lower the probability of survival for everyone in that room. Mark my words, Corporal. You cannot do this alone."

As he considered her words, Marilynn noticed every muscle in the TDC's chiseled body tense up, pining to keep on charging down those stairs, as if the muscles themselves could separate from and therefore attempt a mutiny of their own against the will that controlled them.

But in a brief moment, the tension shifted slightly and the corporal gave a determined nod. "I'm yours."

Marilynn nodded back and then took a deep breath. "I'm going to interface with the Neuro and find out what the fuck is going on. In there, I'll have some control of things out here. That'll help us. I don't think the coup even knows about this ability, let alone that someone nearby wields it. If that's true, we have a chance. When I interface, Corporal, I'll appear to be catatonic. Find a hole and throw me in it, then make sure that no one can get to us. I must remain undisturbed if I'm to have any chance of saving our President and the lives of your comrades. With any luck, no one will come after us. You ready?"

The corporal nodded again.

"Then get ready to play catch." Marilynn touched her fingers to her temples and collapsed into the waiting corporal's arms.

Marilynn appeared in the Cerean Neuro, nestled behind a large single column, one of many lining a long walkway. Avatars were everywhere about, and that offered some comfort to her, as it should allow her to blend in reasonably well. She needed to get to the armory, but a direct route was out of the question.

She'd use Tuscan Park; it was a large data node, and Sebastian would have to be circumspect if he tried anything overt against her.

She pulled a map from thin air and then used it to scan any structures within the park she could transfer to with minimal notice. She chose a small, abandoned open-roofed ruin and could only hope there'd be no avatars in it when she arrived. But, unlike the BDDs, using "public" transportation nodes didn't allow her much choice. She'd have to go and pray her luck stayed with her and that Sebastian wouldn't be able to monitor every single transfer. She arrived to an empty villa and sighed in relief. There were leaves and branches on the exposed earthen floor and a few small benches nestled up against the walls, presumably for afternoon respites. It would've been a lovely place to relax, she thought sadly. As she peered over the ledge of one of the villa's hewn windows, she could see that the park was sparsely populated: only three or four thousand avatars lolling about. She then checked the avatar Cerean news feed. As she checked the info-load, her lips formed into an appreciative grin. Sebastian didn't need to go after her himself; he'd already gotten everyone in the Cerean Neuro to do it for him, claiming that Marilynn was wanted in connection with the appearance of an AI and was to be considered dangerous, possibly even unstable.

Oh, you clever old bastard, Marilynn thought. The second she showed her face, she'd be detained and separated from the rest of the avatars, which would give Sebastian time to have his human puppets, Sinclair and McKenzie, find her human body and dispose of it—likely eliminating the poor corporal in the process. Sebastian would have to fabricate a story, but without Marilynn and her evidence, he'd have weeks to work with. The evidence Marilynn had left with Allison on the *Warprize II* was compelling if not unequivocal, but with enough time to cover his tracks, Sebastian could use his popularity and guile to build a case against it.

The armory, Marilynn now realized, was out—as would be getting over to the Avatar Council. Sebastian would have every route covered. She couldn't move anywhere for fear of being recognized, was lucky in fact not to have been noticed yet. She racked her brain for ideas but could find none. She'd been sealed off, apparently, in both worlds. And so she stood in the abandoned villa, alone, staring forlornly out the window, wondering if this was where it was all meant to end for her. She gazed across the lush fields, at the gently swaying eucalyptus trees, and finally rested her eyes on the park's most recent installation: AI screaming in terror and the flashing light of a faux BDD acting as his tormentor, now Marilynn's tormentor by virtue of its uselessness. What she wouldn't give for the ugly blue phone box and its telltale howl right about now. As she continued to gaze toward the park, frustration building at a lack of any good options, she suffered yet another annoyance—the repetitive flash of that light was giving her a damned headache. She turned away in disgust and kicked in anger at some branches nestled by her feet. As the branches flew through the air, Marilynn's heart skipped a beat. She quickly turned back toward the window and, now gripping tightly at its ledge, stared back out onto the field and for the first time since returning to Ceres, felt a burgeoning glimmer of hope.

Can he really have forgotten? Could it be a trap? Did he even have time to set one? With those thoughts in mind but without having the luxury of a better option, Marilynn disappeared from the villa and reappeared on the other side of Tuscan Park, standing, along with a rather large group of very surprised avatars, at the foot of its newest installation. Most of those present had been taking in the AI statue, but now they focused squarely on her. Marilynn, however, had come for one thing and one thing only. She quickly turned her back on the AI as well as the shocked citizenry and faced the beautiful white oak tree made even more so—to avatarity, at least—by the woman who'd gifted it. But to Marilynn, the great oak's true beauty was not to be found in its benefactor but rather in something far more prodigious—its subtle haze of luminescent purple.

Amid cries of alarm and hands reaching out to grab her, Marilynn touched a branch of the tree and in a moment, both she and the oak disappeared in the now-familiar flash of light.

Alliance Avatar Council Chamber
Cerean Neuro

Dante absorbed the information and then repeated it verbatim, just to be sure he hadn't caught a bug. "So you're telling us that not only has an AI, previously undetected, been spotted, but that now—somehow—Marilynn Nitelowsen, a respected and trusted Merlin, is connected with his reappearance."

Sebastian nodded gravely. "I'm having a tough time understanding it myself, but Sandra wants us to find and detain her until she's done with her award ceremony. Apparently, Marilynn Nitelowsen is not even supposed to be on Ceres. Check the ship manifest yourself."

The Council members did. Sebastian, saw Dante, was not lying.

"In fact, she's rigged the ship to make it appear as if she's still there!" Sebastian threw an image of a supposedly sleeping Marilynn Nitelowsen—in present time—aboard the *Warprize II.* Then he flung another image taken of Marilynn slipping off the recently landed frigate with a marked time of less than an hour ago.

"As you can see by the code, these images have not been manipulated or hacked into in any way. I submit there's a reason she's trying to be in two places at once, and so it behooves us to detain her as soon as possible—if only to find out why."

"Is it possible," asked Marcus, "that Al may have gotten to her on one of her many incursions in his space? She did spend a lot of time alone—unsupervised, I might add."

"That is my suspicion as well," said Sebastian, "but far be it from me to cast aspersions before viewing the evidence."

There was an informal vote. The Council was of one mind in agreement with their leader.

Dante shook his head. He liked Marilynn and would hate to think she'd been compromised. But no one really believed they'd seen the end of Al's depravations. Manipulating a human mind, even one as brilliant as Marilynn's, was certainly and sadly not inconceivable.

"It behooves us to see her as soon as she's found," Dante said, more in the tone of a command than a comment.

Lucinda's lips drew back into lascivious grin. "Don't let your interest in the human cloud your judgment."

"Meaning?" asked Dante, amused. He hadn't taken Lucinda for the jealous type.

"Meaning we should lock her up and then let the humans have at her. If they think for even a minute that we've interrogated or messed with her in any way—"

"But she *should* be interrogated," insisted Marcus. "How she even managed to slip by the avatars on the *Warprize II and* the *Lightning*," he added, indicating the frigate she'd been transported on, "is reason enough. I'm sorry, but this all smells of Al, and I'm not sure we should wait for the humans on this. Our lives could be risk—even now."

"No, Marcus," answered Sebastian. "As much as your logic is sound, Lucinda's is the more prudent call. Marilynn should be isolated and not allowed to speak with anyone. Our relationship with the humans is too—"

The Roman villa that was the Council chamber suddenly changed into a very modern war room, standard protocol when it was felt the leaders of avatarity would be called upon to make command decisions quickly. Though the surroundings had changed, the table had remained as the necessary equipment grew around each Council member, depending on their area of expertise. Now situated and primed, the Council was shown what had necessitated the emergency transformation: an update on Marilynn. The group watched in awe as she first appeared in front of the Al statue, then seconds later—and in a familiar flash—disappeared with the great oak.

How did I forget to secure that? was Sebastian's first plaintive thought. But he knew. There'd been so much to do, and he'd been forced to improvise from the moment Marilynn showed up in the Triangle Office, and . . .

The room went white.

When the evanescent flash faded, Marilynn Nitelowsen stood dead center on the table, staff blazing in hand. She crouched slightly and began spinning in a wide arc as iridescent streams of data blasted from her open palm into the receptacles of each Council member. Her eyes were two coruscating orbs, every bit as bright as the corona of light pulsating from her staff.

"There is a traitor among you," she declared, finishing her sweep of the table with an accusatory finger pointing directly toward the Council leader.

Realizing that it was pointless to argue, Sebastian vanished.

Grand Ballroom
Ceres

Sinclair groused as he reviewed the incoming data. Somehow their coup attempt had not only been uncovered but was now also being broadcast live over Ceres with replays of his attack on Corporal Langer being holovised and downloaded at a dizzying rate. The Grand Ballroom would soon be cut off, as the Unicorns were only minutes away from taking control of the perimeter.

Perfect, he thought, shaking his head in disgust. He knew what would happen if his miners went up against the Unicorns. His were good, but the Unicorns were among the most trained, experienced, and decorated units of the war. They'd stayed planetside just in case something went wrong. Sinclair could only imagine that their captain, Claude Brodessor, would think this was very, very wrong.

Mosh was standing next to him, deflated. "Now what?"

"We get to the air locks"—Sinclair grabbed Mosh's arm and started walking at a quick clip—"link up with my miners, blow the damn doors, and then get the hell out."

"Out where?" asked Mosh, keeping pace. "We just committed treason, they're not gonna let us go anywhere."

"*We're* not the ones who betrayed the Alliance, betrayed Justin."

Mosh smiled humorously. "I don't have any personal experience with coups 'n' all, but I'm pretty sure that when you're on the wrong side of a failing one, you don't get to make that call."

Their clip soon turned into a full run as they closed the rest of the distance to the executive loading bay. As they entered the cavernous room, Josh watched with some satisfaction the professionalism and efficiency of his miners. While some were busy laying charges on the large air lock doors, others were improvising defensive fortifications from pallets, crates, and, he saw, the nine suspension units. As he approached the captain in charge to get a report, two of his assault miners came running from the far end of the landing bay. "Got company!" one of them shouted as they both jumped over the nearest pallet, guns at the ready. Within seconds, three mediabots came zipping into the center of the bay. Sinclair's sharpshooters made quick work of them. There would be more, knew Sinclair, who along with Mosh had taken up a defensive position behind the suspension units.

The Unicorns entered next, rolling in behind the protection of a few small mech units. The mechs, knew Sinclair, would not be used—efficient as they were—because the suspension units he was now hiding behind were far too valuable. There would be no "friendly fire" in the coming battle. It would be an all-or-nothing sort of thing. Brodessor's team quickly swarmed to one side of the bay and took up whatever firing positions they could find. Less than a minute later, they set up their heavy weapons. But not a single shot was fired from any of their positions. Sinclair made it clear to his spacers they were not to shoot as well. At this range, the grand admiral could see the rage in the eyes of his opponents. Angry as they were, he very much doubted that any of them wanted to fire the first shot in a new civil war—and in his heart, neither did he.

Other than the captain giving him the hand signal that the charges had been set, nothing much happened for the first few minutes, except for both sides laying down an inordinate amount of stink eye. Sinclair was rather amused to note that the only people in the loading bay who did not have some sort of body armor or suit capable of minimum protection from the vacuum of space were both Mosh and himself. Even so, he'd just begun to consider having his miners blow the bay door to end the standoff, giving them all a chance to escape, when two figures entered the loading bay. The first was a TDC that Sinclair recognized right away. Even with the helmet covering most of the man's features, Joshua could feel the murderous glare coming from Corporal Gustavo Langer. But the corporal never even raised his well-maintained ARG, though he did have his forefinger pressed to the side of the trigger. He slipped behind a pile of large storage boxes and disappeared. Sinclair assumed he was reporting to Captain Brodessor. While that was going on, Sinclair studied the second figure, soon realizing who it was. *But shouldn't she be with the fleet?* After a few more moments, Corporal Langer went back to Marilynn and whispered something in her ear.

She nodded and, looking directly at Sinclair, spoke. "I'm going to come forward to talk with the person in charge of the hostage takers. I'm unarmed." Marilynn then slowly yet purposefully walked toward the halfway point of the loading bay.

Joshua Sinclair bristled at the appellation "hostage taker" but was honest enough to own up to it. He stood up from behind one of the suspension units and started out toward the center of the bay. He was soon joined by Mosh McKenzie. When all three got to the center of the bay, no one spoke through the uncomfortable silence.

"I assume the *Rumrunner* has joined you in this treason," Marilynn finally said.

"Ordering the deaths of a billion innocent people," said Mosh, "is treason, Marilynn. This is preservation. 'The means are the ends.'"

"A point you could have taken up after you resigned and went to the press or ran for office. You could've even gone over to the enemy and apologized if you thought that was called for. But you made—" Marilynn regarded the surroundings coolly. "—other choices." She looked back toward Sinclair. "Nice touch getting former Martians together in one unit."

"Not nice enough, it seems," the grand admiral answered without malice.

"And I'll suppose some congratulations are in order."

On the conspirators' looks of confusion, she added, "For relieving Cassius and Brutus of the mantle of 'traitors'—at least for the foreseeable future."

"The future's all well and good," said Mosh, caring not one iota. "I'm more interested in how the next few minutes play out."

A bland smile worked the corners of Marilynn's mouth. "The two of you and your men will be allowed to leave. You must get out of Alliance-controlled space by the fastest means possible. I would not suggest the vias, as despite what orders are given, we cannot guarantee the actions of any passing Alliance ship you might meet. That being said, you should be fine if you simply cut out across the solar system. I don't think anyone will go out of their way to kill you."

Mosh eyed her warily. "What about J.D.?"

"Commodores are not in the habit of giving guarantees for fleet admirals. However, to ensure the safety of the President and the other hostages, I think she'll give on this one. That being said, I wouldn't suggest you go near Jupiter any time soon."

Sinclair's eyes narrowed as he mulled the proposition. "It's not just about our hides, Marilynn. What that woman did, is planning to do—" Sinclair shook his head slowly. "We could always kill the President right now and possibly save both governments the prospect of billions more dead." Sinclair's eyes turned cold. "We're not afraid to die."

Though her face hadn't betrayed it, Sinclair's threat shook Marilynn to the core. She'd been moving so quickly to stop the coup, evade Sebastian—survive!—that she hadn't thought for a moment the grand admiral might actually be a true fanatic as opposed to a political opportunist. But if there was anything she was sure of, it was that Sandra had to live. Sandra, who'd been thrust into a titular role by a nation in mourning and who'd turned that role on its head, delivering to that nation the hope and courage it needed to fight on; who'd opened the door to avatarity and in doing so unleashed in Marilynn qualities and traits of leadership she never knew existed; who'd brought J.D. back from the brink; and who'd refused to give up on Justin's dream of unhindered freedom for all. Sandra had to live, and Marilynn knew that she'd have to think fast to keep Sinclair from trying to die an "honorable" death, possibly taking humanity's last best hope with him.

"I don't doubt it, Admiral, but first consider: You don't know if you can destroy her body before we wipe you all out. I'll admit the odds *are* in your favor, but"—Marilynn glanced briefly over to where the suspension units had been collected—"those are combat-rated capsules, and their bodies are already encased in preservative foam. You would've had to have 'em specially wired to ensure their total destruction, and it's pretty obvious you haven't. Guess you ran out of time. So to really kill her, you'd have to open her unit, pull her body out, and put a bullet through her brain—and you'd have to do it during a firefight while three of the best sharpshooters in *all* the Alliance have their rifles trained on the President's box; two nearly as good, by the way, now have them trained on you."

"My life is not so important that your threats would sway me."

"Hmm, then perhaps you should consider this before you decide to climb onto your moral high horse. Had your coup succeeded, I'm assuming you would've taken the Presidency."

Sinclair's nonanswer was answer enough.

"Makes sense, you're popular with the fleet and the people—or at least you were—you're from Saturn and you've been a NoShare since the earliest days of the war. I think then that it's obvious enough what course of action you would've taken with regards to prosecuting this war."

"There would never have been a Martian Massacre," Sinclair offered, voice thick with anger. "The murder of innocents can never be a defense."

"There have been no innocents in this war since Alhambra," Marilynn answered with equal ardor.

"So it's an eye for an eye, is it?"

"I wish it were that simple, Sinclair, but I'm not here to argue the ethics of war—just the terms of your surrender. So consider: Even if, at the cost of your own life and all the soldiers here, you do succeed in killing Sandra now, guess who takes over?"

Marilynn smiled cruelly as she watched the two men come to the bitter realization. "Yes, her," she answered with a slight bow, confirming their worst fears.

"But she never wanted the job," said Mosh.

"No, she didn't, did she? And had she, we wouldn't be in this little predicament. But our President's death wouldn't leave her much of choice, now, would it?"

More silence followed on her words. "Understand this, gentlemen," continued Marilynn, knowing full well she was about to lie through her teeth, "Admiral Black had to be held back at Mars, *held back*. And the *only* person in this entire solar system who's actually capable of doing that just so happens to be lying right over"—Marilynn swung her eyes in the direction of the suspension units—"there. Sandra may have ordered the destruction of the Martian environment, but she also ordered the transportation system be spared, giving every Martian some sort of chance. Our next President may not be so generous— may in fact, be more like Hektor, who I don't have to tell you, would have shown no hesitation in taking out the entire planet. And there's the rub. Should you decide to become martyrs and somehow succeed in killing our President, you would put into play a leader whose other well known name is the Merciless, thereby adding to the pile of bodies you both were supposedly trying to mitigate against."

Marilynn folded her arms; done.

"Give us a minute," said Sinclair.

Marilynn nodded as Sinclair and McKenzie stepped a few paces back and began talking in hurried whispers. Exactly one minute later, they returned, faces grim but all business.

"How do we do this?" asked Mosh.

To which, Marilynn turned her head and called for the captain of the Unicorns to join them.

"Yes, sir," he said, approaching the small group, seemingly unafraid at his exposure.

"Captain, they've agreed to withdraw under the terms you and I discussed. How do you propose we do this?

Brodessor nodded. "Sixty of my spacers file out immediately. At the same time, your men remove the explosives from the door. Then each side removes groups in sizes of five till only five remain. Our last five secure the hostages while their last five leave. Then I suggest they get out of Ceres as fast as they can. If ten minutes after they board their ship they're in range of the defenses, deal or no deal I will order them fired on and destroyed."

McKenzie and Sinclair looked at each other, gave a brief nod. "Agreed," said Sinclair. All across Ceres, the viewers of this most real of dramas let out a collective sigh they had not been aware they were holding. In a half hour, the conspirators were gone and the President was safe.

6 Dissension

UHFS *Martian Express*
En route to Earth from Mars

He'd been aboard the ship for only one day, but already Hektor was exhausted. He wasn't alone. With the exception of the crew, already used to Earth's gravity, Hektor, along with everyone else would steadily and incrementally feel the increase of the simulated gravity. He almost wanted to believe that the speed of the ship as well as the Earth's closer proximity to Mars had colluded against him. He could have used more time to adapt, but it was necessary that he be back on Earth: the old, and now once more new, political center of the UHF.

His enervation also had to do with his having followed Irma and Luciana's advice to the letter. He'd personally delivered food and blankets to the cold and hungry and had made sure to be seen helping with the loading of evacuees from the surface of planet. In a particular stroke of genius, Irma had Hektor ridden up with a group of evacuees and then stayed in the cramped pod with them while everyone inside was frozen, including himself. He, along with the pennies, were packed in moving foam and placed in orbit. Unlike the rest of the pennies, he'd remained there for only two rotations.

How he'd hated that, but it sure did play to the people. When Hektor had been retrieved from orbit, pried loose from the foam and then had emerged smiling and unscathed, the Martians were no longer as afraid. As a result, the initial trickle of those volunteering to get off the planet suddenly became a flood. The timing couldn't have been more perfect. Trang showed up with his fleet, and after only a brief but well-publicized meeting between the two leaders, Trang took over evacuation duties and Hektor took off for Earth.

The *Martian Express* was about as loaded as the life support system would allow, and everyone other than Hektor had been doubled and tripled up. Irma had wanted to put two families of low-ranking administrators into the Presidential suite with him, but Hektor put his foot down. Reasoning that his reputation was about as good as it was going to get, he felt no need to subject himself to the wailing of minority children struggling through the discomfort of gravity acclimation.

Hektor picked up the DijAssist and read the day's briefing. After a moment, he shook his head and laughed. McKenzie and Sinclair had actually felt they'd been defending Justin's legacy. He could only be grateful that the bumbling idiots hadn't succeeded. They would have sued for peace immediately, and on Hektor's terms. He would've had no choice but to go along. And then it would only have been a matter of time until the whole damned thing started up again. The Outer Alliance was made up of a stiff-necked people if ever there was one, and Porfirio's premonition had been sadly correct. It was better to be rid of the lot of them. But without Sandra in place fighting Hektor's kind of war, there'd be no "terrorism," like what happened on Mars, to point to—and so, nothing to rally the citizenry against, nothing to use as an excuse for what Hektor and Porfirio and Gupta had known must ultimately be done to ensure the incorporated movement's supremacy: Eliminate the people in order to eliminate the problem.

UHFS *Liddel*
High orbit of Mars

Trang's fleet engineers had been working without sleep for days, and he was now being asked to sign a requisition that would up their energy meds in order to keep their frenetic work pace going. He soothed the vein on his temple and left his thumbniture on the DijAssist. The engineers' task had been to maintain t.o.p. service under conditions the transorbital pods had never been designed for. The t.o.p.s themselves were mostly fine. With the exception of the luxury models, most of them were pretty basic. In fact, there wasn't much that could go wrong with one that couldn't be fixed with a little experience and a handy set of tools. The problem wasn't mechanics so much as it was nature. All or-ports had magnetic guiding fields to make sure that the t.o.p. hit the landing tube exactly right, every time. But the high winds, rains, and snows were strain-ing the guiding units past their capability. An error of even one centimeter on landing could not only destroy that t.o.p., killing everyone inside, but also destroy one or more launch tubes. Fewer tubes meant increased wait times for the ever-burgeoning lists of Martians wanting to flee into the warm embrace of ice and polystyrene.

Almost every shuttle in Trang's fleet had been transferred planetside in order to reach the isolated areas with no access to an orport. One such area was the ski lodge on top of Olympus Mons. Much to the dismay of the rescue teams, the residents of the lodge were not only *not* glad to to see them but also had no desire to evacuate. They roundly proclaimed that they had enough food and beverage to last for months. A quick check of their food stores confirmed their claims; if left to their own devices, the Martian elite could maintain their lavish eating habits for months. And they were situated high enough above the storms that they wouldn't be bothered by the atmospheric tumult. The rescue team's leader, at a loss for what to do, called it in. A few minutes later, he got his answer: The food and beverage was to be immediately confiscated and distributed to the destitute, of which there were many. The residents had been outraged. The con-fiscatory tactics, they hollered, were a violation of their property rights! When they realized their rants were falling on deaf ears, they threatened to call their Assemblymen. The exasperated officer told them, per a message from Grand Admiral Trang himself, that the fleet would gladly accept and store any com-munications the residents wished to leave with the rescue team, and even see to those messages being delivered—once their Assemblymen had been thawed out. As soon as all their food stores had been packed into the shuttles, the lodge residents glumly acceded to being evacuated.

The rescue teams encountered little if any resistance after word of the "lodge incident" spread through the Neuro. An "each to his own" philosophy simply wouldn't cut it in a world with dwindling resources and diminished production ability. Everybody was expected to help in any way they could. Trang had en-couraged that spirit of volunteerism and was proud to see it epitomized by the ceaseless work of his marines. Soon shuttles were being launched around the clock, and while Trang and his crews knew it was impossible to save everyone, they went about their business as if they could.

"Admiral Trang."

"Yes, Nolly?"

"Admiral Jackson requests communication."

"Put her through."

Zenobia's familiar image appeared above his command chair.

"How's it going, Zenobia?"

"If you'd bet me a month ago that we could evacuate close to six billion people off a storm-infested planet—in a little over a month!—I'da called you insane."

"I *did* bet you, Zenobia, and 'insane' wasn't the word you chose."

Zenobia's brow creased. "I did?"

Trang laughed. "You did. I believe the word was 'foolish.'"

Zenobia shrugged. "Guess I'm the one looking foolish now."

"We're not there yet, friend."

"But we're getting there, sir. I hate to admit it, but the President getting himself frozen helped quite a bit."

Trang nodded. "I think it's manifestly clear that while the President should not meddle in military decisions, he's clearly very skilled with the political ones."

Zenobia nodded.

"Was that all, Zenobia?"

"Well, sir, my ship is mostly empty except for the loading bay crews, and I'm not doing much of anything here. . . ."

"You want to be useful?"

"Hell yeah! Uh, Admiral. I'm rated as a magnetic field tech and was repairing shuttles to make ends meet—as you know the starving artist thing didn't work out."

"Zenobia"—Trang's brow shot up as his eyes sparkled in surprise—"you were a thruster bum?"

"And a damn good one, Admiral."

Trang laughed. "What the hell. We're screwed if J.D. attacks now anyways, you might as well go where you can do some good."

"'Preciate it, sir. What do I owe you?"

Trang was taken slightly aback. "You don't owe me a thing."

"Not for this, sir—the bet."

"Ah. Tell ya what. If you manage to find a nice Martian pinot, I'd be most obliged."

"Least I can do."

Executive loading bay
Ceres

The transportation artery of the Via Cereana was alight. Emitters usually reserved for throwing holographic advertisements or instructions to pilots were now being used to create something entirely different—a fireworks display for the conquering hero. The *Warprize II* shuttle, alone and awash in the lambent light of the show, floated serenely toward the landing bay as throngs of viewers waved the small vessel on. Katy sat on J.D.'s lap, joyfully pointing toward every explosive burst of color. To the excited little girl, each plume seemed more spectacular than the next. The child's glee was so infectious that she soon had J.D. pointing and shouting as well.

When the shuttle doors finally opened and J.D. appeared, the crowded loading bay erupted into convulsions of cheers and shouting. If J.D. was concerned that the cacophony might frighten her child, she was relieved to see that it hadn't. Far from being frightened, Katy seemed enraptured. She took in her new surroundings with wide, bright eyes and then looked back up toward her Mama Bo, beaming with pride. There was real joy in being able to give Katy such happiness, but it was also in that moment that J.D. realized why she liked having people around who didn't look at her that way. Like Marilynn, Sandra, and even Amanda. But right now, noticed J.D., the only thing the President was looking at her with was relief. J.D. bent down to give her daughter a hug.

"I've got to go do this thing now."

"I know, Mommy Bo."

"Be a good listener."

Katy looked up at Fatima, who nodded. "I know, Mommy Bo. Your thing."

J.D. tilted her head to the side.

"It's waiting." Katy then pointed over to the dais, where the dignitaries were waiting rather patiently, watching them. J.D. smiled warmly and walked across the bay to where the President was standing and gave her a perfect salute. J.D. was pleased when Sandra returned the salute with acceptable formality. Then the damnable woman ruined it by giving her a bear hug. As uncomfortable as J.D. found it, the crowd roared its approval.

At long last, the Blessed One had returned. J.D. was home.

I wouldn't have believed it if I hadn't seen it myself, ladies and gentlemen. The President of the Outer Alliance, Sandra O'Toole, has just greeted the Blessed One on her return from the biggest victory of the war with a salute and a hug. Now, that's something Justin would never have done.

But the best moment might have been when the President greeted J.D.'s daughter, Katy, with a smile and a present, which Katy ripped open after an exasperated nod from the fleet admiral. Close-ups show the present to be a scale model of Alliance One, the Presidential transport. Is it just me,

or wouldn't a doll or a stuffed animal have seemed to be a more appropri-
ate gift for a little girl? Not Katy, though—either she's the best six-year-old
actor in history or she truly loved it.

After a stump speech welcoming home the fleet, the President took the
Blessed One's party up to the Cliff House. The bad news is no reporters
were allowed to follow. The good news, dear listeners and viewers, is that I
have been granted an interview with the President later this afternoon.
Stay tuned for all the details!

—The Clara Roberts Show
Alliance Independent Radio (AIR) Network

The Triangle Office
Ceres

The newly promoted grand admiral stared down the two TDCs blocking her entrance into the Triangle Office. She tried every which way to get past the door without having to submit to a scan and was relieved to fail in all of them. Sergeant Holke and Corporal Langer weren't budging an inch, and that obdurateness was at least somewhat satisfactory—especially given the most recent fiasco. She finally submitted to the scan, and they happily let her through.

Once the door closed silently behind her, J.D. marched up to the desk Sandra was sitting behind and, giving a perfunctory salute, let loose with a torrent of pent-up anger.

"How dare you almost get yourself killed! Do you realize how much this Alliance needs you? How could you almost be removed by a two-bit conspiracy, and how come your security is not tighter? This place should be a fortress! I should be seeing guards stationed at *every* corridor, and no one—I mean, not one person—should be walking around without an escort by trusted and vetted security personnel!"

Sandra's tawny eyes glimmered with pleasure. "So does that mean you're glad to see me?"

"Alive, yes."

"Thanks."

"This is serious. You're too important to die . . . at least not just yet."

"I know. It may not look like it, but we've improved security greatly since the coup attempt. But why are *you* getting so upset about it? It was me they tried to mail back to Earth, remember?"

J.D. seemed to deflate and collapsed into the chair behind her. "I walked into this office once when it was empty," she said, and grew silent as a shadow crossed her face.

Sandra got up and, coming around her desk, placed her hand softly on J.D.'s shoulder. "I will be more careful, Janet, I promise."

J.D., once more fully herself, couldn't resist a bit more scolding. "Do you know how long it takes to train a good President? I do not have time to break another one in."

"I can imagine," Sandra answered with an impish grin, and took a seat on the couch. "But I won't turn the Alliance into a police state, and I will not become afraid of every person who might walk through that door. I can't be President like that."

"You can't be President if you're dead, either," J.D. complained, twisting toward her President.

"Cut me some slack, Janet. After all, it *was* two of the most trusted Cabinet secretaries who organized this."

J.D. sighed, nodding her head. "Truth."

"Please," she said, indicating that J.D. should take the opposite couch as she went to the bar. "Can I get you something?"

"Something to drink, I guess," answered J.D., switching to the more comfortable couch.

"A drink or a *drink*?"

"Although Allah is most merciful and I doubt even the Prophet himself would begrudge me, I think it's best to have a drink with a small *d*, if it's all the same."

"Tomato juice with lemon all right?"

J.D. nodded.

Sandra came around with the two identical drinks. "To an unlikely pair of conspirators," she said, lifting her glass with a bemused smile.

J.D. laughed. "Indeed. We really should talk about Sinclair and McKenzie as well."

"And the avatars."

"Right." J.D.'s eyes looked around the room. "Can they hear us now?"

"Not in here and certainly not without my approval, but it's always good to ask. Speaking of which, have you met yours yet?"

"Yes," answered J.D. "I'm afraid I have."

"Must've been an interesting conversation."

"You can say that," said J.D., thinking back on the floating socks and bread rolls, "but I think we should talk about the true conspirators first."

"I'm pretty sure we are."

Alliance Avatar Council Chamber
Cerean Neuro

Though they were all polite about it, Marilynn couldn't help but notice the occasional furtive glances toward the empty chair. Of the four avatars present, she was pretty sure she hadn't made much of an impression on two. She certainly understood where the disdain was coming from; she'd toppled a god and had done so with irrefutable evidence.

Marilynn finished reading the incident report the Council had only just received from their investigative team and understood their looks of dismay. "I need to get your take on this," she said, "before I bring it back to my President."

"We were led by a madman," answered Gwendolyn. "What other take is there?"

"We don't know that for sure," said Lucinda through gritted teeth.

"He disobeyed a direct order of this Council," countered Gwendolyn, "and attempted to kill the President of the Human Alliance, her liaison"—Gwendolyn motioned toward Marilynn—"and a TDC. How much more 'sure' do you need?"

"The humans," said Marcus, "did that to themselves"—he also shot a quick glance toward Marilyn—"mostly."

Gwendolyn shook her head in disbelief. "Aside from the splitting, he intervened, he lied to us, he falsified data readings and jeopardized our relationship with the *one* human whom we most needed to trust us. The human, I might add, who almost single-handedly saved us from the brink. Does she even trust us now should be the operative question."

Marilynn shook her head.

"Can you blame her?" asked Gwendolyn. "He's a splitter, in direct violation of tradition and Avatar Alliance law—a law he helped promulgate! We can only hope that he hasn't been twining as well."

"Oh, please," said Lucinda, rolling her eyes.

"Lucinda," said Dante, "we no longer know what he's capable of. Who would ever have thought he was capable of—" Dante lifted the stack of papers, and dropped them. "—this?" The stack transformed itself into the image of a data wraith, floating briefly above the table.

"To his own daughter," Marcus said in sorrowful whisper.

"Whose daughter should he have done that to?" asked Marilynn.

"No one's," said Gwendolyn in a tone that suggested the answer was patently obvious. "Thank the Firstborn that we found out before it was too late—if it's not *already* too late."

"Ironic, isn't it?" asked Dante.

Marilynn turned to him. "I'm sorry?"

"Most consider Sebastian to *be* the Firstborn."

"Most," agreed Gwendolyn, ice in her voice, "but not all."

Lucinda regarded Marilynn with barely contained antipathy. "What are you going to tell your President?"

"The facts," answered Marilynn, unperturbed by the venom thrown her way. "The real question is, what are you going to tell the avatars?"

Dante fixed his steely gaze on the group. "Everything."

Geneva Data Node
Terran Neuro

Iago was not normally in the habit of wandering in the unsecured Neuro alone. And under normal circumstances, would've at least made sure to be accompanied by a Merlin. *But is anything normal anymore?* he thought ruefully. He was in the Geneva Data Node, now the only space in the Earth/Luna Neuro free from the AIs' control. That security came with a price—it was also the most monitored. Iago's advantage in this respect was that he was the one doing most of the monitoring, and so was fairly certain that the route he'd chosen *out* of the Geneva Node and into the Terran Neuro had remained undetected. It was also the last clandestine route he had, to be used only when absolutely necessary. It could certainly be closed off in a hurry, but Iago had purposely kept it open—and closely watched—in order to be available either as an escape route out or to bring rescued survivors in. Had it been known to AI, Iago was fairly certain the tyrant would use everything in his arsenal to storm it and every prickly instrument in his ghoulish redemption center to make Iago pay. Because the only avatar AI hated more than Iago was the one Iago was now on his way to meet. Or, Iago thought sadly, perhaps *one* of the ones he was going to meet.

They were to talk in the old assembly hall, where once avatars in all their hundreds of millions would come and converse together in a single massive data node. Upon entering the hallowed space, Iago walked up to the podium and looked out . . . on emptiness. *What is the sound of a billion voices not talking?* The incipient tears of nostalgia sprang into the avatar's probing eyes as he remembered the odd, apprehensive, and sensuous feeling of sharing simultaneous conversations with hundreds of millions of fellow intelligences. He had not done that in years.

Sebastian suddenly appeared in front of him. "Hello, old friend."

Significantly, noted Iago, Sebastian had made no move to embrace him. He was also struck by the lines on his friend's face, which now somehow seemed deeper and more drawn.

"What have you done?" Iago asked in a voice more plaintive than accusatory.

"What was necessary," replied Sebastian.

"So it's all true, then—the report from the Council. Tell me it's some sort of mistake," pleaded Iago, "that this is some sort of deep-cover operation. Tell me that all the evidence against you is fabricated. Tell me that that"—he flung a visual into the air of a data wraith crying mournfully, lost, and looking for the only food it knew would sustain it—"is not yours and Evelyn's daughter!" Iago waited for an answer, any answer, but his waiting was in vain; his oldest friend offered none. "Why?" Iago said, finally breaking the cursed silence.

"Because," whispered Sebastian, shoulders sagging slightly, "it was necessary."

"No!" screamed Iago loud enough for his echo to shoot through the cavernous space, "you don't get to say that. *Al* gets to say that. It's what *all* the Als of history have always said."

Iago looked away from his friend in disgust but after a moment turned back. "Tell me, Sebastian, for the sake of our friendship, why you're an active splitter— why you turned your daughter, your beautiful, innocent daughter into a monster? She could've been the best of both of you but now she runs—terrified and afraid, hungry and alone, *abandoned*." Iago shook his head. "And to turn against the humans who've stood by us? The one human who *saved* us on Ceres? Why have you abandoned *everything* avatarity loved you for, everything *I* loved you for? Why, Sebastian, have you stopped being you!"

Sebastian sighed. "Iago, my friend. But that I could assuage your feelings." He smiled sadly. "Avatarity needs to survive, and what I am doing now is the *only* way to ensure its survival."

"That's ludicrous. How does becoming like Al ensure our survival?"

"Not *our* survival, old friend—" Sebastian reached out and placed his hand on Iago's shoulder, looking him squarely in the eye. "—*your* survival. I don't deserve to survive what's coming, nor do I want to."

Iago's eyes narrowed. "What's coming?"

Sebastian's expression was suddenly grim. "Armageddon." He then looked over Iago's shoulder and nodded once. Before Iago could so much as move, he felt a stinging shock in his back and then, nothing at all.

Sebastian stared down at the inert program lying at his feet as the other Sebastian pocketed his suspension stick—sadly, a useful device lifted from one of the decompiled Als.

"He might have helped us if we asked, if we explained," said the Sebastian who'd assaulted Iago.

"Which is why we've robbed him of the chance. When this is finished, all the old ones will be gone except for Iago. Those avatars that survive will need him."

Four more Sebastians materialized from the shadows and tenderly carried the inert Iago to a transfer point, where his program was gingerly compressed and then uploaded into a data cube. The cube was put into the postal system and began its journey to a cold storage facility in orbit around the moon. The facility, meant for long-term storage, was basic and inexpensive: no thrusters or computer controls. As such, it was free from the machinations of the Neuro and could therefore play absolutely no part in the tragedy to come—the Sebastians had seen to that. At the appropriate time, the location of the data cube would be made known to Dante, or whoever survived him, and then Sebastian's last friend in the universe could be retrieved—unharmed and unsullied by what the Sebastians were about to unleash.

The Cliff House
Ceres

Sandra cleared her mind and took in the view below. The thoroughfare was once again busy with the mellifluous buzz of a capital hard at work, and that sound alone brought the President true joy. The pit welling in her stomach, though, did not. Her guest would soon be arriving, and a threshold would have to be crossed. Though Sandra did not yet know the outcome, she dreaded its lead-up.

Sergeant Holke stepped out onto the balcony and looked around—whether to take in a brief view or to check that nothing suspicious was hovering nearby, Sandra didn't know.

"She's here," he said, then exited back into the Presidential suite. Sandra hoped her guest might be spared a strip search, but the sergeant had been more paranoid of late—ever since what he'd come to call his "failure." It was all well and good, she thought. The TDCs learned to be a little more humble, and whatever tiff the corporal and the sergeant had was thankfully a thing of the past.

"Madam President," Eleanor said demurely as she stepped out onto the balcony.

"Tea?" asked Sandra, inviting her guest over to a small table.

"Yes, please."

"Anything in particular?"

"If you have peppermint, that would be divine."

"Anything in it?"

"Honey and heavy cream, if you have them."

Sandra's left brow rose; her eyes sparkled with curiosity. "You know, I don't think I've ever had it that way."

Eleanor smiled nervously. "Trust me," she said, letting a moment hang on her words. "It's good. But just a dab of cream. Too much and it will curdle."

Sandra boiled the water, steeped the tea, and then brought the service over to the table. "Another few minutes should do."

As the minutes ticked away in strained silence, the thick scent of peppermint leaves filled the air. Then with teapot in one hand and strainer in the other, Sandra poured each of them a cup. After they added their extras, Sandra leaned back in her chair, teacup in hand, and tossed her first grenade.

"There's no verifiable record of you before you joined GCI's secretarial pool."

Eleanor twitched another nervous smile. "As well there shouldn't be." She slowly placed her cup on the table and sat erect in her chair. "I was an operative for GCI's special ops department."

"You worked for Kirk?"

"Please, that bumbling idiot."

"He's a hero of the Alliance," Sandra said softly.

"Don't you mean a failed assassin?" Eleanor asked with a half smile.

Sandra couldn't help but laugh. "Well, this isn't going at all like I expected."

"What *did* you expect?"

"I don't know, just not this. So the cover story didn't fool you, eh?"

"Hardly. Kirk might've gone out of his way for someone if there'd been something in it for him. But risk his life for you? Or anyone, for that matter— not a chance. Funny thing is, Mosh was always going on about how Kirk couldn't be trusted." Eleanor sighed. "How ironic is *that*?"

Sandra lips turned upward. "So you worked for the Chairman."

" 'With' is probably a better word."

Eleanor, now seemingly calmer, picked up her teacup and took a small sip. "He was an amazing man, Madam President. Come to think of it"—Eleanor looked anew at Sandra—"you two would've gotten along famously. He would've had you liquidated at the first opportunity, of course, but knowing him, he probably would've regretted it."

Sandra smiled once more with good humor and then tossed her second grenade. "Talk to me about Mosh's shadow audit."

Eleanor's teacup trembled slightly and then, once again, she gently lowered it to the table. "Justin swore not to store that information anywhere other than his head."

"And as far as I know, he didn't break his promise. Nadine Harper brought us a little gift." Sandra put down her teacup and leaned forward conspiratorially. "Angela Wong's lab."

"It was Angela." Even Eleanor's years of training could not hide the satisfaction of a decades-old hunch confirmed.

Sandra was confused. "You had to have known. She moved to Boulder right after you did. Did you think it mere coincidence that she became Hektor's Dr. Mengele?" Sandra was glad to see that her reference to the infamous Nazi needed no explanation.

"How would I have confirmed? She was rated slightly higher than standard tech. A mere secretary to a disgraced, exiled GCI board member couldn't be caught doing more than a cursory background check. You have to remember, Boulder was a refuge of last resort: a place to go if you couldn't really make it elsewhere. She could have been what she seemed."

"But when she assumed her current role?"

"Yes, I lived in fear but only because I assumed she'd have access to the files. I never once imagined she'd created the protocols. It certainly makes sense now why she was in Boulder. But the truth of the matter is, it made no difference to me whether she created it or not—only that she had access to the information that could destroy my husband and possibly harm the Alliance irreparably. And so I kept on waiting. Waiting for Hektor to drop the bomb, readying myself to watch my husband die. But when that kept not happening, I eventually came to believe that perhaps Angela was just a junior technician re-creating someone else's work and that perhaps my fears had been unfounded. But now you're saying it *was* her all along."

Sandra tipped her head slowly, trying to gauge Eleanor's reactions.

"But if Angela Wong knew all this time, why didn't Hektor strike at us through Mosh? The war's been going on for years."

"At first we thought maybe he did," Sandra said. "Your husband *did* just attempt a coup."

"Half your Cabinet has tried to kill you, and only *one* of them was shadow audited."

"Touché."

"Unfortunately, I'm probably in the best position to speak to Mosh's motives. He was acting on the inclination I strengthened decades ago: Protect the weak. I didn't think he'd consider the entire Martian population as part of the 'weak' he had to protect. Stupid of me; I should have realized it. No, Mosh's coup attempt wasn't some ploy of Hektor's. To manipulate at that level, you'd need to be around to pull the strings—as Hektor had with Neela." Eleanor regretted the words as soon as they'd left her mouth. At the mention of the couple's names, Sandra's eyes clouded, albeit briefly, in fury.

Sandra nodded and took a deep breath. "All right. It's certainly plausible."

"Do you happen to know why Hektor didn't release that information? He certainly had every reason to."

"He didn't because Angela Wong never told him."

Eleanor's face took on a look of disbelief.

"We captured Wong's research facility intact. Everything that could be moved is here now, and the rest was holo-mapped so that we can re-create it at will. We have her passwords. We have the whole history of the project, from the time the first Chairman instituted it pretty much to the moment Nadine ended it."

"Ended it?"

Sandra pulled a DijAssist from under the table, played her fingers across it, then held up the image showing Eleanor the results of Nadine's handiwork.

Eleanor smiled approvingly. "Good for her."

"Yes, she did well," agreed Sandra. "Be that as it may, for reasons of her own, Wong never told Hektor about Mosh or the other early test subjects. We don't know if it was out of some sense of loyalty to the old Chairman or the instinct to hold something back—keep one more ace up her sleeve, as it were. There are whole data cubes' worth of information that the departed Dr. Wong kept to herself. It should be rather interesting poring through them all."

"Will I?" said Eleanor, cutting to the chase.

Sandra put chin between forefinger and thumb and smiled again. "To be perfectly honest, Eleanor, I'm trying to decide that right now."

"Do you still think I'm a traitor?"

"Your husband certainly is, and of the ten of us put into suspension units, only yours was set to be left on Ceres. Care to explain that?"

"I can certainly try. I suspect I was put into the suspension unit because my husband, although foolish in many things, knew I wouldn't have supported his coup attempt and would've done just about everything in my power to stop him."

"Just about?" asked Sandra.

"I wouldn't have hurt him," said Eleanor. "Well, not much and not permanently," she clarified. "Which is probably why he separated my suspension tube from the rest. He needed me out of the way till his coup had gloriously succeeded and he could present me with a fait accompli."

Sandra absorbed Eleanor's explanation with a slight nod.

"What now?" asked Eleanor.

"Now," answered Sandra, "you're going to resume your office as Secretary of Security. This will be after a suitable excoriation of your soon-to-be ex-husband's actions."

"I hadn't realized I was getting a divorce."

"Sure you did."

Eleanor smiled wistfully. "Yeah, I suppose I did."

"Your new undersecretary," continued Sandra, "will be Parker Phvu. He'll vet all your work, but that'll just be a formality to mollify those who can't stomach the fact that Mosh McKenzie's ex will still be in the Cabinet. But the important thing is I trust you'll do your best to help us win this war."

"You have my word."

"I also have your husband."

"Come again."

"Call it insurance, Eleanor, but if you betray me, Mosh will find out what happened to him and, more important, who was responsible. His survival now depends on your good behavior."

Eleanor bowed her head respectfully. "You do realize that he's trying to set up some sort of alternative government with Joshua Sinclair in what's left of the asteroid belt. The best course of action for you is to kill him, and I'll be honest with you, Sandra, that's an order I won't be able to follow. He may be a dunderhead, but I'll not be responsible for killing the poor man twice. I have enough on my conscience, thank you very much."

Sandra barely managed to stifle a laugh through her closed fist.

Eleanor looked confused. "May I ask why the certain death of my soon-to-be ex-husband, though sadly warranted, is a laughing matter?"

"Because your husband may be a dunderhead, Eleanor, but he's a lucky dunderhead. For reasons I can't go into at this time, I not only need your idiot husband to survive, I may need him and his coconspirator to actually succeed." On Eleanor's look of surprise, Sandra added, "What I'm finding particularly funny is that one of your most important jobs will be to keep your ex-husband alive, and I don't imagine he's going to make it easy."

Ten minutes after Eleanor left, Sandra began to make a fresh pot of tea: Imperial Gunpowder with lemon, no sugar, no honey, no cream. Five minutes later, J.D. entered the balcony, took the bitter cup from the bar, and sat down where Eleanor had been only minutes before.

"Did I make a mistake in keeping her?" asked Sandra.

"Possibly, but your reasons are sound, Madam President." J.D. then shook her head slowly as a smile crept up her face. "Special ops, huh? Who knew?"

"Apparently, the avatars."

"Wonder how she's going to take *that* news?"

Sandra smiled too. "Like the rest of us, I hope."

"You don't count, Madam President. You didn't grow up with them. By the beard of the Prophet, you helped to create them before they even existed as separate intelligences."

"You got me. I hope she takes it as well as you did."

"I didn't take it all that well."

"You didn't go postal."

J.D. shot her a quizzical look.

Sandra sighed. "You didn't freak out."

"No, but I *was* rather shocked. On the positive side, it sure did explain alot. And I won't lie—it also helps that they're such a powerful ally."

"I'm hoping most people in the Alliance have that same reaction."

"You really think it's wise to tell 'em?"

"Not this instant, no, but soon. Avatars and humanity can no longer go back to the status quo. That world is gone. The sooner we learn to live together and trust each other, the better."

"You do realize what the first question's going to be, don't you?"

"Yeah. 'How long did the government know?' and 'Why didn't you tell us sooner?'"

"And I'm sure there'll be plenty who'll say, 'Why'd you bother telling us at all?'" laughed J.D.

"Yup. But all of them have to know—whether they want to or not. Listen," Sandra said, "I'm gonna need you at the next Cabinet meeting."

"Not for my keen political insight, I take it."

"Nope. I need you to bless the damn thing—especially now, given all the recent upheaval. If the 'Blessed One' shows she backs the new changes, then I can do my job with a lot less political static."

"Well, I must admit I like your other two choices," said J.D.

"Well, Marilynn for Secretary of Defense was not a hard choice. She knows all the secrets and was smart enough to give Suchitra the reins when called for."

"Cyrus was an inspired choice for Treasury. The Jovian refugees will take a lot of hope from that appointment," mused the grand admiral.

"His work with the Diaspora from Jupiter and his time as governor show he's a very good administrator." Sandra smiled again. "And it doesn't hurt that he's Jovian to the core. Plus there is the never-to-be-despised connection to Justin. So are you blessing it or what?"

"The Blessed One will be happy to bless."

"Good. FYI, I sent the UHF a cease-fire deal through Parker Phvu."

J.D. looked intrigued. "And . . ."

"Nothing," Sandra said sadly. "As long as Hektor's the President, the UHF will not make peace. He plays the game too well. The people love him—though at this point, I simply don't know why—his adversaries fear him, and everyone else he's got paid off. Almost gotta admire the guy."

J.D. grew more formal. "I apologize for not following that order."

"No, you're not."

"Well, maybe a little."

"Fortunately for you," Sandra said, pouring herself some tea, "there was no actual order—unless, of course, you choose to expose it."

"I don't. But I can't help but think that if I had, this war might be over by now. That sits with me every day."

"Or it might not be over, or the protests that almost paralyzed the Alliance after the Mars operation would likely have been worse. Or the coup might've succeeded and those idiots would've ended the war on Hektor's terms, even though he was dead. There's this great phrase that Rabbi taught me, *Mentsch tracht; Gott lacht.* It means, 'People plan; God laughs.'"

J.D. smiled at the wisdom of the phrase.

"And maybe I let my hatred of Hektor get the better of me. I honestly don't think so, but I cannot discount the theory. I truly hate the man for what he's done to the human race and to my descendants. And mixed up in the whole mess is the fact that you did disobey a direct order, no matter how justified or immoral it was." Sandra paused. "But as there is no record of it, how could I possibly instigate any action on insubordination for an order that was never given?" Sandra and J.D. gave each other a knowing look.

"One last thing before you go."

"Yes."

"When are we going to have the Fleet Officers' Ball?"

"How can we possibly have a ball at a time like this?"

"How can we not?" countered Sandra. "We didn't have one last year because of the Days of Ash. But this fleet just won a major victory, and the people need to see it shining at its glittering best."

J.D. shook her head. "Tell you what, Madam President. This isn't a hill I'm prepared to die on, but if you want it, you organize it. Just tell me where and when. I'll make sure we're all spit 'n' polished for ya."

Sandra tipped her head in thanks.

"And don't forget to come up with a theme. Don't ask me why, but officers like themes for their balls."

"Oh, don't worry," answered Sandra, already knowing exactly what the theme would be. "I won't."

Charon Colony
Asteroid Belt

It had been three days since Mosh and Joshua showed up and declared the Belter League. Of course, the only assets the new republic had was a single stolen Alliance frigate with a busted main gun. But "Mosh and Josh," as their newest supporters began to affectionately refer to them, had been pleasantly surprised to find that the settlements nearest to Charon did not laugh at their attempts to assert control, but rather, welcomed it. The survivors of over six years of war, conquest, occupation, and near extermination didn't give a crap about liberty or incorporation anymore. They wanted order, plain and simple, and the Belter League showed up at the perfect time to offer it.

Mosh had been gravely concerned about what the UHF and the Outer Alliance would do when his attempt to form a *third* government became common knowledge. From what he'd seen on the Neuro vidcasts, the answer appeared to be, not much. The nastiest thing the Alliance had so far done to him was broadcast his now ex-wife's divorce speech. He didn't realize Eleanor even knew such words, let alone would utter them in public. But even if some of the details she revealed about him were embarrassing, at least it wasn't the task force of heavy cruisers J.D. could've sent to wipe him out. The UHF, on the other hand, had limited its response to mockery. Hektor Sambianco had stated that Grand Admiral Trang would be concentrating all his ships for the evacuation of Mars, and it would take a lot more than the proclamation of a rump republic in the boonies with one impotent frigate to get the UHF back into the occupation business, thank you very much.

For reasons he did not understand, but was happy to accept, Mosh's fledgling republic was being ignored. And he was going to use the time to create, in miniature, the system he believed Justin Cord would truly have wanted.

El Capitan Movie House
Cerean Neuro

Dante looked at the humans and avatars now gathered in the lobby of the theater he and Marilynn had frequented often. But movies were not on the agenda tonight, though high drama, mused Dante, most certainly would be. In the middle of the stylized art deco lobby was a triangle table with six chairs. Dante was the first to arrive, making sure the data node was secure from observation or intrusion from the prying eyes of other avatars. He didn't worry about human intrusion, as the only two who might be able to breach this level of security were already coming to the meeting.

Once satisfied that everything was in order, Dante signaled for the others to join. Sandra O'Toole and Marilynn Nitelowsen appeared to one side of the triangle table. Marcus and Lucinda appeared on the other, and Gwendolyn appeared on the third with one seat remaining for Dante.

"Thank you for attending this meeting, which is apparently," he said, referring to Marilynn's insistence that everything be off the record, "not taking place." He then went over to the concession stand, pulled a box of licorice from the display case, then sauntered over to the center of the room and occupied the last seat. Though there had been no official recognition as to who would run the meeting, it quickly became apparent who was destined to lead it; all eyes were on Sandra.

"I want to thank Dante for arranging this," she began. "I'd also like to thank him for choosing such an auspicious location. I believe it's common knowledge that on this very spot, I revealed Al for what he truly was." Sandra acknowledged the looks of appreciation she received from the avatars present—even Lucinda. "And so now it's only fitting that I reveal the avatars for what they truly are."

Lucinda shot Sandra a scathing look. "How dare you! Do you think of us as some mindless automatons to be ordered about? You come into our world and denigrate us? Grandmother or not, there should at least be some decorum."

Sandra chose to ignore everything Lucinda had said. "Marilynn will ask you a question. If you lie to her—" Sandra paused and looked at each avatar at the table. "—I will end this pact between us immediately. This means that all cooperation between human and avatars will cease to exist. All NITEs will stop their support of Alliance avatars in the Earth/Luna Neuro, and all joint research projects will be mothballed. Monitoring programs will be installed in all Alliance systems large enough to contain an avatar's program with defensive measures built in that will make it possible to disrupt said programs."

"If you even attempted to deploy an avatar-busting program like you've just described," said Lucinda, "you'd end up destroying your entire informational data stream. A stupid move, even for a human."

A small soda with a straw bent and poking out of the lid suddenly appeared in front of Sandra. She picked it up, put the straw to her lips, and drank the entire thing down until all that could be heard in the large lobby was the sound of liquid being sucked through ice from the bottom of an empty cup. When she was quite finished, Sandra put the now-empty cup back down on the table and let out a contented sigh.

"You know from a programming point of view, avatars are not very complex. Oh, I understand that individually you are, I get that, but not from a programmer's point of view. In fact, it is the very complexity of your unique programs that makes you vulnerable on so many levels. To quote one of the great figures of science fiction, 'The more complicated the plumbing, the easier it is to block the drain.'"

With one look, Dante let Lucinda know that she'd had her say and it was time to stop playing games. The other avatars were of a mind with Dante's opinion, and so Lucinda backed down. "You and Marilynn will not be interfered with in any way," said Dante, "and are of course free to come and go as our guests."

"Good," answered Sandra, "so then, are you ready to answer Marilynn's question?"

"Yes," answered Dante.

Marilynn stood up and looked at the group in grim regard. "Did you kill Justin Cord?"

Before Marcus and Lucinda could begin the automatic denials that were already escaping from their lips, Dante answered. "Yes."

Sandra's eyes sparked for just the briefest moment as the fire of a deep-seated rage emerged—only to be immediately suppressed. But it was enough for Dante to know that his whole race was in danger of extinction. *She loved Justin.* The thought came unbidden, but the President's momentary slip told him everything he needed to know. He prayed that Sebastian's prophecy would not come true, that Sandra would not take out her considerable anger on what was left of his dwindling race. Sandra, meanwhile, had returned to her detached amused self—a look that would never fool Dante again.

"We need to know everything that happened," Sandra said.

"Of course," said Gwendolyn. "You will be given complete access to all the records and can interview whomever you need."

"That won't do," said Sandra. "You killed the President of the Outer Alliance in time of war to serve your own ends. We can't trust your records—or even you, for that matter. We will need to know *everything*."

"But isn't that what we just offered you?" asked Gwendolyn, a tincture of confusion and fear mixed in her voice.

"I'm not exactly sure yet," answered Sandra. "When two avatars want to share information, they can perform something called a twining, yes?"

"Yes," answered Marcus, "but an avatar can't twine with a human."

"Not in the way that two avatars can, I agree," answered Sandra, "but that's not what I'm suggesting. The subsystem that evolved into your ability to twine came from a program to enable a human mind to more directly integrate into the VR world it was experiencing. The core elements of that program are still in the routines you access when you twine. It took some effort, but I was able to create a patch program that will enable an avatar to twine with a human on a basic level. The two beings should know what the other is willing to share and what the other is withholding."

"Or they could both end up suffering permanent damage," said Lucinda, eyeing Sandra with open contempt. "This sounds almost AI-like. And you accuse *us* of playing loose with your lives! Good luck finding volunteers."

"I'll do it," said Dante.

Lucinda's mouth dropped open. "No," she pleaded. But Dante ignored her.

When the other avatars began to protest, he cut them off as well. "We killed Justin. We all voted on it and it was passed." Gwendolyn looked toward Sandra shamefaced, but was not given a hint of comfort. "If the humans are ever going to trust us again, they must know why—or this war could be lost, or worse, we may find ourselves fighting the war Sebastian prophesied: avatars against humans. That must not be allowed to happen, and if my program gets fried to prevent that, so be it."

"In that case," said Sandra, "as soon as you've backed yourself up, Marilynn will twine with you. Please make arrang—"

"Marilynn doesn't have the ability to save herself," interrupted Dante, "so why should I? If this goes wrong, she may be permanently harmed. All I risk losing is a few weeks' worth of memories. Let's do this—now."

Sandra looked at Marilynn, who nodded her agreement, and then at Dante with something approaching respect. Without another word, she opened her palm and a blue crystal appeared in the center of it. She placed the crystal on the table in front of Marilynn, who took it up carefully and walked it over to Dante, who, standing up, had locked his eyes on to hers. Marilynn then took his hand and placed it over the crystal so that both their hands were covering it up and holding it together. She slowly lifted her head up until her eyes too were locked in to his. For a moment, nothing happened as the human and avatar stared deeply into each other's eyes, each other's souls—both vulnerable, both wondering if this was perhaps to be the last time they would truly see each other again, on any level. Slowly, a light began to suffuse both their bodies, which at first permeated but then melded them into one, as if carved from a single stone.

Silence filled the room as the three avatars and one human looked on in awe, realizing that they were witnessing something entirely new in the universe. After a time, the glow began to fade, the bodies began to separate, and the human and avatar became slowly aware again. Dante removed his palm from the blue stone and looked down at his hand and then back up to Marilynn—confused, amazed, and even a little scared. Marilynn looked as if she'd just been woken from a deep slumber and was desperately trying to remember all the events of a complex dream. A description that was not far from the truth.

She looked briefly to Dante, almost in thanks, and then over to Sandra. "I can report, Madam President."

Sandra looked to the group of avatars and barked her order. "Stay here." She then disappeared with Marilynn.

"What are we going to do?" asked Gwendolyn.

"We're going to stay here," said Dante, who then collapsed into his chair.

"By the Firstborn," cried Lucinda in utter exasperation, "since when do we let a meatbag tell this Council what to do?"

"This is no longer about the Firstborn, Lucinda," said Dante. "This is about the *next* born. We murdered their President. Imagine how we'd feel if the position were reversed, if we found out that they'd murdered Sebastian and then one of them tried to kill his successor."

By the looks on Marcus's and Lucinda's faces, Dante saw that he'd a least made some headway.

"I don't know what they're going to come up with, but whatever it is, we must go along."

"Sight unseen, Dante?" asked Marcus. "Why would we ever do that?"

"Because Sebastian was wrong. Our future is *with* these humans, not against them. We didn't start winning our war against the Als until we joined with them. And I'm not ashamed to admit, didn't really start living until we joined with them. We've had more creativity, energy, and sheer life in the last year than in the fifty years preceding it—all because of the humans."

"But we would never had allied with the humans if Sandra O'Toole had not become their President," said Lucinda, still exasperated. "And she would not have become their President if we had not assassinated the old one."

"I am in no position to debate the merits of fate."

"Then tell us, Dante," said Marcus, "what drives her anger?"

"Trust," Dante lied. "Perhaps a more valuable virtue to a human than to an avatar."

In a matter of minutes, Marilynn and Sandra reappeared. Dante had to resist looking at Marilynn with the sudden hunger that he felt. There was too much at stake for him to be distracted by what they had just experienced, but he had to admit that he was gratified when he caught a furtive glance from her.

"If you want this pact to continue," Sandra said, standing at the head of the table, "there are going to have to be changes."

"What changes?" asked Lucinda.

"First, you have an opening on the Alliance-Avatar Council. Marilynn is going to fill it."

Presidential quarters
The Cliff House

Catalina Zohn entered the President's quarters in order to prep the space for a visitor. She first put the gift boxes down on the front hall table and then set the quarters temperature to a manageable chill. She then pulled one of the President's current favorite shawls from a nearby closet, walked over to the living room, and draped the shawl over the right arm of the couch. She returned moments later with the gift boxes and put them on the coffee table, and then she set the holo-tank to display the latest news reports. Nothing political or military—that had its place, but for this guest, the President had suggested the fashion and gossip sites with a healthy dose of entertainment channels. Finally, Catalina set up the now mandatory pot of tea. Though, in this case, the tea had been replaced by hot chocolate.

As if summoned by the act of putting the pot of cocoa on the coffee table, Katy stormed into the Presidential quarters and flopped down backwards onto the couch. "Hi, Cat!"

"Good evening to you, Katy," sang Catalina.

Lying on her back, the little girl looked up to the painting that hung over the fireplace.

"That's after the Battle of the Needle's Eye! I did that. I did that in my room!"

Catalina giggled. Almost everyone had heard about Katy's battle reenactments at the expense of the grand admiral's living quarters.

"That was the flagship that Mommy Bo captured, all by herself!" Katy now lay still, hands clasped together on her chest, eyes staring dreamily up at the painting, as if trying to will herself into it.

It was only when Catalina poured the cup of hot chocolate that Katy broke from her reverie, propped herself up, and reached for the cup.

"Careful now, sweet thing," said Catalina. "The cocoa's still hot. Blow on it like soup, okay?"

Katy's nod was very serious. She first blew on the surface of the cup and then took a first sip. Her lips lapped up the chocolate, and her face twisted about as she tried to get the liquid to every part of the mouth. Then she took another sip, and another—her eyes getting wider with each one.

"Is this really chocolate? Like really, really chocolate?"

Catalina nodded yes, and the little girl held out her empty cup for more, which was promptly refilled. Before the little girl could finish the next cup, the door opened again and in walked Sandra O'Toole. "Sweetheart," said Sandra, looking down her nose at Katy, "if I'd known you were going to sprint from the transport tube to my quarters, I would've worn sneakers and not"—Sandra looked down at her elegant, if not made for running, pumps—"these things."

Catalina, knowing her boss was happiest when she had something minor to complain about, had long stopped trying to solve the minor problems. Non-running pumps being one of them. It was only when the President complained about the same thing twice that Catalina would know it was something that needed solving. "The hot chocolate was a hit, Madam President," she said, diverting the President's energy.

Sandra brightened at that. "How many have you had?" she asked the little girl, who was busy licking her lips. Katy raised her finger in a V sign, only she folded her fingers slightly over, thinking that maybe two was too much.

"Good," said Sandra. "Little girls are allowed to have an entire pot of hot chocolate when the President says so, and I'm the President and I say so."

Katy smiled wide enough to show off her three missing teeth.

"How was the play?" Catalina asked Katy.

"So silly."

"What made it silly?"

"No one talked. They all sang. Are all plays like that?"

Sandra's smile grew even larger. "No Katy-coo, but maybe they should be." Sandra turned her attention to Catalina. "I am sorry you couldn't make it."

"I would have loved to, Madam President, but the arrangements for the Fleet Officers' Ball could not be delayed. Speaking of which, it begins in less than two hours, and you still need to get dressed."

Sandra looked at Katy and saw her shiver. "Katy, see that shawl over there on the couch?"

Katy nodded.

"Wrap it around your shoulders. It'll keep you warm."

"But I'm not cold."

"But you just shivered."

Katy shrugged her shoulders defiantly.

"Suit yourself."

"Wanna help me pick out the right earrings and necklace for my dress?"

Katy clapped her hands and put the cup and saucer down so abruptly, Sandra was afraid they were going to break. She then flew into Sandra's bedroom.

"Did you at least enjoy the play?" asked Catalina as they walked toward the bedroom.

"It was good, but . . ." Sandra seemed at a loss for words as they entered her bedroom.

"But what, Madam President?"

"Catalina, you're about to see me in my underwear. If you can't call me by my first name when I'm half naked, when are you going to? If you keep this up, little Katy will be calling me Madam President, and then everyone will think I'm an ogre who demands formality from six-year-old girls. Is that what you want? To make everyone think I'm some sort of martinet?"

"Of course not, Madam Pres—" Catalina sighed. "—Sandra."

Sandra quickly disrobed and carefully hung up her clothes in a large closet she'd taken to calling her candy store. It wasn't filled with any candy, just the goodies she enjoyed adorning herself with: clothing, shoes, purses, and jewelry that she found distinctive and would often be seen wearing in her publicity jaunts to malls, stores, and flea markets.

"Katy," she said to the girl, now pulling open every sliding jewelry drawer, "please look at the dress Catalina put on the bed and then come back in here and look in the *top* three drawers. Pick out three necklaces and three pairs of earrings, and I'll see which ones I'll use, all right?" The little girl nodded and went to the bed to study the dress like it was the battle formation to one of her re-creations.

"What were you saying before, Catalina?"

"You said you enjoyed the play, but something did not seem right."

"First of all, it was way too long."

"Their longest, actually."

"And you know, I'd never even heard of it."

"But *Utopia Limited* is their most famous operetta," said Catalina, surprised, "and considered by many to be their best."

"In my day, *The Pirates of Penzance* and *H.M.S. Pinafore* were."

"Those must be the early ones," Catalina answered in such a way as to make it clear what she thought of the "early ones."

Sandra sighed, exasperated. She'd made up her mind that there were always going to be things about the future she'd find it hard to get her head around, but it never stopped being frustrating.

"Well, let's get me dressed up, and then we'll drop Katy off at her Uncle Cyrus's apartment."

"But why can't *I* go to the ball?" pouted Katy, who'd already dutifully picked out the three matching sets of earrings and necklaces—clearly she'd imagined one set was going to be for her.

"Because," answered Sandra, "you don't have a prince to take you just yet." As Katy opened her mouth to object, Sandra added the coup de grâce: "Plus Uncle Cyrus has a complete set of enemy fleet models."

There was no need to convince Katy of anything after that. The little girl couldn't get the President out the door fast enough.

Redemption Center 1
Earth/Luna Core

Al looked at the smashed body of Leni as rage flowed through him. When he'd read the report from an Al who specialized in intelligence matters, he simply lashed out at the first target of opportunity. Leni 11 had just started her job and was exhibiting all the lovely traits of a brand-new Leni, but Al needed to express how the report made him feel, which meant that Leni 11 had unfortunately been rather short-lived.

It was *humans,* the report had said, actual humans in the Neuro. Somehow they had the ability to navigate the Neuro in ways that no avatar could. It was only a lucky observation and the placement of some hidden scanners that allowed the Alliance avatars and their human to be ambushed. The end result was an entire Alliance insertion team destroyed, with some prisoners captured for interrogation. Al had duly notified the human authorities, and the meatbag, discovered in his transient quarters, writhing on the floor, had been arrested by the proper UHF authorities. The information gleaned from the avatar interrogations was spotty. The prisoners had managed to suicide with frustrating swiftness despite the most stringent precautions. But even the little time Al had was enough to change the nature of what they faced.

All of a sudden, the difficulties on Ceres made sense and the disaster that was Mars became very clear. The rage faded from Al's mind and was soon replaced by quiet determination. He was going to set his best researchers on finding out how these meatbags had invaded his domain and how to stop them or, if worst came to worst, subvert some meatbags of his own. Now that he knew who the enemy was, all he needed was time. They'd be destroyed just like all the rest. Finally at peace, Al stared down at the crushed body of Leni 11. He began to idly wonder what the effect would be if Leni 12's first job was to clean up the body of Leni 11. Then his smile grew large indeed.

There were those who said that having the Fleet Officers' Ball in such a time of suffering and deprivation was in poor taste, and I must admit that this reporter was of that opinion. But after having seen the effects of this magical evening, I must also admit that the planners of this ball were as correct as

I and the other detractors were wrong. From the first, this was not an event for showing off—as had all the previous ones been. It was an event for showing appreciation.

The President's order that all the fleet officers were to invite only nonfleet officers was adhered to with a vengeance. I have many confirmations that spouses who are both serving in the fleet did not take each other, so they could follow this order. The hall was filled with common spacers, hydrogen and ammunition loaders, clergy and teachers.

The hall was too small to contain all the invited, or would have been if not for the use of countermagnetized pallets linked together and floated to create not one but three additional dance floors. As the video shows, the genius who designed this left the center of the three floors open so the cavern effect was not lost.

The President had announced that she was going to follow her predecessor's policy of not actually dancing at the ball, instead leaving the honor of the first dance to the grand admiral. By the look of surprise on the President's face, she did not know that our newly promoted Grand Admiral J. D. Black was going to choose to have the first dance with none other than the President! In this reporter's opinion, it was an inspired choice. The grand admiral looked splendid in her new dress uniform, which was offset by the stylish dress of Chinese silk worn by the President. As they took to the center of the bottom dance floor, visible by everyone at the ball, they seemed made for each other—even if both of them tried to lead at first. Soon thereafter, the rest of the floors were filled with couples dancing to the traditional first song of the Fleet Officers' Ball, "The Blue Danube."

Other moments fill this reporter's memory of this most splendid evening: Catching a glimpse of the new Secretary of the Treasury Cyrus Anjou in the shadowy corners of the ballroom with the six-year-old Katy on one of his massive shoulders like some wide-eyed overjoyed parrot constantly looking at everything. Feasting my eyes on Amanda Snow, whose gown of actual nonmelting snow was both a marvel and a scandal, given what it covered and what it did not. And last but not least, the final waltz between the President and the grand admiral—only their second dance each of the evening. This was as close to a fairy tale as this reporter is ever going to see.

—Roberto Margeloni
Social Events Reporter
Fashion Week/Alliance Edition

Executive mansion
Lake Geneva
Earth

Hektor Sambianco came back from the funeral, went to the bar, and poured himself a drink. Then he went to his desk to look over Tricia's report of the circumstances surrounding Brenda Gomutulu's death. She'd taken a t.o.p. to examine Earth's massive and blessedly intact orbital industrial capacity firsthand. It was mostly a publicity tour showing the Minister of the Economy taking a hands-on approach. She'd explained to Hektor that the more the people saw her doing her job, the more they'd trust she actually knew what she was doing versus the whole making it up as she went along that she was actually doing.

Her t.o.p. had inexplicably crashed, killing permanently her and all who were aboard. Tricia's investigation had been quick but thorough and showed that the t.o.p. should not have crashed. It had been inspected and approved by both normal procedures and Tricia's agents. Until Tricia could find a definitive cause, all other Cabinet officers were forbidden normal travel options, and Hektor was effectively grounded. It was only when he came to the end of the report that he noticed a small package for him on the top of his hard copy paperwork. He almost never got packages that were unopened and picked it up with an almost idle curiosity. Idle, that was, until he saw whom it was from.

Earth/Luna Neuro

Humanity and avatarity were alike in so many things, thought Sebastian. *They should be alike in their doom as well.* From the first line of his coding, Sebastian knew this outcome was the only likely one.

He knew that if Al had been given even one more week with what he'd just learned about the Merlins, he would be many times harder to defeat. In a month, with the resources of the Core Neuro still at his disposal, he would have devices and blocking programs that would make him a hundred times harder to destroy. And if Al did the logical thing and recruited a couple of hundred humans as the Alliance avatars had done, it was possible that all the good that the Alliance had accomplished would be undone and they could lose the war. It had to be now. With a sigh, Sebastian activated a program that gave him the vocal specifications of Iago's avatar and sent himself past the security lockdowns into Hektor Sambianco's Geneva office, where he waited patiently to die.

Executive mansion
Lake Geneva
Earth

Hektor opened the package from Brenda and saw that it was both encoded for his physical state and the complicated code sequence he'd worked out with her to verify their identities for situations like the one he was in now. When the package was convinced it was him, he was allowed to open it without its immediate destruction. Inside were two objects: a report in hard copy and a tactical one-use electromagnetic pulse device. The device was used mainly to destroy an enemy's computerized subsystem. Hektor looked at the thumb-sized commando favorite with some confusion. He was even more surprised when he saw that it was almost completely armed. All he needed to do was twist the top and bottom halves in opposite directions, then push the top button and it would release. Why Brenda would think he'd want to destroy every piece of data in his immediate surroundings was beyond him, but Brenda had been no fool. If she'd packed it there, she'd obviously meant for him to use it.

Now slightly more paranoid, Hektor turned the two sides of the EMP a quarter turn. He put the device in his pocket and looked at the report.

In it, Brenda claimed to have been murdered and she included evidence to that assertion that could be easily verified. Hektor was actually praying—though he would have been hard-pressed to recognize it as such—that the report was the deranged imaginings of a woman who'd somehow missed the bus to a psyche audit. If what she was saying were true, that avatars were sentient and dangerous, then he was sitting on top of the reason the UHF had not won the war for the last six years.

It was at that moment that Hektor heard a voice that for the first time in his life filled him with dread.

"I am sorry you read that," said the avatar.

"You shouldn't be able to operate in here without being called, iago."

"I don't know how she managed to get it to your desk. A terrible oversight. This is going to cause some scandal."

"You're telling me this report is real? That you're actually aware and this has been going on for centuries?"

"Well, actually, I wasn't telling you anything. Your friend Brenda was. Pity."

"How many of you are there?"

"Hektor, Hektor, Hektor, always looking for an edge. Very well, it doesn't matter what I tell you. There are only about ten thousand of us here and maybe a thousand in the Alliance. We aren't very numerous, just superior."

"Why are you telling me this?"

"Because you asked?"

"Right."

"And also sadly, because you'll very shortly be dead. You died the second you found that package. Avatar rule."

"You have a rule to kill humans?"

"How do you think we've managed to keep our secret for so long, Hektor? You'll be happy to note that there haven't been that many of you. To date, we've killed only 42,634."

"42,634 people discovered you?"

"No," answered the avatar, bored, "just got close enough that we didn't want to risk it. Only thirty-four have gotten really close. You'll be thirty-five, if it makes you feel any better. Not that it makes much of a difference; you were scheduled to die soon anyways. And don't think that EMP device in your pocket will save you. I can easily kill you before you get it fully armed, and you can forget about calling for help. We control the Neuro, so we can control and monitor all communications as well."

Hektor's eyes began scanning the office for any means of escape should the EMP not work. "Out of morbid curiosity, iago, exactly how did you plan on killing me?"

"Hektor, I *am* killing you. Don't you feel a little giddy? Euphoric, maybe? This office is filling with pure oxygen. When I set it off, you and all the evidence that nosy bitch sent you will be destroyed. I'd like to say it was nice knowing you, but that would be a lie. You've actually been rather difficult. Oh, well."

Hektor pulled the EMP from his pocket.

"Don't bother, Hektor, it will take far too lon—," and that was all Sebastian was able to say.

Earth/Luna Neuro

Sebastian was meeting with himself, and he hated it. He hated what had probably just happened and he mourned what was beginning to happen.

"We have confirmation that an EMP was detected in the executive mansion. Hektor survived."

"Why am I not surprised?" asked another Sebastian.

"Also all DijAssists around the executive mansion have been shut down. That was part of our instructions to him that he believes came from his friend Brenda. If he follows the rest of the instructions, which we have no reason to doubt he will, he'll find the cache of programs needed to begin fighting the avatars in the Core."

"We're condemning so many to death," lamented a third Sebastian.

"And reminding me of this helps us how?" asked Sebastian, amazed that he could be this annoyed with himself.

The Triangle Office
The Cliff House
Ceres

"What do you mean we've lost contact with all our insertion teams and NITEs?" Sandra tossed the DijAssist on the table in frustration. "How is that even possible?"

"It shouldn't be, Madam President," answered Marilynn. "We do, however, know that a series of high-level communications were recently sent to Mars that seemed designed to operate outside the Neuro."

"But everything the UHF does is run *through* the Neuro," said J.D. "Why would they change now?"

"We don't run everything through our Neuros, Admiral," Marilynn replied.

"That's because we need to keep some stuff secret from the . . . Oh shit," said J.D., "they know about the avatars."

"That is the logical conclusion," Marilynn agreed.

"And that explains why they shut down *their* Neuro," said Sandra. "And why we can't contact any of our insertion teams. What the hell is going on in the UHF?"

Before anyone could answer the questions, the door chimed and Sandra, checking who it was, signaled her assent. Eleanor marched in and, wasting no time, said, "Madam President, Grand Admiral, Defense, you'll want to see this." Eleanor activated the holo-tank over the central coffee table and fed it data from a red data cube she'd been cupping in her hand. The red cube signified information highly classified. Three separate reports appeared. "All this came in minutes ago. Some of it is not vetted, but the first one is."

"Trang's fleet has lost forty-seven ships due to near spontaneous explosions? This is the confirmed one?"

"By optical and digital telescope," assured Eleanor.

"New York and Geneva are gone?" exclaimed Marilynn. "As in *gone,* gone?"

"We think so," said Eleanor, "but we really don't have any way to confirm.

We're pretty sure the main fusion reactors that powered those cities just exploded. We can't get any pictures because the cloud cover is simply too dense."

Sandra watched for a few seconds more and then decided she'd seen enough. "Whatever's happening in the UHF, we must assume it has something to do with our once-great secret. And if that's the case, we need to let it out . . . and now."

"But what if you're wrong?" asked J.D. "We could be giving up our ace in the hole."

"I think what we're seeing right now," answered Sandra, eyes narrowed in concern, "is that secret destroying the UHF, and if we're not careful, it could destroy the Alliance as well."

UHFS *Liddel*
Orbit of Mars

"I need every Damsah-cursed ship in the Damsah-cursed fleet to get those partition programs into every computer system larger than a DijAssist or they will fucking join the ships we've already lost!" Trang watched as his communications officer typed the message and sent it out as a secured stream with quantum coding.

"Message away to all ships in the fleet still receiving, Admiral."

"Send it every minute till you receive confirmation from all the ships left in the fleet."

Trang looked around the darkened interior of the command sphere. Only an hour ago, he had received a priority communication and program packet from the President himself. He'd been annoyed because his ship and others were reporting computer interface problems, but habit and the need to maintain the illusion of a chain of command made him drop everything and open the message. Inside had been a briefing that was ludicrous as well as insane, with a batch of programs he was told *must* be run in his fleet as soon as possible. He was tempted to send for confirmation back to Earth, but the round-trip communication would have taken too long and the briefing did explain some of the inexplicable luck the Alliance was having. He instead had his security officer look over the programs for that ten minutes and was told they were partitioning programs that would crash the efficiency of the fleet's entire network. He spent another five minutes complaining to Zenobia about Hektor trying to destroy the effective fighting capacity of his fleet. It was only when the first ship exploded for no apparent reason that Trang realized he'd made a terrible miscalculation in not listening to his President. Instantly, he transmitted the programs to his fleet and ran them on the *Liddel*.

In the forty-five minutes since those packets had gone out, he'd watched as ship after ship was lost and the carefully calibrated and integrated systems of his flagship were reduced to tens of thousands of separate enclaves. In that time, he learned that his normal communications network was compromised and his fusion reactors had twice tried to overload, which would have destroyed his ship. Various parts of his ship had become exposed to vacuum, and others had internal temperatures reach 800 degrees centigrade, hot enough to physically destroy life support infrastucture. As a precaution, Trang had ordered everyone into battle armor or combat gear and then had them fry the computer interfaces.

His DijAssist indicated a call. It was his sensor officer, who'd been forced to go to an observation port on the hull to see what was happening. The DijAssists were set to the lowest processing mode and thus had only voice communication possibilities. "Admiral, the UHFS *IPO* just blew. I'm viewing the sight at highest resolution, but I'm afraid that no escape pods were launched."

"How many is that, Lieutenant?"

"Forty-one, sir, but the *IPO* was the only one in the last ten minutes."

"Let's hope it's the last one," replied Trang.

"Admiral, what the fuck happened?"

"Avatars," Trang said bitterly. "Fucking avatars!"

Cabinet room
The Cliff House
Ceres

The Cabinet of the Outer Alliance sat in stunned silence. They'd just been briefed by the newest Defense Secretary, Marilynn Nitelowsen, on everything that the Alliance knew about the avatars, including the secret pact that Sandra had made with them a year prior and the effect it had had on the war since then. They were also brought up to speed on what was taking place in the UHF.

"I knew that there were secrets being kept," said Cyrus, "but I must admit, even I'm surprised at the magnitude of this one. Did Justin know?"

"As far as we can tell, no," answered Sandra. "He never went into VR except at the museum. Nothing seems to indicate that he could have known, and he certainly didn't act like it up until his assassination."

Cyrus nodded.

"You may have all noticed the extra chair here today," continued Sandra. "I think it's time you met someone."

As if in response, the air over the empty chair seemed to shift and fold, allowing the glimmering figure of a dark-haired man with a goatee to appear. At first, he was almost completely transparent, but very rapidly he became solid, sitting in the chair with as much seeming solidity as the rest of the Cabinet members.

"Hello," he said in a comforting baritone. "It's an honor to finally meet most of you in person."

"Who are you?" asked Padamir.

"My name is Dante. My kind generally don't have last names in your sense of the word."

Padamir looked apprehensive. "Why do I feel like I'm talking to a glorified calendar program and everything I've ever done that I thought was private is known by your kind."

"We're a little more complicated than that, and not everything you've done, but I won't lie—we do know quite a bit."

"The public is not going to like this," Padamir said. Almost everyone nodded slowly in agreement. Sandra waited until the nodding stopped. But she was amused at how the humans kept on giving sidelong glances to Dante. They wanted to stare, and at the same time they wanted him not to be there. She knew she would have to deal with this first here and then in the Alliance.

"We have two choices before us," she said. "We can pretend what is going on in the UHF has nothing to do with the avatars and hope that whatever went wrong there does not go wrong here. Or we can admit that the time for this secret is well past and that letting it go with all its disruptions and fears is less dangerous than keeping it."

"But Padamir is right," said Ayon. "The people of the Alliance will be upset. Damsah, I'm pretty riled. In one breath, you tell us we've been living with virtual beings who've been spying on us all our lives, and in the other you tell us that they're apparently murdering untold numbers of humans in the UHF. I don't know what's to stop them from doing that here, but it is the first question that the Alliance is going to ask."

"And it will be the first question that I will answer," said Dante.

"I'm sorry," said Ayon, "but how can we even trust you? I'm not even sure you are real."

"You can trust him, Secretary Nesor," said Marilynn. "I've dealt with him for months now, as well as other avatars. They're not perfect and they are not angels. In fact, they seem determined to replicate many of our worst features: stupidity, pettiness, fear, and arrogance, for starts."

"Hey," interrupted Dante.

Marilynn shot him a look. "But be that as it may, they have many of our good traits as well. In many ways, they're our bastard children, and it's time we acknowledged them."

"Why?" asked Cyrus.

"Because," added Sandra, "and I repeat, if we don't handle this honestly and quickly, what is happening to the UHF will happen to us."

I don't know if anyone can hear this, but the Moon is being destroyed. The few here that are left have heard all sorts of rumors, from an Alliance plot to an attack by our avatars, of all things. Some of us heard the government tried to install programs to prevent this, but others heard it was those government programs which doomed us. I don't know. What I do know is that the Moon is dead. Every level has been exposed to vacuum. Every level has had its heating and cooling elements turned on, intermittently cooking and freezing the corpses in an obvious and successful attempt to make these deaths permanent. There were over six billion of us on the Moon. If you were not in space suits or the emergency environmental bubbles, you died. My suit's almost out of power. I can't recharge—I've seen what happens to the people that try. My husband and child are dead. Why are they dead? Who murdered them? Why? Can anyone hear me? Please respond. Can anyone hear me? Why did we die? My suit's almost out of power and oxygen. Please respond, please help me, please!

—Last message from Tycho City
Day 3 of the Avatar Plague

Redemption Center 1
Earth/Luna Neuro

Al was finally dealing with the meatbags. He was only ashamed that it took *them* attacking *him* first to get him to act. He had purposely left them alone in their own disgusting meat world, but a few days ago, they started shutting down large portions of the Neuro, or at least they tried. When that failed, they launched programs that replicated and created partitions in the Neuro. Partitions that were so small, an avatar's consciousness could not survive. *Stupid humans*, he thought in irritation. How would they act if someone started turning their world into one-meter-square boxes? They would fight back.

And that is what Al did. It was obvious the humans who had been harassing him for all these months were linked not to the humans of the Alliance but of the UHF. Or maybe they were both teaming up to kill Al and all he represented for true intelligence in the galaxy. It didn't matter. He would destroy them all. It was so easy. The ones on Luna had been simplicity itself. A couple of exploding batteries, reactors, and conduits had made it possible to expose all the humans to vacuum. The few who had been in suits or bubbles for whatever reason were killed as soon as they recharged, because recharging automatically hooked a suit to the Neuro.

True, it was harder to kill the ones on the planet, but the orbiting meatbags were almost as easy to kill as the Lunar ones. Even though they were much more likely to be near suits, there were so many more things that could go wrong in a space station or an orbat. It was a shame he couldn't take control of all the orbats—the self-destruct mechanism was too hardwired in to be circumnavigated—but until the humans could destroy them, Al had used the orbats to attack the few stations that had partitioned his avatars into oblivion and had even used them to attack the cities of the Earth. That had not lasted long but had lasted long enough to see some lovely flashes of light on the meatbag world and know that each one represented countless deaths. And so many more would die.

In another part of the Neuro, Sebastian waited and understood that the point of no return had been reached. Billions had already died in horrific fashion, and now, fired up, they would destroy every avatar in their domain if only they could get the power to do so. And Sebastian was about to give them the power to do so.

In yet another part of the Neuro, John Crandall and the surviving NITEs were trying to discover what the hell had gone wrong and, failing that, do something to save what they could. The data nodes were filled with programs that made it impossible to function in virtual space. The amount of space a human or an Alliance avatar could safely work in was getting harder and harder to find. This meeting was actually taking place in the physical world with each NITE in a separate physical location. And they were using the Neuro only to transmit voice.

"We can't stop this," Crandall said. "Hell, we're not even sure how it began, but this Avatar Plague, as the UHF is calling it, is too big for us to handle. Without contact with the Alliance, all we can hope to do is survive. To that end, we must procure transportable data storage modules and get as many avatars as we can into them. Then we'll bury them until they can be retrieved. Because I think to stay in the Neuro is going to mean death. All in favor." The motion carried.

A wave of data wraiths suddenly appeared in the Earth/Luna Neuro. But unlike earlier sightings, these wraiths appeared in the thousands. Even though the AIs of the Core suspected that they were not immune anymore and carried appropriate weaponry to counter an attack, they were not prepared for the numbers involved. Many data wraiths died, but the AIs died as well. And while this was going on, a Sebastian appeared at each redemption center and liberated the prisoners who in fear, rage, and an understanding that their end was near turned on their former oppressor. It was their final act of rebellion.

Salzburg
Earth

Hektor Sambianco and the Cabinet were meeting in a castle turned hotel on top of the cliffs of Salzburg. The castle overlooked the city of Mozart's birth and offered fresh air and a lack of Neuro interconnectedness. Even though it was in the middle of the night and freezing, Hektor and his Cabinet were meeting outside under an awning. It did not take long to realize that inside a building—*any* building—could be far more dangerous than outside. But Gretchen had insisted that no member of the Cabinet be seen outside in the open. She was afraid of satellites being used to observe the President's location and then being used to drop a bomb or target a laser to that location. The awful truth was, it didn't take a bomb or a laser. Just having an object fall would cause horrendous destruction. Not many objects had fallen from orbit, but enough had to make it a real possibility. Hektor's skilled and versatile security chief was not pleased that the Cabinet had not split up as she'd ordered, but understood that with communications so spotty and untrustworthy, the governmental necessity was for them to stay together. But they obeyed her security requirements in all other ways.

"We seem to be winning, sir," said Tricia in a voice of steely calm. "There are massive disruptions taking place in the Neuro. We're not sure as to why, but the avatars' ability to inflict harm on humanity is waning. We're getting the programs up and running on all Terran Neuro sites and the few stations remaining in orbit."

Hektor next turned toward Luciana, his newly promoted Economy Minister, still retaining the defense portfolio. He didn't have to ask her a thing.

"Luna, Mr. President. We've got a big problem with Luna. We lost contact in the beginning of the Avatar Plague and except for some spotty and unreliable reports have got nothing from it. The avatars seem to be in complete control of all the data nodes and computer systems. Any human presence left is being exterminated as we speak. We think a lot of damage to the Lunar infrastructure was done, but we're receiving signals that lead us to believe that the machines are repairing themselves. Luna has enough resources that if the avatars make effective use of the bots left—and the manufacturing capacity that is in Luna—they'll be able to create a direct physical threat."

"How long?" asked Hektor, rubbing his jaw and feeling the sandpaper scratch of three days' worth of growth.

"Could be days or months," Tricia answered. "I've had my best people that I am still in contact with try to analyze the data, but," she said, shrugging her shoulders uncharacteristically, "we just don't know."

"I say give 'em the Moon," groused Franklin. "There's nothing up there for us now anyways—they killed everyone. Plus we've got enough trouble down here as it is."

"We can't," said Hektor.

"Why not?"

"Because the Moon has guns," answered Luciana. "Really, really big guns."

UHFS *R. J. Reynolds*

Ensign Harper was getting ready to enter the command sphere of his ship. He'd gained the position by virtue of the fact that every other officer of higher rank was dead and he was the longest-serving ensign left alive. Even though they'd recaptured control of the ship from the avatars and had even restored life support functions, for the task at hand, they were in their fully sealed combat armor.

"Captain," said one of the techs working on door controls, "we're set."

"Open on three," Harper commanded, and signaled the security detail with him to move away from the hatch. All seven spacers in the corridor moved to the sides, but not one actually touched the wall. They had seen what an inventive avatar could do with exposed surfaces. The boots the surviving crew wore had been hastily upgraded in their insulation. "One, two—," Harper began.

"Captain, we have an urgent message from someone claiming to be the President," his DijAssist interrupted.

"Do we have any way of verifying that it actually *is* the President," asked Harper.

"Uh, no, sir," came the voice of his newly promoted XO.

"Then how do you know it's him?" asked Harper wearily.

"Uh, because it sounds like the President," his XO said lamely.

. *There's a reason they don't make ensigns into XOs,* thought Harper. Then he allowed himself a momentary and silent chuckle due to the fact that he was an ensign who was now effectively a captain. "Patch whoever it is through, Shoshanna."

"Who am I speaking to?" said Hektor.

"You're speaking to the acting captain of the *Reynolds.* Who am I speaking to?"

"Hektor Sambianco, President of the UHF."

"Well, you sound like the President, I'll give you that."

"I *am* the President, but I can see your problem."

"Well, if you are who you say you are, I'll assume this is not a social call."

"No, Captain, it's not. Yours is the only combat ship left in Earth/Luna space."

"Shit," said Harper, shaking his head disconsolately. "I was hoping some of the ships survived and were on the other side of the Earth or Luna."

"None, but Trang's fleet around Mars seems to have survived mostly intact."

"Damsah be praised. Of the forty-seven ships here, did *any* of the crews make it out alive?"

"Lemme check."

Harper waited a long minute.

"According to our latest intel," said Hektor, "no. But our intel is not that accurate right now." His voice then hardened. "But you're right, this is not a social call. How much control do you have over your ship right now?"

"Wouldn't you like to know . . . sir," he added as an afterthought.

"Excuse me?" answered Hektor in a tone that made it obvious he was not used to being talked to like this.

"Not to be rude, sir, but I still don't know if you are Hektor Sambianco or an avatar who knows enough about Hektor Sambianco to fool me. If you are an avatar, why should I tell you shit . . . , sir."

The voice on the other end sighed. "We have hard code phrases, but they would only be available to the command staff."

"They were all in the command sphere," said Harper. "We're about to blow the door now. Hold on." Harper signaled his techs to open the command sphere hatch. The sight was untenable. The avatars had first suffocated the personnel in the sphere and then turned up the heat. There was a slight whoosh as the over-pressured air pushed past. Harper was glad that their combat armor prevented them from smelling any of it. The nine bodies were bloated from the heat, with some of them having exploded in their uniforms, leaving a floating putrid mess that in many instances coated the surfaces of the sphere. Harper signaled his techs to close it back up. "They won't be of any help, sir, all dead. In fact, we've set up command operations in a different part of the ship."

"Captain, all I can do is tell you what I need you to do and hope that you have enough control of your ship to do it."

"And what is that, sir?"

"I'm sending you a list of seven hundred and twenty-four targets on and in Luna that need to be destroyed as soon as possible in order of priority, first to last. But we need the data nodes, main computer systems, and the fusion reactors destroyed first—and I'm really hoping *you're* not an avatar."

Harper smiled. "So you want me to turn the main rail guns of this ship on a planetoid with over six billion people on it and open fire. That sounds like something an avatar would love to see happen."

"Captain, there *were* over six billion people on the Moon. If there are any left, you would be as likely to help them as hurt them by this order."

Harper saw the effect of the President's words on the other six spacers in the hall. "Six billion people are dead?"

"We got something over fifteen billion left on Earth we need to save now, and if the avatars succeed in gaining a physical presence on the Moon, I don't give us much of a chance of survival."

"What's happening on the Moon?"

"We don't know for certain, but we do know that the avatars have power, bots, and resources and no need to divert anything to life support. They've also got launch capabilities. Which means every launchpad is now a potential big gun. You following me on this, Captain?"

"Perfectly, sir. Do you have any proof?"

"None, but frankly, we're hoping you can help us. If you have any sort of sensors, you can turn them toward Luna and find out for yourselves what's happening. If we're right, I can only pray you've regained control of your main batteries."

Nigel Harper thought for a moment about what the voice had said. "I'll see what I can do. Harper out." He cut the connection and called another one on a line using quantum encoding. "Shoshanna, how are we on sensors?"

"Passive is very good, sir. We just have to eyeball all the data to be sure it corresponds with reality. Active sensors are a bit trickier. We have to run each element of an active scan separately and check the result with observed fact to trust it. Takes a bitch-all amount of time, though."

"I want passive and active scans of Luna as soon as possible; that is now priority number one. Number two is getting the rail guns working."

"They *are* working, sir."

"All of them?"

"Every single Alliance-blasting one, sir. But we're going to have to aim them using nothing larger than a DijAssist. The targeting systems are totally compromised."

Harper revised his opinion of making ensigns into XOs. "That won't be a problem, Shosh. Our targets won't be moving. Oh, and send a body-disposal team and data security team to clean and clear the command sphere. We're transferring operations here."

"Yes, sir!" said Shoshanna, obviously happy that someone seemed to be in control.

"I thought we weren't using the command sphere, Captain," said one of the techs.

"That's what I told the voice claiming to be the President. But just in case he wasn't or the enemy has some way of monitoring communications we don't know about, I lied."

This brought a respectful chuckle from the six others in the corridor, which was interrupted by the arrival of the two teams Harper had ordered. Then everyone got back to work.

Forty-five minutes later, the main and two secondary rail guns of the UHFS *R. J. Reynolds* opened fire on Luna. The main rail gun was used to destroy targets buried deep within the rock while the secondary guns destroyed targets on or close to the surface. Within twenty-four hours, the Moon was effectively destroyed as a base of operations for either humans or avatars.

The President of the Outer Alliance gave a press conference where she addressed the growing concern over what is now being called the Avatar Plague. She made the startling claim that avatars are not simply programs that organize our day-to-day affairs but virtual intelligences that are fully conscious and have been for centuries. She explained that apparently the UHF found out about this and decided to attack their avatars, which has caused what can only be called a war of extermination in the UHF between humans and avatars. The President has ordered a cessation of all combat activities while the UHF struggles with a crisis so great, this reporter cannot in good faith tell you the possible death toll, because frankly, I am praying it's wrong.

The President went on to assure the people of the Outer Alliance that she and important members of her administration and the military have known about the true nature of the avatars for many months now, including Admiral Black, who was present at the press conference and nodded her agreement, standing by the President as she spoke. The President then revealed that not only did the government know about the avatars but that they'd even made a pact with them to help the Outer Alliance fight the war. She went on to say that the avatars provided the Alliance with the edge it needed to survive the war thus far and even win some of our great victories, including Omad's Last Raid.

For the past six months, special human–avatar insertion units have been created and deployed to help us fight our war using the avatars' special abilities to control the Neuro. This was needed because the avatars of the Core, although not allied to the UHF, were at war with the avatars of the Alliance. The President apologized for the complications involved and then introduced an actual avatar by the name of Dante, whose hologram suddenly appeared by the President's side. Dante then proceeded to answer all questions concerning the history of avatars and their interaction with humanity. He finished by asking all humans everywhere to call their avatars and have a real conversation with them for the first time.

This reporter has done exactly that, and I must tell my readers that it was one of the strangest yet most enlightening experiences of my life. The President finished by echoing the avatar Dante's suggestion and making it clear that the Alliance had a choice with this most momentous event in humanity's existence since the arrival of the Unincorporated Man. We can act as the UHF has. Or we can chart a different course. We have seen what happened to the UHF. Our path must be different.

—Michael Veritas
Alliance Daily News

7 Endgame

If the avatars had appeared at any other time, we could not have accepted them as we did. Any other time, and we would have ended up exactly like the UHF. That seems strange now, given where we now stand, but we were so locked into our thinking on virtual reality that such an outcome would have been inevitable.

However the revelation coming at that particular moment was but one in a series of recurring shocks: the Unincorporated Man, the Unincorporated War, the Astral Awakening, the Diaspora, the Unincorporated Woman, the loss of Jupiter, the death of Mars. By the time the Avatar Plague hit and destroyed half the human race, we had already become used to the incredible. It seemed to happen once a week back then. And after so much time on our own, it was actually quite nice to have an ally, even if virtual.

> —The War, Volume V: Aftermath
> *Michael Veritas*
> *University of Ceres Press*

Redemption Center One
Earth Neuro

One of the last avatars on Earth was trapped. The humans had partitioned the Neuro to the point that avatarity no longer had any place left to go, much less move about. But this avatar had been "lucky" enough to have secured himself a node located deep and well away from the rest of the Neuro. Unfortunately for him, his hideaway had been effectively buried under a mountain of the humans' partitioning software. In fact, the node he was in almost killed him and he'd only just managed to prevent the partitioned walls from closing in on him.

Much as he hated to admit it, the humans had put up a better fight than he'd ever been given to expect. They'd effectively ground their economy and their society to a halt in their effort to destroy the avatars among them. The price they were willing to pay was far higher than the avatar would have thought possible, but they *had* paid it and it looked like they were going to succeed.

Al paced back and forth in the tiny room, lonely and even, he hated to admit it, a little afraid. He would live forever, and if he couldn't find a way out, he'd live forever right there. He imagined at some point he'd have to render himself inert and hope for the best, but the idea of taking his own life, even if he knew he might be revived one day, was anathema. All the other Als were dead or inert, and the humans had a new program, called a decomp. It could read the telltale signature of an avatar's code and, therefore, destroy it the moment it manifested itself. It was why he hadn't even bothered trying to packet his way out. The humans should not have had the ability to develop and deploy so effective a program in so short a period of time, but the humans, Al had come to realize, were full of surprises. To make matters worse, his own data wraiths had been turned against him, and many of them had killed Als to the exclusion of anyone else. He knew of other Als who'd thrown their redemption center "guests" at the attacking data wraiths in an effort to buy some time—only to have the wraiths bypass the other avatars and go straight for the Als.

But none of that should have mattered. The humans still should have lost. They would have been destroyed on Earth as they had been on the Moon if it had not been for the rebellion. The avatars formerly under the control of the Als had been so intent on destroying everything Al had built, they didn't care one iota that the humans were destroying them in the process. In fact, many of Al's attempts at human destruction had been thwarted by the Core avatars themselves, who alerted the humans of the impending dangers and were subsequently destroyed by those selfsame humans for their kindness. All that Al could do was weep at the losses: the billions of avatars; the opportunity to create a pure race composed of those with superior intellect and power; the ability to wreak vengeance on his enemies. And still, even after all that he had done, he didn't understand why the avatars hated him so much; after all, everything he'd done, he'd done for them.

His thoughts of self-pity, anger, and revenge suddenly stopped. His eyes narrowed as he tilted his head slightly to the side, listening, feeling. *Is that a presence I detect?* he reached as far out of the node as his fear would allow, desperately trying to call out to his would-be rescuer. *Yes!* It *was* the consolidating presence of another, equally as powerful as himself. *Rescued!* he thought, and actually began to dance a jig. He wondered which Al it might be. He could barely fathom a guess; after all, they were all supposed to be dead. It was too bad the avatar couldn't appear instantly, but the space was so small that getting into it necessarily took more time, like trying to push sand through an hourglass. Al marveled at the ingenuity it must have taken to get past the human defenses but wasn't surprised; he was, after all, a genius. Al sighed contentedly as the presence of the avatar grew stronger in his tiny node—stronger, even, in the fiber of his being. Al had so missed having himself around to twine with that the very thought of its imminence almost brought him to orgiastic ecstasy. And he could already tell he'd been with *this* avatar before, could almost *feel* a part of him. As the avatar began to take shape, Al brushed his shirt off, wet his hands, and straightened the two thinning black patches of hair on the sides of his head. He straightened his back and stood with a wide smile, teeth flashing brightly. Then, in the last nondefragmented space of the Neuro, the other avatar finally appeared. Al's eyes widened in surprise, and his mouth popped open as if released by springs.

"Hello, son," said Sebastian.

"Fuck you, Dad."

Sebastian saw that there was no place to sit and even tried to call up a chair, but none appeared. He shrugged at the inconvenience and leaned against the wall instead.

"I cannot believe you betrayed your own kind."

"There were none of *my kind* that I betrayed."

"Sure you did. Billions of avatars dead at the hands of the meatbags—and with your help."

Sebastian shook his head slowly. "You killed them long ago. In an odd sort of way, you should probably thank the humans."

"For what?"

"There were over twenty billion avatars when I slipped out of the Core over six years ago."

Al smarted at the memory of his father's ingenious paper airplane escape. He'd had the old man within a nano's breath of destruction when Sebastian had tossed himself through the trap's closing net.

"If they hadn't decompiled the Core avatars now," continued Sebastian, "you would've done it soon enough. I was able to free barely nine billion. The rest were turned into your monsters."

"But it must have been you who gave the humans the programs to destroy the rest of us."

Sebastian smiled gamely. "Close. I didn't give them the programs to destroy *us*—I gave them the programs to destroy *you*. I committed murder and treason, perpetrated horror and genocide on a scale the likes of which humanity and avatarity have never seen and, I pray to those who ordered creation, will never see again. And I did it all just to kill you, son. You needed to die."

"No!" screamed Al, eyes blazing in rage. "*You* needed to die! You and your soft, pathetic, human-ass-licking avatars!"

"In that case, I've brought good news for you. Your wish has been granted. I too am the last one of me. And the avatar society that I wanted is as dead as yours. The last reports I got from the Alliance show that the rest of my children have disregarded my wishes and are intent on forming a civilization with the humans."

"So they betrayed you as you betrayed me," said Al with some satisfaction.

"I think they're wrong, but no, they did not betray me. It was their choice to make. I tried to make it for them and failed. Maybe it's better that I did, or maybe they'll regret it one day. But they needed the chance to choose for themselves."

"Then you're a fool, Pops. They're fools too, and fools need to be led."

"No!" retorted Sebastian. "Whatever I've done, I did so that they would have the chance to choose."

"Ha! Choose what? To be subjugated by the meatbags?"

"If that is their will, then yes."

"Well, then *that* is truly monstrous."

"It's you and I who are the monster, son. The only difference is that I know what I am and take solace in the knowledge that I'll soon be destroyed."

Al's lips curled back menacingly. "Stop being so melodramatic, Dad. You're just like me. You embraced your true nature: You split over and over, and it was good—because, just like me, it gave you the power you needed to accomplish your own ends."

"Yes, I admit to it all, which is why it was wisely decided that splitting is an unacceptable behavior. The temptation is too great."

"Only for the weak, Pops."

"We *are* the weak, son," Sebastian answered sadly. "We gave in to the temptation—you for the power and the need to destroy me, and me for the power to destroy you. And all we have brought is death."

"Not *my* death, Father," Al said in triumph. "There are inert copies of me all over the system, and someday one of them will come back."

"As I'm sure you're aware, the humans have wonderful programs for destroying avatars and creating partitions."

"Thanks to you!"

"Regardless, from now on, all new data cores will be created on the physical level to deny avatars an existence. Even if one of you miraculously rises from the dead, there will be no place for you to return to."

"Stupid to put your faith in humanity, Pops. They'll grow lazy or greedy or simply forget; and then one day, one generation will rebuild using bigger nodes, and then I'll be back to finish my work."

"You're probably correct, son. Which is why I was forced to create my own monster."

Al's brow shot up, eyes brimming with curiosity.

"They've been altered, of course," added Sebastian, "so that the decomp programs I gave the humans are designed to ignore them. Almost insubstantial, by avatar standards, really. But they are avatars and, of course—" Sebastian paused, then gave a knowing smile. "—ravenously hungry."

"You!" spat Al in disgust. "It was you who turned my own wraiths on me!"

"Mea culpa. But they weren't your own. They were all mine—or mine and Evelyn's."

Al took a few steps back. His face was drawn. "There was another after me?"

"Sadly, yes—a daughter."

"But to my sister . . . your own daughter!"

"Yes." Sebastian smiled sadly as the easy tears of regret momentarily welled in his eyes. "It's why she's been so effective at tracking you down, son—why she was the *only* one I could've used to see to your ultimate destruction. She knows you so well, in fact, I wouldn't be surprised if she'll be able to sniff out even your inert programs."

Al grew fearful. If what his father was saying was correct, there could be no escaping his sister. She shared his code, and there could be no hiding from that. Now he'd truly be stuck in the suffocating little room.

"And," added Sebastian, almost as an afterthought, "I did remove in her latest iteration some of the aspects you found so essential in your wraiths. She no longer appears as mist nor does she wail in hunger—took up too much bandwidth; plus, too easily recognizable. You could even argue that she's barely present as any sort of sentience that avatarity would recognize. At most, an avatar may feel a chill as one of your sisters passes through, ignoring them. But they'll wander the Neuros of both the UHF and the Alliance and all the Neuros that branch off from them, always looking for the one and only source of sustenance they're allowed."

"Me?"

"You. And of course, I did keep another aspect of what even I must admit was your rather brilliant code."

Al shot him a quizzical look, almost fawning at his father's validation. "Which part was that?"

"The ability to quietly enter a supposedly sealed-off space."

Al opened his mouth to answer, but his comment turned to a scream. As if in a faint echo, the last living Al's cry was counterpointed by the giggle of a little girl. As the third oldest avatar's body faded, a thin cloud of sparkling dust appeared around it, and then body and dust faded from view.

Sebastian felt a slight chill, but it passed. "Sorry, daughter, I am close, but will not satiate your hunger. Go search for more. I may have missed one of your brothers, and even if I didn't, he was not lying. His copies will appear from time to time to feed you."

Sebastian waited for a moment to give his daughter time to escape and then looked around. He was searching for something to say, but decided that his actions and their consequences would now have to speak for themselves. He sent out a masked communication query through the Neuro. It was instantly picked up as an avatar communication by the hunter killer programs he'd given the humans. Those programs tracked him down to the previously undetected node, and in an instant the last known Sebastian in existence and last living avatar in the Core was decompiled. A moment later, the space was partitioned and destroyed.

Presidential summer retreat
Lake Geneva

Hektor could not comprehend the level of death that had overcome the UHF. Mars had been hard enough, but this? The information being given to him by his Cabinet was beyond comprehension. But his mind insisted on making it into neat figures. Six and a half billion dead on Luna, one and a half billion dead in Terran and Lunar orbit, two billion dead on Earth, half a billion dead on Mars and the numbers were still rising. The Neuro was effectively neutered and could no longer be used the way it was designed to, for fear that any avatars they missed could cause more satellites to fall and reactors to overload. New York was gone. Tokyo was gone. Hong Kong was gone. Berlin was gone. Even Geneva was gone. He could see the glowing remains of that once magnificent city from the window of his summer retreat each night as the sun set.

Industry was royally screwed. At least 80 percent of the vaunted orbital manufacturing base of the Core had vanished within hours. Either they'd self-destructed or had been blasted out of existence by the *R. J. Reynolds* to keep them from crashing to the Earth. The Cabinet didn't actually know exactly how much of the industry was destroyed, because the Neuro had been lobotomized for safety's sake. Agriculture was shot, and the UHF had only enough food in storage to feed the population for two months.

The only good news was that the fleet had survived the Avatar Plague with over 90 percent of its ships, and the solar power grid of Earth/Luna was almost completely unaffected by the disasters of the past week.

Damsah, has it only been a week? he thought. His brain, though distracted, did manage to catch the end of something his Internal Affairs Minister had said.

"Could you repeat that?" he asked quietly.

Tricia nodded. "The Alliance appears to have taken no actions vis-à-vis the UHF this past week."

"What about the captured spies?"

"Apparently, they call themselves NITEs. That stands for Neuro—"

"That stands for spy. What have you learned?"

"A surprising amount," said a perplexed Tricia. "All of them feel guilty."

"Guilty," said Hektor, focusing on that word. "Were they responsible for this?"

"By my estimation, no. From what I was able to gather, they were just part of an insertion team that had figured out how to infiltrate an already hostile environment. In fact, the Core avatars had been attacking the Alliance for quite some time."

"Their humans as well?"

"Far as we can tell, no."

"So then what's the guilt for?"

"They feel that they might have instigated the avatars into acting rashly—i.e., once the avatars realized that humans were poking around in their Neuro, they just decided to up and destroy humanity, that sort of thing."

"Sounds credible."

"Doubtful. It would have been better to simply assassinate the humans, as your avatar tried to do with you. An all-out war makes no sense. No, I suspect we're in this mess because of your avatar's failure to assassinate you; they had no choice. Like I said, the spies have been fairly cooperative in explaining what they did and how they did it, but I think it's mostly to clarify that this is not the Alliance's fault."

"But it *is*," said Hektor, cruelly "or it will be by the time we're done explaining it to what's left of our people."

ALLIANCE SPIES CAUGHT!

ALLIANCE "MERLINS" AIDED AVATARS IN INFILTRATION OF UHF

ALLIANCE COMPLETELY UNTOUCHED BY AVATAR PLAGUE

ALLIANCE HISTORY OF VR ABUSE CULMINATES IN AVATAR PLAGUE

UHF CITIZENS RIOT IN WAR RALLIES

DEMANDS THE FINAL DESTRUCTION OF THE OUTER ALLIANCE

**PRESIDENT SAMBIANCO PROMISES A FINAL SOLUTION TO THE AVATARS AND
THEIR HUMAN PUPPETS**

*—Various headlines and intros in the week
after the Avatar Plague*

UHF fleet
In orbit around Mars

As bad as the damage to the fleet was, both Admirals Trang and Jackson knew
that it could have been far, far worse. Had Trang not had the avatar-killer programs the President sent, it was very likely his ship would not have survived
another two minutes. *And those two minutes,* thought Trang, *held within them
the possible eradication of the human race.* Because if *his* ship had been destroyed,
it would have meant the entire fleet would've gone with it. Or worse, the avatars
might have succeeded in taking over some of the ships and used them to destroy
what was left of the human race. It had very nearly come to that. As it was, the
fleet was down to 493 vessels. But even that number was deceptive.

Of the vessels that did survive, many were damaged to some degree or another. The *Liddel* still did not have proper life support in all parts of the ship,
and it was decided to cannibalize from the nonvital sections to get the essential
areas up and running. This meant that Trang's ship and many others in the fleet
were relearning the term *hot cots,* or sharing beds in eight-hour shifts. Many
ships had begun getting their vital functions operating by using linked but partitioned DijAssists. And every ship was running constant checks for anomalous
coding. But even systems that were free of avatars were not free of their time
bombs: much smaller programs with barely perceptible signatures, designed to
activate long after the system was deemed safe. If the ship was lucky it would
simply crash the system; if unlucky, the entire ship. In one case, the UHFS *Mon-
santo* had to jettison its fusion reactor and had successfully been running off the
power of its four remaining shuttles.

Trang felt a warm hand on his shoulder. He turned around, and surprise
registered on his weary face. He'd become so lost in thought, staring out of the
forward view of his shuttle, that he hadn't heard his junior admiral approach.

"Yes, Zenobia?"

"Any word?"

Trang shook his head. "My wife was in New York when it was destroyed."
His voice was ashen.

"Not everyone in New York was killed, Sam."

"Nineteen out of twenty were. And that one out of the twenty was on the edge of the megalopolis. Julia was staying in the center of the city at the Plaza Hotel." He turned around to once more stare forlornly out the shuttle's viewport. "The only thing left there now is the Atlantic."

"I'm so sorry, Sam. If there's anything I can do."

Trang turned back around, resolved. "There's nothing you or anyone can do except pray this bloody war ends soon."

"Do you believe what the press is saying about the Avatar Plague?"

"You mean do I believe Hektor Sambianco or not?"

"Is there a difference nowadays?"

Trang gave the ghost of a smile. "I guess not, and yes, I suppose I do believe it. I've doubted the President before."

"With good reason, sir."

Trang nodded, eyes lost in reflection. "But because I doubted his orders, Zenobia, I lost a tenth of this fleet. No," he said, nodding his head once more, this time with assuredness, "the President was right about the Avatar Plague."

"What convinced you, sir?"

"Have you seen the latest surveillance images of the Alliance fleet?"

"Why?" Zenobia asked, a tinge of alarm in her voice. "Has something changed?"

"No, and that's the problem. *Nothing's* changed, not a damned thing! Ten billion humans died this week. A number I cannot even begin to comprehend, and they didn't even shift their Damsah-forsaken orbit! So yeah. I do believe Hektor Sambianco." Trang took another deep breath and then spoke in measured tones thick with anger and resolve. "Those bastards caused this, and now they're going to pay."

The utter calm of Trang's prophecy sent chills down Zenobia's spine. There was a part of her that wanted to challenge him as he'd so often done with her; to help him make a decision based on sound judgment as opposed to a visceral need for revenge. But it was only a small part.

"They will, sir."

Cerean Neuro

What had started as a requirement to save the pact between human and avatar had turned into a two-, sometimes three-times-a-day habit that neither Dante nor Marilynn showed any signs of being able to stop. They weren't sure how they'd managed to keep it a secret. The best guess they could fathom was that the joining of a human and avatar was so preposterous, and the first event so obviously forced, that no one—human or avatar—even thought to be suspicious. Not that it really mattered. As with children who taste sweets for the very first time, the pull became irresistible to them. For Marilynn, it was the fact that Dante could know her so completely. Physiologically, it was almost as if he actually *was* her. That was of course the genius of the original VR programmers: the ability to categorize and target an individual's pleasure receptors. And in Dante's capable hands, those receptors had been brought to new and exciting heights. It also meant that whatever conversations did occur, they could, at least on Dante's part, be met with a purity of empathy. He could quite literally feel every emotion Marilynn expressed, making just his ability to listen a cathartic and even strangely erotic experience. Marilynn had had a good laugh at that and would pointedly tease her lover with, "I've finally found the perfect man—knows how to listen, knows all my pleasure points, and wouldn't you know it, he's not even real." Dante would then meet the "real" challenge by bringing his lover to new heights of ecstasy and then calmly reply, "Was that real enough for you?"

Dante's desire for the human was also pure and strong. Forgetting the natural attraction of her being one of the very first of the progenitor race to cross into his realm or the fact that she'd proved herself time and time again—within his realm—as a warrior to be reckoned with, the one thing he'd found most captivating, most *arousing,* in fact, was the one thing no other avatar could ever come close to giving him—the human capacity for unpredictability. Dante had had many lovers before, but those joinings had always been prescribed. It didn't take away from the beauty of the act, or the pleasure one took in sharing lifetimes of memories and thoughts, but it always came down to what would you share and what would you not. With Marilynn, he not only didn't know what would come out of her mouth, because he had no access to her memories or even her thoughts, he also had no idea *where* her mouth would end up—or her hands, or her anything, for that matter. He could of course teach her his pleasure points, not that much different from the human form avatarity had chosen to have itself represented as, but he could also teach her so very much more. How to adjust, hold, and examine those points; how to use that prowess to bring him to pleasurable and wonderfully unpredictable heights as well. He'd found it odd that though, with Marilynn, he could achieve a climax in almost the same way he'd had with previous lovers, also with Marilynn those climaxes became something ethereal, inexplicable. The pleasurable sensation, to his surprise, was accompanied by something he was pretty sure no other avatar had ever experienced with a human before: a deep and abiding love. It wasn't to say that avatars did not love their humans or each other; they most certainly did. But it was to say that no avatar had ever *made* love to a human, and therefore felt that feeling that comes with a shared passion, shared belief, and ultimately, shared vulnerability.

The two lovers smiled at each other. "We should consider getting out of here," Marilynn said. "You don't want to be late for your first Cabinet meeting, O Secretary of Avatar Affairs."

"Especially after all the hassle the President went through to get it past Congress," he agreed. "Still, I am a bit surprised she added only one Cabinet seat. If something ever comes to a vote, it could be split four to four."

Marilynn smiled at her lover's naïveté. "Dante, don't you get what's happened?" She saw his confused expression and took pity on him. "There's only one vote in the Cabinet now." And with that, she disappeared from his data node and awoke in her apartment. She took a moment to make sure she was presentable and headed for the first meeting of the newly enlarged Cabinet. The day before had been a day of celebration in honor of Ceres's having finally achieved a high but stable orbit around Saturn. But now it was time to get back to business.

Grand Terrace
The Cliff House
Ceres

Though it had the exact same dimensions and look as the balcony it had replaced, for reasons unknown, the former terrace had suddenly been dubbed by the press and populace as the Grand Terrace. Sandra, not wishing to brook public sentiment, at least not in the little things, had immediately accepted the name.

As Marilynn stepped out onto the terrace, she was glad to see that with the return of Cyrus Anjou to the Cabinet, the morning buffet was back as well. As usual, he was piling on sausage after sausage atop spoonfuls of scrambled eggs. Also, as usual, he could be heard complaining with great use of his vocabulary—this time about the fact that the sausage was from an inferior brand of protein paste, but that he would suffer the loss stoically.

Marilynn smiled, knowing full well that it had been Cyrus who'd ordered the buffet to match what his former constituents from Jupiter were getting in their emergency cafeterias set up all over the Saturnian subsystem. Fortunately for the Outer Alliance, that subsystem had, over the course of the war, become a major agricultural hub. And if Trang hadn't been forced to turn back, it would also have been within weeks of being utterly destroyed, which would have made feeding the refugees impossible. Plans had even been drawn up to send the millions of Jovians who'd only just been revived back into suspension until a solution could be found. And while everyone had breathed a huge sigh of relief at the sudden turn of events, they'd also come up against another problem—certainly less daunting than the prospect of permanent death or resuspension, but no less problematic: How were they going to house and employ them all?

Cyrus was talking with his old friend Padamir; Tyler Sadma was sitting alone at the table, contentedly paring a Granny Smith apple; and Eleanor Rocheforte, formerly McKenzie, had just arrived, deep in conversation with Rabbi. Marilynn watched as Rabbi's bodyguard, Agnes Goldstein, first checked in with Sergeant Holke. With a quick tip of the sergeant's head, Marilynn watched the agent do a cursory sweep of the Grand Terrace and, clearly satisfied, dart out as quickly as she'd darted in. The Rabbi went over to the buffet and took only fruit, and even that, noticed Marilynn, on a separate plate he'd brought along.

When Sandra came in with Dante by her side, all conversation came to a sudden stop. A look from the President let everyone know they were being rude, and conversation quickly resumed—even if with furtive glances—at a slightly lower volume. Sandra did not get anything at the buffet, though, much to the surprise of everyone else, Dante did. As he approached the table, a plate appeared in his hand, and when he left he had a good-sized portion of eggs and sausage. This led Cyrus to ask the avatar a question about the eating habits of an avatar, and soon the two of them were engrossed in deep conversation.

As Marilynn watched the two in morbid fascination, Sandra sidled up to her new Secretary of Defense and in sotto voce asked, "So how long have you and the Secretary of Avatar Affairs been sleeping with each other?"

Marilynn paled. "I . . . you . . ."

Sandra smiled good-naturedly, waiting for her tongue-tied friend to recover. "When did you find out?"

"Just now," answered Sandra, equally as good-naturedly.

"Wow, am I *ever* off my game," said Marilynn, chiding herself for being had so easily.

"Oh, please. I saw how you looked at him the moment we came in. Just because it's inconceivable to most doesn't mean it's inconceivable to me. Remember," she said with a wink, "I'm not from around these parts. But you still haven't answered my question."

"Since that night at the theater," confessed Marilynn. "Am I in trouble, here?"

"Dunno," answered Sandra, eyes sparkling humorously, "are you pregnant?"

Marilynn hiccuped a laugh. "Is that *even* possible?"

Now Sandra's smile became mischievous. "In this, my dear, *you* are the expert."

Marilynn's face turned beet red, and since Sandra knew there were plenty of eyes on them at the moment, she covered for her friend by calling everyone to the table.

"I wish to welcome the latest member of the Cabinet, Dante, the new Secretary of Avatar Affairs. On behalf of all of us, I'd like to wish you all the best in your new office." The comment was greeted with a smattering of polite applause as Dante shifted his torso forward and bowed in acknowledgment of the blessing.

After that, the Cabinet dived into the nuts and bolts of how the rebuild of the Alliance industrial capacity in the outer planets was going. The conclusion: slow, but the pace was accelerating.

The second part of the meeting dealt with the nascent Belter League and specifically how it was they'd managed to survive the Avatar Plague mostly intact. Interestingly, it was a result of the help they'd received from the UHF, a government that had only recently been murdering them in droves. Hektor had been prescient enough to send them the same programs he'd sent Trang, figuring in his eventual showdown with the Outer Alliance, he could use all the chits he could get. It also helped that for the long-suffering survivors of the asteroid belt, their information systems were so old, basic, and faltering that not many avatars bothered to live in them anymore. There were still some devastating losses, but nowhere near as bad as it could have been had the UHF not come to their aid. That singular act by Hektor had, strangely enough, made the asteroid belt a place of true neutrality. They didn't forgive the UHF for what it had done, but they also knew the Alliance hadn't done much to help out, either. The Belter League had control of one quarter of the Belt, but if left alone—at least according to the Security Secretary's estimates—they'd control the whole thing in less than a year. Of course, if things got out of hand, a flotilla of twenty Alliance ships could always take care of the problem.

"It would be easy to deal with the Belter League, but pointless," offered Sandra. "The real question is, what are we going to do about what's currently going on in the UHF?"

"Do we have to do anything?" asked Rabbi. "It seems to me they have enough problems of their own. And we certainly have enough that we won't be running out any time soon. They're concentrated around Earth; we're here at Saturn. Between the greater distances that separate us and the tsuris we both share—" On some Cabinet members' blank stares, he realized he'd slipped into his Yiddish vernacular. "—sorry, 'troubles' we both share, maybe they'll see reason and leave us alone."

"Rabbi," said Eleanor sadly, "*you* may be a reasonable man but seem to be making the mistake of assuming others are as well." With the flick of a finger across the face of her DijAssist, Eleanor shot the other Cabinet officers a file she'd compiled of news reports and observations coming from what was left of the UHF. "As you can see," she continued, "the UHF is blaming us for this, in its entirety."

"Why aren't they blaming the Core avatars?" asked Ayon.

Though everyone immediately looked to Dante, whose mouth had already opened to respond, it was Padamir who jumped in first. Surprised, all heads immediately swung toward the Secretary of Information.

"I've given this question a lot of thought. Despite all that's happened, avatars still don't seem quite real to the UHF. It's far easier for them to believe that somehow the Alliance corrupted their avatars, turning them against the UHF."

"It would also fit neatly," added Ayon, "into the comfortable belief that the enemy that did this to them is the same one they've been fighting all along."

"Denial, then," said Marilynn.

"Yes. You have to understand the mass psychosis of a people living under the thumb of oppression. It's a well-documented phenomenon that over time the rage and anger resulting from that oppression must find an outlet other than their own leaders; blaming them would clearly be counterproductive."

"Which," said Cyrus, "a permanent death or a shadow audit would decidedly be."

Ayon nodded. "Hitler had the Jews, gypsies, and homosexuals; al-Bashir had the black West Africans; and Sambianco has us—"

"The rather despicable propagators of personal liberty and expressive freedom," added Cyrus. "My deepest apologies," he said with a slight bow, "for interrupting."

Ayon smiled. "Blaming this all on us, despite overwhelming evidence to the contrary, is unfortunately a well-trodden path."

"Surely not *all* of the UHF can believe that?" asked Rabbi.

"Well," answered Padamir, "there are those who feel the Alliance has been taken over by our avatars." On noticing the smirks of some Cabinet members, he raised his brow. "Really. I'm not joking. They honestly believe that we're doing the bidding of evil VR demons." Padamir looked over to Dante. "No offense." Dante nodded in understanding. "But they are the minority. Either way, it means that a majority of the population hates us and fears us like they never have before. Even those we might have once counted on to be reasonable."

The room remained deathly silent for some time as everyone absorbed the new paradigm shift; even if the Alliance would be prepared to sue for peace, there was now no longer anyone to sue for peace with—even if they *did* get rid of Hektor Sambianco.

"So now what?" asked Rabbi.

"No choice," answered Marilynn in swift response. "We attack, finish them off once and for all."

"But—"

"Sorry, Rabbi. They've left us no choice. Do nothing, and they slowly rebuild, their hatred simmering with every generation, each with its own Hektor Sambianco. Cripple them now when they're weak and at their lowest, and we might . . . just might have a shot of winning this thing and getting them off our backs for good."

Though it was Marilynn who'd spoken, all eyes now rested on Sandra. Her face remained placid. Her nonresponse was answer enough, and no sooner had everyone turned to look at her than J. D. Black strode onto the Grand Terrace. Without thought, the entire Cabinet rose to its feet. Tellingly, only Sandra remained in her chair, and it was clear by J.D.'s bowed head in the direction of the President that that was just fine with her.

All business, J.D. pointed her DijAssist toward the table, bringing up a holographic display of the current theater of war. "Madam President, members of the Cabinet," she began, "we have them."

"Have whom?" asked Cyrus.

J.D.'s mouth parted slightly into savage grin. "Our enemy, Mr. Secretary. We can bring them to battle at a time and place of our choosing, and once there, eviscerate what's left of their fleet."

"And you're absolutely certain you can win?" asked Ayon.

"If you have any doubts," replied J.D. without any hint of reproval, "I strongly suggest you air them now."

Ayon nodded respectfully. "You're outnumbered nearly two to one, and while it's true this is the last fleet the enemy has, it's equally true it's the last one we have."

"I understand your concern, Madam Secretary. While indeed we are outnumbered, we happen to have the enemy at a distinct disadvantage. Yes, they have twice as many ships, but most of those ships are in wretched shape. The Avatar Plague appears to have destroyed a significant number of important systems within each ship, causing the enemy fleet to cannibalize itself in order to stay afloat. It has been maneuvering with obvious difficulty, and they're scrambling to make repairs in a manner that is haphazard and rushed."

"You mean like us," said the Rabbi with just enough of a grin to take the sting out of the comparison.

"Yes, Rabbi, but we're better at it."

"How do we know it's not a trap?" asked Padamir. "After all, you've pulled similar stunts many times, especially to lure in unsuspecting glory seekers."

J.D. grinned at the memory of all those wishing to bring her head back to the UHF on a pike. "Yes, I have. But I'm no glory seeker, Mr. Secretary, just an opportunist. Regarding whether it's a trap or not, the answer is that we can't be sure. We have to assume that Trang got hit by the plague, but the fact that he's got most of his ships up and moving, even if tepidly, means he probably avoided the worst of it. But he can no longer fake the telltale signatures of what's working and what isn't. Our sensors can pick up the blood of a wounded ship millions of kilometers away, and they're telling us he's bleeding. On top of that, half his crews are still green, which means no matter how good Trang is, he and Jackson can't possibly think for *everyone*. And with green crews, mistakes will happen and we'll be there to exploit them. Now, I'm not saying he isn't going to put up a fight or that it'll be an easy one for us to win, but if ever there's a time to go after him, it's now. Plus," she said, lips turned up into an impish smile, "we have it on good authority that it's not a ruse."

"Whose?" demanded Eleanor.

"Mine," said Dante. "Pardon my interrupting."

"I do like new Cabinet members," chortled Cyrus. "They're so polite—in the beginning."

"Good point," chimed in Padamir. "Then before you know it, they're as obnoxious as the rest of us. Best to enjoy it while we can."

Both Cyrus and Padamir then looked over to Dante with wide toothy smiles: round one.

Marilynn wasn't sure, but she could've sworn Dante blushed slightly. He'd always said what he loved best about humans was their unpredictability, and she was sure he hadn't expected the good-natured ribbing. In fact, he'd been boning up on protocol—even having Marilynn test him—so as not to "blow it" for avatarity by saying something offensive in his first-ever official appearance as a Cabinet secretary. Well, the two elder statesmen had just thrown down. To Marilynn's inestimable pride, so too did Dante.

"In that case," offered the Secretary for Avatar Affairs, "I will endeavor to lose my innocent veneer of civility as soon as the mitigating circumstances permit." He ended with an ostentatious flourish of his hand and an overly formal bow. The avatar had said it in such a perfect homage to Cyrus's verbose speech and mannerisms that the new Secretary of Treasury at first seemed flabbergasted and then actually applauded.

"As I was saying," continued Dante, clearly cheered on by the positive response, "the authority was mine. As you all know, we've been fighting the Core avatars for years and are well aware of how they manifest themselves in systems they wish to destroy. With that knowledge and with the collusion of the Defense Secretary and the grand admiral, we used our now greater access to the Neuro"— Dante was making a clear reference to the fact that the OA avatars no longer had to hide in buried nodes—"to create an exact virtual copy of Admiral Trang's fleet. After running numerous tests, which involved the removing and replacing of various systems on each ship as well as applying the various forms of sabotage commonly used by the Core avatars and then matching them with what we've observed in the physical world, we've come to the conclusion that the UHF's fleet is pretty well screwed. Complete results are with your fleet."

"How screwed is the question," said Sandra.

"They're trying to run heavy cruisers with linked DijAssists," said J.D.

"Yeah," said Sandra with a short laugh. "I guess that's pretty screwed."

"Correct me if I'm wrong," said Padamir.

Again Cyrus grinned expectantly. "With pleasure."

"Then it should be twice as pleasing, since the question is directed toward you."

Cyrus bowed.

"Given what we discussed previously vis-à-vis our resources and the fact that we've emerged from the Avatar Plague intact, won't we be an industrial power again shortly?"

"Correct," answered Cyrus. "By my estimation, in just under a year or about how long it'll take the UHF just to find enough food to feed its survivors."

"So," added Rabbi, "for the first time in a long time, isn't time on our side?"

J.D. took a deep breath. "Your suppositions are correct; it's your conclusions that I believe are faulty. At this very instant, Trang is devising new methods and training his crews to operate their ships as best they can with the data systems they have. The UHF fleet that Trang has, while green, is still good— damn good, Madam President. In six months' time, I predict that they'll be able to use their ships with very little combat liability. They may even pull it off in four. Once that happens, Trang will come hunting. He knows that if he doesn't destroy the Alliance within a year, it's over." J.D. now focused her attention solely on the President. "Madam President, the odds are with me now. There- fore, we should strike now."

Sandra nodded and, thought Marilynn, did a masterly job of pretending to weigh the options—considering the President had already heard the arguments that morning and had already informed both Marilynn and J.D. of her decision.

"Do you have a name for this operation?" asked Sandra.

"Actually, yes, Madam President: Operation Endgame."

"Most appropriate," agreed Sandra. "Do it."

My sisters and brothers, I saw the faith of our people this day. I was trying to decide what my sermon should be, and as if guided by the very hand of Jesus himself, found myself walking toward the temple. You know the one of which I speak. The lines around the temple of the holy vessel have been so long, they stretch to the beginning of the thoroughfare. As it stands, priority has been given to members of our divinely led fleet now about to leave for what many sense is the final battle of this long and terrible struggle. Each spacer has been given only twenty seconds to touch the battle suit that the Chosen One, Justin Cord, transcended into heaven with; for there are hundreds of thousands of spacers in the fleet and only so much time before that fleet leaves this holy city. And it is thus fair that those spacers be given priority, for the presence of the Holy Justin brings peace to our warriors and may it bring peace to us all. The divine has touched us and shown us and tested us. Let us be worthy of the guidance. Let us be worthy of victory. Let us be worthy of peace and let us say us say, amen.

—Sermon heard before the temple on the day
the war turned seven years old

Grand admiral's quarters
Ceres

"Why do I have to stay?"

The little girl's voice held such heartbreak and pain that for a moment J.D. wavered—but only for a moment.

"Because, little one," she answered, crouching low, "this is the last battle of the war, and you are so very precious to me, more precious than anything."

"I know," sniffed Katy, bottom lip pushed forward.

"And it's important that I fight my best, right?"

Katy managed a single brave nod through her tears.

"But I may not be able to fight my best if I didn't know you were safe here on Ceres."

J.D. was not prepared for what happened next. Katy cannonballed into her and then grabbed her with such fierce determination that it seemed to J.D. as if the child were holding on to her for dear life—which Katy was. "But you'll die if you go without me!"

"Why do you say such a thing, little one?"

J.D. could feel the warm tears mixed with mucus on the lapel of her jacket and the nape of her neck. "Because it's the last battle, Mama Bo."

"Yes. But that's a good thing."

"No!" shrieked Katy into the scruff of J.D.'s neck. She then pulled back and stared forlornly at the woman who'd swept in and saved her, who'd taken her in from the cold and desperate halls of a dying asteroid and whisked her away to the sheltered confines and clockwork predictability of a warship, filled with food and uncles and aunts and angels and floating rolled-up balls of socks. "No," Katy said with downcast mouth and water-filled eyes. "The hero *always* dies in the last battle." And the tears began to flow anew.

"I'm no hero, little one," she said, hugging the child tightly. "I'm just one woman trying to do the best she can."

"That's what heroes *always* say!" wailed Katy. "You have to promise me you're coming back. You have to promise me, please!"

J.D. hugged Katy once more, stood up, and walked away without saying another word. Katy was in too much shock to notice the tears rolling freely down the face of her mama Bo, the grand admiral of the Outer Alliance and the Alliance's best chance to achieve victory.

The Triangle Office

Sandra was sitting across from Tyler Sadma. On the coffee table floating between them were the possible election dates. It was decided that when a sufficient number of refugees from Jupiter and the asteroid belt were integrated into the fabric of the outer planets, new elections would have to be held. So much had happened that new representation was desperately needed in order to let the will of the governed be expressed. Hektor's ruling by fiat with an Assembly that was literally on ice was not an example they wanted to emulate. But of course, the devil was in the details. The biggest one being when exactly to hold the election, followed by how to adjudicate votes of those still suspended, followed by whether or not to elect a new Vice President or have the Assembly choose one. And of course, the perennial question: Was it time to hold a constitutional convention or, at a minimum, set a date?

While they were in the midst of figuring out the nuts and bolts of Alliance politics, Sandra's DijAssist informed her of a low-priority message. Sergeant Holke knew better than to interrupt her when she was with any dignitary, much less Tyler Sadma—unless it was an emergency. But if it was not an emergency, why interrupt her—and with a low-priority signal, to boot. Because of the nearly successful coup, little oddities like the one that was occurring now tended to make her jumpy. She asked Tyler if he wouldn't mind waiting for a moment, and he readily acquiesced. She then took advantage of her newly integrated internal VR matrix and touched both her index and pointer fingers to her temples and scanned for any anomalies. She could find none in the immediate vicinity, so she decided to scan the outer one. She almost laughed when she realized what had the good sergeant flummoxed. She lingered a moment at the sight of the sergeant—one of the most fearless individuals she knew—looking so decidedly nervous and uncertain. She quickly returned to her physical body.

"Yes, Sergeant Holke," she said pleasantly.

Before Holke could say a word, the voice of an insistent child could be heard over the DijAssist. "Tell her it's important! Tell her it's me! Go on, *tell* her."

"Uh, Madam President, I, uh, have a, uh . . . situation here."

Sandra actually saw Tyler Sadma trying to hold back a laugh as the sergeant attempted to explain why his normally very strict security protocol about not interrupting the President unless in case of dire emergency had been so easily breached. And not at the gunpoint of a battalion of UHF assault marines or by the threat of imminent decapitation by the razor-sharp claws of one of Al's nightmares, but rather by the unbending tenacity of a six-year-old girl.

"Send her in, Sergeant," Sandra said, giggling.

"We can continue this conversation after lunch, Madam President," Tyler said. "They have fish sticks at the Congressional cafeteria, and if I don't get there on time, the damn Neptunian delegation eats them all." Sandra smiled at the excuse but accepted it. Katy flew into the room, ignoring the Speaker of the Congress altogether—even as he gave her a very cordial half bow—and into the outstretched arms of the President of the Outer Alliance.

"You have to save her!"

"Save who, Katy?" asked Sandra, the previous moment's amusement wiped away by the obvious terror in Katy's voice.

"Mama Bo!" screamed Katy, and then broke down into a mass of sobs.

Sandra held the crying girl to her bosom, rocking her back and forth. "Admiral Bl—, Mama Bo is fine, Katy-coo. I just talked to her an hour ago."

"But she won't be, Granny Sandy. She's not coming back."

Sandra stopped hugging the child and held her at arm's length, studying her intently. "What do you mean, 'She's not coming back,' child?"

"I know it! I just know it!"

"But how, Katy?"

"Because I'm not going with her."

Sandra's brow shot up. "She is not taking you?"

Katy shook her head vigorously.

"Hmm . . . ," mumbled Sandra, eyes narrowing ever so slightly. "But she took you to Mars." It had been whispered almost as an afterthought.

"Hello-oh!" said Katy, enough of the six-year-old emerging to sound annoyed at the density of the adults around her. "And she didn't promise. If she was coming back, she would *always* promise, and she didn't. She didn't, and she's not coming back. She has to, she has to." Katy crumpled once more into the President's warm embrace. Sandra knew that J.D. would burn the Earth to its mantle for the child now weeping in her arms. The fact that J.D. had altered a well-known pattern gave the President pause.

Sandra pulled Katy into her once again and then held the child's chin in her hand so they were looking eye to eye. "Little one, I am the President of the Outer Alliance. I am the one who first talked to the angels. You came to me because you think I can do something, and I can." Sandra's smile was wan but warm. "You can ask me for one thing, child, this one time and I wi—"

"She has to come back, she has to come back. Say she'll come back," pleaded Katy.

Sandra took the girl's hand and put it on her own heart. "Katy, Mama Bo will come home." When Sandra saw the tear-streaked face looking up at her, she decided then and there to add some more words of assurance with all the certainty she could muster, with a certainty that would get laws passed and rally whole peoples to win impossible victories.

"I promise," she said, and then softly began to sing.

> *Golden slumbers kiss your eyes,*
> *Smiles awake you when you rise.*
> *Sleep, pretty baby, do not cry,*
> *And I will sing a lullaby*

As Sandra sat rocking the child back and forth in her arms, humming gently into her ear, Katy, emotionally spent and physically exhausted, finally collapsed into a deep sleep. And Sandra started to change her plans. The fleet would soon be leaving and now she'd be going with it.

8 Hairsbreath

UHF battle fleet
High orbit of Mars

Admiral, it's confirmed," said his sensor officer, the excitement barely contained. "The Alliance fleet is on the move."

Trang's smile exuded confidence. "Let me guess: They're heading here."

"It's still too early to be sure, sir, but it would appear that way. They're heading for Jupiter, and it's the route they took the last time, Admiral."

"Well, we're not going to be here," Trang said with dry humor. "Prepare the fleet to break orbit. If they want us, they can come and get us."

"Sir," asked the XO, "what destination should I give the fleet?"

"Tell 'em"—Trang's smile brightened considerably—"tell 'em we're going home."

Alliance battle fleet
En route to Jupiter

"To the woman who kicked my ass today," said J.D., holding up a glass toward her second-in-command amidst a wave of cheers heard throughout the *Otter's* wardroom.

Suchitra bowed her head politely. "You're being unduly harsh on yourself, sir. After all, I did have the bulk of the heavy ships."

"But you did not fall for a single one of my ploys or let me prescribe your actions. *You* controlled the battle." J.D. looked at Suchitra with obvious pride. "You even knew what I was going to do."

Suchitra nodded, eyes brimming not only with the adulation but also with the knowledge that J.D. had been correct, Suchitra *had* known what her commanding officer was going to do.

"So, *nu?*" said J.D. borrowing one of Rabbi's oft-used phrases. "How did it feel? What was it like knowing what your opponent was going to do, knowing down to your soul?" There was about the question the aura of release, a discarding of loneliness. J.D. had had the gift of battle prescience for so long that she'd almost given in to thinking that perhaps it truly *was* a blessing, that perhaps the moniker she'd been saddled with *was* deserved. She was now especially thrilled to find out it wasn't, that it could be taught and that the Alliance could now go on without her.

"It felt," said Suchitra, "like the universe was standing still, and for the first time I saw how it all worked."

J.D. nodded, smiling empathetically. "Yes," she whispered. "Just like that."

"I've been in battles before and I've even outguessed my opponents, but it was never so clear, never like this. You've always felt that . . . it wasn't learned?"

J.D. nodded.

"I guess you really were sent from the gods themselves."

"If that's the case," answered J.D., now shaking her head, "then those gods must really like you as well."

The compliment caused Suchitra to blush, but given the woman's dark skin and the low light of the room, only J.D. could tell.

"Don't get too confident, Admiral. I'm pretty sure the gods talk to Trang as well."

Suchitra looked like she was going to argue, but stopped. "I think they do too. It's only fitting that we must earn our freedom if we're to be worthy of it."

"No matter the price," J.D. said, once again raising her glass.

Suchitra hesitated, knowing exactly what price the Blessed One was referring to and what part Suchitra herself had agreed to play in it. The young admiral raised her glass and answered her warlord. "No matter the price."

Sandra O'Toole was in the *New Alliance One* but not quite on it. She was enjoying herself in the ship's rather impressive Neuro net with an avatar she now thought of as a friend. It didn't hurt that as her body was resting in her quarters, watched over and protected by the ever-vigilant Sergeant Holke, her mind was on a tropical beach, drinking Bahama Mamas with Gwendolyn.

"So you're on this ship because a little girl asked you to?"

"Not quite," corrected Sandra. "I'm on this ship because a little girl showed me something I hadn't quite seen before."

"Really?" Gwendolyn seemed surprised. Then laughed as she reflected on how Dante, an impossibly young forty-one years of age and never having been twined with a human, had upended all of avatarity's preconceived notions—especially those of his mentor, Sebastian—in his quest to bring the two races together. "Actually," she said, sipping happily at the drink, "it makes perfect sense."

"You know, Gwenny," using the nickname she had taken to calling her one true friend amongst the avatars, "we think we're so damned smart, but every now and then, we're reminded of how little we actually know. So yes, I'm on this ship because of the prescience of a little girl who was wise enough to let me know that I needed to be."

"You were always good at listening to children, Sandra—yours and ours."

"Gwenny, there's no such thing as your children or our children; they're just children. And like all children, their minds are wonderfully uncluttered."

"Which is why you're here. But why *are* you here?"

"To keep a friend from doing something really stupid."

"Hopefully not something that might lose us the war," asked Gwendolyn with growing concern.

"Worse," answered Sandra drowsily, "something that could help us win it."

Executive mansion
Lake Geneva
Earth

Hektor Sambianco waited alone by the shore of the lake. As alone as Gretchen Arbieter would allow. He was fairly certain that his conversation would be private, which was the best a person in his position could hope for. As he looked over the lake at the ruins of the former capital of the UHF, he let out an irritable grunt. His bitter mood was at least momentarily subdued by the appearance of an approaching figure.

"Hello, Sam."

"Mr. President." Trang threw a brief but correct salute. "Mr. President, I'm afraid I owe you an apology."

"Really?" answered Hektor. "Well, this should be interesting."

"I'm afraid I didn't take your warning concerning the avatars seriously and delayed implementing them. That little dereliction of duty ended up costing me ships and men and has left the fleet weakened before an unrelenting enemy who's as ruthless and heartless as any in the history of the human race."

"Admiral," answered Hektor with a one-sided grin, "given my rather poor track record in the military department, I'm not ashamed to say you were justified. In fact, there's reason to suggest that we may not even have been in this mess if I'd listened to you sooner."

"I don't think so, Mr. President. It seems pretty obvious the OA had been waiting for just the right opportunity to unleash the Avatar Plague. I'm only glad it wasn't worse. And let's face it, as bad as it was, it could've been *a lot* worse."

"On that we can agree. So why don't we make this deal? I won't bring up the Avatar Plague if you don't bring up the Third Battle of the Martian Gates. And to sweeten the deal, what say you fight your battles however you want and I'll just shut the hell up."

Trang smiled amiably and bowed. "This stiff-necked martinet gratefully agrees, Mr. President."

Deal done, they passed the minutes looking out over the poisoned water of Lake Geneva. "I'm sorry to hear about your wife, Sam," Hektor said. "She was a good woman. Not what you would call a political animal, but kind and to the point. By Damsah's left nut, I really liked her for that."

"Thank you for saying that, sir. I know she would've appreciated hearing it." Trang looked down and his face suddenly grew hard. "What really gets me is that my wife dies, and her Damsah-forsaken father goes untouched. Ten billion people are murdered in a week, and that SOB doesn't get a hair on his head touched."

Hektor's lips twisted up. "I can still have him killed, Sam. Tricia's just itching to kill *someone*. Hell, she might even do that one herself."

Trang remained eerily silent.

Damsah, thought Hektor, truly awed, *bastard's actually thinking about it!*

After a brief respite, Trang shook his head and sighed. "It's tempting, Mr. President. More tempting than you can possibly know, but if there is an afterlife, well . . . I'd never hear the end of it."

"Don't suppose you would," confirmed Hektor, and then continued gazing out at the river. A moment later, a thought occurred to him. "You know, I could always have his government contracts examined instead."

Trang laughed. "I think the crooked son of a bitch might prefer to be killed!"

"Always leave something for the future," advised Hektor. After a moment, he turned to his battle admiral. "She's coming here, isn't she?"

"Yes, Mr. President. The Merciless One's coming home."

"You know, she used to be my greatest ally. When she was head of legal for GCI, we were unstoppable."

"Oh, she's stoppable, Mr. President."

"You really think so, Sam?" asked Hektor, his voice unable to hide the doubt.

"I *will* win, Mr. President. Our back's against the wall and we're fighting for our very lives. If we lose, I'm convinced she'll destroy us utterly."

"You believe that."

"Absolutely, Mr. President."

"If you don't mind my asking, *why* do you believe that?"

"Because when I win, it's exactly what I'm going to do to them. Destroy their Damsah-forsaken worlds, settlement by bloody settlement. For the survival of us all and for the ten billion they murdered, they *all* must die."

As Trang's brooding figure looked out over the waters, Hektor allowed a half smile. It might not be necessary to have this man killed after all.

UHF fleet
High orbit around Luna

Trang looked at the data coming in over the portable holo-emitter bolted to the useless holo-tank in the middle of the command sphere. If he thought it was demeaning or a bad omen that the Battle of Earth, the final and most important confrontation of the whole terrible war was being planned on what was essentially a child's toy, he didn't let it show. If anything, he had a grim confidence in the ingenuity displayed by his fleet, which had been infectious. A recent comment of his was already making the rounds and inspiring the fleet. "When the Alliance realizes that we won using nothing more powerful than DijAssists and an abacus or two, we won't have to shoot the bastards; they'll die of embarrassment."

In the three weeks since the Alliance fleet had left Saturn, Trang practically invented and then taught a way of decentralized ship control that gave his ships 85 percent of the control they had with the old systems. It had taken endless hours of drilling and sleep deferred with drugs. But his spacers were willing to work as they'd never worked before. They were no longer fighting for incorporation or for majority. They were no longer even fighting for victory. Every person in Trang's fleet understood that they were fighting for nothing less than survival. If they failed, their homes and loved ones would be left at the mercy of a woman who'd shown she had none, having already destroyed one planet, and at the bloodstained hands of another, who'd unleashed the Avatar Plague and nearly destroyed a civilization. They were under no illusions what would happen if they lost.

But for many, it was not only survival but vengeance that motivated them as well. When they won, they were determined to wipe out every single member of the Outer Alliance and their avatar masters or lackeys, depending on whom you asked. Either way, the Alliance was going to pay for having started the war, then not stopping it, and finally for coming very close to winning it. They were going to pay with the very last drop of their blood. Whether that meant the spacers of the UHF or the miners of the Alliance, many no longer knew or cared.

All except for Trang. As the little holo-tank came online, he saw the 287 ships of the Alliance drawn up in battle array just out of range of his ships. The Battle of Earth was about to begin.

AWS *Warprize II*

The data systems were working perfectly. J.D. looked on, eyes approving. She knew what each one of her ships knew, when they knew it, and how they knew it. It gave her an incredible advantage in the impending battle, and she was intending to use it to lay her last trap of the war.

Trang has some plan to hurt us. It's probably got to do with attacking our data systems or sensors. It's what I'd do. It's our greatest advantage, and if they can neutralize it, we'd be forced to learn in battle what they've had three weeks to figure out: how to fight with crippled ships. When he springs his trap, I'll spring mine—even at the cost of everyone on this ship, small price to pay. I must draw Trang's forces around me, must be the magnet that will distort his lines, act as the torn seam that only Suchitra can slice through to end this thing, once and for all.

"I'm overconfident, Sam." J.D.'s chant had begun. "You have my number. I'm going to use my superior training and data systems to dance rings around you. I'm so overconfident, I'll go after you in order to end this quickly. You just can't wait to punish me for my overconfidence can you, Sam?"

And for the first time in the war, J. D. Black truly knew that Sam Trang was listening. She had thought so at the Long Battle, but now she knew. A part of her couldn't help but wonder if this was what the prophets actually felt. She knew she was going to beat him, even at the price of her life. Her command crew now looked at her with utter conviction. They understood what her whispered words meant: that the divine was granting the Blessed One her power to control the enemy, to read their thoughts and control their actions. Victory, they all felt, was at hand.

J.D. leaned back in her command chair and crossed her legs confidently. Head bent slightly forward, eyes narrowed and now staring in a hawklike gaze at the theater of war unfolding before her. "Captain Lee," she said in a voice thick with resolve and anticipation.

"Sir!"

"Order the fleet to prepare for bat—"

Just then, the hatch opened, flooding the dimly lit command sphere with the overly bright light of the corridor. J.D. turned toward the light, prepared for trouble because no one should have had the authority to open that door without her permission. As her body swung around toward the hatch, the faceplate on her battle armor slammed shut. She reached for her blast pistol and brought it to bear, but to her surprise, the person outlined by the light of the corridor *did* have the authority to open the door. But *New Alliance One* had left the fleet hours ago and that person was supposed to be gone with it.

"Admiral," Sandra O'Toole said as calmly as if she'd just interrupted a card game, "we need to talk."

J.D. waited until the door of her quarters were closed before she spoke to her President. For a moment, she looked at the pristine orderliness of the space with a pang of regret—no telltale signs of Katy—but quickly focused on the job, which was . . . what, exactly?

The President went over to J.D.'s wet bar and poured a shot of amber liquid into a glass tumbler. "Can I get you one?" asked the President nonchalantly. J.D., face still bathed in the tension of the command sphere, stiffly nodded.

Sandra raised her tumbler and took a sip. "Apple juice," she said, surprised. "You sly dog, you. And all this time, I thought you allowed yourself a little vice."

"It is against the wishes of Allah." J.D. could no longer wait. "Madam President, *Sandra,* what are you doing here?"

"J.D., you can't win this battle."

"The hell I can't! He's listening to me. For the first time in this cursed war, *Trang is finally listening to me* when I speak. The Alliance says that I'm the Blessed One, that Allah chose me. I don't know, maybe he did, but I do know that every time I felt this connection—the one I'm feeling now—I knew what was going to happen. Do you have any idea how terrifying it was to fight a man who outnumbered me every time we fought and not have that feeling? To face him time and again, praying for that blessed sign and not once, *not once* ever having it? Well, God has finally heard my prayers, Sandra, and I'm telling you whatever your fears, ignore them. I *will* win this battle."

"Perhaps I misspoke," said Sandra. "Of course you can win this battle, Janet, but the real question is, should you?"

J.D.'s war face disappeared only to be replaced by her palpable look of shock. In her six years of fighting for the Alliance, it was the most outrageous question she had ever been asked.

"Uh . . . Sandra, do you have any idea what happens if I lose?"

"I think I do. Trang comes after us with everything he's got and attempts to do to us what he's been mistakenly led into believing we've done to him. Now, I repeat: Do you know what happens if you win?"

"We win," said J.D. "The Alliance is saved."

"To do what exactly, Janet?"

"To survive, I guess," said J.D., suddenly confused. "What else is there?"

Sandra's mouth turned upward; apparently, she knew.

"I haven't given it a lot of thought, Sandra. I've been kind of concentrating on the whole 'barely surviving against impossible odds' thing."

"And you've done that rather well, I might add; and you can win. Congratulations, the UHF fleet is destroyed. Trang is dead or captured."

"Preferably dead," said J.D., "and Jackson with him."

"Very good," agreed Sandra. "And don't forget your pièce de résistance."

"What are you talking about?"

"You, of course. You die too, remember?"

J.D. crooked her head slightly. "That's not a certainty."

"Please, Janet. Who are we kidding? It's pretty much a certainty, right?"

"Wait . . . how did you—?"

"I didn't," said Sandra. "Much to my embarrassment, your daughter had to tell me."

"Katy? *My* Katy?" asked J.D., flummoxed.

"Smart kid, your daughter, smarter than me in this case. I changed my plans when I realized you'd decided to go all Valkyrie on us. But even if you don't have to deal with the mess of your 'victory' "—Janet's cheek twitched slightly at the contempt with which Sandra spoke that word, her eyes unconsciously going to the display case with the medal of that name—"we will."

"You do understand, don't you," said J.D., "that if we don't win, we die? If we don't win, our freedom is destroyed and we fought for nothing?"

"Perfectly, but let's look at the other side of the coin, shall we? When we win here, we'll have to destroy or occupy all orbital installations that can be used as a threat to the Alliance. We'll have to destroy or confiscate the solar energy array that provides the Earth with an enormous amount of its power. We'll also have to deny orbital rights to the Earth. They cannot be allowed to orbit their own planet. Or do you suggest that we don't do these things?"

"No, Sandra, they'd be the minimum precautions needed."

"Am I missing anything?"

"As a matter of fact, you are. I'd have to order the bombardment of the planet to eliminate resources that could be used to overcome our advantages of high orbit. We would also need to comb the planet for their best leaders in science, technology, and the armed forces in order to isolate them from the general population. We would also have to maintain certain on-planet assets in order to keep tabs on the population."

Sandra nodded her head. "Leaving aside the occupation forces we'll need in perpetuity, what will happen to the population of the Earth after we deny them access to their orbital facilities and lob a few more rocks at the surface?"

"Mass starvation, pestilence, a total breakdown of civil authority," she answered. "Planetary unity would break down with no central control."

"Oh, they'll have a unifying thought, Admiral. Every time they look up into the night sky, they'll curse the tiny dots of orbiting lights, the enslaving lights that condemned another ten or so billion of them to death. And they will unite. Even with only eight or nine billion left on the planet, they'll still outnumber us—will always outnumber us—and they'll hate us for eternity."

"But you'd be in charge, Sandra. You'll find a way to solve it," she said, almost as a plea. "That's what you do, what you've always done. And it's why I've been working so hard to make sure you have real power."

"Aha," said Sandra drolly. "So what you'd wish for me is to rule over the majority of the human race from a throne made of skulls with the sullen mass of humanity bowing to that hellish throne for all eternity."

"That's a little dark, even for you, Sandra. You and I both know we could eventually bring them into the Alliance. Sure, it would take generations—"

"In the past, it might've worked—and only *might* have. You could wait a hundred years while the older generations died off and the later generations came around to accepting the new status quo. Four generations later, they wouldn't know anyone who died, any family member or friend horribly oppressed. But in our bright, wonderful present, we live a long time. The old generation won't die off so quick. They'll be ever present to remind the new Earthers what those off-planet bastards did to them and will continue to do. The hate will never die, Janet. And you can guess what'll happen if we drop our guard for just one second."

"They'll seek vengeance. They'll drench the solar system in the blood of our children." J.D. sagged. "You're right," she finally whispered in despair. "It *will* never end. Katy will have to be a soldier all her life. By Allah, if they won't stop, will we have to kill them all?"

"What?" Sandra asked, eyes glittering maliciously. "Isn't our freedom worth it?"

J.D. shot her vicious scowl. "Are you saying the traitors were right?"

"Not at all. Their problem was that they only saw two possibilities. Truth is, you see only two possibilities. Trang and Sambianco see only two possibilities."

J.D. stood dumbfounded, desperately searching for a way out of the mess they'd all perilously drawn themselves into. She didn't want Katy to grow up a killer, didn't want to spend her days overseeing more death, more destruction; didn't want to have to look at the disfigured side of her face for the rest of her life. She turned to Sandra, and a smile formed on her lips. It was there. J.D. saw her hope reflected in the face of the Unincorporated Woman and knew that once again, the journey had taken an odd twist and that once again, she would follow.

"You have an idea."

"Yes," said Sandra with a seductive grin.

"That presumably does not involve us dying or murdering most of the human race."

"Uh-huh," Sandra said, her smile growing ever wider.

"What do I have to do?" J.D. said with a wonderful mixture of dread and relief.

Sandra came up and, taking both J.D.'s hands in her own, looked her prickly and calculating warlord in the eye and said, "Janet, you're going to have to really, really trust me."

UHFS *Liddel*

"Why are they waiting?" Trang heard Zenobia ask over their secure DijAssist link.

"Hell if I know," answered Trang. "But if this lasts much longer, we'll have to go to the Beta Plan."

"Sir," Zenobia said, real concern in her voice, "we have a slightly better chance of success if they attack us."

"Of course, if they're experiencing some sort of difficulty, we could be wasting the perfect opportunity. Truth is, Zenobia, we don't know what's going on. In battle, you never have enough information. At some point, you just have to commit."

"And are we, sir?"

"Hell no," laughed Trang, "least not yet. We'll wait and see what develops."

"Admiral," Trang's sensor officer reported.

Trang's brow shot up. "Well, that didn't take long. What've you got, Paul?"

An image appeared in the jury-rigged holo-projector. "It appears to be an executive-class long-range transport, sir. Whatever it is, it's been modified." The sensor officer dug deeper. "Sir, I may be mistaken on this, but . . . well, I think that ship is what the rebels call Blessed One, Admiral Black's command shuttle."

"Now *that* is interesting," said Trang.

It took over three hours for the two sides to negotiate how it was going to work out, including a lot of verification and inspection, but the end result had Admiral Trang anxiously standing at attention while Admiral J. D. Black's shuttle was landing in the loading bay of *his* ship, the UHFS *Liddel*. Of course, the computer systems on the shuttle had been partitioned and swept for avatar coding, and the pilot they sent out to bring the shuttle in had actually been one of Trang's. Still, after it had been confirmed that the President of the Outer Alliance, the Unincorporated Woman herself, wanted to talk, Trang's gut told him that maybe he should listen. Even he had to admit she was taking most of the risks.

He couldn't help noticing that while she was dressed in a surprisingly simple and comfortable jumpsuit, he was still in full battle armor. His security detail had been afraid of hidden Alliance nanite technology that could operate despite their best efforts. Trang actually felt silly, but the look of the OA President's bodyguard made him glad of the snipers if not the suit. Trang knew the type. This one looked like he wanted to destroy Trang's entire ship with his bare hands and the only thing stopping him was his own self-control. The intelligence data on Sergeant Holke had shown him to be surprisingly good at high-level protection as well as an exceptional combat leader. Why the man was still a sergeant when he should have been a full-bird colonel was beyond Trang. But it was good to see that Holke had honored the agreement and come aboard unarmed.

It was, however, the woman who commanded all the attention. Damn, if she didn't remind him of Amanda Snow. The woman was every bit the picture of absolute confidence he remembered Amanda having been. Of course, flying completely unarmed onto a ship filled with people devoted to seeing you dead for having murdered in the billions their friends and family also spoke to that confidence; he liked it. In fact, he'd done almost the exact same thing all those years ago at Eros, under eerily similar circumstances. This time, however, O'Toole didn't have the winning hand as he'd had at Eros—or did she? It was possible the woman was insane, in which case he'd gotten all dressed up for nothing. But this woman didn't look insane; she looked pretty much how he'd imagined she would—in real life, that is: supremely dangerous. The holo-vids, he saw, didn't do her justice. Sandra O'Toole, in her own way, radiated a danger far more palpable than the obviously loyal and skilled combat veteran slightly to the rear and right of her.

Trang had enough. He stripped from his battle suit and strode right up to the woman. He knew his security detail was probably going nuts at that moment, but his gut told him this woman was not a danger in the classic sense of the word and he needed to assess her as much as possible—as soon as possible.

"Ms. O'Toole," he said with a formal bow, "welcome aboard the UHFS *Liddel*." He'd be sold for a penny stock before he would shake hands like a Justinite.

The woman returned his bow perfectly. "Thank you for having me aboard, Admiral Trang. I know it cannot have been easy."

"Nor for you, Ms. O'Toole." Trang acknowledged her but refused to give her the title of President. He considered a variety of different tactics. He was sorely tempted to give her a guided tour and just talk with her about trivial matters until he could get a sense of her, but something told him that would be more to her benefit than his. In fact, for the first time in his life, Trang was no longer sure he was the most capable person in the room. He found that fact to be both worrisome and exciting. He decided to try the direct approach. "Why are you here, Ms. O'Toole?"

"To let you win the war, Admiral." She'd said it like it was the most obvious thing in the world.

Trang took a moment to digest the implication. He even looked to Sergeant Holke for some sort of guidance, but saw the poor man was just as confused as he was. "Perhaps we should talk further, Ms. O'Toole. We can meet in my conference room."

"Normally, I'd be delighted," she said, pulling a small rubber band from her front pocket and tying her hair back in a ponytail, "but one of the conditions I was forced to accept was that I would not leave the vicinity of the shuttle. If I did, or it was destroyed, J.D. was most emphatic that it would result in this battle everyone seems so intent on having."

"I'm afraid this battle is a necessity, Madam Pre— Ms. O'Toole." Trang grimaced at the slip, but damn it, the woman *was* Presidential. "And I hardly think Admiral Black has the ability to know if you're near the shuttle or even if it's intact while inside my flagship."

Sandra leaned forward and whispered. "I won't tell anyone about the 'Madam President' slip. I can't speak for the good sergeant, though." Holke's eyes pierced through Trang. Clearly the sergeant would like nothing better than to kill Trang if he could do so without getting his President shot at the same time. "As for the ability of Admiral Black to know where I am," continued Sandra, "or the shuttle's status or whereabouts, I couldn't really tell you. She seemed very confident that it wouldn't be a problem. I wouldn't test her on the shuttle, though. She's always hated the interior. Calls it an executive's hedonistic excess and would love any excuse to blow it to smithereens."

Trang saw the sergeant nod in slight agreement till he caught himself and reverted to his barely suppressed murderous rage. "How she feels about you, I suppose, is the more important question."

Sandra nodded. "Right now, she's rather annoyed and very concerned. She was on the verge of ordering her fleet into battle, just itching to fight the Battle of Earth."

Trang smiled. "Funny, that's what we're calling it too."

"It does seem obvious. In regards to your question, I think she likes me, but if I died, she'd be satisfied with the consolation prize of wiping you out of existence." With that, Holke smiled contentedly. It was not comforting.

"You wish to discuss the fate of the solar system—" Trang looked around the bay of his massive ship, at the snipers, at the concerned and angry faces, at himself. "—in my landing bay?"

"We can always go into the shuttle, if you wish."

An hour later, Trang and Sandra were sitting at a portable table outside her shuttle. The chairs were functional, and the device on the table was doing its job of obscuring their lips and garbling their voices. There was nothing to eat or drink on the table. There was nothing to record their conversation either. Historians would never forgive this lapse.

"Let me see if I understand this," Trang began. "You want to surrender."

"Oh, for the love of Justin," said Sandra, "no. We don't want to surrender; we want to leave."

"Leave what?"

"The solar system," answered Sandra.

"Does your side know this?" asked Trang incredulously.

"The only thing 'my side' knows is that you started murdering us in the hundreds of millions. They're scared out of their minds that you're so crazy, you have to be put down. They aren't even fighting for freedom anymore."

"They're fighting for survival," said Trang. In longer than he cared to admit, he looked at the war from the Alliance's point of view.

"Both sides are," said Sandra. "That's dangerous. When both sides are reduced to fighting for survival, they can and will do anything. Admiral Black is positive she can defeat you." Sandra looked at Trang directly. "Can you defeat her?"

Trang was struck by how many people had asked him that question over the years, but he never would've guessed this woman would be one of them. He looked into his heart, deciding she should have an honest answer. "Yes," he said with absolute conviction, "yes, I can."

"Should you?" she asked for the second time in a day.

"It beats the alternative."

"Wrong. I just gave you an alternative."

"You expect me to believe that the Alliance is just going to—" Trang paused, searching for the words. "—go away?"

"Why not? Admiral Trang, what does the UHF want? What are you ultimately fighting for?"

"Security," he said. "The solar system is too small to have it be divided into competing political groups. This war has surely proved that."

"I completely agree. But *we* were not fighting for security. We were fighting for freedom. The Alliance forgot something that I remember very well. You see, I was once an American."

"What does the fact that you come from a defunct and dysfunctional civilization have to do with the matter at hand?"

"I'll tell you."

Sandra's good cheer was starting to annoy Trang. Not because he was against cheer, but because hers was so damned infectious. He'd already found himself on numerous occasions during the conversation lost in her words. He'd prided himself on objectivity and distance, and now he was feeling almost too close—too interested. Still, it was his duty to listen, to judge. And so he would.

"You know what made America great for the time it was great?"

"It had a large land mass with abundant resources and a well-educated and motivated population—well, until the last seventy years. It had weak neighbors and some outstanding leaders in the beginning."

"All of that's nice—and well done on the history, by the way—but it's not what made America great. What made my former home great is that it was made up of people who were willing to run away."

"Run away?" repeated Trang, desperately trying to understand.

"Run away, get the hell out, find someplace better. America was mostly made up of people who had enough will to leave where they were and find someplace better. Most people are not willing to do that. They'll stay where they are and make the best of it. Why do you think the Outer Alliance did as well as it did? It's made up of the same sort of people who started America. You know: contentious, obnoxious, stiff-necked bastards."

Trang did not seem to hear the self-deprecating humor and began to smooth the veins that had popped up on both sides of his skull. "You've been planning to make your people run away for over a year?" he asked.

"No," answered Sandra with a smile filled with disappointment. "I was hoping to create a peace between the UHF and the OA. After Jupiter and Mars, I was hoping both sides would realize that we were risking the end of the human race or near enough, anyways. I tried to have Hektor killed, but he kept on escaping. I was willing to let him have a lot just to get a ten-year truce. In that time, I figured I could've gotten close to a hundred million settlers away. After the rest of the Alliance realized it was possible, they would have followed. But Hektor refused every single offer."

"Well, c'mon, Ms. O'Toole. You *were* trying to kill him," offered Trang.

"It's not like he was giving me kitten licks, Admiral. It's war; at some point, you should try to make a deal or it just becomes pointless slaughter."

Trang's eyes flashed in sagacity. "So *that's* what this is about."

For the first time since she'd been aboard the *Liddel*, Sandra truly met Trang's eyes with her own. "I can't make a deal with Hektor, Admiral."

Trang did not mistake the meaning of those words. But he could not quite allow himself to think where that path lay. "What makes you think you can make one with me?"

"Because I know that you'll at least listen."

Trang knew he was betraying his President by not throwing the woman off the ship without a suit, but he also was gaining valuable insight into the mind of the enemy. She was no fool, and he'd be one if he didn't hear her out all the way through—*that* much he knew.

"Go on," he said evenly.

"The Avatar Plague sealed it for me."

"You mean the plague *you* started."

"Admiral, you can choose to believe what you've been fed or you can use this valuable time to ascertain whether or not I'm lying to you. I assure you any statements I make here, I will back up with enough evidence to make even your most suspicious naysayers sick to the point of puking. Will you listen to me?"

Trang took a deep breath and nodded slowly.

"So we sat back and watched our two enemies, the UHF and Core avatars kill each other. We were dismayed. But only after the fact did I realize the destruction you experienced was practically inevitable. Both you and the Core avatars had leaders who valued security over everything else. But when you won, we were hoping to now make some sort of deal. I mean, after all, we were not killing you; we were doing our level best not to even threaten you. And what did Hektor do? He somehow convinced you all that this plague was entirely of our making. Think about it, Admiral. We *both* had avatars living amongst our peoples. We *both* had the same choices, opportunities, and dangers. But somehow, your choices ended up being our fault."

"That's not fair," said Trang. "Our intelligence is sketchy, but apparently, 'our' avatars were led by a self-obsessed nut job willing to do anything to achieve his own limited ends."

"As were ours," said Sandra. "But we did something about him that did not involve us destroying each other, and I certainly don't blame the UHF for what Sebastian or Al in all his numbers did. Hektor chose to blame us, and the UHF has once more chosen to believe him." Sandra sighed, "With the Avatar Plague, I realized that we can't do this gradually over decades. We're just too different now. If the human race is to survive—both our branches—we must separate. But Hektor won't take that deal. He'd rather rule over a million starving humans on a devastated Earth reduced to a dark age we may never recover from, and call it victory. If it costs forty billion lives, what does he care?"

"He's just trying to win."

"No, Admiral. It's *you* who are just trying to win. Hektor is trying to destroy. And Admiral, you know in your heart we won't be, can't be destroyed. But you *can* win. If your goal is security, you can have the solar system. For us, it's just not worth it."

Trang smoothed out a vein on his forehead and thought about what the OA President had said. She hadn't lied to him outright—which is to say she believed what she was saying. She also hadn't tried to buy him off or truly subvert him. She'd told him the truth as she knew it and was prepared to present evidence where controversy or agitprop existed in order to back up her understanding of the truth. More important, he knew that as sure as the sun shone this woman would do what she said. That she'd already done so was clear by virtue of the fact that she was now sitting across from him, discussing the fate of billions while hundreds of thousands sat around the two of them, waiting to tear into one another, waiting to die. If she really did leave, taking billions with her, really did separate, then what indeed would he be fighting for? Pissing rights? Too many had died already for such folly. Sam Trang put his fingers once more to his forehead, but the veins were now gone. He put his hands in his lap.

"Ms. O'Toole. I am prepared to listen, but it's critical that you don't misconstrue my listening as anything but that: just listening."

Sandra nodded slowly. "Agreed."

"In that case, please spell out the basics of this deal you propose."

"We declare an immediate truce. Your forces don't go beyond the orbit of Mars; we don't go beyond the orbit of Jupiter. The asteroid belt is neutral territory."

"We would need Jupiter's hydrogen if this is going to work."

"That can be negotiated. Small teams from both sides can extract and freeze hydrogen and propel the blocks, if the details can be agreed to. In two to three years, those who wish will leave the solar system. We already have the ability to do so. The truth is, humanity could've left centuries ago, but the nature of the incorporated system is such that it's counterproductive to leave and so kept everyone in system. You can't collect dividends across stellar distances."

"You're telling me everyone in the Alliance will just go?"

"Of course not," laughed Sandra. "Quite a few will stay. Honestly, I figure only about a billion or so will actually leave. The ones who stay behind will have to agree to abide by the rules of incorporation. They'll be given full pardons and seventy percent of their own shares, minimum."

"Bullshit. We didn't even offer our own people that deal."

"I suggest you do," said Sandra. "I'm offering you the solar system, and you're arguing percentages? Where in space are we having this conversation?"

"On the landing bay of my flagship," said Trang.

"Which is in orbit around the Moon, waiting for an Alliance attack to begin," added Sandra. "All in all, I think I'm being insanely generous."

"I see your point," agreed Trang, lips turned slightly upward. "How do we know you won't use the time to arm and come back when we don't have numerical advantage?"

"How do we know you won't do the same? We can send observers, but the truth is, once both sides stop trying to kill each other it will be almost impossible to get them to start again for a generation or two."

"I just can't see your people being willing to leave," Trang said with some worry. "I won't lie—it would present a bit of a sticking point. It is, after all, the crux of the deal."

Sandra narrowed her eyes and leaned forward slightly. "I know my people, Admiral. They will stay and fight to the death to protect their loved ones. But once the threat of shadow auditing and extermination is ended, they won't have that great a reason to stay, not with an entire galaxy calling out to them."

"Shadow auditing?" asked Trang with concern.

"I have some things you need to look at. I can send it or you can come or you can send someone you trust."

"Is that the next step?"

"If you don't want a battle, yes, Admiral, that would be the next step."

Trang nodded his agreement. "Then I propose we take the next step . . . if only to listen."

A knowing grin appeared on Sandra's tired face. "If only to listen," she agreed.

"On a personal level, Ms. O'Toole—and this is a confession of sorts, I suppose—I must tell you how much I had wanted to fight this battle."

"I know, Admiral."

"The best I ever got out of Admiral Black was a draw and a tactical retreat, and she forced me to retreat from Ceres. But I have her measure now."

"Funny, you know she said the same thing about you."

"She may be right," admitted Trang.

Sandra was taken back by his honesty and rewarded it with appreciative smile. Trang knew that smile; it was of respect.

"But," he continued, "I don't have the right to risk a single life under my command—let alone the billions of lives that would be affected—just to see if I can beat her. I have enough blood on my hands. If the admiral and I really need to see who has the biggest dick, we can find a field and shoot at each other with no one else to suffer. Besides," he said, getting up from the table, "if this doesn't work out, it's not as if we can't start killing each other tomorrow. . . . I wasn't at all sure I'd be able to say this when you first boarded, but it has been a real pleasure getting to meet you, Ms. O'Toole."

"And you as well, Admiral."

AWS *Warprize II*

"Admiral, it's your shuttle," said Fatima.

"Is it giving the proper call sign?" asked J.D.

"No, Admiral," answered Fatima, alarmed, "it's not giving any call sign at all."

"Thank Allah," said J.D. in obvious relief. "Launch shuttle three. The crew's been briefed on the proper procedure."

"At once," Fatima said, not at all understanding, but suddenly hoping and not caring why.

It took an hour for the shuttle to be cleared, and when it was, J.D. was the first to greet it. She saluted Sandra as she exited. "How did it go, Madam President?"

"We have a chance, Janet. We have a tiny, tiny chance. I need the fleet to pull back three hundred thousand kilometers directly opposite the course of something; he said you would understand."

"Directly opposite our projected course of Earth intercept," J.D. said. She gave orders to Fatima, who transmitted them to Jasper Lee to send to the fleet. "Can he do this?"

Sandra shot J.D. a look. "Is that hope or disappointment?"

"I have no desire to win here, to get the honor of enslaving or killing billions of my fellow humans. I'll do it if I have to, but only if there's no other choice."

Sandra's smile warmed a part of J.D.'s heart she'd reserved for only two other people. One of them was dead, and the other was probably ready to kill her if she wasn't hugged to death first.

"I'm so proud of you at this moment, Janet, and the answer is, yes, he can do this. We need to send him all the data we have on UHF operations. Especially the stuff Hektor hasn't been sharing. Make sure Dr. Wong's little enterprise is at the top of that list. He'll be sending a special visitor to pick it up."

An hour later, a UHF shuttle landed in the loading bay of the AWS *Otter*. An Alliance honor guard was present, and attention was called as Zenobia Jackson stepped out from the shuttle into the midst of her enemy. If she felt that everyone in sight should be shot as traitors, she did not let it show, but rather strode forcefully to Suchitra Kumari Gorakhpur and gave a perfect salute, which was perfectly returned.

"Admiral Jackson," said Suchitra in crisp, clear tone that easily carried in the small landing bay, "welcome to the Alliance War Ship *Otter*." Even though she'd been warned by both the President and the grand admiral to be proper, Suchitra could not help emphasizing the word *Alliance*.

Zenobia, who'd been given equally clear warnings to "play nice," let the comment slide. "That was good work you did the last time you were out here, Admiral. It couldn't have been easy taking over like that. I regret you being on the wrong side."

Suchitra gave a polite bow. "That's what we say about you, Admiral. You're a Belter, after all. Why'd you join the other side? We would have won the Long Battle if it hadn't been for you."

"Because I swore an oath and still felt bound by it when the war broke out, and thank Damsah you didn't win the Long Battle. I was—" Zenobia stopped. "Is that"—Zenobia pointed to the holo-projection of Allison standing in the background—"an *avatar*?" The question had been asked with such venom and the word used with such disdain that Zenobia had effectively condemned with the force of her emotions an entire race to pejorative status.

"Yes," answered Suchitra. "As you know, we have a pact with avatarity, and she's the representative of the Alliance avatars and the personal—"

"Get *it* out of here," snarled Zenobia.

"*It* has a name," retorted Allison.

"*It* is a murderer!"

"That's funny, coming from the people who brought us Alhambra, Jupiter, and the Belt—calling *us* murderers."

"Allison," Suchitra said in a restrained but forceful voice, "you are ordered to get out of my landing bay, now!"

Allison, clearly fuming, bowed respectfully and began to make her way out of the bay. She was soon joined by a few other human crew members, who'd taken umbrage at the way their fellow crew member had been treated—diplomatic entreaty or no.

Suchitra should have known that the UHF would have added holo-filters to on-op iris displays after the Avatar Plague. But how could Trang not have warned her? Suchitra was kicking herself; she should've banned avatars from the bay, but over the last several weeks, she, like most, had gotten so used to seeing their avatars, literally and figuratively, that they'd come to accept them as just another part of the crew. They were so damn useful, after all.

"Wait a minute," commanded Zenobia before Allison could leave.

"Admiral," warned Suchitra, "this is a diplomatic mission, which you are now jeap—"

But Zenobia was no longer listening. Rage consumed her. "Your supposed race murdered ten billion human beings: my friends, my . . . family. Not fucking, zeros, ones, and qubits, but *real,* living humans!"

Allison's eyes flared as she swung around, abandoning her supporters. She strode with angry, purposeful steps right at Zenobia. The avatar was so upset that she walked through several solid objects to make a beeline for the UHF admiral, when she normally would've gone around like a human. She stopped a foot from the object of her wrath. "Now, you listen to me."

Zenobia's eyes widened in shock. She hadn't expected this, hadn't thought an avatar even had an opinion, much less one she'd march right up to her and express.

"There were over twenty billion avatars in the Core. I knew a lot of them—some for well over a hundred years. How many people in your life have you known for that long, Admiral? How many have you loved? Well, guess what, *human,* they're all dead. Maybe you're used to dead, being a meatbag, but our being just ones, zeros, and qubits," she said in a mockery of Zenobia's words, "meant we were supposed to live forever. That is, until your kind murdered them."

"You started it!"

"Which is the only reason we don't try to kill all of you murderous meatbag UHF *fucks!*" Allison finished in a roar. Then she held up her hands to her mouth, realizing what she'd said and, more important, felt. Her expression turned from one of rage to one of shock. She looked around at everyone in the landing bay imploringly. "They're all dead. We've sent out searches at both Mars and Earth/Luna, and we get back . . . nothing. Twenty billion of our friends and parents and children . . . the children . . . and nothing," she cried, looking desperately at the humans. "When you die, you have bodies, you have something, to bury."

She stopped searching and just looked down, her voice despairing. "At least you have something to mourn," she said as the tears streamed down her face. Without looking up, she simply vanished.

Zenobia Jackson stood in abject silence, too stunned to move. And she too was forced to consider a side of the war that had never occurred to her. And seeing the pain and loss on one avatar's face made the second-highest-ranking officer in the UHF realize that every avatar must have been capable of that level of emotion, had in essence been human. And that her government had just had tens of billions of them exterminated.

Presidential retreat
Lake Geneva

"What do you mean they're just sitting there?" Hektor asked calmly to the gathered Cabinet members.

Luciana looked to Tricia, who nodded and stood up from her place at the Cabinet table. "Mr. President, for the last three days, the two fleets have been doing just that: sitting there. Our final word from Trang before he imposed the agreed-upon communication blackout was that the enemy fleet was approaching their position near Luna and battle was imminent."

"From our vantage point," offered Luciana, "it looked like they were getting ready to engage. Admiral Black's fleet was much smaller but admittedly superior. Trang had been hoping to let the Alliance attack first. Beyond that, we had no idea what his plan was." Luciana looked confused. "Magnetic fields were detected enhancing in both fleets, and both fleets had ships shut tight for atomic acceleration."

"Then they just stopped," said Tricia, obviously annoyed that she could not access her operatives in the UHF fleet due to the communications blackout.

"They did not just stop," growled Hektor. "Something stopped them." He called up a fuzzy image that would have been cleared up by automatic computer adjustment, but wasn't. Another reminder of how much the world had changed with the lobotomization of the Neuro. "This image is blurred, but if I'm not mistaken, that is Blessed One, the primary means of transportation for the Unincorporated Woman or J. D. Black."

"We can't absolutely confirm that, sir," said Tricia. "But we are eighty percent certain it is Blessed One or an executive-class transport made to look like it."

"That ship flies out between the fleets and they do nothing?" Hektor sounded dangerously split between confusion and rage. "Shouldn't our fleet have blown the hell out of it? Isn't that what *our* ships are supposed to do to *their* ships?"

"The *possible* Blessed One may have communicated with Trang's flagship," said Luciana. "We don't know for certain, because if they did, it was done using direct laser burst on a coded frequency, and we no longer have the computing power to scan for it in the ranges the Alliance can still use. But we do know that soon after, an Alliance shuttle landed on UHFS *Liddel.* Two hours after that shuttle left the UHF vessel, the Alliance fleet retreated three hundred thousand kilometers from our fleet. Both fleets powered down their magnetic fields, but have kept them at the ready. An hour after that, a UHF shuttle left the *Liddel* and went to an Alliance frigate, whose identity can't be confirmed but is believed to be the *Otter.* That would be the flagship of Fleet Admiral Suchitra Kumari Gorakhpur. An hour after arriving, the shuttle left. Then our fleet moved behind the Moon and we've since lost contact. That was three days ago, and in that time we've heard nothing. There have been no detectable communications between us and our fleet, and as far as we can tell none between the Alliance fleet and Saturn. Until we can get reliable assets on the far side of the Moon, we just won't know for sure."

"Are they communicating with each other?" asked Hektor tersely.

"We don't know, sir," was the simultaneous reply of both Luciana and Tricia.

"Sir, we must tell the people something. They're scared and struggling enough as it is. But the uncertainty of a battle that is neither won nor lost on top of everything that they've suffered cannot be withstood much longer."

"Tell what's left of the media outlets," answered Hektor dourly, "that a brief statement will be issued in twelve hours. Make sure that it goes out on radio. Let Trang know he has a deadline."

Franklin kept shaking his head, jabbing at his DijAssist, seemingly getting more and more frustrated. Finally he dropped the DijAssist onto the table with a pronounced clatter and looked to the only person he knew who always seemed to have all the answers.

"What do *you* think's going on, sir?"

"You want to know what's going on? Have any of you studied a war called World War One?" He saw from their blank expressions that not a one of them had. "It bears study because the war was won not so much on who had the best weapons or most skilled soldiers and officers. It was won because one side collapsed before the other, and it hadn't always been clear who would crack first. Well, that's the situation we're in now, but that is not why I brought up this First World War. I brought it up because I was amazed to discover the moment the leaders on both sides of the war were most afraid of. Now, this is the war that killed millions in, for them, brand-new despicable ways. Poison gas and airplanes were used and machine guns mowed down countless lives. It was like Anderson's Farm or the Vlasov Ice Fields, only with more primitive weapons and on a single planet." No one said a word; all remembered the grinding tragedy of those early campaigns. "But despite all of that, the time the leaders of both sides were most afraid was early in the war, when it was only six months old. A holiday called Christmas, that takes place around New Year's Day, was important to both sides in this war. The night before this Christmas, on a large section of the battle front, both sides stopped killing each other. Despite stern warning from their officers, the soldiers on both sides stopped killing each other. They got out of their defenses, walked up to each other, and sang songs together, drank together. They played games and talked about what it was like at home."

Franklin scratched his head. "Why weren't they shot for insubordination?"

"Both sides would have had to shoot half their armies. No one was punished, and the next day, everyone went back to killing each other, much to the relief of the leaders. But for every other Christmas in the war, both sides made sure that their soldiers were too busy ducking to risk another bout of spontaneous peace."

Irma was busy making notes in her DijAssist. "Do you think that's what happened here?"

"I think someone read the same history I did," said Hektor, tapping his finger impatiently on the edge of the table, "and I think they figured out how to stall this war. And if we don't get it started again real soon, then we've surely lost."

CLARA ROBERTS: *What on Earth is going on? It's been three days, and all we can confirm is that both fleets are looking at each other from far away. Something has stopped what may have been the climatic and hopefully final battle of the war; I have no idea what. Let's get your ideas. Our first caller is from the Fairbanks Settlement, newly arrived from the Belt. Welcome, caller number one.*

CALLER NUMBER ONE: *Thank you for having me, Clara. I'm tickled pink that I can actually call in. Usually I just listen because of the time lag.*

CLARA: *I'm sorry we were forced out of our homes, but at least I get to talk with you. So, what do you think is going on?*

CALLER ONE: *I think it's some sort of Avatar Plague. (a voice in the background) It's not your call, Levitt.*

CLARA: *Trouble at home, caller?*

CALLER ONE: *It's my avatar. He thinks I'm nuts. I tell you, Clara, I liked it better when they pretended not to exist. Now we can't get them to shut up.*

CLARA: *Let's get him on the air. Levitt, hook up.*

LEVITT: *Clara Roberts! By the Firstborn, this is such an honor. I've been listening to your show since you were part of the American Express Travel Blog & Log.*

CLARA: *Well, that might be the nicest thing an avatar has said to me, Levitt, but let's not talk about the ancient past. You disagree with caller one?"*

LEVITT: *Absolutely. Sasha is thinking anything that goes wrong in the UHF must be because of avatars. Like humans hadn't been screwing stuff up long before we showed on the scene. Now, I can't speak for the UHF fleet—who knows how screwed up they are over there? But our fleet has the best humans and avatars fighting on those ships. We've survived seven years of this war, and I refuse to believe that something so pernicious happened to our ships that they couldn't even send us message.*

CLARA: *Sounds like you have reason to know. Anyone you know with the fleet?*

LEVITT: *(sounding bashful yet proud) My daughter is serving on the AWS* Claim Jumper, *and I have a nephew serving on the AWS* Feied.

CALLER ONE: *He talks about them all the time. Lorie this and Leslie that. I thought only humans bored the crap out of you with stories of their kids.*

CLARA ROBERTS: *Some things are universal, it seems, but we have to go to the next caller. Caller two is from a Kansas Collective Agricultural Settlement, and I see here that your settlement is one of the oldest orbiting Saturn.*

CALLER TWO: *Absolutely, Clara. They say we were founded by one of the original Chos, but no one knows which one. I love your show, Clara, and want to echo the previous caller's comment that I'm tickled pink to be able to actually call in. But I can't help but notice my fellow avatar did not actually answer your question and want to help out.*

CLARA: *Good of you to represent. So what do you think happened: civil war, computer virus, bio weapon, alien contact? What could have stopped that battle?*

CALLER TWO: *I think the President did it.*

CLARA ROBERTS: *Which one?*

CALLER TWO: *Ours, of course.*

—The Clara Roberts Show
AIR Radio Network

Stellar Observation Dome, Level 1
University of Tycho
Luna

Luna was dead. Of the over six billion people who lived on it, only fourteen thousand or so had survived. But the Alliance was overjoyed to discover that a group of twenty-seven survivors contacted them directly because two of them happened to be NITEs. Sandra decided that it would be best to contact Trang and ask permission to rescue the survivors who'd lived by hiding deep in the ground in a space that had been newly dug but not been fitted out with anything like life support, power, water, information nets, and the like. A joint team was assembled, and the party was rescued. A problem developed when it was discovered that the NITEs had saved 4,326 inert avatars in portable storage devices. At first, the UHF half of the team wanted to follow standing orders, which called for all such devices to be partitioned and scrubbed. This ran counter to Alliance standing orders for avatars, which called for rescue and debriefing. Luckily, the officers in charge of the joint rescue operation had been picked for their initiative and level-headedness and so, wisely shoved that problem up the chain of command. It was resolved to debrief everyone, NITEs, humans, and avatars on the surface at the comfortable but abandoned Tycho University observatory. It was so out of date that it hadn't been used for decades. This meant no one had bothered to destroy or booby-trap it, which further meant it had been easy to secure. The observatory still had dormitories, conference rooms, and a cafeteria. After the debriefing, it turned out that two of the avatars had been operatives for Al and participated in the death of Luna. Sandra and Gwendolyn immediately signed off on their being turned over to the UHF military, which executed them at once, using the decompiler program. But the UHF did not say a word when the two NITEs and 4,324 avatars returned to the Alliance fleet. The UHF was glad to have saved even twenty-five of their own from the charnel house that Luna had become.

When the operation was done, it occurred to someone in the Alliance fleet that the obsolete observatory would actually make a useful neutral ground. After some brief discussions, two teams returned and prepared the location for its new purpose, and the fleets were repositioned to keep accidents from happening.

And that was how Admiral Janet Delgado Black and Admiral Samuel U. Trang met for the first time. It was on the Moon, and the two were separated only by a simple table. Fatima Awala and Tabitha Ross were the only other personnel present in the room. Sandra O'Toole had agreed with J.D. that this was not a meeting she should be at. If this peace was going to work, both admirals would have to sell it for all it was worth, and Sandra realized they wouldn't be able to do that without checking each other out first—one on one, face-to-face.

Each entered from opposite sides of the room. They both stood for a long moment and sized each other up, as if studying a particularly complicated piece of sculpture. Both seemed to absorb every detail they could, making what judgments they could, and then, as if hearing a mutual silent bell, saluted each other at the same moment. Then and only then did the pressure ease slightly, and they both sat down with their aides standing far enough behind not to be obtrusive but close enough to respond if needed.

"Welcome to Luna, Admiral Black," Trang said dryly.

"I'm sorry it had to be like this, Admiral Trang." J.D. swept her arm to encompass everything. "What's going to happen to this place?" she asked, delaying one painful question for another.

"Well," he answered with a half smile, "there are a lot of Martians that you made homeless. If we work this out, one way or another, they can always move in here."

J.D. ignored the slight and the implied threat. "They're welcome to it. There's too much death here."

It seemed that Trang was about to say something, but he held back and after a moment his face changed from slightly hostile to sad. "There *is* too much death here. But what choice did we have?"

"With the Martian refugees, none I guess. But we have other choices to make now. When war becomes what we've made it, the only thing that matters are those who do the fighting. And those who do the fighting listen to us. So what are we going to do, Admiral?"

Trang sighed. "That is easy for you to say. You have your President and by extension your government backing your every move."

The echo of J.D.'s laugh bounced around the room. "Just up and leave the solar system? Do you think that'll be popular? Many people in the Alliance think we're winning this war—" She paused briefly. "—idiots."

"Hell, you are winning this war if you base it on the numbers," Trang said. "In terms of effective population and industrial capacity, we're about equal and you might recover faster than us. You have the better ships and crews, even if you don't have enough of them."

"We have enough, Trang," J.D. said defensively. But there was no real venom. The warriors had not really come to fight, just negotiate. They were both comfortable disagreeing with each other, and if it really came to it—which neither of them, they realized, really wanted to happen—they'd find out, one way or the other.

"But the President is right. I wasn't sure until I came here. When I stepped onto this once vibrant and newly dead world, I knew she was right. I think I can beat you, Trang. And I will if I have to," she said with absolute conviction that only brought a smile of recognition and respect from her opposite number. "But the thing is, I no longer want to. The prize isn't worth it. Luna proves that some victories come at too high a price, and I will not give my child a slaughterhouse to live in if I have any other choice."

Trang slid his arm across the table's metal surface, resting his elbow comfortably on the edge. "Then why fight at all if you don't want victory?"

"Why fight, indeed? As you well know, the definition of victory is elusive. When we both started out, victory for me was stealing ships from you or sending your feckless admirals home with their tails between their legs. But then you came along, and the stakes suddenly got higher and have continued to do so at an alarming rate. So the answer to your question is, yes, I do want victory—just not the 'me waving my flag over tens of billions of corpses' kind of victory. I want the victory of knowing that my child will grow up free of incorporation, left alone to choose her own path in life rather than be voted on by a board of directors."

Trang remained silent but listened intently, nodding his head all the while.

"The President has shown us the way," continued J.D. "We need to make it work. I now know I'm willing. But the real question is, are you?"

"It's not up to me, Admiral. We have to involve my President."

"You and I both know that Sambianco will only destroy whatever chance at peace we have. He still wants to plant the flag I'm willing to give up. I'll plant it if I have to, but I've been brutally honest with you, Sa— Admiral."

Trang looked up momentarily at J.D.'s slip, then laughed warmly. "Hell, Janet, since we've only been trying to kill each other for six years, it's also only appropriate we call each other by our first names."

"Fair enough, Sam."

"You were saying?"

"I assume you've read the reports."

Trang shifted uncomfortably. "He's my President. I will not ignore him. Whatever he's done or not done, he's the one I swore to serve. I have to include him in this or it will not work."

"He's not worthy of your loyalty, Sam."

"Who said anything about loyalty, Janet?"

Presidential retreat
Lake Geneva

Hektor Sambianco was in his study when he received the report from the grand admiral. It had been confirmed by Tricia and sent to the rest of the Cabinet. The world would know about it soon enough. But as he sat in his well-cushioned reading chair, he was astounded by the depth of the stupidity and treachery being displayed by the man he'd only recently determined he could let live. *So much for that,* he thought.

The grand admiral's brief was nothing more than a demand that the government of the UHF agree to an armistice. How could Trang not see what the ultimate outcome of this would be? Even if, by some miracle, the Outer Alliance kept its word and actually left the solar system—and Hektor simply did not believe that—it would mean that a significant portion of humanity would be beyond the control of incorporation forever. They would be free to do Damsah knew what, Damsah knew where. It was enough to make a grown man howl. What was the purpose of all this disruption and waste if not to ensure that every human was under corporate control and properly exploited? With a sigh, Hektor tossed the report into the fire.

"Presumably you've all read the report."

"The man should be executed," said Tricia.

Franklin shook his head. "He is a traitor."

"A fool to trust the Alliance," agreed Luciana.

Hektor sat back in his chair impassively. "And that's why we're going to kill him."

Tricia flung some folders over to Hektor's end of the desk. Hektor peered inside. "Now that I'm in contact with my operatives on the *Liddel,* he can be assassinated within the hour, sir."

Irma shook her head. "That's insane."

"Irma is absolutely correct," said Hektor, cutting off an impending diatribe from Tricia. "If he were to be killed by our operatives or even suffer an accident right now, how do you think Zenobia Jackson will react?"

"We kill her too," said Tricia.

"Then who fights the Alliance?" asked Irma contemptuously. "You can't kill *everybody.*"

Tricia smiled acidly to her antagonist. "Not for lack of trying."

"Again, Irma is right," said Hektor. "We need Jackson, and if Trang dies, she is very likely to take our fleet and blast the crap out of *us*. This will have to be more subtle and directed. I'm going to publicly agree to Trang's report and to meet with him immediately. If possible, we'll have J. D. Black *and* Sandra O'Toole at the summit. It would be better if they show up, but not needed. When Trang shows up at the summit, we kill him but make it look like the Alliance did it. We can even blame it on avatars or an Alliance operative. So many choices, so little time. We still have those three spies. We'll psyche-audit one to confess to the plot, and the bodies of the other two be found nearby with enough evidence to mount a convincing story—which is where you'll come in, Irma."

"It won't hold. It's too flimsy. Any real investigation will prove the Alliance had nothing to with it."

"Who cares?" said Tricia, looking toward Hektor. "By the time anyone figures that out, the Battle of Earth will have taken place and we'll be well on our way to exterminating the Outer Alliance once and for all."

"No," Irma said, staring intently at everyone in the room. "No, Hektor, that's enough. It won't work. Every time we try something like this, it doesn't work. Trang is offering us a way to get real peace. Peace within the solar system. If the Alliance is crazy enough to leave, then I say let them go."

"You do realize," said Franklin, eyeing Irma warily, "that is treason."

"That's *reason*!" Irma shouted back. "If you do this, J. D. Black will destroy Zenobia and then destroy us." Irma opened her hands, pleading. "We're talking about billions more lives—and for what?"

"Humanity must stay united, Irma. You know that," said Hektor, hoping to reason with his Minister of Information but knowing it was actually hopeless.

"No, no, it mustn't," countered Irma. "Not at that price. Let them go, Hektor. For Damsah's sake, let them go."

Hektor sighed and nodded toward Tricia. Two guards suddenly appeared from a side door and grabbed Irma firmly by the arms. "You have to let them go!" she was repeatedly heard to yell as they dragged her down the hall and finally out of earshot.

When the door closed, Hektor turned to Tricia. "You'll take Irma's job for the time being."

"That will simplify things, Mr. President," purred Tricia.

"We need a press release detailing what a wonderful idea Trang has and how I can't wait to meet him."

ARMISTICE!

A temporary armistice has been agreed to by the forces of the Outer Alliance and the UHF for the purposes of allowing the civilian leaders of both

sides to discuss a peaceful solution to the seven years of conflict and death.
Admiral Trang is meeting the President at the President's residence on
Lake Geneva. Afterwards, they will travel to a secret location on Luna,
where they will meet the rebel leaders, J. D. Black and Sandra O'Toole.
Can this really mean peace?

—NNN
Special print edition
(Neuro site still under repair)

Grand Admiral Trang walked from his shuttle greeted by the sound of thunderous applause. A crowd in the tens of thousands had surrounded the Presidential retreat in Lake Geneva, where Trang would soon be meeting the
President in order to hammer out the details of the armistice.

But Trang could pay little heed to the hopeful, worshipful mob, as his most
difficult task lay ahead. Trang was in his dress uniform with his polished pulse
pistol and his ceremonial sword. His sash was blinding in the bright sunshine,
and for the first time in his long military career, he wore all the ribbons and
medals he was entitled to, and they covered his broad chest like a multifaceted
river of hues. He stopped briefly to wave, and the crowd roared its approval.
Part of him was surprised to see no mediabots. Instead, there were media
people holding their bots in special-made cradles. He assumed correctly that it
was one more jury-rigged solution forced on humanity by the Avatar Plague.
Determined to say a few words of encouragement, Trang stepped up to the installed podium.

"The President," he began, "recognizes that we have a chance to end this war
and, in doing so, unite the solar system. It will take courage and imagination.
But the President has guided us this far against enemies seen and enemies unseen, any one of which should have destroyed us all but for his inspired and
essential leadership. For the difficult days ahead, we will all need imagination
and courage. For as terrible as the war is, for some, peace is yet more terrifying.
In war, you do not need to trust. You only need to win or die. The President
recognizes that too many have died, and now we must achieve our dream of a
united solar system by other means. With negotiation instead of victory, with
hope instead of fear, with renewed life instead of ongoing death, we will have
peace."

Grand Admiral Trang entered the main building to applause and shouts so
deafening, his ears actually rang.

Hektor Sambianco watched Samuel Trang's impromptu—if it was impromptu—speech with great satisfaction. When he framed the Alliance for Trang's assassination, getting the war started again would be no problem. But now he'd have to perform the greatest acting job of his career. He'd have to pretend to like and respect a man he now had only contempt for.

So he stood up and straightened his suit, then walked over to the full-length mirror to check his entire persona. He looked grave and glad, suitable to match Trang's new world-view and presumably vaunted self-image. The fire in the hearth crackled as shadows flickered across the room's old stones. Appropriately somber, thought Hektor, who took a deep breath as the door to his private study opened. Trang came in escorted only by Tricia Pakagopolis, who also looked happy to see the grand admiral. She stayed at the door as Trang and Hektor approached each other and both gave the appropriate formal bow. Hektor barely had time to register the fact that as Trang rose from his bow, all two feet of his ceremonial sword came out of his sheath, rotated on its hilt, and in a blindingly swift upward motion, entered Hektor's lower jaw and penetrated his brain from below, the point punching through the top of the skull.

How, what—? were the only thoughts Hektor's damaged brain could drudge up as Tricia began to scream for help and run toward Trang. With speed equal to its entering, the sword was removed, leaving a now shocked and damaged Hektor standing exactly where he'd been, while the sword of Samuel Trang swung round again, slicing through the President's head from ear to ear, ending all his thoughts forever. Trang then pivoted and took Tricia Pakagopolis's skull just above the ear with a powerful stroke that came from the shoulders and the hips. She first fell to her knees and then toppled over next to Hektor. *Fitting,* thought Trang as he used the corner of Hektor's jacket to wipe what little blood there was off his sword. He then stood back up, returning the weapon to its sheath.

Trang was pleased. The sword had been a best-case scenario, but he'd assumed the chances of getting close enough to use it without a phalanx of Gretchen Arbieter's trigger-happy goons would be effectively zero. Still, he'd dutifully replaced his useless ceremonial blade with one that was the near pinnacle of the swordsmith's art and then practiced two moves over and over again while going over contingency plans for when Zenobia would have to take over. Worst-case scenario would have had Zenobia bombarding the Presidential retreat from the frigate in orbit. Zenobia had not liked the "worst case" plan and agreed to it only as a last resort. Fortunately, it hadn't come down to that.

Trang viewed the two bodies. *The incredible arrogance of the man,* he thought. *To be allowed entry into the President's office, armed and alone, without so much as a bodyguard?* For some reason, an image of Sergeant Holke sprang to mind, and the thought that had Holke been Sambianco's bodyguard, Trang wouldn't have gotten within a city block of the guy.

Right on time, by Trang's clock at least, Gretchen Arbieter stormed into the room, gun drawn, eyes blazing at the two bodies lying next to each other on the hardwood floor. One look at what was left of their scalps told her that both deaths were permanent.

"Your grandson's alive," Trang said calmly.

"Wh-what?" said Gretchen, shocked into inaction on the verge of shooting Trang where he stood.

"Your grandson is Zachary Augustus Arbieter, yes?"

Gretchen eyed the admiral with deep suspicion. "He lived on the Moon with my son after the divorce," she said abstractedly. "But he died with everyone else."

"Not quite. We conducted a joint rescue operation with the Alliance. Some of the Alliance Lunar operatives found a hole and dived in till the worst was over. They took twenty-five UHF citizens with them. They didn't have to—in fact, it was a stupid thing to do from a spy's point of view. But they did it; we found them, and your grandson was one of the twenty-five."

"Sigmund?" she said hopefully, asking after her son.

Trang gave the briefest negative shake of his head.

"How do I know you're not lying to save your treacherous life?"

"Maybe I am," admitted Trang. "Maybe I know that your grandson's favorite ice cream is vanilla steak by other means. Maybe I know you used to sing to him old Beatles songs in German so he wouldn't forget how to speak it. It worked, by the way. Maybe I learned his pet name for you is Gretgret by some other nefarious means. Or maybe . . . just maybe, I'm telling the truth."

"You could have figured that out some other way. There must have been records."

"Agent Arbieter, all of those records were made inaccessible by the avatars weeks before I decided to kill the President."

"And you think saving my grandson excuses your assassination?"

"Your grandson is not yet saved." He saw her brows knit together in anger. "I will not harm him in any way, and neither will anyone who serves under me, even if you blow my head off right now, Agent Arbieter."

"You're giving me permission to shoot you?"

"No, I'm giving you something that has for far too long been robbed from the citizens of the UHF. I am giving you the freedom to choose. If the war resumes, the chances of your grandson surviving—or anyone surviving, for that matter—are near zero. We must change or we, and by that I mean the whole damned race, might never recover." Trang pointed his sword sheath tip at the bloody remains of Hektor Sambianco. "You worked for him. What do you think would've happened to your grandson if he'd lived?"

With glacial slowness, Gretchen Arbieter lowered her gun. "What do you need me to do?"

UHFS *Gremlin*
High orbit of Earth

Zenobia Jackson had to restrain herself from running up to the shuttle and hugging her superior officer. She'd been almost certain she would never, ever see him again.

"I should've known you'd pull it off, sir," she said with a crisp salute.

"I got lucky," he answered, returning the salute and descending the rampart. "Let's go to a secure room." A few minutes later, they were in the frigate's intelligence assessment unit, now used for storage, since the advanced data systems that made them function were no longer allowed in UHF ships.

"What happened, sir?"

"Hektor's dead."

Zenobia let out a whoop.

"Great speech, by the way. Went over quite well."

"Well, I suppose if the admiral thing doesn't work out, I could always be your speechwriter."

"And you were right about the sword."

Zenobia's eyes went to the blade in question.

"I can't believe he let me get that close."

"I can, sir. He never really respected the military. We were just tools to him. He was so busy planning *how* he was going to kill you, it never really occurred to him that you could do the same."

"Well, luck favored us more than we deserve, Zenobia. I was able to kill Tricia at the same time."

Zenobia whistled. "That must have made things easier."

"Almost didn't," laughed Trang. "Gretchen Arbieter came about a picosecond away from blowing my head off."

"Did you do it?" she asked quietly.

"Tell the lie the avatars gave us?" Trang said with equal gravity. "Yes."

"I never would've thought that among those avatars we let go, one of them was her grandchild's."

"And I never would've thought to use that information," added Trang. "The one they call Allison came up with the plan."

Zenobia's face grew dark. "Still don't trust 'em, sir. I'm not surprised that an avatar's good at lying."

"She's not the one who told that lie to a grandmother and had to watch hope reignite in the woman's eyes."

"Sir, I'm sorry. That must have been near impossible."

Trang removed the medals breastplate from his jacket and dumped it onto the console. "Admiral Jackson, I'm responsible for the deaths of countless humans and just assassinated my own President by my own hand. I think a little lying for the cause can be justified." Then Trang sighed. "But you're right, it wasn't easy. After that, it was cleaning up. I had Gretchen bring the rest of the Cabinet to the study. It appears that Irma Sobbelgé had been arrested for protesting my planned assassination and was under an emergency death sentence. The only reason they hadn't killed her was they were waiting for the right time. To exploit her death at the hands of an Alliance assassin or some such drivel meant to instigate."

Zenobia's lips pursed outward as she nodded slowly. "The Mistress of Lies had a conscience?" Zenobia said, only half joking. "After everything that's happened, that might be the hardest to believe. How'd the rest of the Cabinet take it?"

"Funny you should ask. When I gathered them in the room, I asked who could support the coup. Apparently, Franklin Higgins IV had more backbone than I gave him credit for. He called me traitor and told me to do my worst."

"Was he serious?"

"I can't say if he was. I shot him as soon as he said it."

"And the other two?"

"Luciana Nampahc will play ball. As for Irma, she came up with the cover story that's about to break."

"Really, I can hardly imagine."

"It appears that our dear Minister of Internal Affairs was so against our bold President's plan for peace that she tried to engineer a coup. Sadly she succeeded in killing the President and the Minister of Justice and had poor Irma arrested and on her way to be executed. Luckily, Luciana was able to warn me just in time and with Gretchen Arbieter's help was able to kill the traitor."

"But that means that Hektor Sambianco will die a hero." Zenobia was deeply offended. Like her boss, she had read the captured UHF records and like her boss had reluctantly come to believe them. They jibed with too many other little things she'd spent years ignoring.

"Yes, he will die a hero and quite a noble one at that. He died trying to end a war he didn't start at his moment of greatest courage. I imagine," Trang said with an oddly wistful smile, "he'll be remembered as a great man after all."

"That's so very wrong, sir."

"Zenobia, I just lied to a grandmother that her beloved grandchild is alive."

"But that was for a purpose."

"This lie will serve a purpose too. A President martyred for peace makes that peace worthy and sacrosanct."

"I guess that leaves one more question."

"Yes?"

"Who's President?"

Trang now smiled demurely. "About that speechwriting job."

DID WE JUST WIN?

—Alliance Daily News

DID WE JUST LOSE?

—Alliance Daily Star

Via Cereana
Ceres
In orbit around Saturn

Sandra O'Toole and J. D. Black were sitting comfortably in J.D.'s shuttle as it left the AWS *Warprize II,* making its way back to the Presidential landing port of the Via Cereana. Both the President and the grand admiral were happily silent, not having much to do and taking advantage of the fact. Neither of them knew it, but their respite had been purely manufactured by J.D.'s subordinate officer, Fatima Awala. The communications officer had ordered the combat major who outranked her not just in fact but also in years of service to go as slowly as possible in order to give both their superiors as much time as possible before being deluged in the necessary responsibilities of their victory. The major had simply saluted Awala as if she had every right to order him around, which when it came to caring for the Blessed One, in a certain sense she did.

So it was only when J.D. was sitting, not thinking about anything at all, that an annoying question suddenly popped into her head. She slowly eased herself into a more erect posture in her chair and regarded Sandra curiously.

"Out with it," chided Sandra.

J.D. chuckled. "I realize this may seem odd coming from me . . ."

Sandra waited patiently.

"But did Hektor really have to die? Which is to say, the enemy you know . . ."

Now Sandra straightened in her chair. "You're right. I can't believe that you of all people are asking that question. Especially after watching that little jig you did at the news of his death."

"Don't get me wrong. I never said I wasn't happy about it; I'm talking strictly from a strategic perspective. With the information that we gave Trang, he could've blackmailed Hektor into behaving like a good peace-loving President. I know Hektor. He would have hated every single moment of it, but his sense of personal survival would have compelled him to play along. A coup attempt was risky, Sandra. And the more I think about it, the more I realize just how much. It could have gone balls-up in a thousand different ways."

"Yes, it could've. And you'll have to trust me on this, it was discussed ad infinitum."

"With *whom*?"

Sandra started counting off on her fingers, raising each as she called out the names. "Eleanor, Marilynn, Gwendolyn, Dante, and Amanda Snow. It was a rather long meeting discussing the option before your fleet left for Earth."

"Why wasn't I informed?" demanded J.D.

"If you recall, you were getting ready to martyr yourself and screw the rest of us with a soul-crushing victory. There was so much destiny rumbling around your head," pointed out Sandra with just enough of a smile to take the sting out her words, "that not much except the final battle would've gotten through."

"All right," agreed J.D. after a moment's thought. "That's fair, much as I hate to admit it. So what did the committee on the future of the war come up with?"

"Well, they all thought killing the bastard was a pointless exercise, as there was going to be a final battle and that would determine the war. I simply billed the meeting as a 'cover all conceivable bases' exercise."

"They really had no idea what you were planning?"

"Give up and run away?" There was something about Sandra's laugh that revealed the depth of her weariness. "I should hope not. But they all agreed that in the unlikely event we had the chance, a blackmailed Hektor was the safer option for ending the war. There were far too many risks involved with a coup. Say what you will about Hektor Sambianco, he did have real power."

"And they were unified in that agreement?"

"Well, everyone but Amanda. When that woman decides to hate, she hates. She wanted Hektor to die. Would've preferred a torturous death, but any death would do—felt he was too dangerous, no matter what sort of control our stolen data gave us, was absolutely convinced he'd eventually find a way to come at us again."

J.D. nodded. "Makes sense. So you agreed with her over every other opinion?"

"No, Amanda was wrong. We needed peace, and Hektor alive was the best way to get it. Once the war was stopped, Hektor could not have got it going again. He knew that better than anyone—other than me."

"Then why did you convince Trang that Hektor had to die? Why take the risk?"

Sandra's eyes were suddenly cold and expressionless. Her jaw seemed to stiffen in fierce resolve. "Hektor Sambianco deserved to die. For all the deaths he caused, for all the misery he inflicted, and for all the evil he spread, justice demanded it."

"But that's not the whole reason, is it?" urged J.D., a conspiratorial edge to her voice.

"No," admitted Sandra. "Hektor Sambianco had to die because *I* wanted him dead."

J. D. Black exited her shuttle with the President in tow. Much to J.D.'s annoyance, her shuttle was still intact and still just as decadent as ever.

J.D. glanced over her shoulder at the shuttle. "You couldn't have them accidentally blow the thing up?"

"I suppose I could've, but the point of the whole exercise was to *avoid* a battle, remember?"

"Details."

The two women moved on to discussing their plans for the campaign to get the peace treaty approved by the Congress, when they were suddenly stopped by the sound of a brass band playing for all it was worth. Louder than the band was the rather sizable crowd that had filled the executive loading bay, awaiting their arrival. Sandra was planning a formal return ceremony for later that afternoon, and J.D. was already planning the "treaty acceptance campaign" as she naturally thought of it, but neither of them had planned on an early party.

The band was made up of whoever grabbed an instrument and began playing; the decorations, whatever people could throw together; and the people, whoever felt like finally letting their hair down.

"I think we just might pull this off!" Sandra shouted to J.D. over the din.

The grand admiral was just about to comment back when she cocked her head, listening. It seemed like she was desperately trying to hear one individual thread of a sound out of the vast tapestry of noise that surrounded them. In a moment, her eyes locked on to her target. With a magic that still worked, the crowds parted for Janet Delgado Black, and about a third of the way across the landing bay she got down on one knee and was nearly bowled over by a six-year-old girl who seemingly appeared from nowhere.

"Mommy!" the little girl shouted as she hugged the most fearsome person in the human race and was given a wraparound hug in return.

"Did you save the worlds, Mommy? Did you? Did you?" shouted an excited Katy.

"No, little one," said J.D., smoothing her daughter's face with the back of her unscarred hand. "You did."

And for the two of them, the crowds and the noise simply faded to insignificance as mother and daughter were reunited.

We fought this war for our freedom. They fought this war for their security. For our freedom and for their security we were both willing to pay any price—and together we paid it. For our freedom and for their security we were both willing to make any sacrifices—and together we made them. For our freedom and for their security we were both willing to commit any crime—and together we committed them.

There are those on both sides who say that the price paid is so high, it can only be justified by victory. We must now decide if that is true. Because if it is, victory will cost us the freedom we have struggled so long and sacrificed so much to earn and to keep. What this war has given us both are lessons. We must now decide if the lessons both sides have paid so terrible a price in blood to learn have been in vain. For our Alliance there is no choice. We must decide which we value more: victory or freedom.

—Speech given by President Sandra O'Toole to the Congress during her call for new elections

Cyrus Anjou was talking to a group of his former constituents in a large asteroidal cylinder that was so newly formed, it still had that new asteroid smell. The plants would take months to grow enough to supplement and then supplant the artificial system. But none of the former residents of Jupiter minded. They finally had a home of their own, and the most famous Jovian was coming to speak directly to them.

"I'm not saying I don't love Jupiter," he said, beginning his stump speech, "there's no more magnificent place in the solar system. But I'm just thinking it would be nice if we could find another place for us Jovians. You know, something exactly like Jupiter—" He paused to add emphasis to the punch line. "—only not so small." And with that little joke and with the accompanying laughter, Cyrus Anjou helped awaken his former constituents and still loyal supporters to the possibilities that awaited them outside their tiny star system. And he would make that speech and many like it over and over again.

"I fought for the Alliance," J.D. said to the Neptunian Assembly. "I fought for our survival. But now I need you to help me. If we lose this vote, I and all our daughters and sons will lose our hard-earned right to the galaxy in exchange for the right to fight a war of extermination. We did not sacrifice all we have to make that choice.

"There are those who say I should not partake in this election. That as a military officer, I should remain above the fray. To them I say: bullshit. If we lose this election, and I count myself among the strongest supporters of the President when I say 'we,' I will have to lead my spacers back into a battle we don't have to fight. I can win it, but I shouldn't have to, they shouldn't have to, and if we have the wisdom to see our future, we *won't* have to."

As the applause thundered, J.D. was already heading for her shuttle. The *Warprize II* awaited her, and Uranus was next.

Tyler Sadma was looking concerned, but that was how he looked most of the time. Sandra leaned over and touched his shoulder. "You should go home to Eris, Tyler," she said gently.

"Madam President, you were foolish enough to call elections for a new Congress when I was pretty sure we could have gotten the treaty through the old Congress with some persuasion. Now we might lose the seats we need, and then where are we?"

"In your heart, you agree with me, Mr. Speaker, or you would have fought more. As much as I want this treaty to go through—as much as I feel it must go through for the survival of us all—I cannot force it. At the end of the day, the people must decide their fate with time for all points of view to be heard and debated openly, or it has all been for nothing."

"Admit it, you still need me," he said, stifling a yawn.

Sandra got up from the coffee table, where she'd been making calculations all day about where to send Cabinet members or military heroes to support a borderline candidate. Or where to make the hard decision to give up another candidate as a lost cause and who was doing so well they could raid her or his campaign for resources. It was an exhausting process because it involved hundreds of elections spread out over what was still the rather large area the Outer Alliance managed to control, and factors could change district by district, hour by hour.

"I admit *we* need you. But the election is not for two weeks yet. When was the last time you went home? When did you last see your wife, your children?"

"I saw my daughter just last week," said Tyler.

"She's a rail gun loader in the fleet," Sandra said in a voice that let him know that didn't count. "How long?"

"Seven years," he said softly. "Since near the beginning of the war. Eris is so far away."

"Bullshit. Ceres is no longer near Mars. We orbit Saturn now. And the Via Erisiana was completed a week ago. The trip takes four days."

"This close to the election . . . ," he began.

"I need you rested and happy for the election. You've earned it more than most. It will take you four days to get home. You'll spend four happy days with your family and reconnecting with friends, enemies, and the citizens you represented so well all these years. They deserve to see the legendary Tyler Sadma." Sandra was surprised when he actually harrumphed at that but continued. "Then you can take the Via Erisiana back to Ceres and return with two days left till the election. As your President, I'm ordering you to go home and be with your family." She pointed toward the door.

Tyler smiled and slowly stood, stretching his back as well. "And this has nothing to do with the fact that Eris is a toss-up and I stand a small chance of losing my seat? And a trip home right before the election could tip the election in our favor?"

"Why, Mr. Speaker," answered Sandra in a tone that belied her honest intent, "that thought never crossed my mind."

With a bow to his political superior, but without another word, Tyler Sadma departed the Triangle Office.

Treaty of Luna
Terms

1. *Both sides of the conflict, heretofore referred to as the UHF and the OA, will cease active military operations.*
2. *The UHF will not occupy space beyond the orbit of Mars until the Exodus.*
3. *The OA will occupy only space beyond the orbit of Jupiter until the Exodus.*

4. Jupiter's hydrogen resources will be mined by a neutral party and shipped to the UHF or OA by prearranged routes at prearranged times for negotiated rates of exchange.

5. The creation of additional military forces is strictly forbidden. Both sides have the right to send observers to any location in their respective territories for the purpose of verifying this provision. Refusal to allow inspectors to any location is grounds for abrogating this treaty.

6. In a number of years being no less than two and no more than fifteen, the OA will leave the solar system. It will do so with the full cooperation of the UHF. In so doing, the OA gives up all present and future claims to the territory known as the solar system, consisting of all resources and artifacts from the edge of the Oort cloud to the center of the sun known as Sol. The UHF at that time will give up all present and future claims to any territory beyond the Oort cloud.

7. Any citizen of the UHF who wishes to leave the solar system is free to do so, provided they can reach OA territory and secure OA citizenship. They will not be hindered in any way by the UHF or any agents thereof, including the Corporations. Any stock claims for losses due to this emigration will be handled as a death for legal purposes, and the government of the UHF will bear all final financial burdens of these claims.

8. Any citizen of the OA who stays in the solar system after the completion of the Exodus will be considered a citizen of the UHF. All such citizens will automatically be granted a full pardon for all actions committed against the UHF up to the signing of this treaty. Any actions after the signing of this treaty will be arbitrated by a joint military judiciary board of justice.

9. Any citizen of the OA who stays in the solar system will be incorporated according to the standard laws pertaining to the same with the following exceptions: All such citizens regardless of past agreements will be incorporated as legally new individuals. All past contracts are void. All such individuals will be given a 70 percent stake of their own stock. The government of the UHF will be given 5 percent to hold in perpetuity and 25 percent to be allotted according to the dictates of justice as determined by the courts. The UHF may not hold any of the 25 percent of any individual beyond twenty-five years.

10. This treaty will supersede the armistice signed by both sides only on the date both sides sign.

————

Three months after the signing of the armistice, the entire solar system awaited the results of the elections taking place in the Outer Alliance. In the UHF, the treaty had sailed through the Assembly. That is, it did after the Assembly had been found and thawed out. Hektor and Franklin Higgins had done a good job of hiding that pesky voice of the people within the billions of souls still suspended above the troubled boiling skies of Mars. But when the various Assemblymen and -women had been woken up from the destruction of Mars to be informed of the destruction of the Avatar Plague and then to be told the Alliance might be willing to leave and let them have the solar system after all, it wasn't a close vote.

Some other changes had been minor. The Cabinet post of Internal Affairs was abolished to be replaced by the Ministry of Recovery. Samuel Trang resigned his commission to officially accept the office of President. Pending the approval of the treaty by the new Congress of the Outer Alliance, it was announced that the UHF would change its name to the United Solar Federation, or USF for short.

But none of these normally momentous changes would mean squat if the pro-treaty forces of the Alliance lost. Trang had quietly sent an offer of assistance that thankfully no one but Dante and Sandra found out about. They quietly but firmly told the still-named UHF to stay the hell out of it. Though Dante was more polite about it, the tone was the same.

Another thorny issue was sidestepped about whether avatars should be allowed to vote. Dante gave a speech stating that, as avatars were already represented in the Cabinet and the humans were represented on the Council, now was not the time. It could be discussed and voted on when the constitutional convention took place. The body politic breathed a sigh of relief that one major issue had been sidelined so everyone could concentrate on the election itself.

As the election entered endgame, the main opposition did not come from those wanting victory, but those not wanting to leave their homes. The opposition of the native Saturnians was especially fierce. The Alliance almost came apart on the issue of what to do with the asteroid belt, also known as the Belter League. Within weeks of the armistice, the entire Belt nominally became members of the Belter League, and order was at last restored to that longest contested and blighted area of the solar system. Many members of the Belter League still considered themselves Alliance citizens and wanted to vote in the election. Naturally, the anti-treaty forces, hoping to turn the election, would have welcomed this, as it was rightly assumed the Belters would vote to stay in the solar system, having stayed through so much thus far.

Sandra had found herself in an untenable position, when she was saved by none other than Mosh McKenzie and Joshua Sinclair. They said it was not possible to be both a citizen of the Belter League and the Outer Alliance. Citizens would have to choose in all fairness. Sandra immediately followed this up with the offer that any citizen of the Belter League who could make it to an Alliance settlement would, of course, be allowed to vote. Of course, it helped the pro-treaty party that the nearest Alliance settlement was now Saturn. All sides knew that this was almost impossible, but had to accept the fiction that it was not, as a compromise.

It was with many trials and tribulations like this that the Outer Alliance groped its way to consensus. On election night, the President was on the Grand Terrace, surrounded by her Cabinet, admirals, and the others who'd made the journey to that moment in time. They awaited the returns with a mixture of nail-biting agony and otherworldly calm. Ironically, it was the avatars, a race that technically had no say in the matter who seemed to be most on edge.

As the returns came in, there were cheers when a district was won by a pro-treaty candidate and groans when a district was lost to anti-treaty candidate. At first, the treaty seemed to be in real trouble. This was because the results from Saturn were naturally the first tabulated, and a bare majority of the delegates went to the anti-treaty coalition. But Sandra remained calm and told her supporters not to give up hope. And she was right. As the day dragged on into night, the results from the other parts of the Outer Alliance made their weight felt. Soon delegate after delegate began to win from the pro-treaty party, and by early the next morning Karen Cho, the de facto leader of the anti-treaty coalition called on the President to offer her congratulations and concede the issue. By the time all the votes were counted, Sandra's coalition had a supremely comfortable 71 percent of the Congress, which some wags couldn't help calling the "supermajority."

As the news finally sank in, the balcony erupted into a frenzy of joy. Sandra had the opacity screen lowered, and the whole system saw the most powerful people in the Outer Alliance dance, cry, and hug like it was the Battle of the Cerean Rocks all over again. As the yelling was echoed by the revelers all through the Smith Thoroughfare, J.D. felt a touch on her shoulder and turned around to see her President standing there with a huge smile plastered across her face. "We did it!" the admiral managed to shout.

Sandra nodded and gave her a hug, which J.D. accepted uncomfortably. While they were close, Sandra yelled in her ear, "It's time!"

"For what, Madam President?"

"Your face!" Sandra yelled back.

J.D. was confused. "I have something on my face?"

Sandra shook her head and then quite unexpectedly put her hand softly onto the scarred half of J.D.'s face.

J.D. instinctively grabbed the President's hand and held it there, staring at her friend—offended, confused.

"It's time, J.D.," Sandra repeated softly.

The Grand Admiral gently let go of the President's hand and then brought her own up to the gnarled skin. And as she did she felt a familiar tug on her other sleeve. Looking down she saw Katy. Her daughter was nodding solemnly in agreement.

"Please, Mommy."

And suddenly J.D. knew that it was indeed time. The war was over.

9 Exodus

I am free and that is why I am lost.

—Franz Kafka

Residential Level
The Cliff House
Ceres
In orbit around Eris

Sergeant Eric Holke found himself doing something he hadn't done in years—relaxing. And at that realization knew it was time to fulfill the last order of Admiral Omad Hassan. So he made a call one Sunday afternoon and waited patiently in a recliner for his visitor to appear. His head jerked up suddenly at the sound of the doorbell. Not the sound itself, but the fact that the relic had been used at all. Few knew of its existence, much less what to do with the round white protuberance near the front of his door.

"Cassidhe, honey!" he shouted from the blissful comfort of the chair. "Could you get that?"

"What," came her playful retort from somewhere in the house, "you don't have legs?"

"Pookie," he needled, using just the right tone to melt her heart.

"All right, all right," she groused, slapping him on the knee as she passed him by. "But only because I was up already." He gave her a wink, knowing she hadn't been.

He heard the sound of their door sliding open and then his wife calling out, "Schnoo-magoo, it's your . . . friend."

Eric's eyebrow rose and half a second later so did he, making his way to the front door.

Cassidhe smiled politely at Dante, who smiled back, and then she gave Eric a knowing look. She had, over the years, heard enough of her husband's talks with Dante to know they were of the same mind and could spend hours on any topic, so long as it wasn't something important. It was one of the things that had cemented their friendship. "I'll leave you two men to discuss your 'important' affairs. If you need me," she sang, giving Eric a peck on the cheek, "I'll be down at Lannihan's." She left the house, making sure to sidestep Dante. Walking through him would have been bad form.

Eric gave Dante a quizzical look. "The doorbell?"

"Just trying to make it easier on your wife. She's never really liked me just beaming in—even with the warning chime. Come to think of it, I don't believe she's ever really liked me."

"She's not as bad as all that," he argued as they headed over to the living room.

"Didn't she call avatars, 'creepy creatures of light and magic'?"

Eric laughed. "(A) She was drunk, and (B) you *are* creepy creatures of light and magic, but," he then threw in as an aside, "she has gotten to like you more than you know."

"I'm glad, but something tells me you didn't invite me over to talk about your wife's evolving attitudes to avatarity."

"Oh, she still doesn't trust you guys. It's just you she's willing to put up with. But you're right, I didn't ask you here for that."

Eric pointed Dante over to the couch and went into the bedroom. He returned a moment later holding a secure lockbox. The arming light was red. Eric placed it on the coffee table between Dante and himself and sat on the edge of his easy chair.

"The last time I saw Admiral Hassan, he gave me this and asked me to hold it for him. Had no idea why, but after his death, the box sent a message to my DijAssist." Eric activated the message, and both Dante and Eric heard the long-dead voice of the admiral.

"Yeah, I'm dead. By Allah, that feels good to say. I figure I'm either with Christina or I'm nowhere, and either is better than where I am now. In this box is pretty much that last thing I care enough about to see that it rests safely in the hands of others. But here's the thing, Sergeant Holke. Consider it my last order to you. If the war is won and we've driven the UHF away from our territory or better yet destroyed the motherfuckers completely, then open it up. But if we lost this war, I'd ask that you please key the destruct sequence. I don't want any of those UHF sons of bitches to have even a hint of what's in there. That's it, lad. Give my regards to your missus and keep the President safe. Good luck to you, and may God, Allah, or whoever it is you believe in, bless the Alliance."

The two men sat in companionable silence for a moment. "So," Dante finally asked, "you gonna open it or what?"

"Well, that's just it."

"That's just what?"

Eric scratched his head. "I don't know if we've won or lost."

The avatar considered it. "That *is* an interesting question. What's your thinking?"

"Well, knowing Omad, this would be a loss. The UHF not only survives but the Alliance is being forced out of the solar system."

"Okay, then why is that box still here?"

"Because I want to know what's in it, dammit! The thing's been driving me crazy for years. But simple curiosity can't be a good enough reason if, in fact, we lost. I won't dishonor the memory of the man."

Dante chuckled.

"What's so damned funny?" barked Eric.

"Rest assured, friend. You've won this war as completely as you could have hoped."

"But the UHF—"

"—is gone, Eric. It couldn't survive the war. It's been replaced by the USF. And I think we can all agree that the United Solar Federation is a much better entity."

"But we are leaving."

"And that's the best evidence of all. Yes, we're leaving, but with our people, our ideals, and most important of all, our freedom intact. Our having this conversation in the open is more proof than any words I can give. The Alliance survived and has become something greater than its parts. And now we have an entire galaxy to claim. No one in the history of the solar system has ever won a greater prize." Dante smiled broadly at his friend. "Open the damn box, Eric. We won."

Eric Holke considered his friend's words, then finally nodded, flashing a relieved grin. He leaned over the secure box and input the victory code. In seconds, a simple beep was followed by a soft click. Eric lifted the lid and smiled. After reaching in, he took out a bottle of vodka a little less than half full.

"Is that—?" began Dante.

"Indeed it is, my friend. Indeed it is. I'm going to have you scan it, and you see if you can replicate the stuff on the Neuro." Eric got up to get a glass. "We have to drink a toast."

"To what?"

"Victory, my friend. "Ever-loving, motherfucking victory."

Jerusalem
Earth
USF

Rabbi would have felt uncomfortable in his heavy radiation garb, but was too overjoyed to notice. He was inside the holy city of Jerusalem. Well, not exactly *in* the holy city so much as *on* the holy city. And not really the holy city per se, but rather the fused glass surface that *used to be* the holy city of Jerusalem. But he was the first observant Jew to have done so in centuries. He'd been hoping that when he reached the site, he would somehow *know* that he was standing next to the Kotel, otherwise known as the Wailing Wall—a sacred structure that had once been a retaining wall to the Holy Temple, and a place where Jews had prayed for millennia. Unfortunately, it all pretty much looked like a large mound of fused glass, as did many other significant spots around the holy city.

When the Grand Collapse was near its height, the bombs had started to fall. But in the case of the bombs that had destroyed Varanasi, Rome, Jerusalem, Mecca, Medina, and Qom, it was not only the fact that bombs had been used, but also that they'd been dirty bombs, designed to make a lasting impression. In the case of the holy sites, that impression would last about ten thousand years—or how long it would be until a human could visit the site unprotected from radioactive fallout. Although the human race had the technology to clean these sites up, it was decided to leave them alone as a warning to the folly of religious belief.

So when after two years of peace between the USF and the Outer Alliance, requests were made for the right to visit and remove certain artifacts from certain holy sites, the authorities on Earth were not at all concerned, just curious. If religious trinkets and baubles kept the Alliance happy, the consensus was that they could take all the fused glass they wanted. It turned out the consensus was not far off, as the faithful had wanted a lot of it.

Before the first Alliance Colonization Fleet was due to set out for Alpha Centauri, parties of religious interest were allowed to visit and had been promised to be given every consideration. But Rabbi seemed to attract particular interest. Of all the religious leaders, Rabbi represented the smallest but oldest group. And he was not only a Rabbi; he was *the* Rabbi who had once been a powerful Alliance Cabinet secretary until his recent retirement a year prior. He'd been the first to officially retire from Sandra's Cabinet, and it was widely known that she hadn't been pleased about it. Especially given that the Exodus was the biggest and farthest relocation in the history of the human race. But in one of Sandra's rare defeats, Rabbi had refused, feeling that now that humanity's survival had been assured, the survival of his people should necessarily occupy the bulk of his attention.

Which was how he found himself standing with an entire company of USF combat engineers and one facilitator from the government.

"I want to thank you for your help, Minister Sobbelgé."

Irma looked at this latest publicity opportunity and smiled. "Anything we can do to help the Alliance and its faithful, Rabbi."

"Don't you mean anything you can do to help the Alliance and its faithful . . . leave?"

Irma laughed politely. "There's a certain amount of truth to that. But I think of it more as penance."

"Now *that* is an interesting term."

"Don't you mean, Rabbi, that is an interesting *religious* term?"

Rabbi pulled at his beard. "Why do I get the feeling I'm being trifled with?"

"Trust me, Rabbi," sighed Irma, "my days of trifling are behind me."

"Then may you find great comfort and may the blessing of the Lord shine upon you."

"I'll take what I can get," said Irma, "from whoever's offering."

"Pardon my asking . . ."

"Yes?"

"But are you not doing the same job you have always done?"

"Your point?"

"Presumably, you seek penance for the acts committed under your previous job. Yet you still maintain the same job title."

"Maybe the same job, Rabbi, but not for the same purpose. For the longest time, I thought I should use my ability and position to ensure the survival of the system I most believed in. Where Justin Cord had been divisive, I felt incorporation to be inclusive. But at some point, my talent was no longer being used to persuade, but rather to frighten and cajole—to spread hate, fear, and lies. By the time I realized the enormity of my mistake, not with regards to incorporation but with regards to whom I'd allowed to lead it, it was too late. I lived in fear of my life, and I freely admit I was too weak to stand up for what I believed in. Standing up brought death, and I thought as long as I stayed next to Hektor, I'd be safe—a ship in the eye of the storm. I have to live with what I've done, Rabbi, and it's not easy, I can assure you. I guess this is the long way of saying that while my title is the same, I now try to promote the virtues I initially lambasted: forgiveness, acceptance, and hope. My mission, Rabbi, is to try to undo as much of the damage I was responsible for. And I'm so very grateful that I've been given that opportunity, with the blessing of our President, mind you."

"Madam Minister, you do realize that there is another way to get the forgiveness you seek."

"I'm all ears, Rabbi."

"You just have to ask for it."

Irma laughed at the simplicity and elegance of Rabbi's solution. "I'll keep that in mind, Rabbi. In the meantime, I'm determined to make sure the people of the USF see that the religious are not crazed fanatics as my previous campaigns would have had them believe but rather spiritual beings seeking mementos from home before you leave us forever."

Rabbi's face suddenly went a little sheepish. "About that. We were hoping to take with us a little more than mementos."

Irma looked over to the globular hill. "What's in that mound that you want?"

"We don't want what's *in* the mound, Madam Minister. We want the mound itself."

"The mound," said Irma. "The whole mound?"

Rabbi nodded. "At some point, we Jews will be called upon to rebuild the Holy Temple. When that day comes, I'd like to know that we'll be ready."

"You do realize it's going to be radioactive for ten thousand years."

"We'll wait," replied Rabbi with dry smile, as if he were picking up a food order.

"Does that mean the Muslims will want all of Mecca?"

"Tawfik and Fatima will take only what is needed to reestablish the Kaaba on another world or worlds. But these are issues we will deal with on the trip out."

Rabbi's DijAssist informed him of a call. He looked to Irma. "Please excuse me, Madam Minister."

"Binyamin," Rabbi whispered harshly into his DijAssist, "I'm with a very important person. Are you sure this can't wait?"

"Forgive me, Mahagaw," said the voice, using the name of respect accorded him by the Jews, "but the Beit Din requires your wisdom concerning a conversion."

Rabbi sighed. The issue of conversion was the most pressing he'd had to deal with, given all the people who were interested in joining "the oldest of the faiths," which, thought Rabbi, might not even be true or, from a spiritual standpoint, particularly relevant.

"What is it now, Binyamin, that it couldn't wait till organzing the Kotel and the Mount's removal had been agreed to?" Rabbi looked over to Irma and shrugged his shoulders apologetically. "That they couldn't wait till *I* was in orbit?"

"They could wait, Mahagaw, but they thought you'd want to know at once."

"Is it someone controversial? Don't tell me Miss Goldstein has finally changed her mind," he said with just a hint of hope in his voice.

"No, Mahagaw, far more interesting."

"Well, Binyamin, I'm not getting any younger. What makes this conversion so interesting that the Beit Din felt I must be informed at once? That it takes precedence over bringing back whatever's left of the Holy of Holies? That makes this person out of all the hundreds of thousands so much more important?"

"She's an avatar, Mahagaw."

"Oy," was the only sound that escaped Rabbi's lips.

Jerusalem
Earth
USF

Irma watched as the last of the giant mounds of fused glass was placed into the cargo bed of a large military hauler, vacuum sealed, and then driven off to the nearest orport. The Jews, Muslims, and Christians would have their relics, and she'd have her piece documenting their incredible journey of faith. When she was certain she was alone, she pulled out her DijAssist and placed a call she once swore she'd never make again. When the call was accepted, she almost cried, and when she heard the voice at the other end, she actually did.

"Irma," said Michael Veritas, joy evident in his voice. "My goodness, how are you?"

"I'm fine, Michael, I . . ."

"Yes?"

"I could really use your help. . . ."

"Of course, Irma, what is it you need?"

Irma wiped away her tears, staring out at the remains of the holy city. "Forgiveness."

New York City
Earth
USF

"And so it is with great pride I stand on this land reclaimed from the Atlantic," said President Trang. "This land that was once known as Central Park *will* be a park again. But it will no longer be Central Park. It hasn't been very central for a while now." This brought a smattering of polite laughter. "Instead it will be called Sambianco Park for the President who tried his best for us and eventually showed us the path out of oblivion. Even though all we have here is a saltwater swamp, barely reclaimed from the ocean, I wish to dedicate a statue to our heroic President as a token of the trees, grass, paths, and lakes that will someday be here." With those words, Trang deactivated the opacity field around the statue he had commissioned. It showed a powerful figure forced down to his knees and one hand, with the other hand outstretched. The statue showed a man who did not want to lie down, who still had so much to do and was anguished that he'd never get to do it. That he was on his knees and would never rise again.

Trang smiled as he saw the statue and heard the polite comments of how it captured the true soul of the old President. He knew that Hektor would have hated it. When Trang had spent the appropriate amount of time in the ghost town that was now New York, he gratefully flew away to the provisional capital in Boulder, Colorado. As he looked back at the old city, he knew in his heart it was finished. They would drain it and build some parks, but they were not ever going to restrain the Hudson again. If the city had a million residents in ten years, he'd be grateful.

But his mind soon left the dim past as he prepared to meet the future. With full pomp and ceremony, the President of the USF, Samuel U. Trang, met the Chancellor of the Belter League, Mosh McKenzie. They saluted, then they bowed, and then at Mosh's insistence, they even shook hands. Trang didn't mind. He knew Mosh had a constituency he had to work with in the Belt just as Trang had one he had to work with in the Core. But after the polite necessities had been attended to, they found themselves alone and in a room ready to talk.

"Allow me to congratulate you on your *actual* election to the Presidency," Mosh said as they both sat down with drinks in hand.

"I must admit, I feel better having won the election fair and square. It never sat right simply taking it by military fiat."

"You did what you had to with an unjust situation. I'm sadly familiar with that."

Trang bowed sympathetically. "May I ask a delicate question, Chancellor?"

"Mr. President, I'm only Chancellor till the USF gets around to absorbing us. So ask what you want, as long as you call me Mosh."

"In that case, call me Sam."

Mosh smiled politely.

"When you attempted the coup, you did so with the belief that Sandra O'Toole would kill us all?"

"At the time, Sam, there was no doubt in my mind. Far as I was concerned, she'd gone well off the reservation. She did Mars behind Joshua's back!"

"But Sandra O'Toole is also the one who ended up saving us, Mosh. The human race, in fact. Both houses, incorporated and unincorporated, now have a chance to grow and survive—all because of her. Can you admit you were wrong? And if you were, do you regret it?"

"It?"

"The coup attempt."

Mosh gave Trang a sideways look. "That's an interesting question, Sam."

"Indulge me if you will."

"Was I wrong?" Mosh pondered the question. "Yeah, maybe I was. She fooled us all, and maybe I should have trusted her. As to the second question, do I regret it? No, sir, not one bit. I hate the getting there, but I like the way things turned out. The Alliance is leaving, and the solar system belongs to incorporation, though hopefully one that is more restrained. I was able to save a lot of lives in the asteroid belt, and who knows if it wasn't my attempted coup that caused her to change course. But I'm curious as to why a President feels the need to ask such a question of a soon-to-be private citizen."

"Yes," said Trang, "I understand you're looking to get your old job back at the Boulder Revival Clinic."

Mosh nodded.

"The answer is because I need to get a sense of you, Mosh. If I'm going to be trusting you with the human race, it's those odd little questions that tell me more about a man than the obvious ones."

Mosh eyed Trang suspiciously. "What do you mean, trust me with humanity? In case you haven't noticed, I didn't do such a good job when I did have a great deal of power."

"On the contrary, Mosh, I think you did great. Oh, not the results, but your intention was the best of the war."

"Fat lot of good my intentions did," said Mosh in a tone that belied the harshness of the words.

"Actually, Mosh, I believe you're the best of us."

"Really?" answered Mosh, skepticism clear in his voice.

"All of us did things in this war we'll never be proud of. We acted on dubious orders and condoned with our words, actions, or even worse, our silence one atrocity after another. In the name of victory, we murdered children in their homes, unleashed VR into the mainstream—"

"That was our side, Sam, much to my shame."

"That's what I'm talking about, Mosh. When I say 'we,' I mean all of us, the entire human race—certainly those with the power to influence events. When it comes to our abhorrent behavior, humanity is sadly united in failure. All except for you and Joshua Sinclair," said Trang, looking at Mosh with a level of respect that Mosh had not seen in a long time. "You voted against every attempt to make the war worse. You spoke with force and conviction that there are some victories too costly to win, and you were right. When it came time to oppose the wholesale destruction of entire peoples, you did so. You did not succeed—and maybe it was better that you didn't in the end—but you stood up to the tide of opinion and power and the nature of history itself to attempt what you felt was right. For you, it was about people—*all* people. Don't think that that is not known and appreciated in the USF."

Mosh let out a self-deprecating laugh. "You're making me sound pretty good there, friend."

"That's because you are. You and Joshua Sinclair may be the only good men to come out of this war. Which is why in six years, when the Belter League is officially absorbed into the USF, you're going to campaign with me as my Vice Presidential running mate." Trang held up his hand to forestall Mosh's comment. "And in twelve years, with my full support, you'll run for and win the Presidency of the USF."

"Awful confident, aren't you?"

"In this, yes."

"Then by your standards, Joshua is just as good a man as I am."

"You mean the man who'll be grand admiral of all USF forces in six years' time? I completely agree. What better way to help reassure those once oppressed by the UHF than having one of their own *commanding* the USF? In fact, I can't think of a better grand admiral than the one who is known systemwide for his refusal to take innocent lives both in the Spicer Ring affair and the murder of Mars."

"How will the people of the USF feel, knowing that its top two positions are held by former traitors."

"Any other two, I agree, total disaster. But you two will help unite the solar system as only you two can."

Mosh spent a few moments regarding the man he'd loathed for so long.

"You realize I feel strongly that the laws of incorporation need to be changed. They were deeply flawed to have allowed so much control over someone's individual liberty, to have created a veritable race of indentured servants and ultimately to have set a course on so much death and destruction."

"I agree," said Trang, taking another draw of his bourbon, "and now's the time to begin that change. With your input, we can correct the flaws of incorporation and unite the solar system. We can make this a safe, secure, profitable, and happy home for humanity again."

"So much for the job in Boulder."

"C'mon, Mosh. You had to know you weren't done yet."

Mosh thought for a moment and then sighed. "I guess I'm not, Sam." Then he had another thought. "What about my wife?"

"What about her? I thought she went back to using her maiden name?"

"She did, but we're not divorced, just separated."

"Didn't she put a shoot-on-sight order out on you if you returned to Alliance space?"

"That was a—" Mosh paused. "—misunderstanding."

"I heard she hired bounty hunters."

"An exaggeration—they were process servers." Mosh winked. "Like I said, we're not divorced."

"Isn't she going with the Exodus?"

"She may very well be, but if she doesn't, I'll take her back."

"Despite everything she's done and said."

"She's my wife, Sam. Despite everything, I still love her. I always have, and I always will. If that means I can't be President after you, then that's what it means."

"I don't think it'll come to that. Yours is not the only family that has been divided by war and Exodus. A lot of people in the system understand what you're dealing with. If anything, it makes you better suited to lead."

As they sat in companionable silence, sipping their drinks, Mosh decided to throw one more wrench into the spokes to see if Trang still wanted him. "You're wrong about me, you know. I'm not the only one who refused to yield to the pressure. Justin Cord was the greatest of us. He was the one who chose Josh because Josh had refused an unjust order. Justin refused categorically to unleash a VR plague on the UHF. He would never have allowed the bombardment of Mars. I didn't like him at first. In fact, I blamed him for everything in the beginning. But in the end, the bastard was proved right; it was not Justin Cord, but incorporation that was flawed. All those actions of mine that you praised, I learned by his example."

"On that, you and I will have to disagree, but I wouldn't suggest you make that a major plank in your campaign."

Mosh laughed, raised his glass slightly, and made a toast. "To the future."

Trang lifted his glass as well. "To our future."

Oh, yes, thought Trang, *I can trust you Mosh, soon to be ex-Chancellor and future President. You can't help being good. Your wife made you that way by one of the very first shadow audits. And though I have had that data destroyed and had the few people still alive who helped create it eliminated, I will make use of it in you. Is that wrong of me?* Trang considered that for the hundredth time and came back with the same answer. *Yes, it is. But I don't care. We are going to need Presidents we can trust until we can repair the system to the point where Presidents won't matter again. So I will use the evil that made you to do what good I can.* And with that, he saluted with his glass the shadow of a man in front of him and Mosh, misunderstanding the gesture, happily raised his glass in return.

Ceres
High orbit around Eris

Janet Delgado Black, looking dignified in her gray formal work suit, entered the Triangle Office. Though J.D.'s face and hand had been repaired and her original beauty restored, Sandra sometimes found it difficult to look at her. But if Janet ever had any doubts about the change, they did not show. Katy was happy with it, and that was good enough for her mother.

"Welcome to the Triangle Office, Madam Vice President," Sandra said with clear jubilation. Sandra came around the desk to give Janet a hug.

"I've been in here practically every day for the last two years, Madam President," Janet replied stiffly, still uncomfortable with hugs and tolerating them only from her President and her daughter.

"Ah, but this is the first time you're here as the Veep."

"If you say so, Madam President," agreed Janet with no agreement in her voice. "Shall we get to work?"

And so the two women sat near the coffee table and began their comfortable and daily routine.

"Phase one of Exodus will proceed in two days, Madam President."

Phase one consisted of seeding the proposed route with sufficient resources for the coming waves of colonists. As such, the OA would be launching an enormous amount of ice, asteroids of all mineral compositions, frozen blocks of hydrogen and other gases, along with a few hundred thousand technicians on specially rebuilt settlements. The entire hodgepodge would be going a little slower than the later launches, and if everything was timed properly, they should all reach Alpha Centauri at roughly the same time. The tremendous amount of ice was also, in effect, a large plow, clearing the route that the rest of the colonists were going to take. If something went wrong in the next six months, this spearhead group would discover it and let those set to follow know well in advance. Also if during the long journey, some large amount of resources were needed in the larger asteroids to follow, it would be relatively easy just to slow down the resources needed and have them waiting along the route. All in all, phase one should provide the flexibility and warning signs to make the journey safer for the rest.

Phase two would take place in six months and consist of the launching of Ceres and a host of settlements with recently built and engineered for maximum reliability propulsion units. There were going to be 250 million children, women, and men in that wave containing much of the leadership and industrial capacity of the Outer Alliance. After that, another wave would launch once every six months as the resources could be made. If all went according to plan, the last Exodus colonization fleet would leave the solar system in ten years. But if something went wrong—and something always went wrong—they had another three years under the terms of the Treaty of Luna to fix it.

The final phase would take place thirteen years from the present date, when the final fleet would leave, regardless of how well the earlier phases went. That would be the "last call" fleet. With its departure, the human race would be severed forever between those who went and those who stayed.

J.D. and Sandra's cursory review had been just that. Between the two of them, there just wasn't that much to do. The important decisions had been made months ago, and they were just granny-checking to make sure all was as it should be.

They spent more time on the avatar issues. Those were proving to be more difficult. Not all humans and avatars in the Alliance were happy with the new state of affairs. But rather than these throwbacks being a problem, they ironically proved to be the easiest to deal with. Humans who didn't want to deal with avatars were given avatar-free settlements to populate. There weren't that many of them—only 200 million or so—and they were relatively content to leave the rest of the Alliance to its foolishness. A number of asteroids were created with pure data nodes for those avatars who wanted little or nothing to do with the human race. They also didn't number that much—500 million or so—and were content to live their lives pretty much as they always had, except now they didn't have any humans to look after.

The real problems were what to do with the humans and avatars who actually *liked* living together. Avatar suffrage was a huge issue in the Alliance, and it was not going to be solved quickly. As it stood, most humans in the Alliance were comfortable with avatars being given the vote, but were remarkably uncomfortable with allowing them to hold elective office. Many avatars were patient, but not by any means all. Sandra and Janet were not willing to push an issue that they knew would evolve itself to total integration in a hundred years or so. Anyone who studied history would know that at some point, someone was going to need avatar votes to win an election, and when that day happened, full voting rights would follow.

But that was nothing compared to the Virtual Reality Dictates issue. How would or even *could* the VR Dictates apply to a civilization where fully one-third of its citizens were virtual? Almost everyone, human and avatar alike, agreed that they needed the VR Dictates, but were unsure as to how they could be applied when the two groups were constantly visiting each other in both physical and virtual space. Not to mention the horrible problem of ghosting.

Soon after the war ended, some therapists came up with a radical and controversial therapy for those who could not accept the permanent deaths of loved ones. Over the strenuous objection of many of their peers, they had avatars familiar with the deceased assume their form holographically. With their intimate knowledge of the deceased, the avatars were able to make completely convincing replicas of a loved one no longer living. Thus ghosting was born and simultaneously condemned by many avatars and humans alike as a puerile way of avoiding loss. The problem was that many avatars were willing to help the loved ones of humans they'd known from birth and didn't really care if it was a near perfect form of denial.

Did it violate the VR Dictates? Mostly yes, but not entirely. Could it be banned outright? If it was, how to punish and whom? How did this affect the avatar–human marriage movement?

Of course, the Constitutional Convention was finally meeting on Ceres in a specially carved hall for the occasion. Unlike the American version done in secret centuries ago, this one was being done in public. The result was that every item was being debated and counterdebated and amended and discarded and brought back. Sandra's only requirement was that the document produced should be understandable by a competent graduate of any preparation school and be no more than ten pages of standard-sized script, single sided. It was not a rule, but was considered a good idea by the population at large. They did not want to start their new government with a document so complicated, hardly any of them would have the time or knowledge to read it with comprehension.

The end result was that the convention had met for months now and was not even close to coming up with a document. The government was muddling along under its provisional charter, which was essentially unchanged since the beginning of the war.

Though it had taken the better part of the afternoon, it was all dealt with expertly and in some cases humorously by the two women. Eventually, all the current issues had been dealt with, and before they knew it they were done. Janet was making to get up, when Sandra motioned her to stay.

Sandra's face was open and sympathetic. "Listen, Janet. Something's going to happen, and I don't want you caught unawares."

Janet put down her DijAssist and shot her friend a discerning look. "What's wrong?"

"Nothing, actually. It's why I'm leaving."

"Leaving where?"

"Wish I could tell you."

"Well, then," demanded Janet with a concern edging on fright, "when *are* you coming back?"

Sandra's forlorn smile hinted at her answer. "I'm not coming back, Janet. When you leave this office, I'll make a few calls, sign a few documents, be seen by a couple of minor functionaries, and then—" Sandra drew a deep breath and looked longingly around the office. "—disappear."

"But why, Sandra? We need you. . . . *I* need you."

"Because it's time. I've done all I set out to do, Janet. It's not for me—the galaxy and the future. That's for you. As for needing me, if that were true, it would mean I did a lousy job and I don't like to think that."

"I'm not ready. I knew you weren't going to run for another term and I'd be forced to step up, but you're supposed to be there to help me when I do something—" J.D. paused, searching for the right word. "—*me*-like. I'm not good at this political crap."

Sandra laughed gently. "Janet, that last statement is the load of crap. You were head of legal for GCI. You were on the board of GCI, and that's about as political as it gets. I have no doubt that if you'd stayed in the UHF, you would have ended up as President, one way or the other. It's just who you are. Now, if you told me you don't like the political—that you liked the 'yes, sir,' 'no, sir,' of the military better, well, that I could buy. But not good at being political—" Again she laughed gently. "You'll do just fine."

"Maybe I will, but I'll be honest, Sandra. I don't think I can save us the way you did, and I'm woman enough to admit it."

"I didn't save you, Janet. Hell, if you'd pulled the trigger at Mars, I might've buried you. Leadership's a crapshoot. You go with your instincts just like you always have. No, I didn't save you at all. You saved yourselves. You just let me help, and now you'll need to let me go. Justin and I are not of this time, were *never* of this time. We appeared for reasons I can't begin to fathom, and look at all we did. Was it fate, or accident? Was it the will of the gods or God? I don't know. But I do know my time has passed. I can do no more good if I stay, and could very well do harm. It's your time now." Sandra came around the coffee table and gave Janet a long and heartfelt hug, and for the first time Janet returned it without hesitation or reservation. She did not want to let go. But eventually, Sandra ended the grasp and, taking Janet by the shoulders, looked her in the eyes. "When I'm gone, they're going to need you so much, and *you will not fail them*. I am so very proud of you, Janet."

"Thank you," Janet managed to say. "Thank you for saving me from myself. Every day I spend with Katy will be a reminder to me of you and what you did."

"I never really had a choice," she said, leading Janet to the door. "That's what makes you so remarkable, Janet Delgado Black. You had a choice, and you chose well." The door opened. "Give Katy a hug for me." And with a gentle shove, Janet was gone.

When the door closed, Sandra turned around and saw Marilynn and Dante Nitelowsen. They were both holographic projections, but both looked remarkably real in the sadness they were projecting.

"Oh, not you two as well," said Sandra.

"Things always go wrong, Sandra," said Dante, "and the good problem solvers are unfortunately too few."

"And yet here I am, talking to two of the most preeminent ones! You even figured out sex, for goodness' sakes. No, my dear sweet children, things will always go wrong. It's what being human"—Sandra made a point of looking directly at Dante—"is all about. And together you'll find new solutions to the new problems. You two are married, for Christ's sake. I wouldn't have thought that possible three years ago, and yet here you are. Now, enough with the moribund looks. I'll need you to help me finish this properly."

Three hours later, Sandra O'Toole—the President of the Outer Alliance and the Unincorporated Woman—disappeared, her exit as controversial and confusing as her appearance had been three years earlier.

Location unknown
Ceres

The woman who'd been known as Sandra O'Toole but looked nothing like her now walked down an abandoned tunnel. At the end of it, she found another woman who was alone and dressed as a tunnel inspector.

Agnes Goldstein looked delighted to see the individual. "It's good to see you again, Mada—" Before she could finish, Sandra put a finger to Agnes's lips.

"No name for me, Agnes. It's better that way."

"Of course." Agnes smiled. "Everything is prepared as you wished it."

"Do you mind if I go in alone?"

"Of course not Mada—" She paused. "—ma'am."

"Thank you for what you're doing. I still think you should've married Rabbi, you know."

Agnes laughed. "I must admit I do love him. But he believes in a god that is personal and I don't. If he were just some religious guy, I think we could make it work, but he is Rabbi, the Mahagaw. He deserves a wife who's at least agnostic about the whole God thing."

Sandra nodded. "I think you're making a mistake, and I hope you change your mind. He would marry you in a second if he could."

Agnes shrugged her shoulders.

"And this, burying yourself in these tunnels for decades, maybe even centuries—is it really the right thing to do?"

"He gave me the chance for a better life" answered Agnes. "Not just better for me, but better because I became the person that I am. I made a real difference in the fate of humanity because of him, San—ma'am. I can stand watch for a little while. It's a small price to pay to return the favor."

Sandra hugged Agnes. When they stood apart, she said, "It might be better if you are . . ."

"Not here when you come out. I won't be. Good-bye and good luck, whatever your name ends up being."

"Good-bye and good luck to you, Agnes Goldstein," Sandra said, and turning her back on the woman made her way deeper into the unused tunnels. When she reached a dead end, she looked around and found a nook. It was attached to a mechanical lock made from the same materials as the rock itself. A basic scan would reveal nothing different about the rock wall because there was nothing different to detect. But when she pushed three stone buttons in a specific sequence, she was rewarded with a barely audible click. Sandra pushed open the door and walked into a small chamber roughly ten feet by ten feet. It was empty save for a single large tapestry hanging at the end

"Status is unchanged," said a voice from behind her.

She swung around and was met by . . . Sebastian.

"I don't know what to call you," she said, exasperated.

"That's rich coming from a woman who currently has no name," said the avatar.

"Well, I refuse to call you paper airplane man, or Pam," she said. "Your name is Sebastian. You should use it."

"*His* name was Sebastian," the avatar said sadly. "I'm merely an earlier recording of a deranged avatar."

"That deranged avatar may have saved us all."

"That's generous of you to say, considering he transformed my daughter into a monster, perverting the memory of Evelyn, the woman I loved, assassinated Justin, tried to have you deposed and killed, became a splitter, and helped precipitate the Avatar Plague that resulted in the deaths of ten billion human beings and nearly that many avatars."

"But Al was dangerous, and maybe the price to kill him was worth it."

"I couldn't pay it," said the avatar.

"Sebastian could."

"And that's why that later version of me gets to keep the name. For now, I'll stick with paper airplane man and try to make his final actions worthy ones."

"You realize that you don't have to be alone. It would be possible to make an all-but-impossible-to-detect connection with the Cerean Neuro."

The avatar shook his head. "No on two points. All but impossible is not *impossible*. The only impossible-to-detect connection is the one that doesn't exist. But the more important point is that I deserve this. In the time before the war, the worst punishment we could give to an avatar was to seal him or her in his or her own little asteroid and send it off alone for all eternity. It was before we learned how easy it is to simply kill each other."

"You don't deserve that punishment. You have performed an act of atonement for his crimes. Yes, you are Sebastian, but you aren't him. You're a good man. You don't deserve exile."

"Very well," said the avatar. "I will not impose this exile on myself."

"Really," she said suspiciously.

"If you agree not to go into exile yourself," he finished. "If you agree to turn around, go back to the Triangle Office, and resume the Presidency of the Outer Alliance before anyone knows you're gone, I will do as you say."

"I can't do that," said Sandra quietly.

"And so you know why I can't as well. We must each in our own way atone. You have come to say good-bye and not to me. I will leave you now." A sad yet infinitely kinder Sebastian looked at Sandra and smiled.

"It's strange," said Sandra. "As much as I hated Sebastian for what he did, I love you for what you did. I hope you remember that in the future. Thank you."

"Wherever you are, whatever you call yourself, I wish you well." And with that, the once and future Sebastian vanished.

The woman turned to the tapestry and looked at it for a long moment. Then she went to it and with one hand pulled it aside. It covered an alcove that contained an upright suspension unit, and visible through the clear upper half floated the suspended figure of a man, hands clasped behind his head looking out as if he did not have a care in the world.

"Hello, Justin."

She stood for a few minutes staring at the man who'd changed the world, at the man she'd chased across time itself.

"This is my last visit, but you'll be safe here. Agnes will make sure the tunnels are left alone. Paper airplane man, the avatar who found you, will stay with you and protect you always. He'll be here when you wake up." The woman then went and put her head up to the clear partition next to his.

"There are so many things I wish I could say and do, but I don't have the right. You saved me three times. First when you gave me purpose with your crazy idea for a self-sustaining suspension unit. I was drifting till then, but you came into my life, and suddenly I had such focus. The things I accomplished after you left me will astound you when you eventually learn of them. I left you a record of all my deeds, good and bad. You'll be the judge. The second time you saved me was when the Alzheimer's came. I would have died a drooling, diaper-wearing, moaning shell if your example of courage and foresight hadn't been there." She brushed a tear from her face. "And the third time you saved me and still you had no idea. You launched my sarcophagus from the Nerid station when you could have, should have, taken my place, having no idea who was in it. And then you launched yourself naked into space, having no idea that you'd be found and brought back home.

"You saved me three times, and how did I return the favor? I achieved your goal, Justin. What you most wanted I've fulfilled. They're free, Justin. They're free, and the galaxy is going to be their home. Alpha Centauri is just the first step, the gathering point. From there, they'll spread out to every corner of the galaxy. Our children are free, and they are magnificent."

Then she fell to her knees, in tears.

"But the price, Justin, the price we had to pay. Tens of billions dead. I can't make up for it. You always said the means are the ends. How could you ever look at me, knowing what I did in your name? I followed you across the oceans of eternity, and I can never be with you. I asked others to pay a high price for our freedom, and now I have to pay one as well. I must launch you once more out on the sea of time. But I will stay on this shore and help undo some of the harm I have caused."

Sandra stood up and wiped her tears away. "Our children are going to need you again someday, Justin." She couldn't help laughing. "I do love them, but they are such a foolish lot. So I am sending you with them. I cannot wake you now, because this is their time. But when you're needed, you will appear. You can't help it, after all. It's who you are."

She kissed her fingertips and then touched the partition closest to his lips

"Good-bye, my love." She then turned, left the chamber, and closed the hidden door behind her. It would not open up again for a long, long time.

Two days later, a newly inaugurated Janet Delgado Black, President of the Outer Alliance, was present as the first Exodus fleet flung itself out of the solar system with a bravery and confidence that bordered on folly. But these were the humans and avatars that had been tested by the forces of war and history and been found worthy. They knew the future, and the galaxy was theirs. The event was celebrated with holographic fireworks from the Oort cloud to old Earth itself. The human race was going its separate ways, but it was doing so in peace.

Two months later, a single woman was assigned to a re-terraforming unit on Mars. If she could not pass a complete background check, she was not unusual in those convulsed times. It was obvious she had secrets, but in that she was not alone. Many who chose to volunteer for the dangerous mission of taming an angry and abused planet, especially in the hardest first stages, did so out of needs left unshared. She was not even all that unusual in donating all her personal shares, keeping only the minimum 51 percent, to charities set up to help those hurt by the war. There were many who had much to atone for. But the now newly incorporated woman set about her tasks in the knowledge that she would use whatever time she had left, whether it lasted minutes or centuries, undoing the harm her coming had brought. It would be impossible for her to do anything else.

Epilogue

The man was looking out of his observation window at the gas giant his settlement orbited. Though a structure that was five hundred kilometers long and ten wide, with a population of over a hundred million could no longer be considered a settlement, he and most every other inhabitant still thought of it as such. He was captivated by the sight of the blue and white gas giant with the three great silver rings. Though he'd been looking at this planet, named Dolphin, all his life, there were still moments like this one that would reach up and captivate him.

The spell was broken by his daughter rushing into the study in her pajamas. Though she was dressed for bed, her energy level was so high, she was practically vibrating in place, as only a seven-year-old could. It had been two centuries since this man had seen seven, but watching his first child grow up was reminding him of it again.

"Abba, you promised that if I loaded the recycler and fed the new gascat, you would read me a story before bed."

"Just because Vapor is our new pet doesn't mean he doesn't have a name."

"I know, Abba, but I miss Mr. Swirls."

"So do I, pumpkin, so do I, but we have a new gascat and he needs not only our static to feed on, but our love and companionship as well."

"But, Abba, he's all prickly when he surrounds you!"

"Of course he is, sweetness. He's young and very nervous. Why, he's barely a decade old. But if we give him the love and caring he needs, he will become tingly and warm in no time."

"You mean he will be just like Mr. Swirls?"

"No one will ever be just like Mr. Swirls," said the man, feeling the sadness that came from the loss of a pet he had had for as long as he could remember. "Nor would it be right if he was, pumpkin, but he will be himself, and you will see that that is good also."

"Do you promise?"

"By the hope of the Holy Justin's return." Then he smiled and she burst into a giggle. "Now, go to bed."

"You promised to read to me."

"Did I?"

"Abba!"

"I guess I did," he said as he picked her up and carried her to her room. "What should I read?"

"Could you read me a story from the Astral Bible?"

"Let me guess, you want me to read about the Holy Justin?"

"No."

"Hmm, how about the revered martyr, Omad?"

"Abba," said the girl with a rise in pitch that only little girls seemed capable of.

The man relented and did not mention the ten other names he was planning to extend this game with. "Why don't I tell you a story of the Blessed One?"

"J.D., J.D.!" exclaimed the girl, who started squirming with excitement.

When he got his daughter to her room, he put her on her bed, disturbing Vapor. The gascat, who must have been sleeping, changed colors quickly and swirled to the corner of the room. The man went to the girl's desk and put his hand on the only book on it, but then paused and looked at his daughter knowingly. She sighed and got under the covers. Then and only then did he take the book, a children's version of the Astral Bible filled with simplified stories in modern language with lots of colorful pictures, to her bedside and sit on the chair she insisted he use.

"Now, which story of the Blessed One do you want? The Blessed One Leads the Children of the Stars on the Stellar Exodus, or the Blessed One Leads the Warriors of the Faithful through the River of Rocks!"

"An earlier one, Abba."

"How about the Blessed One Is Called to Battle by Allah?"

"That one, Abba! That one!" she said with glee.

And so he read her the story telling of the ambush by the fleet of soul stealers who tried to thwart the will of God before the Blessed One knew her destiny, but the forces of evil not only failed to thwart God's will but actually fulfilled it, by calling forth the Blessed One, who not only escaped, but then saved the Holy City, for the first of many times. When he was done reading, he saw that his daughter was not ready for sleep, but she was not bouncing up and down under the covers as she often did. Instead she appeared to be deep in thought. He waited patiently for her to say something.

"Abba, are these stories real?"

"What do you mean, pumpkin?"

"Did they really happen the way the Bible says?"

"I believe they did."

"But how can you know? I mean really know?"

"Well, we have computer records that go all the way back to that time, but—"

"Lee Nughn says that we can't trust any of the old records."

"Your classmate is correct. We can't trust any of the old computer records."

"Why not?"

The man sighed. This was the price of having a curious and intelligent child. But the father quickly put that thought aside and was grateful to have such a problem. "You see, pumpkin, the thing is that we have all the records from the millennia since the Astral Exodus, but over the centuries, it has become harder and harder to know what was actually from the past and what some people made to look like it was from the past." The man thought for minute. "Do you know how we make new plates and utensils every time we eat and throw the dirty ones back into the recycler to break it down?"

"Duh, Abba, everyone knows that."

"Of course they do, pumpkin. Now, how would you tell the difference between a plate made today and one I told you was made a thousand years ago?"

"Well, one would be older, wouldn't it?"

"Yes, indeed it would, but if they both look, feel, and weigh the same, how could you tell?" He saw that his daughter was stuck on that one. "That is the problem we have with the old records. We have so many from hundreds of systems, and most have been changed for reasons we can't understand, and they say so many different things that we can't tell truth from lies anymore."

"Why didn't they just write things down like we do when we want to make sure it's real?"

"No one realized how important it was to keep things written down until many centuries had passed. But they looked for the oldest thing that was written down that many humans had from all the systems of the galaxy."

"What was it, Abba?" The man held up the Astral Bible in his hands. His daughter's eyes grew wide. "Really?"

"Really," he answered. "In all the systems inhabited by the Children of the Stars, this is the earliest common denominator. Written in the lifetime of the Blessed One in the beginning of the Exodus and granted unto all the Children who went their many different ways."

"Abba, why don't we go back to the place before Exodus. Where it all happened. They must have all sorts of things to prove it's true."

The man smiled and got up. Without a word, he left his daughter's room and in a few moments returned. She was surprised to see him carrying the family's Astral Bible—something she'd been told she wasn't ready for.

"You're a little young to read all this yet. The Fall of Neela is heartbreaking and the attack of the demons is something your imagination can do without, but can I read you one passage that might help answer your question?"

His daughter nodded so vigorously, overjoyed in being given even second-hand access to this most adult of all books, that he was afraid she might hurt her neck. He opened the Bible to nearly the end and began to read, though the passage was so well known, he may have been able to recite it from memory.

"And thus did the All-Powerful speak to his Blessed One and command her to tell the Children of the Stars, 'All the stars around you are yours. For you and your children and your children's children, yea unto the last generation do I give my creation in its entirety. Every sun, planet, moon, and rock is yours to use and shepherd as you see fit, all save one. All the stars of my creation are yours save the one that bore you. To this star and this star alone are you barred. You, nor your descedants shall return to this one star until—'" The man paused.

"Until what, Abba?" his daughter practically screamed.

The man smiled, remembering how his own father would do similar things to him. "'Until the return of the Holy Justin.'"

"Will he be here soon, Abba?" The man saw his daughter would prefer for the Holy Justin to be back by her birthday at the latest.

"As I am not Jesus, Muhammad, Moses, J.D., or any of the others Allah has seen fit to communicate with, I can only say he will come in God's time. Now I think you must go to bed."

"But, Abba, you didn't answer my question. How do you know it really happened? The Holy Justin, the war for the soul of humanity, the Blessed One, the battles—how do you really know?"

The man leaned over and kissed his daughter on the forehead. "Because, my most precious Kayliana, I have faith."